COLLECTION – EPISODES 1-4

THE ANTICS OF

EVANGELINE

MADELEINE D'ESTE

EVANGELINE

AND THE

ALCHEMIST

MYSTERY AND MAYHEM IN STEAMPUNK MELBOURNE
(THE ANTICS OF EVANGELINE BOOK 1)

CHAPTER 1

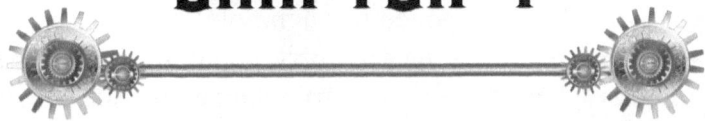

I T ALL STARTED WITH A rat-a-tat-tat on the Professor's laboratory-workshop door. Evangeline and the Professor looked up from their inventing to see Miss Plockton in the doorway.

"Chief Inspector Pensnett ta see you, sir?" she said.

Evangeline perked up on her stool. A policeman here at 56 Collins Street? Something exciting was surely about to happen.

"Ah, yes. I plum forgot."

Evangeline's father stopped adjusting his new, improved auto-chariot and walked over to the wooden bench, placing his trusty brass screwdriver with the ivory handle down beside neat stacks of brass cogs, wheels and pins. Her father, Professor Montague Caldicott, the pre-eminent horological-engineer in all the Colonies, smoothed down his humongous moustache with his real hand.

"Your lesson is over for today, m'dear. Follow Miss Plockton upstairs and continue with your embroidery."

"But Father..." Evangeline groaned. "I could be of some assistance."

"Police matters are not for the ears of impressionable young ladies. All those dead bodies and smugglers and swarthy criminals. Far too sordid."

"I never get to do anything interesting," Evangeline grumbled as she stowed away her rosewood-handled screwdriver in the pocket of her dress, along with a handful of brass pins. The smaller and more delicate screwdriver was a recent gift from her father, an encouragement to pursue her own inventions.

Evangeline's plain bottle-green day dress, buttoned to the neck, was not the latest fashion but it was better than she had ever imagined in her previous life on the grey foggy streets of London, when her toes poked through holes in her boots. Cold was something she had yet to worry about since she arrived three months ago on the dirigible from Singapore. She wondered whether Melbourne could be anything less than sweltering.

"Out. Out."

The Professor shooed Evangeline and Miss Plockton from the laboratory-workshop, before carefully locking the door behind him.

There was a time when a visit from the police would have frightened Evangeline. She would have hurried to hide her loot, but not today. Today she was a reformed character, setting aside her urchin ways and learning to be a proper young lady. But being good all the time was a bit dull.

Evangeline sulked all the way up the stairs, clumping her feet and dawdling. Her father passed her, continuing up the oriental carpeted hallway into his study, closing the door behind him. The conversation of men was muffled by the closed oak door.

Evangeline loitered in the hallway, waiting for Miss Plockton to drag her into the sitting room to complete her crudely stitched handkerchief. Whilst Evangeline was proficient in many skills, needlecraft was not one of them.

Rather than bustling Evangeline away, Miss Plockton did something curious. Her father's personal secretary produced a large brass key from her pocket and opened the small closet adjoining the Professor's study. The room where all the house linen was stored.

The house on Collins Street, where Evangeline now lived with her new extended family, had many secrets. Built by a gold prospector with some alleged unsavoury tastes, there were many hidden passages and nooks within the walls and floors. Evangeline was yet to be trusted with a set of keys, her attempts to explore the house thoroughly hindered.

Inside the small room smelling of lavender and camphor, Miss Plockton pushed aside a stack of damask curtains, revealing a pencil-sized hole in the wall. An audito-projector, one of the Professor's best-selling patented inventions, appeared from under another stack of bedsheets. Miss Plockton wound the key, placed the brass tube over the hole and the audito-projector sprung into action. The sounds of male voices emerged through the horn, as clear as the Melbourne summer sky outside.

"Eavesdropping, Miss Plockton?" Evangeline gasped.

"On occasion, a secretary needs ta take initiative," Miss Plockton said.

Impressed by Miss Plockton's rebellious act, Evangeline squeezed into the tiny room beside her. There was little room in the linen cupboard with the two women's fulsome skirts.

"Thank you for seeing me, Professor," Pensnett said. His voice was gruff with a tinge of the Black Country.

"My pleasure, Chief Inspector. Anything to help the Constabulary."

"I understand you are responsible for inventing the auto-chariot, sir?"

"Oh, yes. One of my many tinkerings."

"Actually, we've had a few problems with auto chariots. Reckless young gentlemen racing along Flinders Street."

"Oh, I know nothing about that..."

"Not to worry, sir. I am here for your assistance with another matter entirely. I have rather a curious case on my hands."

Evangeline's skin tingled. She knew there was something exciting in the wind today.

"We have reports of new unusual shipments of gold hitting the market of Melbourne."

"I am a humble horological-engineer, sir. Although I occasionally branch out into other experimentations, I know nothing of rocks and minerals from the ground. Why is this gold 'unusual'?"

"There have been reports of strange activity. It does not behave as gold should. Apparently gold purchased from a reputable merchant in Goldsmiths Lane has blackened. Overnight."

Evangeline heard a familiar clicking sound. It was the brass fingers of her father's clockwork hand. He was probably stroking his proud whiskers as he often did when he pondered.

"Allegedly, on Monday, the gold was bright and yellow, and yesterday, the nuggets looked more like iron. Dull and grey."

"Of course. Alchemy. Fool's gold."

From her hiding place in the cupboard, Evangeline's eyes widened. But before a gasp of surprise could emerge, Miss Plockton deftly placed a ladylike hand over her mouth. On first inspection, with her tight steely bun and pinched face, Miss Plockton appeared pure hell or high-water Highland Presbyterian, but Evangeline wondered whether she owed some of her efficiency to a touch of the fey.

"We understand you dealt with similar occurrences in London, Professor."

"I assisted the Goldsmiths Guild by developing a device to identify the offending alchemical material. I can't remember whether I brought it with me. I'll have to rummage through my trunks."

"Was the perpetrator apprehended?"

"The device was a success...But alas, we were too late to catch the fiend on that occasion."

Evangeline listened greedily to the details of the Professor's colourful past. Perhaps he was not as boring as he appeared. They had only been reunited for three months, and there was so much she did not know about her long-lost father. She had not even heard the full story of his missing arm. She vowed to grill him at the next available moment.

"Do you have any clues to the identity of this scoundrel, Chief Inspector?"

"Unfortunately not. The heights of the gold rush are over but Melbourne is still a transitory town. It is hard to keep up with all the comings and goings."

"And there is still plenty of money to be made by unscrupulous characters."

"Indeed. I thought I'd come out to the Colonies for a quiet life."

The Chief Inspector and the Professor chuckled.

"Clues are scarce, I'm afraid," Pensnett continued. "When we spoke with the goldsmith in question, he claimed he could not remember the person who sold it to him. The poor fellow was very flustered by his shoddy memory."

"As though his mind had been erased?"

"Quite. He blamed some type of phantasm."

"A ghost? And you believe him?"

"I'm not a man of science. It might sound ridiculous to you..."

"Not entirely..."

"But I have seen enough unexplainable things in my time to keep an open mind. The goldsmith is a reputable businessman."

"Hmm...intriguing."

"And the case gets even more peculiar."

"Do tell."

"The goldsmith surrendered the remaining gold, but when my Constables checked the evidence again this morning, the whole lot had turned grey. Not a speck of gold left."

"Transitory augmentation. How devious."

The linen cupboard door burst open.

"Hallo. What is going on here?"

It was Uncle Augie.

Evangeline and Miss Plockton both blushed red, caught in the ungenteel act of eavesdropping.

"A game of sardines? How fun. Move over." Augie's voice boomed as he pressed his generous frame into the cupboard. Evangeline cried out as a heeled boot squished her delicate toes.

"Uncle Augie. You do have big clod-hoppers."

"Miss Evangeline." Miss Plockton scowled. "Language, please. This is not a fish market."

"Ssh," Augie hissed. "You are both terrible at this game. I would have expected better from you, Miss Plockton."

The door swung open again.

The Professor and Inspector Pensnett stood in the doorway, frowns etched into their foreheads.

"Oh drat. They found us. Squeeze on over, Miss Plockton. We must make room," Augie said.

"What is going on here?" The Professor stood with hands on hips.

"Sardines, my old chum. Join in."

The Professor spied the audito-projector clamped against the wall and roared.

"You have been spying on me."

"Please forgive me, Father..." was all Evangeline could say. Miss Plockton was white as the damask sheets beside her. "I only wanted to..."

"Why is everyone in the linen cupboard?" Uncle Edmund appeared in the hallway, dabbing a handkerchief at his damp forehead, glistening from the outdoor heat. "Is it time for tea?"

"I must be off, Professor," Chief Inspector Pensnett said. "I am grateful for your time and advice."

"Yes. Yes. Let me show you out. Please excuse my impertinent daughter and my secretary. I shall dismiss her at once."

Evangeline gasped again.

"Don't worry, Miss Evangeline. He gives me my notice at least once a week. Usually on Thursdays," Miss Plockton said as she bustled away to fetch the tea.

Evangeline's stomach rumbled loudly. Augie glanced at her, horrified.

"What a beastly noise from a young lady. How can I present you to the Normanbys if your bodily functions speak so loudly?"

"I can't help it," Evangeline retorted.

"You take after your Uncle. Always hungry."

Augie looked fondly over at his best friend. Edmund and Augie had accompanied Evangeline to Melbourne on the long dirigible journey from London to Rome, Rome to Delhi, Delhi to Singapore and then finally Singapore to Melbourne. The Professor's younger brother, Edmund, was an accomplished architect. He was called to Melbourne to design many of the modern sandstone buildings springing up on every street corner, in preparation for the World Exhibition in 1888. Edmund and Augie were constant companions, they shared a room on the dirigible and even had adjoining rooms here in the house.

Augie, or August Beauchamp, wasn't Evangeline's real uncle. He had recently taken over the Prince Albert Theatre on Lonsdale Street and knew all the fashionable people in town. When he wasn't managing the theatrical types of Melbourne, he was Evangeline's strict etiquette master.

A triangle chimed down the wooden hallway.

"Goody. Tea. I'm famished," said Edmund as they all emptied the linen cupboard and traipsed down the hall to the conservatory.

Evangeline smiled to herself. She hoped there would be more talk of the mysterious alchemist over tea. It would be awfully exciting if the Professor would let her help.

Or perhaps she could catch this rascal on her own.

CHAPTER 2

AFTER THREE SCONES WITH APRICOT jam and cream, a wedge of seed cake, a raspberry tart and a disdainful look from Augie, Evangeline recalled her table manners. She easily forgot. For the first seventeen years of her life, using the right fish knife had not been a high priority. She sipped on her tea in a manner she hoped was elegant, her little finger extended gracefully.

"So we have an alchemist in our midst? Melbourne is becoming quite the bohemian town," Augie trilled, as he caressed butter and golden apricot jam on a sliver of white bread. As plump as an overstuffed armchair, Augie had the appetite of a bird. "You have a contraption to catch this naughty man?"

"Somewhere in my trunks."

"I shall help you look, Father." Evangeline piped up, excited by the opportunity to rifle through the locked trunks in the laboratory-workshop. Who knew what treasures were hidden amongst her father's discarded wheels and dials, cogs and engines? Perhaps she might find a daguerreotype of her mother as a young lady or a letter from the woman she barely remembered.

"This is not a matter for young ladies. I have not forgotten my disappointment at finding you spying on me. I am considering a suitable punishment."

"It was Miss..." Evangeline started, before Miss Plockton gave her an icy glare over the teapot.

"Spying is frightfully common," Augie said. "It is not at all becoming."

"Leave the poor child alone, Augie. You of all people," Edmund scolded. "Now, tell me more of this alchemist, Monty. How will the police find him?"

Augie cried out.

"Oh Augie, have you bitten your tongue?" Edmund leaned forward, gently touching his friend's arm.

"I heard a tale at the coffee house only this morning. Apparently, there was a particularly powerful session at Madame Zsoldas's salon last week. There was a flurry of wind in the room, like a tornado, completely messing up all the ladies' coiffures. Mrs Flookburgh-Storth was livid. Then a spirit-presence appeared, clear as day and warned everyone in the room about the arrival of a dark stranger. By all accounts, it was absolutely spine-chilling."

"Poppycock," said Edmund through an ungentrified mouth filled with raspberry tart. "That Zsoldas woman is the presence and everyone's coin purse is a present to her."

Evangeline soaked up every word of gossip and scandal across the table. If she remained quiet, they usually forgot she was in the room and continued talking.

"Ghosts and magic. Who would have thought it under these blue Antipodean skies?" the Professor said. "Now Evangeline. It is time you returned to your lessons with Miss Plockton. You have many years of learning to catch up on. Household management is a mandatory skill for any eligible young lady in the Colonies."

"You are seventeen now, Miss Evangeline," Uncle Augie said. "We need to prepare you to be presented to society."

Evangeline nodded dutifully while grimacing inside. She did not want to be an eligible young lady. Being married off to some bore, or some Boer, was the last thing on her mind. Especially when there were swindling alchemists on the loose. She dabbed the corners of her mouth with a linen napkin.

"Excuse me," she said demurely as she rose from her seat.

She moved around the table to embrace the gruff Professor, his wiry whiskers grating against her cheek.

"No need for all that." He flustered. "Don't get any ideas about this alchemist."

"Oh no, Father. I wouldn't dare."

The three men beamed as she closed the door behind her.

Safely in the hallway, Evangeline opened her palm to reveal the key to the Professor's laboratory-workshop. Some of her less than ladylike skills were not easily forgotten.

CHAPTER 3

RATHER THAN SEEKING OUT MISS Plockton for her lesson, Evangeline slipped out of the servant's entrance, through the courtyard and into the laneway behind the house. Holding her nose against the stench, she leapt over pools of rubbish and night soil. The Colonies were upside down, and, although it was January, the air was as hot as an oven. There was an unseemly dampness spreading under Evangeline's arms and down her back, reminding her of the old days.

She landed on the opposite side of the laneway and waltzed through the back gate, where neat rows of white linen blew in the hot wind and a man in a conical bamboo hat squatted beside a pail of water. The man called out something indecipherable and Mei appeared.

"Here she is," Mei said. "Gracin' us with your presence?"

"The Professor is keen on lessons at the moment." Evangeline flopped down on a basket filled with linen, her skirts puffing around her. "He seems obsessed with useless topics like needlecraft this week."

"You could come work 'ere for me and darn some socks."

"Not likely."

Mei tossed a bundle at Evangeline. She caught the package and hid behind a billowing white sheet to remove her heavy skirts.

Out of her frock and into a red Chinese jacket and trousers, Evangeline was ready for her own lesson with Mei.

A few weeks after her arrival at 56 Collins Street, Evangeline escaped into the laneway to practice her cartwheels, unobserved. After a few twirls on the cobblestones, Evangeline saw a petite Oriental girl her own age, leaning against the back fence with a smirk. Without a word, the girl sprung into the air, landing on the fence like a cat. Evangeline stared open mouthed with admiration. Tumbling was her forte, she always struggled with aerial feats.

"Teach me," she said.

Mei and Evangeline had been friends ever since.

On occasion, the Professor could be quite modern. He approved of Evangeline's friendship with Mei.

"Admirable race, the Chinese," he would say. "Extremely advanced in their science. Just got a bit lost in recent times but some remarkable inventions. I am positive, they will get back on their feet soon."

The Professor approved of matters which broadened Evangeline's horizons in the sciences and the arts. Evangeline failed to mention her lessons from her friend down the lane were in the fighting arts.

Evangeline made the first move.

Her bare foot thrust outwards on an angle, destined for Mei's solar plexus. Mei swiftly blocked the kick with a swiping elbow and followed through with a punch at Evangeline's delicate jawline.

Evangeline ducked with a deep curtsey, avoiding Mei's fist and retaliating with a sweeping kick.

"You've got to be quicker than that," Mei said as she leapt in the air, her waist length black plait swinging like a whip behind her.

The man in the courtyard stopped scrubbing to admire the two young ladies pirouetting and exchanging blows across the cobblestones.

Evangeline narrowed her eyes.

Mei advanced.

A flurry of left and right strikes followed by uppercut jabs pushed Evangeline backwards.

Evangeline flipped into the air, cartwheeling three times before landing behind Mei and finishing with a sharp kick to the back of her knee.

Mei groaned as her knee gave way.

"Who's too slow now?" Evangeline said with a smirk, before steadying back into a defensive stance.

Mei said nothing. Her face was calm. Evangeline should have known she was in trouble.

Suddenly, Mei flew through the air like a gust of hot wind. Both feet ramming Evangeline in the stomach, shoving her backwards onto the linen-filled wicker basket.

"Don't get too cocky," Mei said, smoothing a stray hair from her face.

"Bloody 'ell," Evangeline wheezed.

"Oh, my," Mei said. "What language from a cultured young lady."

Like an overturned turtle, Evangeline struggled to her feet with an unrefined grunt.

"Tea?" Mei said, reaching out her hand to her friend.

"Giving in?" Evangeline replied.

"Not likely, circus girl," Mei said. "I thought you might be fryin' in this 'eat."

"I am perfectly comfortable," Evangeline said as a drip of perspiration rolled down her nose.

"I could kill a cup of tea, meself."

"Well, if you are surrendering. I shall join you."

Evangeline grinned and followed Mei into the back of the Chinese laundry, which doubled as both shop and Mei's home.

Like many of his countrymen, Mei's father came to Australia for the gold rush but never went home again. Mei was Melbourne born and bred.

The narrow hallways were piled with clean white sheets, smelling of soap and starch. The dust storms of recent weeks turned every sheet across Melbourne a reddish brown, and had been a boon for the Fang family. Evangeline followed Mei through the house to the boiling room.

Mei poured a boiling kettle into a white teapot, decorated with exotic Chinese script, spooning heaped teaspoons of fragrant brown leaves inside. Evangeline grabbed two cups without handles and the two girls headed further inside the house to escape the heat. The house was plain, without the flourishes of the Professor's home. Uncarpeted floors and plain walls, bare apart from a golden shrine in the corner of the sitting room

"I have an idea," Evangeline said.

Mei rolled her eyes as she poured tea into a cup with a sweeping arc.

"A policeman came to visit my father. Apparently there's a magician causing havoc in Melbourne. Making fake gold and swindling people."

Mei raised a black eyebrow and nodded appreciatively.

Evangeline took a ladylike sip from the tea cup, remembering to hold up her pinkie finger. Uncle Augie would be proud.

"Alchemy?" Mei asked.

"You know about alchemy?"

"We invented it."

Evangeline screwed up her face in disbelief.

"You say that about everything."

"We did invent everything."

"If I remember correctly, you have some goldsmiths as customers?"

"The Harts." Mei nodded.

"Will you introduce me?"

"And ask if they have been visited by a magician?" Mei pulled an unbecoming face.

"You doubt my abilities to charm men? I am quite the conversationalist. I can talk all about watercolours and how to do a Double Algerian Stitch. Or even about how to keep a ledger of your accounts with the general store."

"Your fingers are quicker than your tongue."

Mei was right. Evangeline's years as a pickpocket on the streets of London had trained her fingers but her stepfather had the honeyed words. But there was no need for persuasion when Evangeline slipped her hand inside a lady's purse or a gentleman's jacket.

"Please? Take me to the Harts," Evangeline said with big eyes. "You know them already. They will be caught off-guard and tell us everything that happened. I am sure of it."

Mei rolled her eyes again before slurping heartily from her cup.

"What's in it for me?"

"A sense of community pride? Assisting with a police investigation and bringing criminals to justice?"

"Pfft."

"Doing good for your fellow man?"

Mei shrugged.

"I'll take you to Faversham's House of Tea afterwards for cake."

"You're on."

"But you will need to dress appropriately."

Mei groaned.

"I know. I hate bustles as much as you do. But we must look the part of trustworthy young ladies. It is all part of the plan."

There was a knock at the door and a rustle of activity, Miss Plockton appeared in the doorway with her parasol folded in her hand.

"Good afternoon Miss Fang. Sorry to interrupt your tea," she said, her face crimson from the heat. "Evangeline Caldicott! What are you wearing? Come home right this instant. The

Professor is in quite a state. He has misplaced the key to his laboratory-workshop."

The key was, of course, carefully squirrelled away in Evangeline's pocket. She scolded herself, she should have headed downstairs immediately rather than taking a detour to visit Mei. Now where would Evangeline locate the last remaining materials she needed for her secret invention?

"I'll help him look," Evangeline said, ducking aside to change back into her cumbersome day dress.

As she fastened the buttons on her bodice and planned tomorrow's visit to the goldsmith, Evangeline grinned with excitement.

Cake and capturing a magician. What could be more delightful?

CHAPTER 4

MISS PLOCKTON MARCHED EVANGELINE HOME. The sun was dipping low in the sky yet the heat was intensifying. One of Melbourne's many quirks was the heat peaking at the end of the day.

An auto-chariot roared down Exhibition Street and the traffic bustled with penny farthings, hansom cabs and a rattling modern steam tram. A telegraph kiosk sat on the corner, a top-hatted man tapped away furiously in Morse code. Evangeline strained her ears towards the kiosk, making out the words 'pudding' and 'elbow'. Morse Code was a skill Evangeline picked up on the dull dirigible journeys from London to Melbourne. The Captain, a rather modern gentleman, had taken a liking to Evangeline. He said Morse Code was a necessary element in the education of any practical minded young person. It had turned out to be quite the handy skill.

"You mustn't walk around by yourself, Miss Evangeline," Miss Plockton scolded. "It's not becoming for a young lady."

"No one saw me," Evangeline replied, as two young men strolled past and tipped their hats. One of the men had the most magnificently manicured moustache and dancing blue eyes. Evangeline hid her smile under her hand and worried about the state of her coiffure.

Miss Plockton tutted loudly.

"Yes, Miss Evangeline. You are practically invisible."

"I am only being polite, Miss Plockton. Would you prefer I was rude to the gentlemen?"

Miss Plockton continued to simmer with disapproval until they reached the iron railings of 56 Collins Street and opened the large oak door.

"There you are." The Professor was pacing up and down the hallway. "What took you so long?"

"Apologies, Professor," Miss Plockton said meekly.

"Are there any scones left?" Evangeline felt a little peckish after her bout with Mei. Kung fu was hungry work.

"Have you seen my laboratory-workshop key, Evangeline my dear?"

"Did you try your study? I remember watching you lock the door when Inspector Pensnett arrived."

"I can't locate it anywhere. It's useless, I'll have to break the door down."

Evangeline moved closer to her father.

"Are you sure it's not in your jacket?"

"I've checked everywhere, I tell you!" he blustered.

Evangeline stepped forward, opening her father's jacket. The Professor floundered, unsure how to behave when touched by his new seventeen-year-old daughter.

She reached into his inside pocket and extracted the brass key.

"Is this the key you were looking for?" she said innocently.

"But. But. But. It was not there before. I'm positive." He grabbed the key from her hand. "I'm absolutely positive."

The Professor stomped down the stairs to the laboratory-workshop, muttering to himself.

"It wasn't there before."

Miss Plockton shot a dubious look at Evangeline but said nothing. Evangeline smiled back sweetly and skipped off downstairs to join her father.

"Are we looking for your alchemist device, Professor?"

Evangeline was not quite used to calling him Father. She shuddered when she thought of Charlie Drigg, the man she thought was her father until the true story of her heritage was revealed.

The Professor rifled through a stack of suitcases at the back of the laboratory-workshop. The thick bluestone walls protected the room from the summer heat outside and the temperature was deliciously cool. A long bench ran down one side of the windowless room, topped with neatly arranged brass scales, clamps and drills. A selection of different sized wrenches, set squares and screwdrivers were attached to the wall, each in their right place. A row of green glass gas lamps blazed overhead.

The Professor's current project was splayed out in the middle of the room. Cogs, like intestines, spread out along the floor. The Professor was refining the next generation of his clockwork auto chariots, the latest personal travel device for one.

In the far corner was the Professor's secret project, covered in a dusty beige sheet. So secret he would not speak of it to anyone. Not even Miss Plockton, his personal secretary, knew what it was. Evangeline knew this secret project had brought the Professor to Melbourne from London, under the insistence of Governor Normanby himself. The sheet was fastened tight around the invention and secured with locks even Evangeline could not pick. She itched with curiosity. One day her father would confide in her but patience had never been one of her virtues.

The Professor grunted in reply as he flicked open the locks on another suitcase with his thumbs.

"How did you identify the alchemist? The one in London?"

"There are two types of alchemists."

The Professor pulled out a stuffed crow from the suitcase.

"Oh, I had plum forgotten about you." He placed the crow on the workbench. "Granville. You poor neglected fellow."

The Professor smoothed down the bird's feathers before returning to the enormous suitcase, large enough to hide two bodies.

"Go on, Father," Evangeline said, eyeing the crow suspiciously. Granville's beady black eyes seemed somehow perceptive and spooky.

"Two types. The type who run with those mountebanks like Madame Zsoldas with all their mesmer mumbo-jumbo."

"Charlatans?"

Evangeline was familiar with the ways of charlatans. In one of Evangeline's circus troupes, Agnesa the fortune teller promised to teach her the tricks of the mystic trade. But before she had a chance, her stepfather had been kicked out of the troupe for drunkenness and frightening the monkeys.

"Absolutely. They string fools along and claim magical powers to turn iron into gold and quadruple their money."

"And the others?"

"Proper men of science misunderstood by superstitious people. Wrongly accused and tainted by charlatans. Ah, here it is."

The Professor cried out in triumph, holding up a polished wooden box. He immediately followed with a hefty sigh.

"But where is the probe? It must have snapped clean off."

He dove into the deep suitcase, only his legs protruding from the top. Evangeline picked up and inspected the curious box with two small brass cylinders fixed on either side, a turnkey underneath and a swivelling broken brass rod at the front.

"Bother," said a muffled voice coming from the bottom of the suitcase, as the Professor tossed a fez, a glove stretcher and a bird scarer out onto the floor. "Must be here somewhere."

"What equipment do they use?"

From what the policeman had described, Evangeline knew she was looking for the first type of alchemist; but one capable of performing some type of glamour spell.

"Some ordinary equipment like a still and a mortar and pestle. And a pear-shaped device called an aludel. And of course, chemicals."

"Special chemicals? Could you find them here in Melbourne?"

"Oh, easily. From a farm supplier like Snodgrass & Sons."

Evangeline was tickled with anticipation. Tomorrow would be quite the busy day, with a visit to the Jewish goldsmiths and now Snodgrass & Sons, as well as tea and cake.

The Professor poked his head up out from the suitcase.

"Why so many questions? This is a matter for the police. Not something you should be concerning yourself with. You have many other matters to fill your time. Like your mathematics instruction and completing your miniature auto omnibus over there. This alchemy is dangerous business and not something to be trifled with."

"Yes, Father," she said meekly, looking over to her half-built wind-up car. The Professor was unaware of her more ingenious and useful invention hidden inside her bedroom. "You are right, Father. I should go upstairs and complete my lessons. If you don't need my help any further..."

"Of course. Of course. Don't let this folly keep you from your books. Retire to your room, young lady. And ask Miss Plockton to bring your supper up to you."

"Thank you, Father." Evangeline reached forward and planted a peck on his bristled cheek. He smelled of pipe tobacco, dust and tea.

Evangeline found Miss Plockton sitting at the kitchen table, hard at work writing tomorrow's list for the butcher boy.

"I'll bring up your supper soon," Miss Plockton said, without looking up. Evangeline had not said a word.

"No pressed tongue, please," Evangeline requested, before climbing the stairs to her own small but perfectly appointed room.

Evangeline loved the company of her new family, but each night she cherished the moment when she closed her bedroom door. A room of her own. After years sleeping in caravans, crammed into squats or doss houses with rats, damp and cold draughts, she now lived the highlife with a four poster feather bed, a rug, a bookshelf with books and a desk and chair. Even her own gas lamp.

There was a discreet knock on the door. Miss Plockton presented her supper on a tray, a brown boiled egg, two slices of bread with anchovy paste and a glass of lemonade. And in a small crystal bowl, a sight so lovely, she was inspired to cry out with delight.

"Oh, Miss Plockton. Strawberries and cream!"

She wrapped her arms around Miss Plockton's waist. Miss Plockton disentangled from Evangeline's embrace with the hint of a smile and ducked out of the room without a word.

Finally alone in her own castle, Evangeline retrieved her own battered suitcase from under the bed and unlatched the locks. It was time to work on her own device. She unfolded the rivet extracting pliers from her dress pocket and laid out her invention on the desk. She needed to finish her contraption post-haste. It may come in handy when capturing the alchemist.

She grinned, imagining how pleased her family would be when she captured the magician. The Professor would forget all about his misgivings once she saved the day.

Life was not so boring at 56 Collins Street after all.

CHAPTER 5

T HE NEXT DAY EVANGELINE WOKE early, determined to complete her construction before breakfast. She was screwing in the last bolt when she heard the wailing of a grown man outside her door. She hid away her half-finished invention, before running excitedly from her desk to see what the kerfuffle was all about.

The howl was coming from Uncle Augie's bedroom. The door flung open and Evangeline's not-real Uncle rushed into the hallway in his stocking feet, his round face distorted in anguish.

"No," he cried.

Evangeline picked up her skirts and rushed towards him.

Augie was clutching something in his palm.

"Where is he?" Evangeline darted into Augie's chambers, expecting to see a burglar or some ruffian. She checked behind the door but there was no one there. She peeked under the feather bed but there was nothing to be seen, not even dust. It was even clear under the writing desk. The room was empty.

There was one last possible hiding place in Augie's room. Evangeline crept up, placed her hand on the brass handles and flung open the wardrobe doors, but all she found were starched white shirts. She came back out into the hallway, disappointedly.

"It's ruined. His birthday is ruined," Augie wailed.

Miss Plockton suddenly appeared at the top of the stairs in her ghostly way. She seemed to be everywhere at once in the grand house on Collins Street.

"Have you taken ill, Mr Beauchamp?" she said with her soft Scottish burr in her harsh Scottish face.

"It cost me a month's wages and now look."

Augie pried open his fingers. He held a dull grey metal pocket watch in his soft skinned palm.

Evangeline and Miss Plockton crowded around for a closer look. Tears were rolling down Augie's bare cheeks. Evangeline had purloined many pocket watches in her time and she had never seen one made of such basic metal. The front was etched in decorative scrolls, inscribed with the name 'Edmund Caldicott'. In contrast, the face was of the highest quality, white and clean. The numbers clear and strong.

"Is it made of iron?" Evangeline said.

Iron was most certainly not to Augie's taste.

"What is this sorcery?" he wailed. "Edmund's birthday is on Friday. I cannot give him this!"

Augie tossed the iron watch aside, striking the wainscoting with a clatter. Evangeline scurried to pick it up. It did appear to be iron. Miss Plockton peered over Evangeline's shoulder, touching the watch gingerly with her finger.

"It was gold! I ordered it from Hart's. It was beautiful. He was going to be so handsome with it displayed from his waistcoat."

"Did they swap it without your knowledge?"

"I collected it the day before yesterday and packed it away myself. I was preparing to wrap it in this lovely grosgrain paper, when I saw it had gone from gold to grey!"

Evangeline nodded. Gold could not dull in this way overnight.

"The alchemist."

"I am calling the police!"

Uncle Augie stormed off down the stairs in his stocking feet, almost slipping on the oak stairs.

Another reason to find the alchemist. He should not be allowed to continue in Melbourne. Evangeline vowed she would catch the charlatan for Edmund and Augie. He would pay for ruining her Uncle's birthday.

CHAPTER 6

A T 56 COLLINS STREET, THE household breakfasted in the conservatory, overlooking the garden. The once lush greenery was now brown and crisp around the edges like the toast on the table. Even the Professor's wind-up automatic watering system could not save the periwinkles, Queen Anne's lace and snap dragons from the harsh weather.

All alone at the breakfast table, Evangeline snacked on thin toast and tea, leaving plenty of room for Faversham's cream cake. Perusing the headlines of The Argus, she read of the construction of the grand new Exhibition Building and vowed to take a stroll to Carlton Gardens to inspect it for herself. But her sight-seeing must wait, she was far too busy for such a leisurely pursuit while the alchemist was still at large.

"Taking an interest in current events? Very good," said Uncle Edmund. Augie followed closely behind in a particularly stylish sea-green ascot.

"But a young lady can know too much." Augie yanked the paper away from Evangeline, handing it to Edmund.

Edmund rolled his eyes at Evangeline and she giggled into her tea cup.

Miss Plockton appeared with a fresh pot and a plate of smoked kippers. Evangeline took her cue to leave. She did not want to waste any more time this morning, her carpet bag was packed ready to go.

"Join me in the sitting room, Miss Evangeline," Miss Plockton said. "We can resume our household accounts lesson."

"But I have an appointment," Evangeline stuttered.

"What did we discuss last night?" Miss Plockton said with thin white lips. "About leaving the house unescorted?"

Miss Plockton would spoil everything. How could she capture the alchemist with a chaperone in tow?

"With Mei. For tea," Evangeline blurted, instantly regretting her words. She should have taken her time to construct a better alibi.

"I must concur with Miss Plockton," Uncle Augie said. "Young ladies cannot go gallivanting around Melbourne unaccompanied, Miss Evangeline."

Now Augie was ruining her plans too. Augie could be such a bore sometimes, a stickler for tradition and etiquette. It was 1882 in the Antipodes, surely people no longer cared about such things.

Evangeline closed her mouth, unable to think of a truthful plea in her defence. Augie would not understand that she was determined to avenge the wrongdoing, seeking amends for Edmund's ruined birthday watch. Augie would be grateful once she apprehended the swindler. But if she told the truth now, she would not be permitted to leave 56 Collins Street.

She glanced at Edmund for support but he was too engrossed in The Argus.

Evangeline was stuck. Mei would have to visit the goldsmith's alone. But would Mei go without the bribe of cream-filled chocolate puffs? This was Evangeline's adventure after all.

"Now, where could you find a suitable escort?" Augie's eyes twinkled. "I may know someone who is available this morning."

Stay home or go out with Augie in tow? It was an easy choice. She and Mei could easily slip away from her uncle in the bustling streets. He would also pay for the tea.

"Miss Plockton, I'll gladly chaperone Miss Caldicott and Miss Fang today."

"Oh, Uncle Augie. You're the best." Evangeline wrapped her arms around her uncle.

"That's what they say," he replied.

CHAPTER 7

MEI EMERGED THROUGH HER FRONT gate in a pale green dress. Her glossy black hair piled up in a fashionable chignon, rather than her usual pigtail. She grimaced as Evangeline smiled appreciatively.

"Miss Fang, you have met my Uncle August before?" Evangeline jumped in before any stray word from Mei gave away their plans. "Uncle Augie will be accompanying us this morning."

"Mister Beauchamp." Mei extended her hand.

Augie bowed in a flamboyant flourish and placed his lips on her gloved hands.

"A pleasure to see you again, Miss Fang," he said. "Your dress is the most delightful hue. It does wonders for your eyes. You are quite the vision."

Mei blushed as she pulled her hand back.

A dappled grey horse and carriage clopped to a stop alongside the house.

"I called a hansom cab. The weather is far too beastly for promenading."

"I thought we could catch the steam tram?" Evangeline suggested.

"Don't let your father hear you mention the tram." Augie shuddered. "You know how he feels about this whole steam fad.

At any rate, a hansom cab is far more elegant. Who wants to be squeezed in with all the riffraff?"

Augie offered his hand, assisting Evangeline and Mei into the narrow cab. The three squeezed into the seat, the cover pulled up to shield their pale faces from the sun.

"Where to, sir?" the driver asked.

"Snodgrass & Sons," Evangeline said.

"The farming supplier?" said Augie. "Is Snodgrass the new place for young ladies to congregate? I must be behind the times."

"Oh no, Uncle, Mei needs to run an errand for her mother."

"The life of trade! How practical," Augie said and stroked his chin. "Actually Edmund could do with a new pair of riding boots. Yes, an excellent birthday gift. After what happened this morning..."

"I'll explain later," Evangeline whispered to Mei as the horse and cab took off down the cobbled street.

The cab passed the gentrified homes of Upper Collins Street, until the houses gave way to trading establishments, shops and the new banks with their grand sandstone arches. Two children in ragged trousers juggled on the corner of Elizabeth Street. Evangeline's heart leapt. Theirs was a life Evangeline knew well, filled with fleas, empty bellies and backhanders. She rummaged in her purse for a coin, to share some of her good fortune and stop them filching coins from unsuspecting passers-by. But the cab was travelling too fast and they swept past the boy and girl. Evangeline looked back helplessly as the people walked by, ignoring their tricks. Her new life was a world away from the streets but the memories were still fresh.

Snodgrass & Sons stood majestically on the corner of William and Bourke Street, taking over an entire city block. Under the wide verandah, the store front was piled high with silver buckets, sacks of seed and saddles. Shop assistants in navy striped aprons darted in and out, balancing brown paper parcels in their arms before loading up waiting traps and cabs. Sturdy farming folk fresh off the train streamed into the store or wandered dangerously into traffic, discombobulated by the busy city.

Evangeline, Mei and Augie stepped down from their hansom cab and a red-haired boy stopped to stare open mouthed at Mei.

"Boo!" Mei said, and the young boy scattered away to hide behind his mother's skirts.

"Oh, these people are rather rustic, aren't they?"

Augie looked down his nose at the ruddy farmer's wives with their wide bosoms and Sunday best hats.

They fought their way through a crowd outside, gathering to watch a demonstration of the latest pneumatic plough. Plumes of steam billowed into the air as the machine jerked into action.

"The finest new invention from Bavaria. The deepest furrows of any machine available in the world. And quick! An acre an hour." The salesman bellowed over the roar of the plough. "Your crop yields will sequentially improve exponentially. The rosiest tomatoes, the plumpest pumpkins, the tallest wheat..."

Evangeline, Mei and Uncle Augie entered Snodgrass & Sons through the large grand doors.

"Why are we 'ere?" Mei whispered.

"This is the place in Melbourne where an alchemist could buy their apparatus."

"I thought it was magical? Why not the Theosophist Store?"

"The Professor told me that they use everyday items. We're looking for something called an aludel."

"A what? I thought you said everyday items?"

The girls squeezed through the shopping crowds, easily eluding Uncle Augie, trapped behind a rotund family.

"This way."

Evangeline pointed to a sign hanging from the ceiling by a chain. 'Brewer's Wares'.

"May I help you, young ladies?" said an older man in a crisp striped apron, with a broom-like moustache accenting the uppity expression on his face. "A gift for your father, perhaps?"

"Indeed," Evangeline responded in her poshest accent. "My father's birthday next week. He is interested in an aludel."

"An aludel. Are you sure?"

"Quite sure."

"Perhaps he meant a ladle and you misheard."

His smile dripped with condescension.

"No. I remember quite distinctly," Evangeline tutted haughtily. "Perhaps they have aludels at Clunbury & Daughter."

Evangeline turned on her heel to leave.

"Oh, aludel. Of course," he said. "Let me check whether we have any in stock."

The snooty man rushed back to the long wooden counter and whispered in the ear of a round balding man. Bored by the lack of action, Mei strayed from the Brewer's Wares and inspected the array of rifles mounted on the wall.

"My apologies, Miss..." said the bald man, as he approached. He had the wettest lips Evangeline had ever seen.

"Prendegast. Miss Gwendoline Prendegast."

"Pleasure to meet you, Miss Prendegast. I am Mr Bletchley. Now, this is an odd kettle of fish. We receive very few requests for aludels. In fact, we have never had aludels in stock before. Until last month when a customer ordered one specifically. It was a tall terracotta specimen imported all the way from the Occident."

"Excellent. I shall take one."

"Unfortunately, Miss. We are out of stock at this present moment. I can order one for you. It can be here within two or three months."

Evangeline pouted.

"But I need it for Father's birthday. He will be so disappointed."

"We have some very handsome hip flasks? They are a perfect present for a father."

"That will never do. Father is a teetotaller."

"Your father sounds a practical gentleman. Perhaps one of our new shaving devices. Straight from the workshop of the famed inventor, Hank Buchanan of Buffalo, New York."

Evangeline winced as Mr Bletchley gestured towards a device which looked more suited to medieval torture than facial grooming. There was a brass cage for resting the chin with six cut-throat blades on a revolving barrel on each side. The Professor would detonate with rage if Evangeline brought a Hank Buchanan device anywhere near the house. There was some story about a stolen idea which Evangeline had yet to hear all the details.

"No. No. Oh, what am I going to do?" Evangeline sniffed, taking her handkerchief from her purse and daintily dabbing at her eyes.

Mr Bletchley and the snooty man shuffled awkwardly.

"We are most terribly sorry, Miss Prendegast."

Evangeline dried her fake tears.

"Perhaps you can help me. By chance would your customer want to sell me their aludel? For the right price?"

"That is possible."

"Yes, perhaps." The men nodded.

"I remember the customer quite distinctly. He appeared to be a high-minded gentleman." Mr Bletchley nodded. "Impressive grey whiskers..."

"You are very much mistaken, Mr Bletchley," said the snooty man. "I'm certain the customer was a lady. Tall and thin with jet black hair."

"You are the one who is mistaken. I would most definitely remember a female customer."

Evangeline deflated. The men were obviously victims of the alchemist's glamour. She was getting so close, yet the alchemist was slipping through her fingers again.

"I'll prove it to you."

Mr Bletchley sneered at his colleague before scurrying back to the counter and returning with a large ledger book. He opened the book. Evangeline leaned forward, memorising the names of the Melbourne residents who had been buying brewing supplies. One never knew when this type of information may come in handy.

"Here."

Mr Bletchley jabbed a stubby finger at a messily scrawled entry.

"I can't read it. What does it say?"

Evangeline peered closer. The writing was like a knotted thread.

"Ergh." Mr Bletchley flustered. "I think..."

"Whose handwriting is that? I don't recognise it."

"I was sure I served the gentleman." Mr Bletchley scratched his head.

The name was an ink blot but part of the address was legible.

"Wellington Parade, East Melbourne?" Evangeline said.

"That appears correct but I can't decipher the house number."

Evangeline squinted. Neither could she. Was it 57 or 81?

"Why thank you, gentlemen. My mother will be wondering where I am."

She stepped away, as the two shop assistants continued to bicker about the aludel buyer.

"It was a woman. I am certain of it."

"You must be going mad. It was most definitely a man..."

One thing was certain. The alchemist knew how to create a glamour. Evangeline was excited to have seized one vital yet incomplete piece of information.

CHAPTER 8

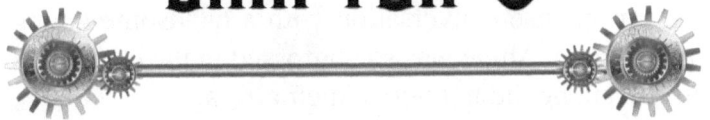

EVANGELINE TOOK ANOTHER DETOUR BEFORE seeking out Mei, locating the 'Clock Mechanics' department. Small woven baskets of differing sized cogs, nuts and springs, in warm brass and dull iron, lined the aisles. She searched until she found a basket of six-inch brass springs. She pushed the springs between her palms as hard as she could to test their strength. Satisfied, she selected four springs.

"An unusual purchase for a young lady. Are you shopping for your father?"

"No," Evangeline said. "This type of spring is ideal for...er... creating the perfect ringlet. It's in all the fashionable papers. I don't suppose you have the time to read The Girl's Own Paper."

The perplexed shop assistant blushed and wrapped her purchases in brown paper and string. Evangeline paid with the money the Professor had given her for a new lace handkerchief. Springs were considerably more useful. The Professor would understand, eventually.

Evangeline found Mei admiring the blade of a large hunting knife, while a shop assistant spied her curiously from a discreet distance.

"Let's go find Uncle Augie. Then our next stop is Hart's. I want to see the scene of the crime."

"Cake first."

"But Mei, every moment is vital."

"Cake. Or no Hart's."

"Very well." Evangeline sighed. "I have to admit, looking for clues is quite thirsty work."

The girls found Uncle Augie holding a strong leather riding boot and in intense conversation with a handsome young man with golden hair. Augie was so engrossed in the company of the beautiful man, he did not notice their arrival.

Evangeline coughed tactfully and Augie looked up with a broad smile.

"Ah, ladies. There you are."

"Sorry for interrupting, Uncle. But shopping is a thirsty endeavour. We were hoping it was time for tea?"

"Absolutely. It must be time for elevenses. Whilst these boots would make a fine gift for Edmund, I have spent more than enough time in this establishment."

Augie turned to the handsome man standing beside him.

"May I introduce my colleague, Mr Everett Foxton? Mr Foxton is one of the actors at the Prince Albert. You may recall, he played a marvellous Blood-Red Bill in Claude Duvall. Outstanding reviews in The Argus. Mr Foxton, please meet Miss Caldicott and Miss Fang."

Mr Foxton briefly smiled with gleaming straight teeth, Mei and Evangeline giggled into their hands and swooned.

"Oh, you flatter me too much, Mr Beauchamp. Charmed, ladies."

"Pleasure." They blushed and murmured, as he politely took their hands one after another, before turning his full attention back to Augie.

"May I tag along?" Mr Foxton said. "I'm awfully lonely here in Melbourne."

"I find that very hard to believe," Augie fussed.

Evangeline agreed. A man of his beauty would be a desirable commodity for every eligible young lady in Victoria, and her mother.

"Girls, would you mind if Mr Foxton joined us for tea?"

Evangeline found her tongue and her senses. An attractive gentleman must not distract her from her investigations.

"It would be an absolute pleasure, Mr Foxton."

They hailed a cab for four and travelled down Bourke Street. Past the street barrows stacked with red apples and yellow bananas, the steam tram covered in advertising placards and the construction of impressive new buildings on every corner. The sun had woken up this morning with a bad temper and the strong wind whipped up clusters of dust. Evangeline held her handkerchief firmly over her nose, thankful for the lavender scent, as the heat sizzled the mounds of horse dung, rotting apples and night soil, bringing the stink of Melbourne to new heights of revulsion.

It was a tight fit in the cab, Mr Foxton and Uncle Augie conversed quietly, their bodies pressed firmly against each other. Evangeline knew theatre people worked long hours together and became very close. Their exclusive conversation gave Evangeline the chance to whisper to Mei.

"After tea, let's escape from Uncle Augie."

"I could knock him out?" Mei offered.

Evangeline was impressed with Mei's nerve but an unconscious Uncle may be a little difficult to explain.

"Maybe next time," she said.

CHAPTER 9

THE PARTY OF FOUR WERE ushered to the last available table in Faversham's House of Tea. Evangeline breathed in deeply, savouring the warm scents of cinnamon and melting butter. The room was white, bright and cool with large windows facing the street, perfectly appointed for observing and being observed. Every table was crammed with mothers and daughters taking a well-deserved break from the toil of shopping along Bourke Street.

As they took their seats, the room rippled with whispers. Every woman in the room glanced up admiringly at Mr Foxton.

"Excuse me for interrupting, Mr Foxton." A woman with a wobbly double chin approached their table.

"I saw your performance in HMS Pinafore seven times. You were simply entrancing. Could I bother you for your autograph, Mr Foxton? For my daughter."

"Of course. Of course."

Mr Foxton replied graciously as she slipped a copy of The Argus in front of him.

"So very lonely," Uncle Augie teased and Foxton fobbed him off with a wave of his hand.

A frilly capped waitress poured tea from a white and gold curlicued teapot. Evangeline was wary of touching the delicate china cups for fear of breaking the handle clean off.

"Remember your manners," Uncle Augie whispered as he passed the silver sugar caddy.

Evangeline immediately raised her pinkie and Mei copied diligently. The two girls feeling like starlings in a room full of peacocks.

The waitress placed a tiered cake stand laden with sugary delights on the crisp damask tablecloth. The girls tucked into slices of cream cake with pink icing, glossy chocolate eclairs, wobbly orange jellies and golden scones with chunky marmalade. Mr Foxton barely nibbled on a piece of dry toast.

"I must maintain my physique."

Augie nodded knowingly. Mei frowned. Evangeline expected Mr Foxton was nothing like the hard working trade men in Mei's family.

The conversation turned to the strange tale of the faux gold watch.

"How intriguing," Mr Foxton said.

"I know. We're going... Ow." Mei howled as Evangeline kicked her under the table. Mei must learn to be more discreet.

"Yes, but extremely tiresome," Augie said. "I shall leave it to the police to handle. But I must find Edmund another birthday present."

"Have you been to Hugglescote's Gentlemen's Outfitters? They have recently opened off the Block Arcade. Finest French accoutrements this side of Paris."

"No, I haven't had the pleasure."

"Perhaps after our tea?"

Evangeline tried not to smirk. Thank heavens for Mr Foxton.

"Oh, but the young ladies. I cannot leave them unchaperoned."

"Of course you can..." Mei said.

"...if you must continue on," Evangeline interrupted, with a glare at Mei. "You can place us in a hansom cab bound for home. I do have lessons to attend to."

"That sounds like a sensible plan," Augie said.

Pleasantly jammed with cream cake and tea, the group settled their bill and stepped out to face the searing heat. Augie hailed a cab and placed the two girls inside, instructing the driver to 56 Collins Street.

"Are we givin' up?" said Mei once Augie was out of earshot. "Thanks for the eclairs, but I was hopin' for more of an adventure. You should've let me knock him out."

The horse clipped down the street. Evangeline swivelled around to watch Augie and Mr Foxton saunter away towards the Block Arcade, deep in discussion.

"Stop!" she exclaimed.

The driver skidded to a halt, jolting the two girls forward, almost toppling out of their seats.

"Are you alright, Miss."

The driver turned around, a worried look on his face.

"A change of plans, sir," she said. "We shall disembark here."

"But the gentleman said..."

"Nevermind what the gentleman said..."

"But you don't want to be goin' down there, young Miss."

"You can keep the fare. I won't tell a soul."

"Whatever Miss wants. Thank you kindly." The driver deposited the two young ladies onto the footpath and Mei led the way to Goldsmith's Alley.

It was time to hear the story from Mr Hart himself.

CHAPTER 10

E VANGELINE AND MEI TURNED UP the narrow
Goldsmith's Alley.
"You start the conversation and get him talking. He
knows you and won't suspect a thing. I'll ask questions once
he's explained his side of the story."

In Goldsmith's Alley, half of the shopfronts were boarded
up. Business was slow now the gold rush had turned into a slow
trickle. But not at Hart's. Their brightly painted sign, sparkling
clean windows, marble flooring and red velvet display cabinets
showed business was still strong. A gold pocket watch was a must
for every gentlemen and especially the newly rich land boomers.

The shop bell tinkled as Mei pushed open the door. A young
man with flashing dark eyes rushed out from behind the front
glass counter.

"Ah, Miss Fang. What an unexpected surprise? How lovely
you look today."

"Mr Hart. You are too kind. Have you met my companion,
Miss Evangeline Caldicott?"

Evangeline was still getting used to her new name. Caldicott
was so much more elegant than Drigg. But who was she? On
some days, Evangeline was not quite sure.

"I have not had the pleasure. Welcome to my family's modest establishment, Miss Caldicott. How may we be of assistance today?"

"We were in the vicinity. Taking tea at Faversham's. When I told Miss Caldicott of your wares."

"Why, thank you for your recommendation, Miss Fang. Is there a particular item you are interested in, Miss Caldicott? A gift perhaps."

"I presume you have pocket watches? I am looking for a lovely gift for my father's birthday."

Mr Hart stumbled.

"Ordinarily, yes. However, a buyer came in yesterday and bought up our entire stock. A land boomer with an unexpected windfall. So unfortunately today, I have nothing to show you."

Mei and Evangeline shot each other a sideways glance.

"May I suggest a gold ring? Or a cravat pin?"

Evangeline laughed a little as she thought about her father wearing a gold ring on his clockwork fingers. Gold clashed terribly with brass.

"My father is not the ring wearing type."

All of a sudden, the shop door burst open and a familiar voice cried out.

"Evangeline Caldicott. What are you doing here?"

Evangeline spun around to see Uncle Augie's angry face.

"Knickers," she muttered under her breath.

"I told you to have nothing to do with these men! These charlatans!"

"Excuse me, sir. Please lower your voice," Mr Hart said. "There is no need to shout."

"How dare you speak to me like that? After what you've done."

A stooped man with a long flowing beard, white shirt and black waistcoat appeared from the back room.

"What is all this noise about? Asher?"

"Father. This man is causing a ruckus."

The older Mr Hart whispered to young Asher and his face paled. Augie glowered at both Evangeline and the two men.

Evangeline wished she could run out the door and escape her Uncle's wrath, but she would not be able to run far in these skirts.

"We are terribly sorry, Mr Beauchamp. My son did not recognise you," said the older Mr Hart. "Please be assured we had nothing to do with the incident. We were as duped as you were. Please accept a refund, or perhaps you would like to choose another of our fine gentleman's accessories?"

"I will never own a piece of your tat! You should be closed down. Mark my words, I will be reporting you to the Governor. Personally."

Augie leaned his ample frame over the glass counter, pointing his finger into the faces of the two Mr Harts. His face as ruddy as the velvet display cushions.

"Birthday ruiners! I don't know how you can live with yourselves?"

"Hear him out, Uncle. Please." Evangeline placed her arm on her not-real Uncle's arm. She hoped to coax more information from the old man.

"The police confiscated all our watches and found the trickery for themselves. The gold turned to iron inside the police station. We have removed every item from the particular shipment of gold from sale. We were tricked like you. It was some kind of dybbuk," the older Mr Hart said.

"Dyb-what?" said Mei.

"An evil spirit from the old country. Cursed ghouls who delight in harming innocent people. The dybbuk must have possessed us both and convinced us to pay a high price for the fake gold."

"So if the dybbuk didn't sell you the gold..." Evangeline said. "Who did?"

The father and son shook their heads with downcast faces.

"We cannot remember," the old man said

"It was like a dream," Asher said. "Every now and then, I catch a glimpse of his face in my mind but before I see him clearly, it vanishes."

"Dybbuks? A likely story. Why not blame the goblins?" Augie scoffed.

"I promise you, sir." The old man cowered.

"You orchestrated the whole swindle and you will pay for this. Believe me. No one crosses August Beauchamp," Augie spluttered. "Come, Evangeline, we're leaving."

"But..." Evangeline said.

Augie grabbed Evangeline by the elbow and pulled her out of the door.

CHAPTER 11

BANISHED TO HER ROOM YET again, Evangeline could hear Miss Plockton behind the closed door, pacing the hallway like a sentry. Evangeline slumped on one elbow, staring out the window, plotting her next move. She knew the alchemist resided somewhere on Wellington Parade. Knocking on every door looking for an alchemist was out of the question. She could not even leave the house. Yet she needed more information on the identity of the mysterious aludel purchaser.

The heat was stifling and prickled Evangeline all over. She mopped her damp forehead and wished the bothersome sun would go away. It was so unfair to be confined upstairs. How could she find the alchemist from her bedroom? Then Evangeline remembered. It was Wednesday night.

"Of course!"

She bounded out of her seat and opened her bedroom door.

"Miss Evangeline. You are not ta come out of your room. You heard the Professor."

"I know, Miss Plockton. I am terribly sorry for all I've done today. I only wanted to help."

She opened her eyes wide, attempting a beseeching look. Miss Plockton's face was as blank as the wall behind her.

"I've had time to think about my wicked deeds. I must turn over a new leaf and mend my ways. I would like a chance to repent for what I've done."

"Repent?" Miss Plockton said with a raised eyebrow.

"If only I could be as good as you, Miss Plockton. You are quite the paragon of virtue."

"I am no different to you. I am a sinner, doing my best to live by God's laws."

"Exactly. I need to know more about God and his laws and so on."

A flicker of indecipherable emotion ran across Miss Plockton's face. Evangeline hoped she was being convincing.

"You want ta learn more of God's word?"

"Oh yes, Miss Plockton. I have been reading the Bible you gave me and I would like to seek God's guidance on how to be less wicked."

"Your interest is rather sudden."

"Oh no, I have been wondering about God and the Bible for days. Weeks even."

Miss Plockton fixed Evangeline with a long and hard stare before replying

"I will speak with your father. There is a service this evening at St. Andrew's. The Reverend gives a wonderful sermon. You would greatly benefit from hearing his words. Your father's lack of attendance is worrisome, I often pray for your soul."

"Thank you, Miss Plockton," Evangeline said solemnly.

Evangeline closed the door. She felt a pang of guilt, but once she captured the alchemist, Miss Plockton would understand her white lies were for a greater good.

Like her education, Evangeline's religious instruction was patchy. Before the death of her mother, when Evangeline lived in a normal house and went to school, her family attended church every week. But after her mother's death, when her life and her stepfather spiralled out of control, God was another part of her life to fall by the wayside.

She pushed aside the red and amber oriental rug beside her bed and pressed on the short floorboard, revealing the secret hiding place beneath. She reached in and grabbed a brass telegraph key.

"Meet me tonight at ten o'clock. In the laneway." She tapped in Morse code.

"Why?" was the instantaneous response.

Whilst rifling in the laboratory-workshop two weeks ago, Evangeline found two basic telegraph key devices coated in dust. Recognising the devices from her travels in the dirigibles from London to Melbourne, Evangeline took them upstairs to study further, before handing one over to Mei. There had to be ways for young ladies to speak with one another without their parents knowing. They agreed to keep their conversations short in case someone intercepted but Mei was succinct at the best of times.

"We're going to catch the alchemist."

"Ten o'clock," Mei responded.

Evangeline was smoothing the rug over with her boot when Miss Plockton rapped on her door and entered with a tray.

"Your father has agreed. You can accompany me to this evening's service. It begins at six."

She placed a tray on Evangeline's writing desk. Her tea comprised of slices of pink ham, a speckled boiled egg and a piece of seed cake, accompanied with a small pot of Darjeeling for one.

"I am so pleased, Miss Plockton. I am very much looking forward to it."

A brief smile graced Miss Plockton's lips, showing a handsomeness in her father's secretary's face never visible before. She looked almost pretty.

Again Evangeline felt guilt at her falsehood. But she was curious to see Miss Plockton's beloved church and glimpse her life outside the house on Collins Street.

Alone once again, Evangeline unwrapped her brown paper parcel from Snodgrass & Sons and set to work completing her new invention. With her rosewood-handled screwdriver, she fastened the two large springs on either side. There was no time or space to test her new invention properly, she only hoped it worked.

CHAPTER 12

S LAPPING THE REINS AGAINST THE horse's rump, Miss Plockton proved to be an accomplished horsewoman, guiding the chestnut mare through the dust clouded streets. Ordinarily, Miss Plockton walked to church but today she borrowed a horse and cab from the Nibthwaites next door.

They must have looked quite a sight. Their faces clad in the Professor's newest prototype, a device to keep out the dust and stench of Smelbourne. The leather straps were hot and sweaty against Evangeline's scalp but the fine mesh around the nose and mouth blocked out the terracotta dirt.

They travelled for ten minutes through the hordes of workers returning to their homes from their shifts on the wharves and in the factories. Shop assistants travelling out to their homes in Collingwood and North Melbourne. The cab stopped for a moment, at one of the new clockwork traffic controllers on the corner of Exhibition and Little Lonsdale Street. Nefarious types loitered around the entrance to the sinful streets of Little Lon, with its brothels and opium dens. Miss Plockton's hand graced the small gold cross around her neck as the traffic moved again and the horse passed the lascivious laneways. Evangeline had not ventured into this part of Melbourne, but she knew the similar streets in London well and had no desire to walk those depraved streets again.

They arrived at St Andrew's, a small bluestone church with a slate roof, simple and unadorned with an iron cross above the front doors. They removed their nasal protectors and wiped their faces with handkerchiefs, before walking up the stone steps. Miss Plockton nodded at the other men and women as they entered but she did not stop to chat. There was a heavy air of seriousness.

Inside, they found a seat on the long wooden pews. Evangeline wriggled to get comfortable, she lacked the natural padding of some of the other women in the congregation. The air was cool inside the stone church, a welcome respite from the stuffy air outside. Men wiped their faces with handkerchieves and women fanned themselves with their hymn sheets.

The church was not what Evangeline expected. The new cathedral on the corner of Swanston and Flinders Street had high ceilings, pointed decorated garrets and stained glass windows in red, amber and green. Miss Plockton's church was plain, more like a meeting hall, yet filled with an understated sense of grace.

"It is not like the gaudiness of those Catholic churches." Miss Plockton read Evangeline's mind again. "We do not need such extravagance to show our devotion to the Lord. He looks down on such showiness."

Evangeline nodded, although thinking a bit of colour would be nice.

The room filled with people and hushed murmurs. A few notes belched from the church organ and everyone rose to their feet. Miss Plockton pulled Evangeline up to her feet by her elbow. She handed her a hymn book open to the right page. The room burst into song, including Miss Plockton in thin reedy notes. Evangeline opened and closed her mouth silently, pretending to join in with the unknown song.

A short balding man in a white robe emerged at the altar and the room fell silent. His clear Scottish voice boomed up to the vaulted ceilings and echoed off the back wall. Evangeline was overwhelmed by the power of the small man's voice.

She glanced around at the other parishioners as the sermon started. Was there going to be more singing? What should she do? She copied Miss Plockton and listened intently to the man's words.

"And Jesus met the ten lepers on the road..." the Reverend roared.

During her life in the circus and on the streets as a pickpocket, there had been no time for God. On the worst nights, when her stepfather spent all their money in the inns, leaving her hungry and alone in a squat, coming home drunk and beating her, she would curl in a ball and ask her mother for help. Evangeline's pleas went unanswered for years but eventually the Professor appeared. Whether this was God, Evangeline did not know. She only knew now was the time to repay the favour. Investigating and capturing the alchemist was her way of making amends.

She pulled herself away from the thrall of the Reverend's word and put her plan into action. It started with a tickle in her throat. A few modest throat clearings.

"Ahem. Ahem."

Miss Plockton glanced across, Evangeline covered her mouth demurely.

Then again. This time, a deeper cough.

Miss Plockton looked again, her displeasure clear across her face.

Then Evangeline coughed harder.

The parishioners on her left and right began to shuffle in their seats. Any sign of sickness in a crowded place was a cause for concern. Miss Plockton scowled deeply but Evangeline kept coughing, louder and louder.

"Excuse yourself, Miss Evangeline. Find a glass of water," she hissed.

Evangeline, red faced with exertion, nodded. She stood up and shuffled past the knees of her fellow parishioners.

"Sorry. Excuse me. My apologies."

She hurried up the aisle, coughing along the way for full effect. She slipped through the thick wooden doors into the hot Carlton streets.

The area between Sorrel and Ferguson Street was known as the Cast Iron district. Lacy cast iron work decorated every verandah, pillar and fence post in the fashionable parts of town. If a person wanted to source supplies of iron, this is the place they would come. For instance, a person who lived on Wellington Parade.

Evangeline grimaced. It was after six o'clock and the Cast Iron district was closing for the day. If only she had been able to escape the house earlier.

She walked up to the first Iron Works. A sweaty redheaded man with rolled up shirt-sleeves and a tweed jacket over his shoulder was locking the gate.

"Ain't you open?" she said. This was not the place for her new lady voice.

"Finished up for the day, duck," he replied. "Come back tomorra."

"Oh heavens. My employer will be rotten angry. I shouldn't've dallied on the way up here." Evangeline covered her eyes with her hands.

"Sorry. I've got to get home for me supper."

The man walked up onto the street, heading away from the Iron Works. Evangeline ran after him.

"My employer, they're a bit soft in the 'ead. They ordered some iron from one of the works here and they can't remember which one."

The man screwed up his face and guffawed.

"There's over a hundred works around here. Needle in a haystack, duck."

Evangeline was not pretending this time, when her shoulders slumped.

"What will I do?" she sighed. "I can't go back with nothin'."

"Sorry, love. It's been a bad day for all of us. Must be somethin' in the water."

"What happened to you?"

"My guvnor is mad as a wet hen. Some customer ripped him off royally."

"Nothing to do with gold, is it?" Evangeline said.

"How do you know?" the ironworker said with surprise.

Another victim of the alchemist.

Across the quiet streets, the church bells of St. Andrew's pealed. There was no time to grill the ironworker further, she could not chance getting into deeper trouble with Miss Plockton.

"Thank you, sir," Evangeline said and dashed away, running along the street as fast as she could, back to the church. She bolted across the street, narrowly missing a milk cart led by two black horses, and rolled her ankle in a divot in the road. Grimacing, she kept running until she flopped down on the church steps, frantically fanning herself with her skirts, as the main doors creaked open.

Miss Plockton emerged with a face as dark as her dress. Evangeline jumped to her feet and rushed over to her.

"I am so sorry, Miss Plockton. It was something in my throat. Maybe a fly or something. The Professor's nasal dust protector needs a few more tweaks."

Miss Plockton pursed her lips tightly, yet burst into a wide smile as the Reverend approached. This was a revelation, Evangeline never knew Miss Plockton could smile.

"Father Inverpepper. A lovely sermon as always." She gushed in a not very Miss Plockton way. Evangeline smirked as she watched Miss Plockton's girlish excitement.

"Thank you, Miss Plockton. And I see you have brought along a bonny new face."

"Yes, this is the Professor's daughter, Father. Miss Evangeline Caldicott."

Evangeline awkwardly curtseyed, unsure of the correct etiquette for meeting a man of the cloth.

"Welcome, Miss Caldicott. I hope you enjoyed my sermon and our church here. We are a simple, honest congregation. Living by the word of the Lord."

"Oh yes, it was very inspiring, sir."

"I hope we will see you again."

He turned to the next parishioner, holding up a rosy cheeked child.

"Now, home with you, Miss Evangeline." Miss Plockton turned back into her regimented soldier voice and marched Evangeline back to the cab.

Disheartened at the prospect of returning empty handed, Evangeline was quiet all the way home. The alchemist was proving more elusive than she anticipated.

CHAPTER 13

B OTHERATION."
The Professor lifted his visor to inspect his welding. The replacement probe on his alchemy detector had failed to meld, clattering to the flagstone floor as soon as he extinguished the blue flame.

"I don't understand. Why is this not sealing?"

Evangeline sat on a stool nearby, her eyes shielded by a visor too large for her small head. Watching her father work was infinitely more enjoyable than her lessons in the sitting room. The Professor's every move was memorised for her own secret experiments in her bedroom. Although, welding in her bedroom may not be the best idea.

"The probe moves when it is touched against alchemised gold?" she asked

"Not quite. When placing an alchemised substance between the two coils, the electric current reads its true nature and the probe responds by vibrating wildly. Well, that's how it was designed to work. Something is not quite right."

"It can detect magic?"

The Professor hemmed and hawed.

"I thought you were a man of science who did not believe in magic?"

The Professor smoothed down his moustache with his creaking brass fingers.

"There are many unknowns in this world. We are only now embarking on great scientific discoveries. We may call it magic now, but I am sure in time, we will understand the true science behind everything."

Evangeline nodded, although she did not completely understand what the Professor meant.

"So you do believe in magic?"

"I have built a few devices which can detect electrical energies. Those energies exist but we do not understand where they come from. Some people can manifest these energies from somewhere within their bodies. Some use it for good purposes and some for evil."

The Professor opened a drawer and pulled out a long brass cylinder, retractable like a telescope. He handed the cylinder to Evangeline.

"My atervis detector. I developed this in England, when investigating a series of... disturbances... in my old home in Bloomsbury."

"An apparition?"

Evangeline's spine tingled deliciously.

"An energy field. This device identifies energy using a gemstone known as nuummite. Some people say this stone allows you to see black magic. In my opinion, there is a perfectly reasonable explanation. The stone identifies unusual energy fields."

Evangeline took the brass cylinder in her hand and looked through the eye-piece.

"I don't see anything," she said disappointedly.

"There is probably nothing to see here. If there was an unusual energy, it glows with a silver aura."

"Do you think there are apparitions in this house?"

"This weather is causing havoc with my joints. Dust everywhere." The Professor chuckled, squeezing oil into the cogs of his clockwork hand. "I have been living in this house for over a year now and I have not experienced anything out of the ordinary. Has Miss Plockton mentioned something? The Scots tend to be a superstitious breed."

"No one has mentioned anything supernatural in the house. But maybe there is something creeping about behind the wainscoting."

"I see no harm in exploring. But don't take the detector out of the house. There are many bad eggs out there, people who know how to use these energies. Those who take pleasure in wickedness."

"I know that," Evangeline muttered, looking down at her boots. Her stepfather's face appeared in her mind. Although he was thousands of miles away in England, the mere thought of him filled Evangeline with dread.

"Of course, my dear." The Professor blustered, reaching out a clumsy, comforting hand. "I only want you to be safe. I can't make up for those years we were estranged. But now you are under my protection, I want to ensure you are happy."

"And I am," Evangeline replied.

She had everything a young lady could want. A loving family, all the food she could eat, pretty dresses and a warm comfortable bed. She no longer had to beg or steal or perform on the streets. Her gratitude to the Professor was endless. Many men would have denied their paternity but the Professor was a good man, welcoming Evangeline into his family.

Evangeline took another look through the magic detector.

She gasped.

Through the eye-piece Evangeline saw a faint glimmer of silver, emerging from one of the Professor's trunks in the corner.

"There! I see silver."

The Professor leaped to his feet and with the speed of a man half his age and size, slammed the trunk lid closed.

"Time for bed, young lady. Don't stay up too late looking for ghouls."

"But Father. The trunk?"

"Good night, Evangeline," the Professor said firmly.

"Good night, Father," she said, defeated.

Another secret for another time.

Evangeline pecked her father's cheek, feeling his hard metal fingertips against her shoulder blade.

"I am glad you are here," he whispered in her ear.

She smiled and closed the door behind her, the magic detector in her hand. It would soon be ten o'clock.

CHAPTER 14

A
T THE FIRST STRIKE OF the Town Hall clock,
Evangeline slipped out the window, shimmied down
the drain pipe and dropped to the ground with the
stealth of a cat. The house was quiet. Lights glowed from Miss
Plockton's room in the attic and Uncle Edmund's study, windows
wide open, desperate to catch any whiff of cool night air. The
Professor was underground in his workshop, still mending the
probe on his alchemy detector. Evangeline hoped he would be
pleased when she returned having solved the mystery of the
alchemist and not too annoyed that his repairs were in vain.

Crossing the courtyard, she opened the door leading to the
back laneway. Evangeline winced as the hinges squealed in
protest. The new gaslights did not extend to the back lanes so
Evangeline treaded carefully to avoid any piles of night soil.

Mei was leaning against the brick wall, waiting.

"Ready?" Evangeline whispered.

"You're the late one."

Mei was dressed in a traditional black Oriental jacket and
trousers. Evangeline cursed her full skirted dress with its boning
and reams of fabric, wishing for her practical, yet immodest,
acrobat's leotard. But her skirts had deep pockets, perfect for
holding magic detectors.

They followed the laneway to Spring Street in silence. This was a genteel area filled with good families, but the scoundrel filled slums were only streets away. Evangeline was not concerned, she and Mei were no ordinary young ladies.

Stepping out into the gaslight, they dashed across the street, past the doric columns of Parliament House and the building site for the new Ministry for the Advancement of Profitable Enterprises. The building commissioned by the Governor and designed by Evangeline's very own Uncle Edmund. She smiled proudly at the blocks of sandstone and could not wait to see the final result. She was blessed with such a clever family.

They darted through the shadows, avoiding cabs clipping down the road and drunks weaving back and forth along the footpath. Evangeline's heart palpitated in her chest, twittering with excitement. They crossed into the wilds of Fitzroy Gardens, their senses on high alert for bandits or robbers. The Argus was filled with daily stories of bushrangers hiding in the Gardens and a park keeper was now permanently employed to keep out the criminals. Evangeline and Mei evaded the light, scurrying from tree to tree and bush to bush.

Then the most awful noise blared, an inhuman screech sounded from deep inside the park. A spine-scraping wail like nothing Evangeline had ever heard before.

"The Bunyip," Mei exclaimed. "Hurry."

"The what?"

"Quick."

Evangeline grabbed the brass atervis detector from her pocket and peered through the lens, scanning the park in the direction of the frightening screech. She gasped as a blur of silver darted through the darkness. Something was out there.

"Run," Evangeline squealed.

They bolted past the statue of Diana and the Stag and kept running until they safely crossed the walkway over the creek and into East Melbourne. The friends scurried like mice between the bushes, past the mansions circling the Gardens, until they reached the wide, tree lined boulevard of Wellington Parade. Evangeline spied a round wide bush, perfect for hiding two slight young females, and pulled Mei into the protection of its branches.

"What's that telescope?"

"The Professor lent me one of his inventions. It is called an atervis detector. You peer through the end and it reveals the aura of magic."

"Magic detectors?"

"He designed it especially for seeking out dark energy."

"And he let you borrow it?"

"I wasn't to leave the house with it. But how could I not? It is the perfect implement to find the alchemist."

"We're gonna walk down the street with the telescope looking for magic?" Mei scoffed. "Crafty."

"Do you have a better plan?"

Mei shrugged.

"And when we do find this magic? What then? We call your friends, the police?"

"Pfft. Police. This is our chance to be heroines, Mei. We could be on the front page of The Argus solving the crime. It's so exciting."

"Sounds like a wild goose chase to me."

"We know the house address is in Wellington Parade and had two digits. And here's number 10. Let's start."

Evangeline walked along with the atervis detector firmly attached to her right eye, inspecting each home from top to bottom, looking for any hints of the silvery aura of black magic.

"How long is Wellington Parade?" Mei yawned.

They had only walked past three mansions. Evangeline shrugged. Mei began to dawdle behind her, dragging her flat slippers against the iron gates of the palatial homes.

The minutes turned into half an hour as Evangeline and Mei scoured Wellington Parade for any evidence of magic. But there was no trace of a silver aura through the lens. Her arm was tiring and a sore spot was wearing under the ball of her foot. Her boots were not designed for traipsing such distances. Mei plucked leaves from nearby trees and lagged further and further behind.

"Look out," Mei hissed.

She pushed Evangeline into the nearest shrubbery.

"Look. On the other side of the street."

It was a bobby on patrol, twirling his truncheon and whistling.

"Someone has spotted us and called the police."

"He looks like he is out for an evening stroll, rather than searching for marauders." Evangeline giggled. "But we must keep out of his sight."

Evangeline held up the atervis detector again, to get a closer look at the policeman as he walked on the opposite side of the street. As she peered through the lens, a horse and carriage clip-clopped through her line of sight.

"Knickers." She gasped.

"What?" Mei whispered.

Evangeline looked again, following the carriage as it continued down Wellington Parade towards Richmond. Through the lens, the edges of the carriage glowed silver, like a freshly polished looking glass.

"The carriage! Follow it."

"But the policeman will see us," Mei replied.

"It's getting away. I know it is the alchemist."

"Perhaps your eyes are trickin' you. Let me see."

Evangeline passed the detector to her friend.

Mei placed the glass to her eye.

"Blimey!" Mei said. "I see it too. Blazing silver."

The carriage was now fading from view and the silver aura trailing away into the distance. The bobby was strolling in the same direction.

"You go after the carriage," Evangeline said. "I'll get rid of the policeman."

"But this is your adventure."

"We're wasting time arguing. He's getting away and you're faster on foot. Follow the carriage and wait outside the alchemist's house. I'll fob off the policeman and come and find you. Then we can solve this mystery together."

Mei dashed off after the carriage. Her flat shoes were indeed more convenient for chasing alchemists than Evangeline's heeled boots. But then again, Evangeline's boots had other advantages.

Evangeline took a deep breath and dusted off her rusty acting skills. She vigorously rubbed her eyes and headed across the road towards the policeman, sobbing loudly.

CHAPTER 15

"EXCUSE ME, SIR," EVANGELINE SOBBED.
The young policeman, who was cursed with a pathetic and patchy moustache, turned and rushed towards her.

"Miss. Are you hurt?"

Evangeline blubbered and wiped her nose on her sleeve, hiding the detector deep inside her skirt pockets.

"I am so sorry, Constable. Can you help me?" she wailed in her best Irish accent. "I am very lost."

"Don't cry, Miss. Where are you supposed to be?"

"Collins Street, sir. My mistress will be awful angry. I was only supposed to be gone an hour." Evangeline snivelled. "She has such a temper. She'll clip me 'round the ear or turn me out onto the streets. Then I'll have nowhere to go."

"Oh, Miss. You are lost. You are heading in completely the wrong direction."

"Oh, I am an eejit. I've only arrived off the boat from Derry a few days ago."

"It's an easy mistake to make in a new town. Turn around and head back that way." The Constable pointed. "But don't cut through the park. It's not safe at night. Follow Wellington Parade and you'll eventually come to Spring Street."

"I know my way from there. God bless you, Constable," Evangeline said with a curtsey.

"My pleasure, Miss."

The Constable doffed his helmet and continued down Wellington Parade. Evangeline walked in the opposite direction for a few houses, then hid in the shadows, waiting for the Constable to disappear from sight.

Minutes passed but it felt like hours. Evangeline's heart raced with excitement. Mei would be waiting outside the alchemist's house by now. Soon, she and Mei would reveal the identity of the charlatan. Everyone would be so proud.

Evangeline counted to five hundred, then followed the path of the Constable and Mei. She darted from shadow to shadow along the gas-lit street, listening intently for Mei's call.

But she passed house after house, without sight or sound of her friend. Her feet aching.

"Mei," Evangeline whispered into the darkness. "Where are you?"

There was no sign of her friend.

Evangeline's excitement began to turn to panic. She pulled the atervis detector from her pocket and began inspecting the houses for any trace of silvery aura.

"What are you doing here?" said a voice.

Evangeline gasped and turned.

The Constable emerged from a side laneway, chuckling.

"You do have a poor sense of direction, don't you, Miss?"

"Oh, you startled me, sir." Evangeline switched back into her Irish accent and hid the detector. "I must have taken a wrong turn somewhere."

"Never mind. This time I'll escort you back myself."

"Oh," Evangeline said. "There's no need, sir. I'm sure I can find my way back this time."

"I insist, Miss. It's a quiet night. It will only take ten minutes to take you back where you belong."

"I don't want to be any trouble. I can manage on my own."

"It will be my pleasure." The young policeman smiled. "This way."

Evangeline stalled.

If she ran, the sensible booted policeman would easily catch her. And then what would happen, would he escort her home to her father? She pictured the Professor's face, purple with rage.

Evangeline was torn.

"Did you say you were from Derry? My grandfather was from County Derry too. We could be related. I'm Constable Kane."

"Mary O'Malley, sir."

"Pleased to meet you, Miss O'Malley. Now, this way back to Collins Street."

Reluctantly, Evangeline decided to follow Constable Kane. Eventually Mei would get bored of waiting for her and probably return home. Perhaps she had lost sight of the carriage and was already home safe, waiting by her telegraph key for Evangeline.

The policeman escorted Evangeline along the safe route around the outskirts of Fitzroy Gardens, past Parliament House, to the laneway at the Spring Street entrance.

"Will you be safe from here, Miss?"

"I know my way now. I will be in even more trouble if I am seen returning with a handsome young gentleman. My mistress will think even worse of me."

The young bobby blushed violently.

"May I call on you, Miss O'Malley? To ensure you made it home safely. Otherwise I'll worry. We don't want you getting lost again."

"I would like that, Constable. 46 Collins Street."

Constable Kane bowed his head and let Evangeline scurry into the darkness of the laneway.

She stuffed her hand in her mouth to stop herself from giggling, thinking of the poor Constable knocking on the door of 46 Collins Street tomorrow to find no Mary O'Malley.

She scuttled along the cobblestones, through the complaining door and into the back courtyard. Miss Plockton's light was out.

The sounds of hearty male laughter floated down from Edmund's study, Augie must be home from the theatre.

Evangeline scurried up the drainpipe, grabbed the window sill and swung her body through the open window, landing on the floor in a crouched position with barely a sound.

Disappointed with her fruitless evening, Evangeline pulled her telegraph key from under the floor board and sat at her writing desk, waiting for Mei's communique.

The next thing Evangeline knew, there was a knock on her door. The sun was streaming through the open window, she had fallen asleep at her desk. She glanced at her mantel clock. It was after nine. Her neck cricked, and, still in her clothes from last night, she quickly stuffed the telegraph key under her pillow, before Miss Plockton burst through the door.

"Oh, thank heavens, Miss Evangeline."

Miss Plockton sighed loudly.

"Good morning, Miss Plockton. Is something wrong?" Evangeline said.

"She isnae here, Mrs Fang," Miss Plockton replied, as Mei's mother came into the bedroom behind her. Her eyes red.

"Why would Mei be here?" Evangeline asked. A knot clenched in her stomach.

"She's disappeared. We suspected you were together, off on one of your gallivants. But here you are safely in your room."

"Disappeared?"

Evangeline collapsed back onto her bed, her mind reeling. The alchemist.

"She no sleep in her bed. Her room empty," Mrs Fang said.

Tears sprang to Evangeline's eyes. She bit her lip.

"You know where is Mei?" Mrs Fang asked. Hope and worry inscribed across her face.

"No, Mrs Fang," Evangeline said truthfully. "I don't know where she is."

She didn't lie but she didn't tell the whole truth. Mei was somewhere on Wellington Parade.

This debacle was all Evangeline's fault. She should have been the one to chase the carriage. Tonight she would go alone to find the alchemist and rescue her friend.

CHAPTER 16

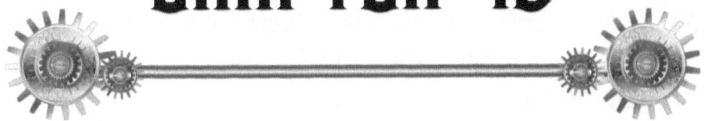

THE DAY WAS LONG AND maudlin. Evangeline moped. Her distracted thoughts were noted during her physics lesson with the Professor and watercolours with Miss Plockton.

"I'm positive the police will find her," said the Professor. "Inspector Pensnett is a splendid chap."

"I've said a prayer for Mei. The Lord will bring her home," assured Miss Plockton.

Evangeline only sighed and nodded in response, her mind wandering into many dark and different places. She pictured the alchemist experimenting on Mei, turning her friend into a statue of fool's gold. Her conscience prickled, yet Evangeline was confident she would rescue her friend. She anxiously awaited nightfall.

Cook baked Evangeline's favourite plum tart for tea. Evangeline smiled weakly and thanked her, but her appetite was ruined. The tart only reminding her of their trip to Faversham's the day before. Augie attempted to lighten the mood with a tale of an actor's jape, the lead actor's moustache wax swapped for anchovy paste.

"Oh, we laughed. Until Vincent was attacked by the theatre cat, Willie. It took three of us to prise Willie off the poor Vincent and his claws left quite a mess. Still, it worked out well in the end. Vincent was perfect for our production of Beauty and the Beast."

Evangeline knew she was spoiling their tea with her long face and excused herself as soon as it was polite.

In her bedroom, she tinkered with her invention, fastening the nuts and testing the release of the mechanism. Evangeline stared long and hard at the atervis detector, her father's invention which led her right to the alchemist. She would have go out alone tonight, without Mei to watch out for her.

"Of course," she said.

Carefully prising apart the four chambers and protecting the nuummite inside, she shortened the optical tubes. Next, she grabbed the nasal dust protector and removed its leather straps. The atervis detector would be infinitely more practical as a monocle.

She slipped the new improved atervis detector over her head and admired herself in the looking glass. She looked rather swashbuckling, Mei would have said she looked like a Chinese Pirate Queen. The thought of her friend made her sigh once again. But Evangeline was ready. It was only a matter of hours until she could escape the house and rescue her best friend.

As the Melbourne day finally ended, thick clouds rolled across the sky, hemming in the summer heat. The temperature barely dropped as the sun disappeared, the heat close and thick. Storms were coming.

Evangeline waited until the house grew silent. Uncles Augie and Edmund had gone to Edmund's club for the evening. Miss Plockton retired to her room in the attic. Even the Professor was at his monthly Horological Engineers' Meeting at the university. A purely academic affair which often resulted in the Professor stumbling in late, reeking of brandy and cigars.

Evangeline steeled herself and thought of her friend. She dressed in her plainest gown, hid the atervis monocle in her pocket and slipped into her new invention. She gathered her skirts in one hand and slid down the drainpipe to the ground. A calico cat scattered across the courtyard as she dropped to her feet. She stopped and listened.

Hooves clattered along Collins Street, piano scales and conversations floated from open windows and groups of people walked the balmy evening streets.

Evangeline placed her hand on the door to the back alley and turned the handle. It was locked. She cursed under her breath in a very unladylike manner, before pulling a pin from her hair and picking the brass lock. A light came on in the conservatory overlooking the courtyard and Evangeline jumped behind the privy, her nose curling at the stench after four days straight of baking heat. The night soil man must be late.

Miss Plockton appeared in the windows, peering out. Evangeline's heart battered inside her chest.

The cat wandered across the courtyard into the light. Evangeline sighed with relief as Miss Plockton turned off the gaslight, reassured the cat was the source of the noise.

Then she heard a voice, so soft Evangeline wondered if her ears were deceiving her.

"Bring her back safe."

Miss Plockton? How could she know?

But there was no time to waste on rumination, Evangeline turned back to the door. With three sharp turns of her hairpin, the lock clicked open and she was out on the laneway.

She ran and ran towards East Melbourne, dodging cat-calling drunken men, groups of women arm-in-arm returning from the theatre, cabs and men on horses.

She only slowed to a walk when she reached Wellington Parade. This time, she was determined to try a different approach. She crept into the laneway running behind the houses, hoping Constable Kane was not on patrol again this evening. She pulled out the atervis monocle, wrapped the straps tight around her head and began her inspection. The grounds of the Wellington Parade homes were grand with outbuildings and stables, the scent of warm hay and horse mess thick in the air.

She walked along the laneway, home by home, seeing nothing of the silvery aura or the carriage from last night.

"Oi, what are you doing, girl?" a voice yelled out of the dark.

Evangeline spun around to see a grey headed man standing in the shadows behind her.

"What's that on your 'ead?"

Evangeline must have looked frightfully odd, like some kind of pirate burglar scoping out the grandest houses in Melbourne.

She ran.

But suddenly there it was. A silver aura jumped out like fireworks in the distance. Evangeline's heart leapt simultaneously with fear and joy. The silvery glow stretched out into the sky around one house. There was no doubting it, she had found the home of the alchemist. But the sheer pulsating strength of the aura was frightening. If only the Professor was here to counsel her.

Evangeline ran towards the house, her heart beating faster with each step closer. When she reached the back wall of the property, she gulped. This was an ordinary wall with her naked eye but through the atervis monocle, the bricks glowed iridescent silver.

She craved excitement and here it was. This was her chance to stop the alchemist, rescue Mei and save the day. She breathed in deeply. She would make her father proud.

"You, girl. Stop."

The grey headed man had followed her down the laneway.

"Go away, old man," she grumbled. "I have more important matters to attend to."

Evangeline inspected the wall. Climbing over was not an option, sharp shards of broken glass were set into the mortar along the top. She turned the handle of the back gate but it was locked. She pulled out her faithful hairpin but there was no lock on this side of the door. Evangeline was not perturbed. In fact, she smiled. Finally, a chance to test out her newest invention.

She clicked her heels together to release the mechanism in her boots. Four large springs discharged from the soles of her ankle boots, two at the toes and two at the heels. She was instantly raised six inches into the air. She giggled. Phase one of her invention was a success. She teetered from side to side on the wobbly springs, rolling front and back, waving her hands in the air to balance.

She bent her knees, testing the compression and the energy in the brass coils, then straightened her legs, up and down, building momentum. In one final push she left the ground altogether, flying through the air and over the brick wall, landing triumphantly on the opposite side, her knees braced.

But the force of her landing sent her straight up into the air again. Up and down. Up and down. She had made a mistake, failing to add a stopping mechanism to her spring heeled boots. Now she was inside the alchemist's home grounds but ricocheting like a jack-in-the box. Up and down. On her next bounce, she had some fun, adding a double somersault. On her fourth, she tried a twist. But she could not stop. The horses whinnied in the stables and a dog started barking from the house next door.

She stopped her tricks and focused on the house. A mansion on two levels, with verandahs running along both floors. She could not stop her upwards and downwards motion but she began to gain control of her direction. She aimed herself towards the house and with one almighty bound, shot towards the first floor balcony.

But her angle was awry. She crashed heavily into a beam with a thud and a smash of glass. Her monocle.

She scrambled to wrap her arms around a wooden post, her legs kicking in the air. Her arms slipped, elbows colliding with the balustrade, legs dangling. She interlaced her fingers around the beam, bringing her fall to a shuddering stop. She bashed her boots together, trying to retract her springs, her arms aching with the strain of her bodyweight. Then the sky boomed with thunder and the first heavy drops of rain splattered onto Evangeline's head.

She kicked her heels together again. This time, with success. Her left boot springs retracted into the sole. But her right boot was stuck, the coils extended. Rain drops, like fat water bombs, splashed onto her head and down the back of her dress.

Slipping her left foot under the railing, Evangeline hoisted herself up on her hands, springing over the wet balustrade. She botched her landing and dropped onto the verandah in an unladylike soggy heap. Grabbing her trusty little screwdriver from her boot, she pressed the springs back into her right sole, fastening the mechanism again. Her invention required a few minor refinements.

Evangeline gathered her breath and considered her next move. She did not have long to think.

"And who are you?" said a voice coming out of the dark.

CHAPTER 17

EVANGELINE SCRAMBLED TO HER FEET.
"Who are you?"
The man was thin and bald with an elongated face. Not quite the alchemist she expected, he looked more like a dour pastor.

"I am here to stop you," she said defiantly.

The man cocked his head with an amused expression.

"And how were you planning to do that?"

Evangeline was lost for words. The sullen man had immediately found a fault in her plan. All her efforts had been focused on locating the Alchemist and she'd completely neglected to plan out what to do once she found him.

Lightning cracked behind them as the raindrops battered on the tin roof.

"Come with me." He gripped Evangeline by the elbow. "Ma'am does not appreciate young girls snooping around."

He dragged her through open French doors and into a bookshelf lined gentleman's study. The man tugged Evangeline through another door, along the hallway and down a set of stairs into a grand entrance foyer with a cavernous ceiling.

He shoved her through a doorway. She fell onto her hands and knees on a plush oriental rug, into a parlour with ruby-red flocked wallpaper and a tinkling crystal chandelier. An angular woman with jet black hair, wearing an azure blue gown lay on a chaise lounge, a book on her lap and a glass of sherry in her hand.

"What have you brought me, Strode?"

With a smirk, the woman closed her book, placing it on a mahogany occasional table.

"She deposited herself on the first floor, ma'am. Did you hear the rumpus?"

"Ah, yes. How rude." She spoke with a clipped upper class accent. Her cheekbones jutting from her face like pyramids. "And she's ruining my rug."

"Sorry, ma'am."

Strode stood close behind Evangeline as she struggled to her feet. He thrust her forward again onto her knees.

"Explain yourself, girl," he said.

The woman inspected Evangeline from head to toe. It was then Evangeline noticed every surface in the room was covered in gold. Edging the sherry glass, embossing the carved furniture legs, the woman's necklace, dangling from her ears, a gold statuette on the mantelpiece.

"I am here to stop you."

The woman laughed throatily and heartily.

"Now, my little reformed street urchin. How did you propose to do that? I have your friend. The little Chinese firecracker put up quite a fight. I have been waiting for you."

Evangeline stared, mouth open.

"You underestimate me, little girl. I sensed your pathetic nuummite crystal before you approached."

Evangeline floundered. She grabbed at her head for the atervis monocle. It must have slipped off as she flew through the air. The Professor would be most displeased.

"Who are you?"

"Lady Violetta Breckenridge-Rice. Descendant of the great Alchemist Nicolas Flamel. I am here to make my fortune in this backward little colony filled with money and fools."

"But you have failed," Evangeline said, her eyes scouring the room for a weapon or an escape route. She could easily slip past this man and woman, but she needed a little more information from the Lady Alchemist before she made her departure. Where could she be hiding Mei?

"A minor setback."

"But the police are onto you."

"My young friend. Those nincompoops are not my concern. I'll be long gone before they get anywhere close. There is more money to be made in Sydney or Hobart Town."

"If you're leaving, I expect you are going to let me go?"

"Of course not. You and your little Oriental friend cannot be allowed to blab to the rest of the world."

The iron front gate groaned and loud footsteps clattered onto the front tile verandah. Lady Breckenridge-Rice and Strode froze and listened. The doorbell rang. Bing. Bong.

Lady Breckenridge-Rice rushed to the mantelpiece and tugged on a velvet rope. An enormous man emerged from a side door, his head wide like a ram. He was easily thrice Evangeline's size. She opened her mouth to scream. Before a single sound escaped, the giant clamped a huge hand over her mouth, stinking of onions.

"Brawby. Put her down in the cellar with the other."

Brawby nodded, and flung Evangeline over his shoulder, her drenched hair slapping against his back like a wet mop. She directed a swift kick to his kidneys with the toe of her boot. But Brawby did not even flinch.

He carried her through the side door into a narrow servant's passage, dimly lit and unpainted, then down a set of rickety wooden steps. Each step groaned under their weight as they descended underground.

The giant flipped Evangeline off his shoulder and onto the ground in front of a row of cages. The cellar was dank, dark and damp, spreading the entire length of the mansion.

"Mei," Evangeline called.

Mei ran to the front of her cage. Evangeline held out her hand before Brawby slapped it back, grunting. He pulled a ring of keys from his belt and unlocked another cage away from Mei, throwing Evangeline inside. He fastened the lock behind her and disappeared back into the darkness.

"Mei. Are you hurt?"

"Sick of this cage but I'm fine."

"I heard you put up a fight." Evangeline grinned.

"It was a trap. They were waiting for me in the street. But I didn't go quietly."

"She is more powerful than I thought," Evangeline confessed.

"What are we going to do?"

Evangeline did not know.

CHAPTER 18

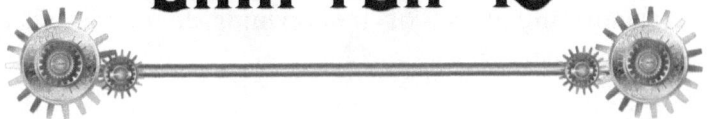

E VANGELINE SCOOTED TO THE FRONT of her cage and inspected the lock. There was no key cylinder on the inside. She reached through the cage bars and with her fingers, traced the keyhole. She grinned, the cage would not contain her for long.

She plucked her trusty hairpin from her bedraggled hair and threaded her arm through the bars of the cage. The angle was awkward, she could only maintain a grip on the pin with the tips of her fingers. She swivelled the pin backwards and forwards, trying to catch the lock but her fingers began to cramp. Evangeline grimaced as the cramp grew worse and her fingers seized up. She pulled back her hand to stretch but the hairpin slipped out of her fingers, clattering onto the floor. She sighed with heavy shoulders before plucking a second pin from her hair.

This time was no different. Her fingers cramped again and the pin dropped from her grasp.

Muffled voices and footsteps creaked on the floorboards above. Who was the mysterious visitor?

"What's happenin'?" Mei whispered.

Evangeline could feel Mei's anticipation weighing on her. She must find a way out.

"Ah ha."

Inspiration struck and Evangeline grabbed for the screwdriver inside her boot. The weightier handle was more comfortable in her hand but the head was larger and less deft.

She struggled, right then left, up then down, tearing at the lock from all sides. Finally, the head of the tool met its mark and the mechanism clicked open.

Mei heard the noise of the opening lock and cheered. Evangeline grinned.

"Ready?"

"Hurry," Mei said.

Evangeline tugged the unlocked door.

But nothing happened.

The door stayed fastened shut.

Confused, Evangeline tugged harder. Perhaps her clumsy tool work had wrecked the lock. She reached around again and felt that the lock was open. But the cage door was firmly closed.

Perhaps there was a second lock. She searched but saw nothing.

"Why are you waitin'?" Mei cried.

"The lock is open. I don't understand."

She stopped for a moment to think. Of course, her escape would not be so easy. Lady Breckenridge-Rice was not only an alchemist. She knew how to manipulate dark energy. She had cast glamours over the shop assistants at Snodgrass & Sons and the goldsmiths. There must be a spell over the cage.

"Can you smell somethin'?" Mei said. The sound of fear in her voice.

Evangeline sniffed the air.

Smoke.

A fire somewhere within the house.

"Hurry," Mei said again.

Evangeline sat back on her haunches. What did she know about magic? Nothing. She swallowed back tears of frustration and her growing feeling of defeat and concentrated with all her might.

Evangeline had escaped her stepfather and found the Professor. Travelled across the world to a new life in the Colonies. She had overcome so many obstacles in her life. A little spell was not going to stop her now. The power of determination welled within her.

She was only seventeen. There was so much more to do and see. Her life would not end in the cellar of an East Melbourne mansion. She would make the Professor and her Uncles proud. She would save Mei and herself. Her mother, Peggy, was watching over her.

Her determination was so strong, she could sense it crackling through her fingertips. So strongly, she swore her fingers glowed with amber light. Perhaps it was a vision caused by a mixture of gaslight and fire smoke but Evangeline knew within her heart, within her soul, this was not going to be the end.

With all her will, her courage and might, she tugged at the door one more time.

This time the door opened effortlessly, as though perfectly oiled. The door practically opened itself.

Mei burst into applause.

"How did you do that?"

Evangeline sat inside the cage for a moment, bewildered.

"I think it was magic."

"Ballocks," Mei replied. "Get me out of 'ere."

Evangeline jumped out and headed to Mei's cage. With three swift clicks of her screwdriver, she unlatched the lock and pushed. But the same thing happened. The lock was open, but the door was closed.

Mei groaned in frustration. The scent of smoke grew stronger, Evangeline felt the tickle of ash in the back of her throat.

Evangeline stood back and tried to gather up the same feelings. She had broken the spell once, she could do it again. She breathed deeply, gathering up all her determination, picturing her mother's face, evoking the power again. Her fingers began to tingle and the cage and Mei's expectant face took on an amber glow. What was this strange feeling?

Evangeline drew all her strength again, clutched at the door and pulled. The door swung open with ease.

"Hoorah," Mei yelled, scurrying out of the cage.

The friends embraced, bouncing up and down in a joyful jig.

"Let's get out of here." Evangeline giggled.

There would be plenty of time to talk when they were back home safely.

The two girls ran up the rickety stairs into the dark corridor. The servants' passage was lined with identical unknown doors.

"Which way?" Evangeline asked

Mei coughed and doubled over. Smoke hung thick in the air.

They kept moving, following the passage, hoping they were heading away from the fire.

"This one."

Evangeline picked a door at random.

"Ouch!"

The door handle scorched Evangeline's fingers, the brass white hot.

They ran back down to the passage to another door, Mei touched the door with the back of her hand, testing for heat.

"It's safe," Mei said.

The second door opened to a heavy curtain and back into the parlour. The room was deserted, smoke crawling along the floor like a fog. There was no sign of the Alchemist, Lady Breckenridge-Rice and her henchmen.

"This way," Evangeline shouted, her hand covering her nose and mouth with her sleeve.

They tore through the parlour and into the foyer, heading for the front door. Mei grabbed for the door-knob, then they heard a wheezing groan above their heads.

The ornate ceiling fell, crashing to the ground.

CHAPTER 19

F LAMING TIMBER BEAMS CRASHED AROUND them. Embers and sparks flew in all directions in a cloud of white plaster dust. Evangeline and Mei were trapped. Burning beams now blocking their path to the front door and the way back into the parlour.

"Bravo, little girls." Lady Breckenridge-Rice applauded from the first floor landing. "I am quite impressed with your gumption. It's such a shame that your endeavours will come to nothing."

Mei and Evangeline stood defiantly as the heat intensified around them. Lady Breckenridge-Rice started descending the stairs towards the front door.

"Sorry I can't stay and chat, little girls but Melbourne has suddenly become very tiresome."

The Lady Alchemist took a few more steps down the stairs.

"The fire will take care of you and any evidence of my operations. I shall fade away into the background like I always do."

The flaming beams blocked Evangeline's way out but Lady Breckenridge-Rice had a clear path through the fire to the front door.

"I must admit this has been a pleasure, my little urchin. The world is such a small place."

The Lady Alchemist leaned over the balustrade with a smirk on her angular face.

"Yes, I know who you really are. I can see through your fine new clothes."

Evangeline frowned.

"How can you know?"

"One meets the most interesting people," the Lady Alchemist said, taking another step towards the front door.

"We have to stop her," Mei said. "She'll get away."

The flames were closing in, licking at them from all directions. Evangeline stared up at the smirking Lady Alchemist. There was one only way they could stop her.

"Tornado?" Evangeline yelled over the roar of the flames.

"Side kick would be better," Mei said. "Yi. Er. San."

Mei and Evangeline kicked in unison. Their right feet slamming into the wooden staircase below Lady Breckenridge-Rice.

"What on earth?" the Lady Alchemist exclaimed, pulling back from the railing.

But their attack had little impact on the carpentry.

"Again," Mei called.

Evangeline took a deep breath and grinned at her friend.

They jumped forward and kicked again. This time, the wood buckled under the force of their strike and the staircase shook like an earthquake. Lady Breckenridge-Rice swayed on her feet and clutched for the balustrade.

"No," she yowled.

"Yes!" Evangeline said, pointing to a particularly bent beam. "Once more. Right there."

Evangeline and Mei pushed forward one more time and with an all-mighty blow, the supporting beam crumpled. The section of stairs tumbled forward, thrusting the caterwauling Lady Alchemist to the ground with a crash of wood, fire and dust.

Mei and Evangeline whooped with glee but there was no time to celebrate. The fire was closing in on all sides.

"How do we get out?" Evangeline implored.

"Flying lotus." Mei pointed to the front door. "Come on, circus girl."

With a grin, Evangeline and Mei took a run up and leapt straight into the air. Together, they cleared the burning beam and landed with a flourish by the front door.

"Next time, trousers," Evangeline said as she noticed her singed hems.

They wrenched open the front door, ran onto Wellington Parade and into the fresh air, not looking back until they reached the safety of Fitzroy Gardens. By then the blaze was lighting up the night sky and the streets rang with the bells of the Volunteer Fire Brigade.

Without another word, Evangeline and Mei brushed the dust and ash from their clothes and headed home wearily, hand in hand.

CHAPTER 20

T HE MORNING SUN WAS STREAMING through her thin lace curtains when Evangeline finally opened her eyes. At her washstand, she scrubbed the soot from last night's adventure off her face. Her hair still scented with smoke, she pinned it back with a secret smile, indulging in last night's triumph for a moment. She had rescued Mei and foiled the mysterious Lady Breckenridge-Rice.

But the more intriguing mystery was the energy which freed them from the cages. The amber glow flowing from her own fingertips. Where had it come from? Could she summon the energy again? What if the energy was dark?

Her stomach rumbled and her thoughts moved to more pressing needs. Breakfast.

Her whole family was at the breakfast table when she entered the conservatory. On the trip down the stairs, Evangeline decided to keep the tale of the Alchemist to herself. It was not quite the triumph she had envisaged. She had imagined herself handing over the Alchemist to the police personally. If she explained last night's adventures, the Professor, her Uncles and Miss Plockton would only worry and banish her to her room until she was thirty-five.

"Our Sleeping Beauty," Augie said as she slipped into the spare chair. Miss Plockton appeared with the tea pot and a rack of grilled toast.

"We have some wonderful news," Miss Plockton said as she filled Evangeline's cup. "Miss Fang returned last night."

"How wonderful," Evangeline gasped, clutching at her heart. "I must go and see her now."

"Our prayers were answered." Miss Plockton squeezed out a little smile and perhaps the barest flicker of a wink. "Sit. I am sure the Professor will let you visit Mei later. First, give her some time with her family."

Evangeline nodded.

Edmund looked up from the morning issue of The Argus.

"The fire last night was a house on Wellington Parade," he said. "They suspect lightning."

"The storm was quite fierce," said the Professor.

"The house was burned to the ground," Edmund said. "But listen to this. In the hours before the fire, a witness reported seeing a strange girl with one eye flying through the air."

The Professor and Augie chortled and snorted. Evangeline pretended to laugh with them as she reached for a piece of toast, remembering the old man in the laneway.

"A Spring heeled Jacqueline?" the Professor guffawed. "Here in Melbourne? Who would have thought?"

"Some old fool was on the lash." Edmund shook his head.

"But what about the poor people inside? Did they escape?" Augie said.

Edmund rustled the pages.

"There is no mention of injuries or loss of life. The occupants must be safe and well."

Evangeline snapped the piece of toast she was buttering in two. No trace of a body? Could Lady Breckenridge-Rice have possibly escaped?

She looked up. Her father, Miss Plockton and her two Uncles were eying her with odd expressions.

"Something wrong, m'dear?" the Professor asked.

"Can you pass the marmalade?" Evangeline said sheepishly. "I am rather hungry this morning."

Evangeline sat, crunching her toast thoughtfully, as her family continued talking about last night's storm. Yet again, she underestimated Lady Violetta Breckenridge-Rice. Evangeline had a hunch, the Lady Alchemist would return to take revenge, but next time Evangeline would be ready.

But for now, Evangeline looked forward to a quiet day at 56 Collins Street. Her thirst for excitement appeared to be quenched. For a few days, at least.

"Oh my stars. Did you see this?" said Edmund, flapping the pages of The Argus. "The Bunyip has struck again. Another poor dead boy."

"How terrifying. A murderous beast roaming the parks of Melbourne," said Augie with a shiver. "Someone should do something."

Evangeline smiled to herself. She had another idea.

EVANGELINE AND THE BUNYIP

Mystery and Mayhem in steampunk Melbourne
(The Antics of Evangeline Book 2)

CHAPTER 1

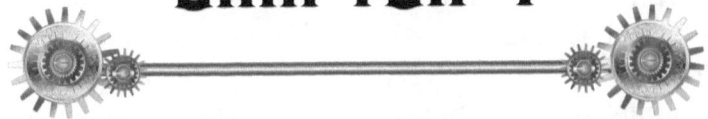

A ND ANOTHER THING, EVANGELINE. YOU mustn't eat too much. There'll be ample food and I know you have a... healthy... appetite," Uncle Augie said.

Evangeline glanced at the buttery shortbread in her hand. What could Uncle Augie possibly mean? It was only her third.

"It's rather unseemly for a lady to eat heartily in public," Augie continued.

Miss Plockton nodded vigorously.

"Aye. Overeating in corsetry is very dangerous," she said. "You dinnae want an attack of the vapours."

"Or worse." Uncle Augie curled up his nose. "I heard a terrible story of a young lady who was forced to 'evacuate' in the nearest potted palm. She didn't see the Duke of Windsor standing on the other side. One too many blancmanges. Let that be a lesson to you, Evangeline."

Evangeline sighed into her cup of coffee, then shoved the shortbread into her mouth whole.

Miss Plockton and Augie recoiled with a gasp, their hands fluttering to their chests.

"I'll need my strength for tonight's Ball," Evangeline replied, but only after the delicious buttery treat was gone from her mouth. Evangeline would never win an award for deportment but she knew not to speak with her mouth full.

Uncle Augie, Miss Plockton and Evangeline had been shopping all morning, finalising the last minute details for Evangeline's Easter Ball ensemble. Now they were resting their weary feet at the Royal Coffee Palace, with a restorative brew and a biscuit. Or four.

"Excuse me." A white aproned waiter leaned across their table, turning down the blue flame on the tabletop percolator. As the coffee erupted like brown lava into a glass jug, Evangeline inspected the device closely, the latest advancement in coffee technology from Zurich.

The Coffee Palace stood near the corner of Swanston and Flinders Streets where hansom cabs and steam trams rattled by, overlooking the gothic facade of St. Paul's Cathedral. The Coffee Palace bustled with lady shoppers piled with purchases and respectable families enjoying a Saturday morning outing, the rich aroma of freshly brewing coffee wafting up to the high vaulted ceilings.

"Now, don't be nervous," Uncle Augie said, once their cups were replenished and the waiter glided away. "But you are ever so lucky. Not everyone is invited to the Easter Ball. It is the exclusive ticket in Melbourne this season. I whispered in the ears of all the right people to get you an invitation. But there's no need to thank me."

Tall and rotund Uncle Augie was not Evangeline's real uncle. August Beauchamp was the constant companion of her father's brother Edmund. They all resided under one roof at 56 Collins Street with her father and his personal secretary, Miss Plockton.

"Only last week, at that appalling performance of the 'Reanimator of Rouen', I put in another good word for you with Mr. Dolwyddelan and Miss Kircubben-Jones. All about how delightful you are and how they couldn't possibly have a Ball without you. And taa-daa, an invitation arrives."

While Augie's business was in the theatre, his main pastime was instilling etiquette into Evangeline.

"This is a great opportunity for you, Miss Evangeline. Mr. Beauchamp has been very kind," Miss Plockton said, adding another layer of guilt before sipping her coffee, black with no sugar of course.

There had been far too much fuss already associated with this Ball. Evangeline knew the Ball was important to Uncle Augie but she took after her father, she was more interested in clockwork than quadrilles. Her father was the famous horological-engineer Professor Montague Caldicott, inventor of many patented best-selling devices including the audito-hearing device and the auto-chariot.

"I am ever so grateful for the invitation, but..."

Miss Plockton issued a scalding glare and Evangeline closed her mouth. In all honesty, she was a little grateful. Her morning embroidery lesson had been cancelled for today's preparations. The day was not a complete loss.

"There is one last errand." Miss Plockton crossed an item off her list with an efficient stroke of violet ink. "Collecting your gown from Madame Brisbois. Then we can return to the house."

The revolver pen was a bespoke invention and Miss Plockton's pride and joy. A gift from the Professor with four different coloured inks, the revolver pen was acknowledgement for Miss Plockton's ten years of service as his personal secretary.

"Then I can go back to the laboratory-workshop?" Evangeline brightened. "I want to finish my new mechanical fly-swatter. It's ever so clever, I got the idea from the Venus..."

"Of course not, Miss Evangeline," Miss Plockton tutted.

"There'll be no time for inventing today, my dear girl." Augie smiled condescendingly. "The day has barely begun."

"There is far too much to do," Miss Plockton added. "We must wash your hair."

"And style it." Uncle Augie nodded.

"Put the finishing touches on your dress trim."

"Practice your Grande Chaine."

"Fasten your corsetry."

"And test you on the right curtseys. Today will be a very busy day." Augie clapped.

Evangeline turned away and grimaced. How dull. She stared out of the large windows, ignoring the talk about Balls and noticed a young boy running up the street. A boy running was nothing out of the ordinary. Like London, Evangeline's home until five months ago, the streets of Melbourne were filled with young ragamuffins. Then a woman ran past with her child bundled close to her chest, her eyes fearful, followed by a well-dressed family; wife and husband and three crying children in tow. The mobile cog-grinder, known for his off-colour songs, frantically pushed his cart through the crowds without a sound. Like a change in the tide, more and more people started rushing up Swanston Street away from the edge of the Yarra River.

The hum of conversation in the Coffee House hushed, as the patrons turned to watch the waves of people outside. Some leaving their seats to crowd around the windows for a better view. Finally, something exciting was happening.

"What's all this commotion?" Uncle Augie said.

"I'll find out." Evangeline was quick on her feet, squeezing past the other customers towards the front door.

"Where is she going? Evangeline!" Uncle Augie said. "I can't chase after her. I've already laced my stays."

"Pardon, sir?" Miss Plockton cocked her head with a frown.

"Never mind. Stop her!"

"Come back, Miss Evangeline!" Miss Plockton called, but Evangeline pretended not to hear and slipped out the doors.

She skipped down the sandstone Coffee Palace steps and ran out into the street. Police whistles pierced the air. Shutters clattered as the barrow girls and boys scrambled to close their stalls. A woman screamed. Spooked horses neighed and bucked. People pushed and shoved, arguing and yelling as they fled the river with fear on their faces. Evangeline's heart raced.

What could be frightening the people of Melbourne on this fine March Saturday?

"What's happening?" Evangeline said.

"Oh it's 'orrible," said a voice in the crowd.

"Is it a fire?" She questioned each person as they hurried past but no one met her eyes. "An escaped lunatic?"

There was a firm grip on her arm.

"You're going the wrong way, Miss," said a gap-toothed young man.

"What is going on?" Evangeline tugged away from his grip, resisting the urge to throw him to the ground. Evangeline may look like any other respectable young lady but if circumstances required, she was more than capable of looking after herself.

Before the young man could answer her, a loud bellow roared up from the river. A screech so horrid, so unnatural, goosebumps rippled up Evangeline's spine. A sound she had heard once before and never forgotten.

"No. It can't be?" she whispered to herself. "In broad daylight?"

CHAPTER 2

T HE BUNYIP." EVANGELINE GASPED.
The bellow of the beast incited a fresh round of screams from
the fleeing crowds. Somewhere, a gun fired into the air.

"Run!" shouted the gappy-mouthed man.

Losing their nerve, the last remaining people bolted away
from the river. But not Evangeline. She pushed through the
throng, unwilling to miss a chance to see the monstrous Bunyip
with her own eyes.

Evangeline had heard the screech of the Bunyip once before.
A few months earlier, while on one of their midnight raids,
Evangeline and her best friend Mei heard the creature's ungodly
yowls in Fitzroy Gardens. That night they'd run in the opposite
direction, but Evangeline would not run today.

The swarm of people knocked over an old woman.
Sprawled on the ground, she cried out as a stampede of boots
squashed her fingers. Evangeline fought through the crowd
with her pointy elbows, helping the bewildered woman back
to her feet.

"Lord save us... demon... a devil," the woman babbled.
"Deliver us from evil."

Evangeline deposited the old woman safely by a shop front,
before turning back to the Yarra. She shoved and jostled through

the crowds, until the numbers dwindled and the cobblestones met the wooden wharf.

"Get away, Miss."

A pair of hands grabbed at her arm but Evangeline pushed closer to get a better glimpse. Then she saw it, the cause of the commotion, a mere twenty feet away, and her heart stopped. Her eyes widening like full moons as her mind struggled to comprehend what she was seeing before her.

The Bunyip was like no animal Evangeline had seen before. Standing on four feet and bigger than four men, its muscular shoulders rippled as it lunged forward with gnashing teeth, its pewter-grey skin shimmering in the sunlight. Part animal, part fish with webbed toes and an elongated eel-like neck, it surveyed the crowd, splattering saliva in all directions. His cannonball eyes rested on Evangeline and her blood ran cold.

The beast paced up and down the wooden jetty, growling. Six helmeted bobbies rushed towards the creature, their old-fashioned muskets at the ready and determined fear on their faces.

"Ready! Aim!"

Shots rang out with a cloud of gunpowder haze.

The beast roared and pounced from its haunches, the policemen surging back out of reach. All except one, a lone bobby slipped, losing his footing in the commotion.

Evangeline gasped.

He was alone on the ground, scrambling backwards on hands and heels.

"Someone help him," Evangeline shouted, but no one moved.

The Bunyip surged forward, snatching the man by the foot. His blood curdling screams echoing along the wharf.

"Help! Help!" The man yelled, flailing his arms uselessly as the beast dragged him towards the river.

"Do something," Evangeline glared at the crowd of trembling men. "Cowards."

She lunged forward, grabbing hold of the man's collar but the Bunyip easily yanked him from her grasp. Her grip was no match for the creature.

The beast backed away towards the water, his eyes fixed on the crowd, growling with a deep rumble. The man's body lolled like a rag doll, his head bouncing on the wooden platform.

"We must help him," Evangeline said with a choke, but the Bunyip was already at the edge of the jetty, slipping into the murky brown water of the Yarra and taking his prey with him.

For a few moments, the man's boot trailed along the surface of the water, the last trace of the policeman as the creature pulled him under.

Evangeline's heart thumped like a brass band, barely believing the scene before her eyes.

"The Bunyip is real," she said to no one in particular.

"Aye, Miss. And another poor dead lad," the same gap-toothed man replied. "The bobbies are useless. Someone needs to do somethin'. Or they'll be more deaths. Mark my words."

Evangeline's family tried to shield her from the horrible tales of the Bunyip, Uncle Augie claiming the stories were not suitable reading material for eligible young ladies. Her overprotective family were a mystery, conveniently forgetting she spent the first seventeen years of her life in less refined circumstances. Evangeline had resorted to stealing the discarded newspapers from the kitchen to read the latest accounts. Evangeline knew the Bunyip was a monster native to Australia, living in swamps and billabongs and feared by the local Aboriginal tribes since time immemorial.

The creature was gone and the wharf was deathly quiet. Evangeline drifted back to the Coffee Palace in a daze. When Miss Plockton and Uncle Augie found her, she was sitting on the stone steps of the Cathedral.

"Thank heavens, Miss Evangeline." Miss Plockton said breathlessly, a tightly twisted white handkerchief in her hands. "Are you hurt?"

"You gave us quite a fright, young lady. Miss Plockton practically wore out the Lord's Prayer and I was all prepared to throw myself at the mercy of the Royal Artillery." Uncle Augie watched a pair of smartly dressed soldiers marching towards the wharf.

"Why did you run off like that?" Miss Plockton frowned. "It was very foolish."

"I saw the Bunyip."

Miss Plockton clasped at her throat and Uncle Augie placed a large comforting paw on Evangeline's shoulder

"It took a poor man," Evangeline muttered. "I couldn't help him."

Her mind whirling, Evangeline trailed after Miss Plockton and Uncle Augie as they collected her gown and returned home for an afternoon of cinching, primping and rouging.

After a few hours and strong cups of Darjeeling, Evangeline's pluck was gradually restored. Yet the Easter Ball was far from her mind. The young man was right, someone must do something to stop the Bunyip. And naturally, Miss Evangeline Caldicott was the perfect young lady for the job.

It was only a question of how.

CHAPTER 3

O H MY WORD. LOOK AT Lavinia Armitage's gown," Jemima snickered. "How could her mother allow her to leave the house in such a state? Reminds me of a sausage stuffed in silk."

Jemima's own ensemble was an explosion of pale pink rosebuds, from the top of her golden head, across her shoulders and over her bustle to the floor.

"And the colour." Albertine wrinkled her nose, another one of Evangeline's classmates from her weekly watercolours class at the Royal Academy of Art. "If I had her sallow skin, I would never dream of wearing such a washed out green. She looks positively pestilent."

Albertine was as dark as Jemima was fair. Her own gown, in the finest ruby-red satin, was puffy and ruffled like a washerwoman's mob cap. The girls stood at the edge of the dance floor, strategically positioned to see and be seen, yet close enough for the orchestra to drown out their barbed observations.

"Don't look now," Jemima said with a smirk. "Caroline Casellton is wearing the most obscene neckline. I never knew she was one of those actresses."

The two girls cackled into their gloved hands while Evangeline disguised a yawn behind her fan. Uncle Augie and

Miss Plockton put hours and hours of effort into her deportment and accoutrements, in preparation for her first formal Ball. Now Evangeline stood in the largest ballroom in the Antipodes, with her hair coiled and pinned, in an arctic-blue gown of silk and duchess lace, with her manners in check and she was bored beyond belief. After seeing a real live monster this morning, the Easter Ball was quite an anti-climax.

The newly renovated Royal Exhibition Building was filled with all the fashionable people of Melbourne. According to Uncle Augie. Evangeline spotted her not-real uncle across the room, flirting with a group of fleshy older ladies.

"And then I said, 'I didn't mean two cans. I meant toucans.'" Augie's voice boomed across the floor. "But her boorish husband still challenged me to a duel. Can you imagine me? Pistols at dawn and all that palaver? Anyway you won't believe the scar. It's uncanny. An exact replica of Michaelangelo's David but on my..."

The ladies hooted and snorted, slapping Augie playfully with their fans. Evangeline and Augie's eyes met and he made a flicking gesture with his fingers. He wanted her to mingle. She sighed.

Evangeline stepped away from the malicious watercolour girls, towards a tall palm by the wall with perfect fronds for unobtrusive people watching. Less than an hour into the Ball and yet to take a single step on the dance floor, Evangeline's feet already hurt. Why did her beautifully ruffled ball slippers have to be so impractical?

The centre of the room was filled with couples. The gentlemen standing tall and straight with finely groomed moustaches, in their black or burgundy tails or golden braided Royal Artillery uniforms. The ladies in a myriad of pale pinks, greens and blues, cinched waists and flowing skirts, twinkled with jewels.

As the couples bowed and curtseyed, commencing the quadrille, Evangeline smirked. Their mannered movements reminding her of her own martial arts lessons, only with less punching and grunting. Evangeline wished Mei, her best friend and kung-fu instructress, could be here to share the joke.

The music swelled, the orchestra was half man, half steam-organ. Men played violins and cellos, while another solitary man replaced the whole woodwind and brass section. He rushed madly from pedal to key, commanding the wheezing organ like the bridge on a dirigible. The steam-organ man lifted his head and waved frantically in the air, as the music and the dancers began to sag. A footman hurried over, throwing a pail of coal into the organ's under-chamber, restoring the orchestra's tempo with a feisty blast of steam.

An army of serving staff darted amongst the hundreds of guests. Footmen in white tails slid across the room, laden with silver trays, lighting cigars and collecting plates and glasses. Two particular footmen caught Evangeline's eye, not only for their impressive height and handsome faces. The two footmen, on opposite sides of the room, shot each other sideways glances when they thought no one was looking. There was something familiar and suspect about their behaviour. She vowed to keep a close eye on these shady characters. If only she'd brought her latest invention with her.

"I will!" a young gentleman announced loudly. "Mark my words."

His companions guffawed heartily, slapping him on the back. The watercolour girls turned, looking down their noses at the men and their boisterous display.

"Isn't my brother odious?" Albertine rolled her eyes.

On the other hand, Evangeline was quite envious. The gentlemen seemed to be having a rather jolly time.

"I tell you, I'll catch the Bunyip myself," Percy Sharpthorne said.

Evangeline's ears pricked up.

"Monsters." Jemima smoothed one of her golden ringlets with a gloved hand. "How vulgar."

Evangeline could still hear the policeman's screams for help echoing in her ears, picturing his face twisted with fear. If only his collar hadn't slipped through her fingers. She was determined to be better prepared next time.

Taking another two steps away from the watercolour girls and towards the rowdy gentlemen, Evangeline eavesdropped on their monster hunting plans.

"The £500 will be mine, I tell you. It'll be an absolute doddle." Percy continued his chest beating while his friends shook their heads. "I hunted with Father in India before coming out here. Lions. Tigers. Crocottas. The whole lot."

With a quick glance, Evangeline assessed Percy Sharpthorne's credentials. With such round cheeks and baby-like skin, Percy would make a fine supper for the Bunyip. He did not stand a chance.

"You'll need to deliver it alive," said Basil Mawdesley.

"Easy peasy, old chaps."

"Better men than you have failed already," said Barnaby Rippingale.

This was the first time Evangeline had heard Barnaby Rippingale speak, his calm cultured voice creating a funny quiver in her tummy. She tried not to stare at his heavy eyelashes and chocolate brown eyes. The watercolour girls often giggled and swooned about Barnaby Rippingale, now Evangeline understood why. He was quite the belle of the ball.

"My driver claims he saw it one night," replied Albion Middlehall. Albion's face was dominated by eyebrows, two thick black slugs asleep above his small eyes. "Twelve foot high, he said. Black as night, with sharp claws and red eyes."

Evangeline's tongue tingled but she kept her mouth firmly closed.

"I heard it has wings like a dragon," Percy said.

"My uncle saw one years ago," Basil added. "Sunning itself on the banks of the Yarra. He said it was covered in feathers, like an enormous bird."

"You are all mistaken," Evangeline said, stepping forward.

The four young gentlemen swivelled around, Basil and Percy with a sneer, Barnaby and Albion with curious looks on their faces.

"And you are an expert in all matters Bunyip? Miss?" said Percy.

"Caldicott. Miss Evangeline Caldicott," she replied.

Even Evangeline knew this was not the correct way to become acquainted with a young gentleman, but manners were not important now, there were more interesting things to discuss. Monsters.

"I saw the beast on the Yarra this morning. With my own eyes."

"You were there?" Albion said with awe.

The men crowded around her, firing questions from all directions.

"Tell us. Every detail."

"I expect you were extremely frightened. Did you faint?" asked Percy.

Evangeline lifted a disdainful eyebrow.

"I heard it took three people."

"Only one. I tried but I couldn't save him," Evangeline said with a slow shake of her head. "The creature tore him from my grasp."

Albion whistled long and low through his teeth. The other three looked on, with slackened jaws.

"You mentioned a prize?" Evangeline asked.

"A reward for the Bunyip's capture is being announced in tomorrow's edition of The Argus."

"And it will be mine," said Percy.

Evangeline smiled sweetly.

Percy Sharpthorne should not count his winnings yet. It did not pay to underestimate Evangeline Caldicott when she put her mind to an adventure.

CHAPTER 4

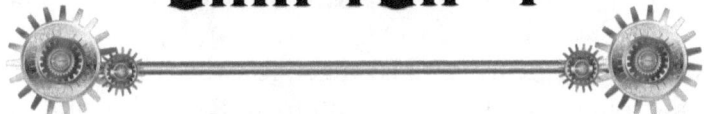

A
ND HOW WILL YOU GO about catching the creature?"
Evangeline asked, taking a seat with the four gentlemen
at a table by the dance floor, hoping for an inside scoop
from Percy the hapless braggart.

"Well..." Percy started.

"Gentlemen. Good evening," said a voice. Evangeline
winced. It was Uncle Augie. She knew this was not the type
of male attention Augie had envisaged for her. "I see you have
met my niece."

The young gentlemen all nodded.

"May I steal Miss Evangeline away to dance?"

"Of course, Mr Beauchamp. Delighted to make your
acquaintance, Miss Caldicott," Albion Middlehall said, taking
Evangeline's hand. "I hope we get a chance to finish our
discussion soon."

Uncle Augie smiled graciously before gripping Evangeline
firmly by the elbow and tugging her away from the table.

"What are you doing talking with a group of gentlemen,
unchaperoned?" he hissed. "People will talk. There are many
wicked tongues and old gossips in this room. I should know.
Most of them are my friends."

"No one cares a whit about me, Uncle." Evangeline shrugged. "I'm a nobody."

"Nonsense. You are my niece! And the daughter of the most well-respected horological-engineer in all the Colonies. I didn't procure this invitation for you to talk monsters all night. What will people think? Come, let's introduce you to a few respectable ladies."

As Uncle Augie ushered Evangeline away from the men, she spied the long tables towering with food. Beef, ham and tongue sandwiches, oysters, sliced chicken and goose lay on silver trays. Crystal glasses filled with wobbly jellies, blancmanges and custards on automated cake stands, slowly revolved around three towering cream sponge cakes, dotted with strawberries. Deliciousness was on display from every angle, yet no one appeared to be eating. Evangeline vividly remembered her urchin days with an achingly empty belly. She could not bear to see food go to waste.

"Cake," she said, tugging Augie towards the feast.

Augie tutted.

"Only a bite. Remember how tightly we laced you into that dress."

Evangeline gazed over the wonderful selection on the table. Choosing only one was nearly as bad as having nothing at all.

"Um," she said, dithering.

"Hurry," Uncle Augie said through clenched teeth.

Evangeline chose a delightfully wobbly pink blancmange with a red glace cherry in the centre.

"Ah, Mrs. Gorseinon," Augie called out to a woman in a violently purple gown, displaying an acre of bosom. "How handsome you look this evening."

Evangeline managed a single heavenly spoonful before Augie grabbed her by the elbow.

"Time to dance."

With a heavy sigh, Evangeline said goodbye to the blancmange and her not-real uncle whisked her into the middle of the dance floor.

"Remember how we practiced," he said through a forced smile. "Now, try and look as though you're enjoying yourself."

In spite of his great height and ample girth, Augie twirled Evangeline effortlessly around the dance floor. She desperately tried to keep up with the steps, while on the other side of the room, Barnaby Rippingale glided across the polished floorboards, tall and straight in perfect step with his golden-haired partner. Evangeline deflated when she recognised a beaming Jemima Lydlinch on his arm.

The song ended and someone tapped her on the shoulder. It was her Uncle Edmund, her father's brother and Augie's best friend.

"May I?"

"I'd be delighted." Evangeline smiled.

Augie made a melodramatic humphing noise before slipping away with a cheeky grin to join another group of ladies.

Uncle Edmund's steps were slower and less theatrical than Augie's, but in his arms, Evangeline finally relaxed.

"Apologies for my tardiness. There was a late appointment at Parliament House. A few minor changes to the design of the new Ministry Building. Philistines. Are you enjoying yourself, my dear?"

Evangeline paused, taking too long to concoct the right words.

"I suspected as much. Just like your father." Edmund chuckled. "It would be a cold day in hell before you caught Monty at a Ball.

"It's so unfair." Evangeline pouted. "Why are these events mandatory for me when Father gives them a wide berth?"

"There are different expectations for a young lady." Edmund shrugged.

"I'd much rather be tinkering in the laboratory-workshop. I'm wasting precious time." Evangeline humphed and looked away. Glancing across the room, she noticed the two shifty footmen again, sharing a subtle conspiratorial glance. There was something going on between the men, but they were no amateurs, they blended into the background as though nothing was awry.

Evangeline and her uncle continued to twirl around the room, coming within earshot of Albion Middlehall and his chums again.

"If you think you can do this, Percy old fellow, I'm willing to make this Bunyip business even more interesting. I'll put down a wager of £100," Albion Middlehall said. "In addition to The Argus prize."

"I see the rum is talking already," Uncle Edmund whispered. "Although if anyone can afford such a folly, it's a Middlehall."

"You're on, old man." Percy puffed out his chest. "Six hundred pounds is a tidy little sum. With the winnings in my pocket and my photograph in The Argus, I'll have every eligible young lady in Melbourne rivalling for my attentions. The ladies adore a man of action."

His friends collapsed in laughter around him and Evangeline suppressed a little smile.

A hand appeared on Uncle Edmund's shoulder.

"Mr. Caldicott. May I cut in?"

"It would be my pleasure." Edmund said, with a raised eyebrow. "I assume you have made the acquaintance of my niece, Miss Evangeline Caldicott. Newly from London, like myself."

Evangeline's stomach quivered and her mouth ran dry.

"We have not been formally introduced, no."

Barnaby Rippingale picked up Evangeline's gloved hand and pressed his lips just above her knuckles. She braced her legs, in case her knees gave way.

"Miss Evangeline Caldicott, may I introduce Barnaby Rippingale? Barnaby's a member of my Club. Studying to be a barrister?"

"Hoping to follow in my father's footsteps."

"Me too," blurted Evangeline. Her heart fluttering like a hummingbird under her corsetry.

"You are studying for the bar? How very modern."

Evangeline flushed ruby red.

"No. An inventor."

"Really? How interesting. You must tell me more as we waltz."

The next song struck up and Evangeline found herself in Barnaby's careful arms. She wanted to gaze up at him, but she did not dare.

"Miss Caldicott, I do not believe I have seen you at any other events this season." Barnaby swept her gracefully across the floor. "Your uncle mentioned you are new to Melbourne. Where were you in London?"

"Oh, here and there," Evangeline said. "We moved about a lot."

"With your father's profession?"

"Yes."

In her former life with the circus troupes and the street performers, Evangeline had no permanent home. After the death of her mother, she was dragged from hovel to hovel, from one swindle to another by her drunken stepfather, Charlie Drigg. The man she thought was her father for almost seventeen years, until she learned the truth about the Professor.

Barnaby flinched ever so slightly and Evangeline realised she was gripping his shoulder like a vice. The memories of Charlie Drigg's belt were still fresh in her mind. She loosened her hold and Barnaby continued.

"I thought the Professor was strictly a King's College man. I didn't realise he moved about."

"Oh. Um. No." Evangeline stopped before she tripped over her own lies. Barnaby did not need to know about her unwholesome past. Evangeline never lived with the Professor in London, their first meeting was the day she arrived in Melbourne.

A look of confusion passed over Barnaby's handsome face. Evangeline would have kicked herself if she hadn't been dancing.

Avoiding Barnaby's glorious eyelashes, she glanced across the room and caught sight of the suspicious footmen again. She craned her neck awkwardly to keep watch over the characters as Barnaby whirled her around and around.

The dark-haired footman was slipping something under his jacket. His face was calm and composed while his hands moved swiftly, but his loot caught the light from the overhead chandelier. It was a beaded purse, not the typical accessory for a footman.

Barnaby swivelled Evangeline around the other side of the crowded dance floor and she lost sight of the dark rogue. But his mousy-haired crony came into view, with a silk jacket folded over his arm, far too expensive for a footman's wage. Evangeline pursed her lips. There could be a perfectly innocent explanation, perhaps the footmen were collecting the guests' belongings for safe keeping, but Evangeline smelled a rat. And she knew the scent of vermin all too well.

Evangeline narrowed her eyes. What were the footmen up to?

CHAPTER 5

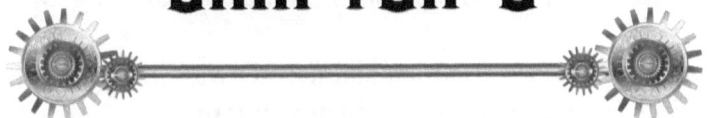

T HE DARK-HEADED FOOTMAN MOVED TOWARDS
the door with a silver tipped cane now in his hand.
He signalled to his pal with an ever-so-slight jerk of
his head. Evangeline recognised the routine from her own
cutpurse past; the footmen were fleecing the ball. Someone
must do something.

"They're getting away," Evangeline said, tearing herself
from Barnaby's arms and dashing across the dance floor.

"Who?" Barnaby called after her. "Miss Caldicott?"

Something was holding Evangeline back. She heard ripping
fabric and looked down to see her pale blue gown caught under
the foot of a portly gentleman.

"Frightfully sorry," the man said, through his walrus-like
ginger moustache.

With a tug and a tear, Evangeline freed her gown from under
his foot and continued running, torn skirts and petticoats for
all the world to see. These silly impractical gowns, how was a
young lady supposed to catch a thief in such an ensemble?

"Stop," she yelled. "Stop them."

Evangeline's voice was drowned out by the orchestra and
the increasingly inebriated laughter of the guests, bouncing off
the high ceilings and wooden floors.

The two footmen were reunited in the doorway and slipped out into the night.

"Thief. Someone stop them!"

With everyone else distracted, it was up to Evangeline to catch the pilferers. Ignoring her pinching shoes, she broke into a sprint and sped through the door into the cool evening air.

Outside, the two footmen sauntered away into the distance, following the gravel footpath towards Fitzroy.

She picked up speed and plunged into a cartwheel. Lifting her arms with a tear of her ridiculously restrictive gown and whale boning stabbing into her ribs, Evangeline flipped three times across the gravel, quickly catching up to the men. But the dastardly footmen heard her coming and started to run.

Evangeline tumbled forward, launching herself at the dark-haired footman. She grabbed hold of his ankles and tackled him to the ground. Unfamiliar with the nuances of rugby, Evangeline crashed on top of him with an unseemly groan.

"Get off me, you slapper," the dark-haired man yelled with a kick. "Enright. Help!"

Enright bolted off into the darkness. Evangeline placed her knee into the small of the footman's back.

"What's going on?" Augie said. "Evangeline! What are you doing down there. Get off that man, this instant."

Evangeline looked up. Quite the crowd had come out of the Exhibition Building and down the path, including Edmund, the Bunyip-catching fellows and the watercolour girls. Evangeline smiled awkwardly at her audience. Even she recognised that her current position sitting astride a footman was rather bewildering.

"Get off me. I'll have you for assault," the footman protested, his face pressed into the gravel.

"Playing the innocent, are we? Go ahead and call the constabulary. I'd like to talk to them myself."

"Evangeline. What is going on?" Edmund said with a serious tone. "Please remove yourself from that footman."

"I dunno what she's on about, sir," said the footman. "Are you responsible for her? Is she a loony?"

"He's been stealing from the guests."

The footman cackled with laughter. The watercolour girls gasped, clutching at their jewelled throats while the gentlemen patted down their own jacket pockets.

"You got any witnesses, Miss?"

"Me."

He squirmed and writhed, knocking Evangeline off his back. She landed with an unladylike thud and reached out to grab his ankles again. The footman managed to scramble to his feet, but a mahogany pipe, a brass mobile telegraph key and a silver snuff box tumbled out of his pockets. The crowd inhaled sharply and tutted.

"I don't think we need any other witnesses," said Albion Middlehall. "I doubt these items are your personal possessions."

"Off to the watch house for you, boy," Percy said, as a steam engine driver and another footman grabbed the thief by the elbows.

"Your gown!" Albertine gasped, horror across her pretty face.

"A small sacrifice for justice." Evangeline shrugged, glancing down at the torn dirty remnants of her dress. Albion Middlehall held out his hand.

"Well done, Miss Caldicott."

Evangeline rose to her feet unassisted and brushed herself off.

"Why, thank you, Mr. Middlehall," she said. "By the way, I overheard your little wager with Mr. Sharpthorne. I want in."

Albion smirked.

"You?" Percy Sharpthorne and Basil Mawdesley scoffed. "A girl?"

"Absolutely, Miss Caldicott. We'd been honoured." Albion elbowed his friends and bowed to Evangeline. "If this little incident is anything to go by, the Bunyip doesn't stand a chance."

"Young lady. Look at your gown. We are leaving right now." Augie humphed, pulling her away from Albion and the others toward the row of waiting hansom cabs. Edmund removed his jacket and handed it to his niece.

"I was only trying to help," Evangeline said.

"Wait until your father hears about your high jinks," Augie said, with quivering jowls. "You've ruined the whole night and embarrassed us all."

Evangeline's cheeks blazed red.

"Uncle Edmund, I was doing the right thing."

"Oh, Evangeline." Edmund shook his head with a tired smile. "What will we do with you?"

"How will I live this down?" Augie sulked as they boarded the cab and the horse clip-clopped towards 56 Collins Street.

"What were you saying to Albion Middlehall?" Edmund said, narrowing his eyes and sucking on his self-combusting pipe.

"Nothing, Uncle Edmund."

Evangeline was in enough trouble already. She dared not mention the Bunyip.

"No more scrapes," Edmund said firmly. "Twice today, you've put yourself in danger. Your luck must be wearing thin."

Uncle Edmund did not understand, Evangeline could not possibly stop now. She must design the perfect contraption for capturing the Bunyip and rid the blight from Melbourne. Edmund would be proud of her. Eventually.

She kept quiet all the way home, plotting out her new invention.

Balls, blancmange, Bunyips and Barnaby. It had been quite the busy day. And with a Bunyip to catch, tomorrow would be busier still.

CHAPTER 6

B ANISHED TO HER ROOM AFTER last night's incident,
Evangeline put her imprisonment time to good use.

She lay on her feather bed with her eyes firmly closed.
She screwed her eyes up tight and focused her mind, gathering
all her determination. Evangeline concentrated as hard as she
could, gritting her teeth with effort. Ever since the night in the
Lady Alchemist's cellar, Evangeline had tried to recreate the
strange power she'd conjured to free herself from the cage. The
mysterious magic which broke the Alchemist's spell.

After a few minutes of intense fixation, Evangeline gasped.
She felt a faint tickle. It was weak but she swore there was
something there. The power was back.

With a grin, she opened her eyes and stared down at her
outstretched hands, ready to admire her handiwork. But there was
nothing, only a perfectly ordinary pair of hands. No amber glow,
no tingling sensation, only a dull ache behind her right eye.

"Knickers," she sighed. The power she conjured at the Lady
Alchemist's mansion remained elusive.

There was a sharp rap on her bedroom door and Evangeline
quickly shoved her new contraption sketch under her pillow.

It was her father, the Professor. He opened the door
cautiously, rarely venturing into his new daughter's room.

Evangeline produced a wan smile. Her ears still stinging after a tongue-lashing from both Uncle Augie and Miss Plockton.

Her father cleared his throat, pursed his lips and tugged his waistcoat over his belly with his real hand.

"When I granted you permission to attend the Ball," he began with a deep breath. "I pictured a refined, but dull, affair. Polite chit-chat and a little light waltzing. I did not expect ruffian wrangling."

"I am sorry, Father," she said, perching on the edge of the bed, her hands clasped at her chest. "I saw the footmen stealing and someone had to stop them. I suppose I got a little carried away."

Her father sat down, the lady-sized chair groaning under his weight.

"I know you want to help, m'dear. But you must be more careful." He sighed. "I probably should've made you stay at home after the morning's terrible incident. The shock obviously affected your judgment."

"I called out for help but no one stopped them. I couldn't let them get away."

"It was very reckless of you. Who knows what could have happened to you if the other men had not arrived."

"I was fine, Father." She folded her arms. "I had already apprehended him. I am not like other young ladies. I know how to conduct myself."

"Perhaps in the past. But you are away from all that wickedness now. You do not need to take matters into your own hands. A quiet word and it would have been sorted out without such a scene."

"But didn't I do the right thing, Father?" Evangeline said, staring directly into his eyes. "Should I have stood by and let the thieves get away?"

The Professor stroked his ferocious black moustache with his clockwork fingers.

"Yes. No." He sighed again. "Your antics will be all over Melbourne by elevenses."

"I thought you deplored idle gossip, Father?"

"I don't care a whit. Generally. But I care about people speaking ill of my daughter. A lady has to be careful of her reputation."

"I thought of all people, you would be proud of my initiative," she said, holding her chin high.

"Unfortunately this is the way of the world, whether we agree or not. People are illogical these days, with their ridiculous manners and useless protocol. You don't want to end up an old maid, like Miss Plockton."

"I wouldn't mind," Evangeline said with a half-shrug. The world of beaus and bairns sounded awfully dreary. But obviously she would dress more fashionably than Miss Plain Old Plockton.

"You don't want to live the rest of your life with a stuffy old duffer like me."

"Father, I don't have time for courting silly young men and such nonsense. I'd much rather spend my time learning from you."

"And you shall. But one day, you will leave me. If you manage to stay in one piece and don't go running after robbers or get eaten by the Bunyip. You were lucky this time. But you never know what might be around the corner. Foolish acts can have consequences. I know...."

Her father took a fleeting glance down at his clockwork hand. Evangeline's eyes widened, finally the opportunity to ask the question.

"Is that what happened to you? A foolish act? Is that how you lost your arm, Father?"

"To a degree..."

"How can I possibly learn from your experience, if you won't tell me the story?"

"Very well," the Professor sighed in defeat. "It all began shortly after my twenty-fifth birthday...."

CHAPTER 7

T HE PROFESSOR CONTINUED.
"It was a gloomy London day, back in the days of proper pea-soupers. I had recently completed my examinations and was finally a fully accredited horological-engineer."

"I was brash in those days, as young men often are. I thought I knew everything. I was going to build the best clocks in the world and quash those Swiss fellows at their own game. Make Britain strong again in the horological arts!"

The Professor slammed his brass fist against his thigh.

Evangeline looked at her father's full moustache, round belly and ruddy cheeks. She could not imagine her father as a young whippersnapper. He gave the impression of being born middle-aged.

"I devoured every piece of information I could find. Spending months memorising the positioning of each individual pin and cog in every great clock in Europe. From the astronomical clock of Strasberg to De Lucia's rebuilding of the Venetian St. Mark's Clock. Nothing else existed. I was relentless."

Her Father's eyes were glassy and faraway, a smile curling on his lips.

"Not even my mother?" Evangeline asked.

Her father did not reply. Mentioning her mother was a bold move. It had taken over five months for her father to divulge the details of his missing hand, let alone the story of how he met her mother. He continued, as though Evangeline had not said a word. She shuffled her position, laying on the bed on her belly with her ankles crossed and her chin resting in her hands.

"I was voracious. I wanted to know everything there was about clocks. And what was the biggest clock in London?"

"Big Ben?" Evangeline lifted a hesitant eyebrow.

"Of course. Or to be precise. The Great Westminster Clock. Big Ben is the name of the bell."

"One of my fellow students from Horological School had secured a respectable position with the master watchmakers firm, Dents. Fergus was a funny-looking chap. Beady little rat eyes but awfully nimble fingers and sharp as a whip."

"Dents had the maintenance contract for The Great Westminster Clock and I pleaded with Fergus to let me come on his rounds. After months of pestering, he agreed to let me accompany him on his next maintenance round. I was excited beyond belief. Here was my chance to inspect the largest mechanism in London up close. I was convinced I would learn all its secrets and perfect them myself. But life does not always unfold as we plan."

The Professor chuckled to himself, his eyes bright.

"The mechanism room was up inside the Tower near the clock face. We had to climb up hundreds of winding steps into the clock room. As I said, I was a foolish young man. I imbibed a few cleansing ales before meeting Fergus. Perhaps one too many. The steps were a little slippery under foot but I pressed on, buoyed by the excitement of seeing the clock."

"Half way up, I started feeling a little woozy. Fergus, in his rat-like manner, had no trouble with the steps and raced up ahead. I dismissed my malaise as a general lack of physical fitness, my studies had been my singular focus for months. I stopped for a moment to catch my breath and promised to take more exercise. In those days I rather fancied myself as a pugilist."

The Professor threw a few punches in the air and Evangeline sniggered, imagining her portly father in a boxing ring stripped to the waist.

"When I finally arrived at the clock room, I was extremely warm and a trifle dizzy. I remember mopping my brow despite the chilly November night."

"Fergus was already at work. His supervisor was known for his fierce temper and Fergus could not waste a moment. But I didn't mind, I only wanted to see the room for myself. And what a beauty she was. I stood back in awe, admiring the magnificent steel creature with her enormous interlacing cogwheels, some over six feet tall. I started sketching, creating my own schematic. I circled the mechanism from all angles, taking notes from each point."

The Professor leapt from the chair, flailing his hands and painting a picture of the mechanism in the air.

"Denison's design was truly top notch. Fergus ignored me, oiling the individual cogs and checking the time against his own pocket watch."

"I was particularly fascinated by one component, set right inside the large wheels, barely visible through the moving parts. I was not sure whether my eyes were deceiving me but it appeared to be a white gemstone, the size of my fist. A stone inside a clock? This was like nothing I'd seen before in all my horological studies. I leaned in to get a better view."

Evangeline switched to a cross-legged position, she leaned forward, her eyes never leaving her Father.

"I've thought about this moment many times over the years. I am still not certain what happened next." The Professor flopped back down on the small chair. "Did I slip? Did I lean too close? Did I take my eyes off the moving parts while I tried to take notes? Even Fergus couldn't understand how or why it happened. But for some reason, The Great Westminster Clock didn't like the look of my right arm. Or she liked the look of my new Saville Row coat, a graduation present from my father and step-mother."

"Before I comprehended what was happening, my sleeve was caught and I was dragged towards the crushing metal cogwheels. How I screamed as my coat was pulled further and further inside. "

"'Help,' I cried."

"'I'll get you out.' Fergus grabbed my shoulders, pulling me back but the clock was strong. I tried to tear off my coat but the jacket was of exceptional quality and the stitches would not tear. I was being dragged closer and closer into the machine."

Evangeline's eyes were as wide as dials, her mouth open.

"I cannot describe the pain as my fingers met the cold steel..."

There was a knock on the door, Miss Plockton poked her head inside.

"Apologies for interrupting, sir," she cooed, in the calm voice she used for the Professor. She used quite a different voice for Evangeline. "But there is a Mr. Wilberfoss here to see you."

"What? Old Wilby here? By Jove." The Professor heartily slapped his knee and jumped to his feet with a smirk. "Bring him into the parlour. And find Edmund. And rustle up some tea. It's a little early for whiskey, I suppose."

The Professor walked towards the door, muttering and chuckling to himself.

"Old Wilby, eh? What are the chances?"

"But, Father. You haven't finished the story. Big Ben tore your arm off?" Evangeline pleaded.

"Not quite. It was far worse than that. But I'll finish the story another time. Wilby is here!"

The Professor waved with a jerky flick of his brass fingers and closed her bedroom door.

Evangeline collapsed into her pillow with an exasperated sigh.

CHAPTER 8

T HE PROFESSOR INSISTED YOU JOIN them," Miss Plockton said through tightly held lips and led Evangeline downstairs to the parlour. Evangeline skipped along the hallway, not caring why, only glad to be released from her exile.

Miss Plockton opened the parlour door to peals of raucous laughter and clouds of tobacco smoke. Uncle Edmund, her father and a fair-haired stranger stopped sucking on their self-combusting pipes and smiled up at her.

"So, this is the new addition to the family," boomed the unfamiliar man, leaping to his feet. "This is the secret you've been keeping, Monty you old dog."

Evangeline smiled shyly. The man was tall and broad with a thick blonde moustache and khaki tweed knickerbockers.

"This is my daughter, Evangeline," the Professor said.

Evangeline offered her hand and Wilby pushed past a spindly-legged table to her side. He bowed low and graciously.

"Pleasure to make your acquaintance, Miss Evangeline. I am Willoughby Wilberfoss. But you must call me Wilby. You're part of the family after all."

Evangeline could not help but smile.

"Sit, sit, my dear. Your father was telling me all about your arrival and how you've started to follow in his footsteps. I simply had to meet you for myself." Wilby gestured to the settee as though the house was his own. "Miss Plockton, my Scottish heather. Bring Miss Evangeline a cup of tea and more cakes, if you have them."

"Of course, sir," Miss Plockton said in a girlish manner.

"Miss Plockton. What did we agree earlier?" Wilby chided, pointing a playful finger at Miss Plockton

"Of course, Wilby."

"That's better." Wilby nodded with a big toothy grin.

As Miss Plockton scuttled off with cheeks as red as the velvet settee, the Professor leaned over to Evangeline.

"Wilby is an old family friend. He lived on the neighbouring estate and Wilby, Edmund and I grew up together."

"Remember the scrapes we used to get into," Wilby guffawed. "The time you fell into the pond mid-winter. I had to jump in and rescue you."

"It was not all that funny."

It was the Professor's turn to blush as Edmund joined in with Wilby's laughter.

"What brings you to Melbourne, Mr. Wilberfoss?" Evangeline said.

Wilby held up a finger and stared her in the eye.

"Wilby," she corrected.

"I like a lady who speaks her mind. We shall get on famously."

"Wilby is a professional hunter. He is here to catch the Bunyip," Edmund said with a gush and big eyes on Wilby.

"I heard you were having a little trouble with beasts here in the Colonies. So I thought I'd pop down and sort it out. A good excuse to visit my old chums, the Caldicotts, while I was here."

A professional game hunter here in 56 Collins Street. Evangeline was immediately all ears. She could learn so much from Wilby and refine her own Bunyip-catching device.

Miss Plockton arrived with a fresh pot of tea and a tiered cake stand, piled with jam tarts. Uncle Augie entered the parlour, close behind Miss Plockton.

"Oh, everyone is in here," Augie said with a touch of umbrage. "Edmund, I have been looking everywhere for you."

"Oh, Augie, you must meet Wilby." Edmund beamed.

"So, this is the famous Wilby I have heard so much about," Augie said flatly, glancing Wilby up and down. "A pleasure to meet you, sir."

"Wilby was just telling us about his tiger-catching in the Malay," Edmund said. "Sit, Augie."

Augie eased himself down onto the settee with a pout. Evangeline popped a tart into her mouth and writhed happily as raspberry jam burst onto her tongue.

"Came face to face with a large female." Wilby jumped to his feet and tiptoed around the back of the settee, acting out his latest adventure like a game of Charades. "Nothing more ferocious than a mother protecting her kittens. The sharpest teeth you've ever seen. She tore a great hole in one of the local guides. Could have done with one of your inventions, Monty. When are you going to build me a gun?"

Wilby slapped the Professor across the shoulder. The Professor was mid-sip and spluttered tea out his nostrils.

"Wilby, you know how I feel about guns. After what happened."

"How could I forget? But this new pipe invention of yours is capital. You always were a clever clogs. I lost my favourite full bent apple while hunting Old Shuck in Littleport."

"Just one piece of advice. Don't store it in your pocket."

Wilby and Edmund grimaced and nodded solemnly. The room was quiet for a moment and Evangeline seized her chance to steer the conversation in a more helpful direction. This was an invaluable opportunity to gather information for her own hunt.

"How do you capture the beasts, Wilby?" Evangeline said.

"Far too dangerous for capturing. I don't want to lose an arm like old Monty here. A big gun sorts them out, quick sticks. I quite fancy a Bunyip head mounted on the drawing room wall of Wilberfoss Manor."

"I hear there is a sizeable reward," Evangeline said.

The Professor and her uncles quickly turned and glared at her.

"I heard people talking at the Ball." She shrugged.

"Not the most impressive purse but not too shabby. The newspaper men are being a trifle reckless in my view. They need to consider public safety. A bunch of amateurs traipsing about can be extremely dangerous. You seem to have a keen interest in the Bunyip, Miss Evangeline?"

"I saw it myself."

"Oh really." Wilby leaned forward. "How interesting. Details, old girl."

"Yes, tell him all about it," Edmund encouraged, grinning at Wilby. Augie crossed his arms.

"I don't know if..." the Professor said.

"Fiddlesticks, Monty. Let the girl speak," Wilby said.

All eyes were on Evangeline.

"I saw the creature take a man and drag him into the river."

"How big was it? As big as me?"

"A little bigger, possibly eight foot long and amphibious. Like nothing I've ever seen before."

"Impressive but not insurmountable." Wilby leaned back in his chair with a nonchalant grin. "No Antipodean monster scares me."

Evangeline snuck another jam tart into her mouth. No one would dare tell her off while Wilby was here.

"So tell me, clever Miss Evangeline. You saw the attack. How would you apprehend it?"

Evangeline paused for a moment, not wanting to give away any of her ideas.

"Some type of net. But it would need to be very strong. The Bunyip had sharp claws."

"Good observations, young lady. You're a lucky fellow, Monty. A good head on her shoulders."

"Most of the time." The Professor nodded.

"Right!" Wilby launched to his feet. "I best be getting my gear and my men together. This Bunyip won't capture itself. I told the Governor, I'd have this beastie dead by tea time. Now, Monty. I have an idea."

The Professor raised an eyebrow, nervously.

"Hear me out." Wilby smirked. "I have one more spot left in my team. I could do with an extra pair of hands."

"You know I've always been a terrible shot, Wilby." The Professor winced. "The outdoors have never been my cup of tea."

"I'm keen," Edmund said, almost exploding from his armchair. "I can be ready in five minutes."

"Thank you, Eddie, old fellow. But I was thinking of someone else."

The Professor and Uncle Edmund looked perplexed. Evangeline held her breath. Did Wilby mean...?

"Now, this might sound a little unorthodox but Evangeline seems a clever and capable young woman. Just what I need on my team."

For a brief moment, Evangeline soared high. Here was a chance to do something really exciting, hunt with a famed adventurer. She pictured herself with a rifle in hand, catching mother tigers in the Malay.

"No!" the Professor and her uncles said in unison.

"But I..." Evangeline blurted.

"No."

"I have..." She tried again.

"No."

Evangeline deflated.

"Don't be so old-fashioned, my good fellows. I had a marvellous American lady join my expedition in the Congo. Remarkable woman. Degree in physics and the best aim I've ever seen."

The Caldicotts shook their heads vigorously.

"Just a thought." Wilby shrugged. "Sorry to disappoint you, Miss Evangeline. I would be honoured to have a sharp-minded girl like you in my expedition. Another time, perhaps."

Wilby took her hand and, with a flamboyant kiss, marched out of the parlour. The Professor and Edmund scurried after him.

Evangeline consoled her disappointment with another jam tart. With a shrug, she reverted back to her original plan of catching the Bunyip herself, but with Wilby on the chase, she'd have stiff competition.

She leaned across for one last tart, raspberry jam always helped her think, and started to plot.

CHAPTER 9

T HE HOUSE WAS QUIET AFTER Wilby's departure and luckily everyone had forgotten Evangeline's punishment. She was chewing on a mustard and cress sandwich, staring out the Conservatory windows, when the back courtyard door opened.

"May I be excused? I must get back to my reading."

Her father nodded, barely looking up from his academic paper and self-combusting pipe.

Evangeline ran through the kitchen, out the back door and into the courtyard.

"Doing the deliveries yourself?" Evangeline said.

Mei dropped a wicker basket filled with sharply folded white sheets by the kitchen door.

"An excuse to hear about the Ball," Mei said with greedy eyes. "Tell me all about it."

The best of friends, Mei and Evangeline made a striking pair. Mei in her cream-coloured traditional trousers and jacket, flat slippers and long snaking plait, Evangeline in her slate-grey day dress buttoned to the neck and skirts grazing the toes of her heeled boots, her brown hair coiled at the nape of her neck.

"It was awfully dull. Except near the end, when I got myself into a bit of trouble. That was rather exciting and absolutely justifiable."

"Did you knock someone out?" Mei said.

"Almost. But never mind about the Ball." Evangeline looked around and lowered her voice. "I have much more exciting things to discuss, like catching this Bunyip creature. It was terrifying, Mei. I still can't believe my eyes. The poor policeman, drowned and gobbled up by that horrid beast."

The girls both shuddered.

"I brought today's Argus," Mei said.

"Splendid. They still won't let me read the stories. Even though I've seen the creature in the flesh. An old family friend of Father's, a famous adventurer, invited me to help him catch the creature but they said no. They never let me have any fun."

Mei unfurled the paper and the girls sat side by side on the stone step in the autumnal sunshine.

"*FAILURE TO CATCH THE BUNYIP,*" the headline read. "*After another day and night of terrorising the people of Melbourne, the Bunyip of Yarra Park is still at large. Four different groups of hunters scoured the Park last night and none were able to apprehend the beast.*"

"*He's more slippery than you'd expect,*" said Brigadier Lionel Thackthwaite, (retired) from Richmond. "*We had him in our sights but he disappeared at the last moment. We will be back tomorrow. I do not give up easily.*"

The bellows of the creature were heard echoing along the Yarra. Was it laughing at the poor attempts by the hunters?

A local Aboriginal man told The Argus that the Bunyip hugs its victims to death. So the tip of the day for any would-be hunters, is to keep your distance. The reported victims of the Bunyip now totalling five after two missing Aboriginal girls were confirmed dead, dragged from their fishing on the banks of the Yarra."

Evangeline gasped.

"How old were the girls?"

"Only a few years younger than us. Twelve and thirteen."

"The beast has to be stopped."

"Let me read the next part... '*The Argus has posted a reward of £500 for the capture of the Bunyip of Yarra Park. Dead or*

alive. Who will be able to rid Melbourne of this fearful monster?'
Blimey, £500!'"

"And Albion Middlehall laid a bet for another £100,"
Evangeline added.

"Middlehall? The sheep station family? His father is the richest
man in Melbourne. You are movin' in fancy circles these days."

"I guess he must be well-to-do if he's throwing around
wagers like that. He has these awfully big thick eyebrows. Like
two black puddings."

The girls giggled.

"Seriously, Mei. We have to catch this creature. A policemen
is one matter but eating girls off jetties is inexcusable."

"The dead bodies are pilin' up." Mei gulped. "Bunyip huntin'
is dangerous business. Five dead already."

"Are you chickening out?"

"Of course not," Mei said defiantly. "Unless you are."

"Never. We found the Alchemist. We can capture a monster."

"She got away."

"But we stopped her. She hasn't been heard of since,"
Evangeline said, but she was not completely convinced they
had heard the last from Lady Violetta Breckenridge-Rice. But
the Alchemist could wait, there were more pressing threats to
thwart. "I have been thinking."

"Here we go."

Evangeline unfolded a piece of paper from her pocket, the
schematic for her new patent pending invention.

"I estimated the creature was at least eight foot long. I'll need
steel netting. Something strong enough to withstand his sharp claws."

"I'm more worried about being hugged to death," Mei said.

"But aren't you excited? Just think, two young ladies proving
they are more capable than a group of fusty old Army men."

"Three hundred quid is a lot of money." Mei stroked her
lower lip.

"Pish posh," Evangeline scoffed. "Think of the girls and the
policeman. It's an act of charity."

Mei arched an eyebrow.

"Will your new thingamie be ready by tonight?"

"Hopefully. I need your help too. Do you have any bangers?"

"Just because I'm Chinese?" Mei crossed her arms. "You want a bamboo hat too?"

"I didn't mean to offend you with my presumptions," Evangeline said. "But do you?"

"Yes," Mei replied. "How many do you need?"

"All of them."

Mei smirked.

"I'll bring them tonight. Did you finish your other invention?"

"Oh yes, and I am ever so pleased with the result."

Evangeline darted inside, grabbing her pale pink parasol with the cane handle from the grand blackwood hall stand by the front door.

By the time Evangeline returned, Mei was upside down, balancing in a handstand against the wall. Her best friend did bore easily.

"Is that it?" Mei said. "Nice colour, but not quite what I was expectin'."

"It's innocent at first glance. One click for a parasol."

Evangeline pressed the button and paraded up and down the courtyard, twirling the handle between her fingers. The parasol was a pale pink whir above her head.

"Two clicks. And it becomes infinitely more practical."

Evangeline pressed the button twice. A sharp thin blade with teeth emerged from the metal ferrule at the top.

"A saw would have come in handy when we were stuck in those cages in the Lady Alchemist's cellar."

"But you got us out. Have you worked out how you did it?"

Evangeline chewed on her lip and shrugged her shoulders.

"Perhaps it was just a fluke?" Mei said.

"Whatever it was, it's unreliable. Unlike the vicious parasol."

"Good name." Mei nodded.

Evangeline grinned.

"And you haven't seen the best part. Three clicks..."

The thin saw retracted and a bayonet blade thrust out.

Mei jumped back.

"Wow. Where did you get that?"

"There are all kinds of interesting bits and pieces down in the Professor's laboratory-workshop. With my vicious parasol, I shall be prepared for any eventuality. Rain, hail or strife."

"Miss Evangeline? Who are you talking to?" Miss Plockton called through the kitchen door.

"Better go," Mei whispered.

"I'll see you this evening. We'll try out my newest contraption and catch ourselves a Bunyip."

"My mama has put locks on my windows. She's worried I'm sneakin' out to meet young men."

"How tedious. Our work is far more important than silly old courting."

"Don't worry. I'll find a way out."

Mei slipped out of the back door and into the laneway.

It was a simple plan. All Evangeline had to do was distract her father, construct her contraption, sneak out of the house and capture the Bunyip. What could possibly go wrong?

CHAPTER 10

TICK. TOCK.
Tick. Tock.

The mahogany grandfather clock ticked with a deep bass voice, standing like a sentinel on the first floor landing. Evangeline tiptoed along the hallway, listening intently for any whisper of her family or the stealthy Miss Plockton.

She swung open the clock's side panel and peered at the inner organs of the magnificent time piece. Evangeline reached in, extracted a single brass bolt and popped it into her skirt pockets.

"Father," Evangeline said, entering the laboratory-workshop in the cellar.

He mumbled in reply, bent over his work bench as usual. A bright gas-lamp illuminating his intricate work.

"Clarence has stopped ticking."

"What!" the Professor's head jerked up immediately. "Impossible. Clarence is the most reliable time piece in the Southern Hemisphere."

"I haven't heard him tick. Ordinarily he ticks so loudly."

"This is unheard-of." The Professor leapt to his feet. Evangeline had never seen her stout father move so quickly before. "How long has he been silent for?"

"I don't know," she said, as he rushed past her, brandishing his trusty ivory handled screwdriver.

Evangeline rubbed her hands together, now she was alone in the laboratory-workshop. She pulled her sketch from her pocket and began searching through her father's well-stocked inventory. She started with the tall dressers sitting along the bluestone wall, pulling open the brass-handled drawers one by one.

"These will do nicely," she said as she came across a collection of magnets. "But will they be strong enough?"

She took the largest magnet of the bunch and wedged it into the workbench vice. She stood back, holding out another magnet in front of her and waited.

"Nothing."

She took one step closer to the vice.

"Rubbish," she said, looking down at her magnet. She did not feel one iota of pulling power. "Do these work?"

Evangeline took three steps closer.

She squealed. Her arms were tugged from their sockets as the magnetic force propelled her forward. She dug her heels into the floor but the power was too strong and she slammed into the wooden workbench at full tilt. The magnets connected with a metallic clank and she crumpled into a heap on the ground.

"The answer is yes," she said, dusting herself off and inspecting a scrape on her forearm.

She continued to search the laboratory-workshop for supplies, building a stockpile of cogwheels, gaskets, pistons, valves and a crankshaft.

"Perfect," she said to herself as she found a yard long steel rod and ticked another piece off her list.

"Last one. Steel netting."

Evangeline rifled through her father's trunks, searching every nook and cranny, finding spoon warmers, a biscuit pricker and a fluting machine but nothing resembling steel netting.

There was one last possible place. She looked up towards the forbidden end of the laboratory-workshop, where the Professor kept his top-secret project. So secret, no one else knew what lay beneath the sheet, not even the uncanny sleuth Miss Plockton. The lumpy carriage-sized object was covered with a beige tarpaulin, fastened down with locks even Evangeline could not pick. Yet another mystery at 56 Collins Street.

Whatever lay underneath the cloth, it was very important indeed. The top-secret project was the raison d'etre for bringing the Professor to Melbourne. The Professor reported personally to Governor Normanby himself, visiting Government House monthly to update on his progress.

Evangeline burned with curiosity and swore she must uncover the secret. But this mission would start tomorrow, after she'd caught the Bunyip, of course.

Footsteps pounded down the stairs and Evangeline flinched, she was not allowed to be in the laboratory-workshop unaccompanied. The Professor would be hopping mad if he found his daughter poking about in his inventory.

Evangeline dashed behind a dresser and pressed herself against the cold bluestone wall, suppressing a gasp as a sticky cobweb pressed against her cheek.

"Where? Um...yes. Over there...hmmm," her father muttered to himself, banging open drawers, dropping tools with a clang and swearing rather colourfully as he stubbed his toe on something.

"There you are, you old bastard." He laughed, before stomping back up the stairs and locking the door behind him.

"Knickers."

Evangeline's shoulders slumped. She was locked inside the windowless workshop. There was no way she could escape without facing the wrath of her father.

After a brief moment of despair, she pulled herself together. This was a wonderful opportunity to make a good start on her invention, every possible tool she needed was within arm's reach.

Evangeline sat cross-legged on the floor and got to work, dismantling valves, unwinding nuts and inspecting each piece for decay and damage. She weighed the crankshaft in her hand, chewing on her lower lip. Her designs were rough and raw, she was an engineering novice, yet when she held each piece of brass and steel in her hand, she instinctively knew where each piece should go. The metal spoke to her and told her where it needed to be. Was she mad or was inventing in her blood?

She began to have second thoughts about her design. At full scale, the device would be rather difficult to sneak down the drainpipe. The Bunyip catcher must be portable.

Evangeline paused. A shuffling sound came from somewhere behind her but she did not turn around. After years of living in less than salubrious accommodations, Evangeline was familiar with vermin and she was in no hurry to see another mousy face. Instead, she waited and hoped her visitor would leave soon.

The noise went away and Evangeline completed her disassembly. With her faithful screwdriver in her hand, she squatted like one of Mei's uncles and began connecting the brass and steel components, creating the skeleton of her new improved device. But she was still missing a net. Perhaps a fishing net would suffice? Her father collected everything. There must be a fishing net here somewhere.

Evangeline froze again. More rustling came out of the darkness from the secret corner of the workshop. An object too large to be a rat, more like person-sized.

This time, she turned with a palpitating heart. She was sitting in a pool of gaslight, beyond was inky darkness.

"Is there somebody there?" she said with a stutter.

Logically, no one could be there. There was only one door and only one way in and it was locked. What could be rustling in the darkness?

CHAPTER 11

"WHO'S THERE?" SHE DEMANDED. "SPEAK up. Now."

But no one replied.

This was ridiculous. Evangeline was no child, she was seventeen years old. She had escaped her evil stepfather, travelled half way across the world and evaded the bobbies more times than she'd like to admit. She was preparing to face the feared monster of Yarra Park. She was not afraid of a noise, no matter how inconceivable.

Taking hold of the steel rod, she took a gas-lamp from the work bench and began to investigate. Nothing seemed out of the ordinary; the trunks, the benches, the dressers and the lump under the tarpaulin, all as they should be. Footsteps clumped on the floorboards above her head, her family walking about on the ground floor. She wondered if her absence had been noticed.

Again, a rustle of fabric and a jangle of metal.

She gulped, her mind rushing to dark and silly places. Could it be ghosts, rattling their chains?

Evangeline remembered, there was a source of dark energy in the laboratory-workshop, she had seen it with her own eyes.

It was the day her father lent her the atervis detector. Another of the Professor's inventions and a type of telescope, the atervis detector displayed any traces of dark energy with a silver aura. Evangeline had peered around the workshop and to her surprise, saw something glowing from one of the trunks. But the Professor closed the lid and shooed her away before she could get to the bottom of it.

Evangeline took a deep, character-building breath and moved towards the sound.

It was coming from the secret project.

The tarpaulin was moving.

She froze, watching the writhing under the oilcloth. The object moved, bulging up and down, in and out. Tied down with locks, the object could not move forward. What was her father's secret project? What could he possibly be building? She gulped as a batty idea flew into her head. Was it alive?

Evangeline inched forward, her steel rod held aloft, her heart galloping. She was determined to expose whatever lay beneath the covering. But she was so engrossed in the rustling object, she failed to hear the turning of the key in the lock. The door opened and her father's heavy boot steps clumped down the stairs. Holding a lamp, Evangeline was bathed in light and he instantly saw her, his face turning purple before a word escaped from his mouth.

"It's moving." She pointed.

"Out. Out now," he bellowed.

"It was an accident, Father. You unintentionally locked me inside. I called out but you didn't hear me."

"Out!"

The steel rod still in her hand, Evangeline grabbed a reel of copper wire and a battered leather apron, before scurrying up the stairs and away from her father's wrath.

Evangeline swished past Miss Plockton in the hallway. The afternoon had turned chilly and Miss Plockton had an ivory shawl draped across her shoulders. Evangeline was struck by an idea.

"What is going on?" Miss Plockton scowled. "What do you have there?"

"Oh, I am helping Father with one of his inventions."

Miss Plockton stared back with disbelieving eyes.

"Your father sounded rather cross. I hope you weren't interfering. Some secrets are best left alone."

It was not the first time Evangeline wondered whether Miss Plockton could see through walls.

"Clarence is broken. You know how he loves that clock," Evangeline said, ignoring Miss Plockton's spooky intuition. "Actually, Miss Plockton, as a matter of fact, I was looking for you."

"Teatime isnae for another few hours, Miss Evangeline."

"Not that. Are you busy right now, Miss Plockton? I was hoping you could teach me how to knit?"

CHAPTER 12

"IS MISS CALDICOTT AT HOME?"
A male voice carried down the hallway from the front door. At the sound of her name, Evangeline jumped from her chair and crouched by the doorway for a better eavesdropping position.

"Whom may I say is calling?" Miss Plockton said primly.

"Here is my calling card. Mr. Albion Middlehall."

"Wait here, Mr. Middlehall. I shall see if Miss Caldicott is receiving visitors."

Evangeline scampered back to her place on the overstuffed armchair, knitting needles in hand. Albion Middlehall here to see her? What could he possibly want?

"There is a gentleman here to visit you, Miss Evangeline," Miss Plockton tutted.

"Who is it, Miss Plockton?" Evangeline said with all the innocence she could muster.

"Mr. Middlehall. I doubt your father would approve of young gentlemen calling. But your father isnae home to ask. Or your uncles."

"Never mind. Send him away. I am busy here." Evangeline held up a lumpy brown square of woollen stitches.

"But I presume he is one of those Middlehalls."

"Why does everyone keep asking this?"

"It would be terribly rude to turn him away. I shall set up tea in the parlour and personally chaperone his visit. Wait here until I collect you."

Evangeline rolled her eyes and turned back to her stitches.

There was a flurry of activity as Miss Plockton marched up and down the hallway, three or four times from the parlour to the kitchen and back again.

"We are ready for you now, Miss Evangeline," she said.

"Can I bring my knitting? I've almost got the hang of it."

"Please behave, Miss Evangeline." Miss Plockton exhaled.

Entering the parlour empty-handed, Evangeline found Albion gazing out through the lace curtains, his hands neatly folded behind his back.

"This is a pleasant surprise, Mr. Middlehall," Evangeline said.

He smiled brightly under his bushy eyebrows.

"I was in the area and hoped you would be accepting company. May I say what a lovely home you have, Miss Caldicott."

"Yes, isn't it?" Evangeline said with all truthfulness. She was grateful every day for her new home, her memories of her previous lodgings in dank, dark squats were still fresh in her mind. "Please, take a seat."

Evangeline sat down on the red velvet settee and Albion took one of the ornately carved armchairs. Miss Plockton, like a sentry, was stationed discreetly by the door.

The room settled into an awkward silence. The mantelpiece clock ticked loudly and nothing was said. Evangeline glanced about the parlour, tapping her fingers on her lap, waiting for Albion to say something.

Miss Plockton politely cleared her throat and broke the silence.

"Perhaps Mr. Middlehall would care for some tea, Miss Evangeline?"

"Tea. Tea. Oh, of course." Evangeline jumped to her feet, glad for something to do. "Sugar?"

Evangeline picked up the intricately engraved silver teapot from the spindly-legged table and poured. As she watched the tea swish around the delicate cups, she was struck with a brilliant idea, an automatic clockwork tea-making machine. This device would be revolutionary, imagine the thousands of hours saved across the British Empire for more productive pursuits. No more waiting for tardy service, piping hot tea would be available at exactly your preferred time. Evangeline was certain even Miss Plockton would be pleased with such a labour-saving device.

"Two please."

Evangeline filed her idea away for another time and measured out two lumps with the silver tongs.

"Why thank you." Albion took the saucer from her hand and Evangeline offered him a plate of ginger snaps.

"These are awfully good," she said, taking one herself and crunching away merrily.

"Apologies for my imposition, Miss Caldicott. I hope you don't mind but I came specifically to hear more about your experience by the Yarra. We were interrupted and did not finish our conversation at the Ball. You mentioned seeing the Bunyip? What was it like? Only if revisiting the ordeal is not too traumatic?"

Miss Plockton shuffled in her seat, but Evangeline ignored her disapproving wriggle. Miss Plockton had forced Albion upon her, this gave her no recourse to control the conversation.

"Yes, it was truly horrid. I can't stop thinking of that poor man, screaming as he was dragged into the river by the creature."

"You were awfully brave, Miss Caldicott. And have you thought much about how you are going to capture him? Mr. Rippingale said you were an inventress too. Are you building something?"

"He talked about me?" she tittered, feeling giddy all of a sudden. "What else did Mr. Rippingale say about me? What were his exact words?"

"He said you were taking after your father," Albion said with a perplexed look.

Evangeline fanned her face and then remembered Miss Plockton, seated in the corner of the room. If Miss Plockton caught wind of the Bunyip wager, Evangeline could say goodbye to any adventures.

Evangeline shrugged at Albion.

"Perhaps he misheard you? Ripples can be a bit muddleheaded."

"Not quite," Evangeline mumbled.

Albion's brow furrowed, his thick eyebrows threatening to take over his whole face. Evangeline jerked her head towards Miss Plockton.

"Sorry, Miss Caldicott. I am confused. Are you an inventress?"

She widened her eyes and tried to surreptitiously point towards the door and more importantly, Miss Plockton.

"I don't understand." Albion shrugged.

Evangeline sighed, she had obviously overestimated Albion's intelligence. Lucky, he was rich.

"I thought you agreed to be part of the..." He started.

Suddenly Evangeline stood up, knocking over the spindly-legged table, splashing hot tea into Albion's lap. He jumped to his feet with a yowl, pulling the hot wet fabric away from his unmentionables.

"I am so sorry. So incredibly clumsy. A cloth, please, Miss Plockton?"

Miss Plockton was already half way down the hallway.

Clarence the grandfather clock chimed four times, the Westminster bells echoing down the stairs. The Professor must have replaced the missing bolt inside Evangeline's pocket.

"Is that the time? I must be off," Albion said hurriedly, pulling his own solid gold pocket watch from his waistcoat. "Thank you for the tea, Miss Caldicott."

"I am sorry. I didn't mean for..."

"No need to apologise. It was an accident. I really must be going. It was delightful to see you again. May I enquire if you will be attending the Soldier's Benefit?"

"Another one so soon? Sounds absolutely awful... "

"Awfully exciting. Of course she will," interjected Miss Plockton, cloth in hand.

"Excellent. I look forward to seeing you there and perhaps you will reward me with a dance." Evangeline nodded and Albion pressed his lips against her outstretched hand. "I can see myself out."

The front door closed and Evangeline grabbed two more ginger snaps. This batch was terribly scrumptious.

"Now, Miss Evangeline." Miss Plockton narrowed her eyes and began stacking the tea tray, snatching the plate of biscuits away before Evangeline could take another.

"It was an accident!" she lied with a mouthful of ginger snap.

"I dinnae know what you are up to, but..." Miss Plockton said.

"It was truly an accident, Miss Plockton. Me and my butterfingers," Evangeline said, turning to leave the room. "I must get back to my knitting."

"God sees all, Miss Evangeline."

Evangeline felt a shiver down her back under Miss Plockton's icy glare. It wasn't only God who saw all at 56 Collins Street. Evangeline would have to be more careful.

CHAPTER 13

E SCAPING MISS PLOCKTON'S GLOWER, EVANGELINE ran up to the privacy of her bedroom. She sat on her bed with the cricket stump sized needles from Miss Plockton's sewing basket and the spool of copper wire, all ready to start knitting a Bunyip-catching net.

Evangeline's mother taught her to knit many years ago, together they knit squares from red wool scraps by the kitchen hearth. But like the memories of her long-gone mother, her memories of knitting had faded. Luckily Miss Plockton was a knitting virtuoso, and after a few pointers and lumpy false starts, Evangeline's fingers quickly remembered the basics.

She cast on and mastered the first rows, her tongue jutting out of her mouth in concentration. The copper wire was hard and quickly gouged a red divot into her ring finger. With gritted teeth, she kept knitting and eventually picked up speed. She tingled with excitement as the net began to grow and another of her inventions came to fruition. With this new device, she would save innocent lives, win £600 and show Melbourne what an inventress was capable of.

Within the hour, she was threading magnets through the copper wire net and casting off. She begrudgingly acknowledged her needlecraft lessons were not completely useless after all.

With her little hand saw, she nervously sliced the steel tube in two, fearing her grinding would be heard by the acoustically gifted Miss Plockton. She fed the net into one tube and put the other aside, turning to the battered leather apron. She laid the apron on the floor, cutting out an oblong shape, before slashing the leather and inserting the steel rods. She connected the rods with spools of copper wire and for the finishing touch, she added a pair of boot laces.

Evangeline held out the device and admired her own handiwork. Portable, powerful and practical, her new invention was ready to test in the field. A touch too utilitarian for her tastes, perhaps a decorative rivet or two would make it more aesthetically pleasing.

"What shall I call you?" she said, but then the triangle chimed for tea and Evangeline put aside her invention for a well-earned break, hopefully with crumpets.

"Afternoon, Father," Evangeline said as she entered the dining room and pecked her father's bristly cheek. "I hear Clarence is in full voice again. You managed to fix him?"

Her father grunted and unravelled the evening's edition of The Herald. Evangeline shrugged her shoulders and sipped her tea. Then all of a sudden, the Professor's face brightened like the sun coming from behind a cloud.

"By Jove. The old fellow's done it!" he exclaimed. "The man works miracles."

The Professor turned around the front page for Evangeline to see "*BUNYIP KILLED*" in big bold letters.

"The Bunyip didn't stand a chance with old Wilby on the case." The Professor grinned.

"Knickers," Evangeline muttered under her breath.

"Did you say something, my dear?"

"Thank heavens," Evangeline said loudly, but inside she deflated. Wilby had beat her to the monster and her afternoon's endeavours had been futile. Luckily, there were crumpets and honey on the table, so the afternoon was not a complete loss.

Her belly filled with comforting crumpets, Evangeline slumped back upstairs to her bedroom. Closing the door, she kicked aside the oriental rug beside her bed and pressed the short floorboard. The house at 56 Collins Street was built with secrets in the walls. The enigmatic house perfectly suited the Caldicotts, who brought their own fair share of secrets with them.

Evangeline pulled the brass telegraph key from the hiding place under the floor. Last week Evangeline added her own innovative component to the telegraph key, an alphabetised typewriter keyboard. So much more convenient than silly old Morse Code.

"Are you there?" Evangeline's fingers flew across the keys.

"You must have heard the news," Mei replied.

"Wilby beat us to it."

"At least, it's dead." Mei tapped back. "No more deaths."

"Yes," replied Evangeline. She knew it was selfish and all that mattered was the culling of the beast but she wished she'd been the one. She glanced across the room at her new contraption, ready to go but no monster to catch. "I finished my new contraption and everything. Such a shame."

"To be honest, I wasn't keen on facing the Bunyip but the reward would have been nice."

"I guess our meeting is off. I'll try to sneak out tomorrow. You promised to teach me more of the tiger moves."

"Let's go out by the Yarra anyway. We haven't gone for a late night stroll in ages," Mei replied. "And I have something to show you."

"We could test the device. It may come in handy for a future endeavour. Same time?"

"In the laneway."

"Don't forget the bangers. It's always cathartic to blow something up."

CHAPTER 14

U NLIKE MEI, EVANGELINE'S FAMILY HAD not resorted to locking her bedroom window, so she slipped out and down the drainpipe once again. Hitting the ground with barely a sound, she hurried across the courtyard, past the privy and through the back door.

Mei was waiting for her in the laneway, with a smug look on her face. A forest green vehicle stood beside her, with one small wheel at the front and two large wheels at the back, a red and gold sign with 'Fang's Fine Laundering' swinging from the rear.

"Like it? We got it last week for deliveries. We won't have to walk." Mei grinned. "Queen Victoria owns one exactly like it."

"Can you really imagine the Queen riding a tricycle?" Evangeline said.

The girls giggled.

"Jump on." Evangeline slipped into the velocipede seat behind Mei. "Where's your invention?"

"Here." Evangeline gestured to her forearm wrapped in brown leather, steel rods running down her arm.

"That?"

"I call it my beast catcher."

"Nifty."

"Not only for Bunyips. It was inspired by the vicious parasol, with a few alterations." Evangeline pointed to her parasol, strapped to her back like an archer's quiver. "Did you bring the bangers?"

Mei pointed to a paper sack on the seat next to Evangeline. She inched gingerly away, ensuring a gap between herself and the explosives.

Mei stepped on the pedals and off they went. Both girls shuddering and jolting as the tricycle bounced over the cobblestoned laneway. Evangeline winced with every bump, glancing with a grimace at the bag of fireworks beside her.

Mei steered the tricycle out into Spring Street, passing the horses and cabs and down towards Flinders Street. An auto-chariot hooned by, noisily overtaking the tricycle with its eight stampeding clockwork legs. The fresh autumnal wind blew through their hair and Evangeline began to tell Mei the story of the mysterious movement in her father's laboratory-workshop.

"There's something alive down there."

"Creepy."

They pedalled past Fitzroy Gardens and Mei turned off the paved road down a dirt track into Yarra Park, running along the banks of the snaking Yarra River.

The town was now gone and the sky was dark. The ghostly white trunks of the grey-green eucalyptus glowed in the dim light. Mei followed the track until a dead end.

"We have to hide the tricycle. I'm more scared of my mama than the Bunyip."

They pushed the Salvo tricycle deep into the bushes and covered it with fallen branches. The leaves leaving an astringent, crisp scent behind on their hands.

"This way." Mei pointed to a narrow path into the thick bush. "That's where the Bunyip lives. Or lived."

"I'm still miffed Wilby beat us to it."

"I'm not."

"Where's your courage, young Mei?"

"I've got courage. I'm just not stupid."

Evangeline followed Mei along the overgrown path, stumbling over clumps of long-haired grasses. Despite the chill of autumn in the air, the foliage was thick and green. They pushed past red-stemmed bracken, spiny-leaved bushes and pale trunked trees, while all around them, the bush heaved with croaks and squawks, rustles and shakes. Her heart pounding in her throat, her eyes darting left and right. Everything around her, so strange and unfamiliar.

A throaty rasping hiss started above their heads. Evangeline stopped short with a choke. Do Bunyips climb trees?

"What is that?" she stuttered.

"Scared, are we?" Mei stopped with hands on hips.

"Of course not," Evangeline said. "I am merely on alert for the Bunyip."

"It's only a possum."

"Surely not. That sounds far too ominous to be such a small animal."

"Come on, circus girl." Mei shook her head and set off again down the path.

"What are you doing out here?" said a voice out of the bushes.

Mei and Evangeline squealed.

CHAPTER 15

"WHAT ARE YOU GIRLS DOING out here?" A tall grey-bearded Aboriginal man stepped out of the bushes.

"Bunyip," Evangeline blurted, with a tremor in her voice. She had seen the Aboriginal people clustered around the outskirts of Melbourne but had never spoken to a native Australian before.

"You looking for the Bunyip?"

"We were going to catch him. But we're too late."

"With what?"

Evangeline gestured to her beast catcher and the man stepped forward to inspect her arm.

"Have you seen one before?" he said, poking at the steel rod with his gnarled walking stick. "He's too strong for this."

"It's the latest in engineering innovation," Evangeline said, thrusting out her chin. Mei nodded from behind her friend's skirts. The man sucked on his teeth. "We were going to the river to test it. Although it is a little pointless, now the Bunyip is dead."

"He not dead."

"It was in the newspaper," Mei said with a raised eyebrow.

"Lots of white fellas running about here. Trying to catch him." The man chuckled. "They all too slow. Bunyip knows this bush. He's smarter than them."

"But they said they killed one." Evangeline narrowed her eyes.

"No white fella is gonna catch the Bunyip."

Mei and Evangeline exchanged baffled glances. Who was right; this man or The Herald?

"You know the Bunyip well?" Mei said.

"I seen him a few times. When I was a young fella, he was here. Me and my cousin stood on the bank down there. He tore one of our hunters clean open. Claws straight through his skin and bones. Blood and guts spilling all over the ground. I can still hear the man's screaming. Long time since I come back here."

"Blimey." Mei swallowed.

"No sign of him for a long, long time. But now he come back. Maybe you white fellas disturbing his territory. No one likes strangers coming into their home."

"Do you know where he lives?"

"He is around here. I know, I can feel him. I seen his tracks. But I don't want to find him. I leave him be."

The man shrugged his shoulders.

"But the Bunyip is killing people. It must be stopped."

"You are silly girls." He shook his head. "You won't beat the Bunyip. You'll be dead in the water like the girls from my mob. Nice girls. Bunyip ate them up."

"Why not take your revenge?" Evangeline tilted her head to one side.

"I want him gone but I don't want to kill him. I want him to move on somewhere else. There's much better fishing down the river. He'd be happier there. You white fellas just making him angrier. You should leave him alone. There'll only be more dead."

"But it's not only us. He is killing your people too."

"It's the way it's always been. You best to leave him alone. Keep away. You can't beat the Bunyip. This is his home. You should go back to yours."

Without another word, the man slipped back into the bush like a ghost.

"Wait," Evangeline called, but she and Mei were all alone again. Her shoulders slumped. "We need to know more."

"Who do we believe?" Mei said. "Did they kill him or not?"

Evangeline chewed her lip.

"I know who my money is on. Who is more trustworthy."

"Who?"

"The one with no money."

"I hate riddles. Is he dead or not?"

"Who has the most to gain? Wilby, of course. Five hundred pounds. Not the elder."

"So the Bunyip is still alive?"

"Maybe," Evangeline said. "We're here now regardless. Let's test the beast catcher. I didn't get a chance for a proper trial in my bedroom."

"The river's this way."

Evangeline and Mei continued down the track through the scrub. Then a fearful sound filled their ears. A guttural, terrifying shriek, tearing a trail up their spines.

"Is that what I think it is?" Mei stuttered.

Evangeline gulped.

CHAPTER 16

M EI GRIPPED HOLD OF EVANGELINE'S arm, both
friends stifling their screams.

"The man was right," Mei whispered.

"It's still out here."

The howl sounded again. A flock of screeching white
cockatoos burst out of the trees. The best friends jumped.

"It's comin' closer."

"This is our chance, Mei," Evangeline said, puffing out her
chest while desperately trying to lock her shaking knees.

"He sounds really big."

"We can catch him. Stop him from eating any more young girls."

"I hope he hasn't got a likin' for it." Mei said, rubbing the
back of her neck. "I don't fancy being someone's supper."

"Don't fear, Mei. We have the beast catcher." Evangeline checked
her leather gauntlet and unscrewed the main chamber. "Bangers?"

Mei handed over the sack. Evangeline slid handfuls of the
small red firecrackers down the large tube.

"So, this should work?"

"Absolutely," Evangeline said. "I think."

"You've tried it?"

"Not exactly. It all makes perfect sense in theory. There's
only one way to find out."

"Why do I let you talk me into these scrapes?" Mei said, with a sigh.

"Because you have an adventurous spirit." Evangeline grasped her friend by the shoulder. "And I need you."

"Alright." Mei grimaced. "The noise came from this direction."

They left the track and pushed through the bracken towards the howls, Evangeline's heart rate accelerating with each step. The sounds of croaking frogs growing louder, the clumps of grass thinning to bare dirt.

Splash.

It sounded like a large stone falling into the river. The hairs on the back of Evangeline's neck stood up to attention. She reached out and grabbed her friend's hand, Mei's palm was damp and Evangeline squeezed back in support.

Another screeching yowl echoed through the bush, this time even closer. The bellow was deep and powerful. It resonated through her rib cage, forcing her heart to skip a beat.

"It knows we're here," Mei whispered.

It was now unclear who was the hunter and who was the prey.

"Are you ready?" Evangeline said. Mei nodded pensively. Evangeline pushed through the last remaining trees to the river, her beast catcher arm outstretched before her.

From the rocky banks, Evangeline could see in all directions for the first time. The river seemed so calm as the dark brown water ambled by.

"There," Mei stammered.

Further down the bank, a large shape emerged from the river. First, the head with the black eyes, then the undulating neck, then the strong solid body with a lashing tail. Water pealed from its smooth grey-black skin as it stepped onto the banks with clawed webbed feet. Evangeline had no breath in her chest as she watched the Bunyip stride onto the shore, muscles rippling as it moved. The beast immediately locked eyes with Evangeline and, staring straight at her, opened his mouth and screeched, saliva dripping from his pointed yellow teeth.

"Ready?" Evangeline said, her heart thumping.

"No." Mei replied.

The beast took small languid steps towards them, his neck swaying hypnotically. Evangeline steadied her aim and pressed the ignition button. The beast catcher crackled, electric sparks spraying from her wrist. The Bunyip flinched. Evangeline licked her lips, a new wave of confidence coursing through her. The beast was not invincible. She waited for the bangers to ignite. The Bunyip crept closer and closer. But the beast catcher stayed silent.

"Quick. What are you waitin' for?" squeaked Mei. "Shoot."

"Um." Evangeline flustered. She felt the electric current, but nothing was happening.

The Bunyip was within twenty feet. The catcher should have fired by now. Evangeline's confidence crumbled into panic.

The Bunyip roared. His foul breath reaching their nostrils and the scent of rotting meat filling the air. Evangeline's stomach turned at the thought of the dead girls inside his belly.

"What's happenin'?" Mei yelled.

"I don't know," Evangeline said. She pressed the ignition button again. But nothing, not even a sizzle.

Was her invention a failure? Would she and Mei be the next victims of the terrible Bunyip? Or would her catcher explode and blow Evangeline into a million pieces? Is this how the Professor lost his arm? Was she doomed to repeat his mistakes? If only he'd finished the story.

Boom!

The catcher fired.

The blast was powerful, knocking Evangeline backwards, jerking her arm and shifting her aim up at the sky, instead of towards the Bunyip.

"Run," she yelled but grey firecracker smoke clouded the air. She did not know which way was the river and which way was land.

"Ouch."

The next thing Evangeline knew, the zap of the electrified net pressed against her face. She was thrown off her feet and tossed to the ground as the magnets snapped shut, wrapping her in a ball. Her fall was cushioned by some other object.

"Get off me."

The object was Mei.

Evangeline and Mei were trapped inside their own net, wrapped up like a Christmas ham, while the Bunyip roamed free on the banks.

"Knickers," Evangeline said.

CHAPTER 17

"BALLOCKS," MEI SAID.

"We know the beast catcher works," Evangeline said. "Just a slight kickback problem. And perhaps a loose wire."

"I'm the one with a loose wire. Why did I let you talk me into this? Again."

Mei and Evangeline scrambled to their feet carefully, any sudden movement would send them toppling over.

"Where is he?" Mei said, as the smoke cleared.

The Bunyip was nowhere to be seen. The river bank was empty.

"The noise must have scared him off," Mei said.

"Let's hope so." Evangeline sighed. "It appears we're safe for the moment."

"If he hasn't gone to get a friend," Mei said. "Get us out."

Evangeline tugged at the magnets along the bottom of the net, groaning as she tried to prise them apart. But the magnets were fixed, holding firm and fast.

"Let me try." Mei tugged and tugged with all her might, without success. They were stuck inside.

"It's useless," Evangeline said. "My invention works too well."

"The parasol?" asked Mei.

"Silly me."

Evangeline pulled the vicious pink parasol from the strap across her back. She clicked the button twice, ejecting the thin saw blade and began sawing.

"I hate ruining my own handiwork," she grumbled.

"Either that or we end up as dinner."

Evangeline tore a large hole in the copper net, reminding herself she could always knit another. They crawled out and onto the bank.

"Are you hurt?"

"I'll live," Mei replied.

Evangeline nodded, the only thing injured was her pride.

"Where has he gone?" Evangeline said, inspecting large footprints in the mud.

"I don't want to know. Let's go home." Mei wiped a smear of mud from her face. "I could murder a cup of tea."

"I agree." Evangeline tucked a wayward strand of hair behind her ear. "Let's come back tomorrow. Better prepared."

"With double the bangers."

She folded the torn net into a bundle and they headed back into the bush, muddy but with all their limbs. The night was quiet again, the noise of the beast was gone and Evangeline began to breathe once more.

"Did I tell you Albion Middlehall came to call this afternoon?"

"Oooh," Mei teased. "Gentleman caller."

"He wanted some information."

"Of course," Mei said. "Mrs. Middlehall."

They continued to traipse through the bracken and bushes, discussing nice normal topics, until they realised the path was nowhere to be seen.

"This way." Mei pointed.

"Are you sure?" Evangeline said. "I'm positive, we came from this way."

"You must have bumped your head. It's this way."

"I clearly remember. We went past that tree."

"You're wrong. They all look the same to you."

"I am very observant, I'll have you know," Evangeline said, with hands on hips.

"Except for now."

The friends crossed their arms and glared at each other.

"Mei Fang. It is this way I tell you."

"Evangeline Caldicott. You're mistaken."

Suddenly the peaceful night was shattered by a bellowing roar. Mei and Evangeline inhaled sharply, their eyes darting in the direction of the cry.

"He's back," Mei breathed.

CHAPTER 18

B
RANCHES AND LEAVES IN ALL directions, there were
no visible landmarks, even the moon had hidden herself
away. Evangeline wished she knew more about the stars
in the upside down Australian skies.

"This way," Mei said again firmly.

"I am telling you, it's this way," Evangeline said, raising her voice.

"Shhh. He'll hear us."

Mei spoke too soon.

The beast bellowed again. The frightening sound coming
from their left.

"Let's go this way?" Evangeline pointed in the opposite direction.

"Yes. Hurry."

Mei took off into the bush. Evangeline picked up her skirts
and started running, branches scratching her face and grabbing
at her hair. Mei led the way but then suddenly stopped short.
Evangeline skidded to a halt, bumping into Mei from behind.

"What's wrong?"

"No." Mei cried, her chest caving in.

"What?"

Evangeline moved alongside her friend.

It was the river bank again. The same place with the same
footprints running along the mud. They had run in a circle.

There was a thundering snap of branches as the Bunyip came crashing out of the bush. He lunged forward, snarling, only ten feet away. With black eyes, dead and dangerous, he leaned back on his haunches like a cat ready to pounce.

Evangeline and Mei clung to each other.

The Bunyip inched forward. A smirk on his grey lips.

Evangeline and Mei stepped backwards but there was nowhere else to go. They were trapped on the river bank, the massive creature blocking their way back to the track and the Yarra River flowing behind them.

They took another step backwards. Mei stumbled on a rock and rolled her ankle. She grimaced in pain and Evangeline helped her back to her feet.

The creature roared.

They took one more blind step and Evangeline's heart was banging like a hail storm. A cold rush swarmed around her feet and she glanced down. They were ankle deep in water.

The Bunyip jumped.

Evangeline tumbled into the river, arms flailing, her skirts ballooning around her. Quickly water-logged, the sodden fabric dragged her down below the surface. The river was deeper than she expected. She kicked, trying to get a foothold on the bottom but her feet found only water.

"Swim!" called Mei, balancing precariously on a pointed rock and clutching an overhanging tree.

"My lessons start next week." Evangeline gulped, choking between mouthfuls of water. The Bunyip slid into the river.

Evangeline propelled herself backwards, using her arms. But the Bunyip lunged forward, his teeth snatching hold of her skirts. He started to reel her in.

Evangeline thrashed in the water, shouting and splashing, but his grip was strong. She reached across her back for her parasol, but it was gone. The pink umbrella was laying on the river bank underneath the lashing tail of the Bunyip.

"Over here," Mei yelled. "You big ugly thing."

The Bunyip ignored Mei, dragging Evangeline onto the shore.

Mei leaped from her rock with a lump of driftwood as thick as her arm. She swung with all her might, the lump of wood thwacking the Bunyip across the face.

The Bunyip growled, but did not let go of his grip on Evangeline's skirts. He began to shake his head, to and fro, jerking Evangeline around in the water. She spluttered and coughed as her head bobbed under the surface again and again, filling her lungs with water.

Unable to take a breath, her heart thundered in her chest. She thrashed and fought, but the Bunyip was too strong, the water too deep. Evangeline began to lose consciousness. Was drowning a worse fate than being eaten by the Bunyip?

Mei struck again. But the rotten piece of wood shattered across the creature's face, crumbling into a million pieces.

"Ballocks."

The Bunyip, surprised by the hit across the jaw, stopped pulling for a moment. Evangeline leaned back and her hands touched the bottom of the river. She had never been so glad to grab a handful of mud.

"Go for the snout!" Mei said.

Evangeline kicked, her hard heeled boot striking at the monster's black wet nose. Her genteel shoes did have some advantages over Mei's flat slippers. Mei joined Evangeline in the water.

"Go," yelled Mei.

The two friends pummelled at the creature with feet and fists, a furious avalanche of small strikes. The creature shook his head, confused and irritated. He opened his mouth to roar and let go of Evangeline's skirts. She tumbled from his grasp and scrambled to her feet. Evangeline and Mei moved forward and the friends started to kick at the Bunyip in unison.

The creature began to back away onto the bank.

"Punches and kicks aren't enough." Mei shook her head.

Evangeline turned, grabbing hold of a log floating down the river. Her fingers slipped, the log was so heavy she could barely lift it. This would be an ideal time for the strange power to return. She grabbed the log with both hands and gathered all her determination. She screwed up her eyes for a moment and tried to summon the magic again. But nothing.

Evangeline would have to resort to her natural brute strength. Straining and grunting in an undignified manner and with one almighty swoop, she lifted the log and bashed the creature across the head.

Thwack.

His eyelids fluttered and the mammoth creature crashed into the water in a heap.

The girls glanced at each other with disbelief, frozen for a moment. It was suddenly very quiet. The Bunyip did not move. His head slumped in the shallow water.

"Is it dead? Did we kill it?" Evangeline asked.

"Looks dead to me."

Mei poked the scaled body with a stick.

"We did it! We managed to kill it." Mei cheered, breaking into a little jig on the riverbank. "We're the best!"

"Thank heavens," Evangeline said flatly, as she trudged wearily out of the water and onto the river bank. Her limbs were heavy and she started to pine for her comfortable feather bed. She wanted to escape the bush and the river as quickly as she could.

"You don't seem very excited? What about the dead policeman and the two girls? You ought to be proud."

"That was far too close for my liking. Perhaps I'll feel more victorious after a good night's sleep," Evangeline said. "Let's go home."

"What about the reward?"

"We'll stop at a telegraph kiosk and report it on the way home."

"What are you goin' to do with your 300 quid? I might get myself an auto-chariot. Do you think the Professor could get me a discount?"

Evangeline finished wringing out her soaked skirts and headed into the bush.

"Wait." Mei grabbed Evangeline's arm. "Can you hear somethin'?"

Evangeline frowned.

Something large was moving through the bush. Something, or someone, was coming.

"Don't tell me," groaned Mei.

CHAPTER 19

MEI AND EVANGELINE GLANCED AT each other
with dilated eyes.

"Two Bunyips?" Mei said, saying aloud precisely
what Evangeline was trying not to think.

"Let's hide."

Before Evangeline and Mei could reach the trees, a group of
men came crashing into the clearing. Evangeline shielded her
eyes against their blinding gas lamps.

"Miss Caldicott?"

"Mr. Middlehall. What a surprise."

"Blimey." Percy Sharpthorne and Basil Mawdesley crowded
around the lifeless body of the Bunyip. A flash bulb blasted as
another unfamiliar man snapped a photograph.

"I guess I owe you £100, Miss Caldicott," Albion said.

"Ladies, may I take a photograph of you with the Bunyip?"
Interrupted another man with a notebook. "I'm from The Argus.
This way, please. Everyone in Melbourne will be desperate to hear
the story of the two young ladies who beat the dreaded Bunyip."

"Don't forget the £500," said Mei.

"Of course. Miss?"

"Fang. Mei Fang." Mei puffed out her chest. "Of Fang's
Fine Launderin'."

"I want to hear every detail of how you slayed the creature. Believe me, ladies. This will be the biggest story of the year!"

As the gentlemen praised and complimented her, Evangeline's tiredness was replaced by a warm glow. As she posed with Mei on the bank, Evangeline recalled the policeman and the two Aboriginal girls. Mei was right. They had saved lives with their courage.

Evangeline's thoughts suddenly turned to her mud-caked hair and wet torn dress. This was not the ideal image for the front page of The Argus. But being a heroine was not all Balls and Coffee Palaces, sometimes it was messy work.

"Ladies, please step back a bit further."

Mei and Evangeline edged towards the grey body.

"My word. What a monster," the journalist said.

"How did you manage to defeat it?" Albion asked, with a curious smile.

Basil and Percy were quiet, seething over their loss of the wager.

"With Evangeline's invention," Mei replied, winking at her friend. Evangeline smirked back.

"I knew it," exclaimed Albion.

"Ready, ladies."

The photographer focused the camera on Mei and Evangeline. They struck their best respectable poses, upright and proper, the way one should appear in photographs. The flash exploded with a white puff and the girls blinked, blinded for a moment.

Evangeline felt a shuffle of movement behind her.

"Bloody hell!" yelled the photographer. "Move!"

Evangeline screeched as a massive tail swooped around and knocked her from her feet. She collapsed with a thud on the dirt.

The Bunyip was back on his feet, snarling with his tail slapping in the water. The journalist and the photographer sprinted backwards to the other men, bumblingly loading their weapons.

The Bunyip roared.

He stared down at Evangeline, laying defenceless in the mud. A splatter of saliva struck Evangeline on the face. She wiped her cheek with shaking hands, her heart hammering. The Bunyip lumbered forward, looming directly over her. Evangeline's lumpy throat filled with tears. She stared into the Bunyip's dead black eyes. She was certain this was it. Her luck had finally run out.

"Three clicks?" Mei yelled.

Evangeline was so frightened, she could barely reply.

"Three," she managed to croak.

Mei clicked once. The pink parasol opened.

"What is she doing, silly girl?" said one of the men. "That's not going to help."

Mei clicked twice. The thin toothed saw emerged.

"That's no ordinary parasol," said Albion.

Mei clicked three times. The saw retracted and the bayonet blade extended, glistening in the light.

With her own blood-curdling battle cry, Mei took a running jump. She leaped forward, stabbing the blade straight through the Bunyip's left eye.

The creature flailed backwards and forwards in the river, shrieking and crying with pain. Mei had struck deep. Only the cane handle of the parasol was now visible, poking out of the Bunyip's eye socket. Waves of water splashed in all directions as the Bunyip tossed his head from side to side. Mei grabbed Evangeline's hand and pulled her to safety. Then the Bunyip's gigantic head dropped onto the river bank with a crash, shaking the ground like an earthquake. His right eye was open but unseeing, his thick grey tongue lolling from his mouth.

Everyone on the river bank was silent. They watched and waited. After a few long minutes passed, Albion crept forward.

"Blood." He pointed to a dark red puddle flowing from the bank into the Yarra.

Then the body shuffled and Albion skirted backwards with a girlish yelp. The current of the river pushing the body downstream.

"I think it's dead," Albion said. "Properly dead this time."

Evangeline hugged her best friend.

"Thank you," she said with tears in her eyes.

"It was my turn to save you." Mei grinned. "Now we're even. I think I ruined your parasol though."

"Miss Fang. May I say, that was magnificent." Albion Middlehall stepped forward. "Jolly impressive."

"Fantastic sword work. Where did you learn how to do that?" said Percy.

"Where do you reside, Miss Fang?" The journalist said, pen poised in the air. "What will you do with the £500?"

The men crowded around the beaming Mei.

Evangeline stepped back with a grin, watching her best friend, the heroine.

"My grandmother was a kung-fu grandmaster and taught me everythin' I know. I started as soon as I could walk..."

While the others were distracted by Mei's increasingly tall tales, the water stirred. Evangeline instinctively flinched.

The grey body was moving again.

She opened her mouth to call out, but the Bunyip looked up, staring straight at her with his one remaining eye. Their eyes locked and Evangeline did not speak. This time the anger and brutality had gone, his black eye was filled with sadness and pain.

With a single glance, Evangeline understood. What had she done? She'd allowed trivialities like money and fame to entice her. The Bunyip was only protecting his home. He was not her enemy.

She lowered her eyes, saying nothing as the monster slipped away under the surface of the water, disappearing completely from view.

"Another photograph, Miss Fang? With your trophy," said the reporter. "Wait a moment. Where has it gone?"

The others turned and looked. The river bank was empty. Evangeline shrugged her shoulders.

"It appears the Bunyip is not dead," Percy Sharpthorne sneered. "What a shame."

"No body. No reward. I'm afraid," said the reporter. The photographer began packing up his equipment.

"You did fight valiantly, Miss Fang. What rotten luck," Albion consoled.

"Come along, Middlehall. There's still a chance to catch this thing ourselves," Percy said as Basil and the newspaper men headed back into the scrub.

"There goes my auto-chariot," said Mei, her shoulders drooping. "I was looking forward to promenadin' down King Street."

"There are more important things than auto-chariots," Evangeline said.

"More important than auto-chariots?" Mei frowned.

"Like honour and intestinal fortitude."

"Oh, you mean cake. Or is it bangers? Cakes with bangers? I told you, I hate riddles."

"I'll explain later." Evangeline placed a hand on her friend's shoulder.

"We could have bought a lot of cake for £600." Mei shook her head.

"Let's go home."

Wet and weary, the best friends found the right path through the bush and headed home, Bunyip-less.

CHAPTER 20

A week later

A T THE SOLDIER'S BENEFIT BALL, everyone was still talking about the Bunyip.

"Your father knows the Bunyip catcher? The Wilberfoss chap?" The same questions, over and over, from every person Evangeline met. "Have you met him? I bet he's awfully impressive."

Evangeline smiled and nodded with gritted teeth. Only she and Mei knew the truth. But since the night at Yarra Park, the Bunyip had gone into hiding and Wilby had taken all the credit. And the reward.

To make matters worse, Mei's mother caught her sneaking back into the house covered in mud. Mei was confined to her room until further notice. Their hasty snippets of conversation over the telegraph were no substitute and when anyone mentioned the Bunyip, it reminded Evangeline how much she missed Mei. Her brave friend who saved her life.

Evangeline wandered aimlessly through the Ballroom of the Travancore Estate, wishing she was with her cogwheels and flanges in the laboratory-workshop.

"Apparently the body of the Bunyip went missing in transit on the way to the Museum. The rumour is a private collector had it stolen," Percy Sharpthorne said loudly.

Evangeline screwed up her face as she overheard the discussion. This was the missing piece of the puzzle, Evangeline had wondered how Wilby managed to produce a Bunyip body to claim the reward. He must have stacked lie upon lie, culminating in the convenient theft of the body. Evangeline grimaced. Some hero Wilby turned out to be. He better not show his face at 56 Collins Street.

Evangeline sighed and continued ambling through the cavernous room. Not even the sight of a table heaving with strawberry flummery could lift her spirits.

Jemima and Albertine eyed Evangeline suspiciously, she could sense their snide comments behind their gloved hands. But when she caught their eyes, they smiled and waved. Barnaby ignored her entirely, dancing more than three times with Jemima, not that Evangeline was counting.

"I was hoping to see you this evening, Miss Caldicott." Albion Middlehall approached as Evangeline stood alone by a potted palm, watching the dancing.

"I guess I owe you £100," she said lowering her chin to her chest, wondering where on earth she would find such a sum.

"Forget the wager. Terrible shame your Bunyip got away. I presume the parasol was one of your inventions. Do you have more? I would like to hear all about them."

"Ahem." Uncle Edmund cleared his throat. "Can I whisk my niece away for a waltz?"

For a brief moment, a dark look flashed across Albion's face, as though he was not happy to see Uncle Edmund. Evangeline could not understand why.

"I would be delighted." She beamed and Uncle Edmund led her onto the dance floor.

"I have been hearing some interesting stories about you, young Miss Evangeline," her uncle said with a mock stern tone, as they took their first steps to the music. "From a mutual friend by the river."

"You should know better than to listen to gossip, Uncle."

"Well, whatever happened, I am very proud of my niece," Edmund said.

The music swelled, Uncle Edmund twirled her around and Evangeline rested her head on his shoulder. Finally she was enjoying the Ball.

"Life is rather peculiar, isn't it?" Edmund mused as they traversed the room. "People are often not what they seem."

"Here you are. I've been looking everywhere for you both," Augie called and waved from the side of the room, his face flushed with excitement. "You won't believe it."

"What's happened now, Augie," Edmund shook his head with a smile.

"Mrs. Picklescott-Smythe has invited us all to a mummy unwrapping soiree next week." Augie clapped his hands. "I went to a few in London. Mummy unwrapping parties are all the rage. It will be the event of the season."

"This may even entice Monty out of the house," said Edmund.

"Am I invited?" Evangeline perked up.

"All the Caldicotts."

"It would be educational," said Edmund.

"I hope it's cursed," Evangeline said.

"Evangeline!" scolded Augie. "How horrid."

Uncle Augie shook his head with a grin.

"What will we do with you?"

EVANGELINE
AND THE
SPIRITUALIST

MYSTERY AND MAYHEM IN STEAMPUNK MELBOURNE
(THE ANTICS OF EVANGELINE BOOK 3)

CHAPTER 1

I T WAS NOT EVERY DAY Evangeline had the chance to witness a mummy being unwrapped.

"I'm so excited, Father." Evangeline skipped to catch up with the Professor. Her father led the way through their front gate, dressed in his best black coat. His prized moustache, waxed and curled perfectly in place.

"Indeed. A piece of ancient history right here in our own street."

"Listen to you both," Uncle Augie said. "Giddy as Christmas morning. Ordinarily I have to invent the most elaborate ruses to get you out of the house."

The whole Caldicott family crossed Collins Street, dodging the carriages and auto-chariots, to the grand residence of Mrs. Picklescott-Smythe. Uncle Augie was not Evangeline's real uncle but rather her Uncle Edmund's constant companion. Edmund and Augie were sporting fashionable ascots while Evangeline proudly wore her new lavender afternoon dress, edged with satin ribbon. Their heeled boots crunching through the amber leaves as the golden Melbourne afternoon sun streamed over the cobblestones.

"This soiree should be highly educational," the Professor said. "Not like your usual frivolous rubbish."

"Do you think there'll be a curse?" Evangeline said.

Uncle Edmund snickered while Uncle Augie gasped with horror, clasping at his ample chin. "Evangeline! Never jest about a curse. Have I told you about the music stand at the Garrick? I still get nightmares every time I hear the scraping of metal."

"I shouldn't think so," the Professor replied with all seriousness. "It's probably some minor member of the royal family. No one too special."

"That's not what I heard..." started Uncle Edmund, opening the iron gate. Augie flinched as the gate squealed.

"Evangeline, please assure me you will not ask once we're inside. Enquiring about a curse is very impertinent. The best families always have the worst curses but no one asks directly. Preferably spoken about when their backs are turned. Now, let me look at you."

Evangeline humphed as Augie inspected her. The Professor rapped on the brass door knocker and adjusted his tie.

"Once we straighten this..." Augie said, pulling up her left glove. A metal object dropped to the ground with a clang and Evangeline winced. "What's this? A screwdriver?"

Evangeline shrugged. "I like to be prepared."

"What else have you got in there?"

The front door swung open, and Augie slipped her rosewood handled screwdriver into his inside pocket and replaced his frown with a radiant smile. A tall butler in white tails and a shiny bald head stood in the entrance.

"Professor Caldicott and family." The Professor handed over the invitation card.

"And Mr. August Beauchamp," Augie added.

Evangeline was still getting used to being a Caldicott. Less than a year earlier, she'd been on the other side of the world, living in squats and flea-pits, tumbling and pick-pocketing under the iron rule of her stepfather, Charlie Drigg. She hadn't a clue about the existence of her real father, living faraway in the Colonies.

"Of course, sirs, miss. Please come this way." The butler peered down his nose at Evangeline, but she lifted her chin and strode inside. He must have seen the screwdriver and was now fearing for the silverware. But the butler had nothing to fear, Evangeline's pilfering days were far behind her. Most of the time.

Mrs. Picklescott-Smythe had one of the largest homes on Collins Street, by virtue of her late husband's iron ore fortune. The house was built of creamy sandstone, wrapped by verandahs and intricate white iron lacework on both levels, spreading over the largest block of land on Collins Street. Evangeline had always wanted to see inside and held her breath as they stepped into the foyer.

Wooden floors gleamed underneath an enormous chandelier with arms like a jewelled octopus. The afternoon light streamed through a white stained-glass panel with red and green accents. A carved balustrade staircase led upstairs, lined with dark, sour-faced portraits.

"My, isn't it grand?" Augie clutched his hand to his heart.

Evangeline nodded but a shiver ran up her spine. The foyer reminded her of the home of the Alchemist, Lady Breckenridge-Rice. Her last memory of the house involved a raging fire and a moment when she feared for her own life.

"This way, please."

The butler opened a set of double doors at the edge of the grand foyer. Evangeline and her chaperones stepped inside the ballroom, with its gleaming floors and rich oriental carpets, four times the size of even the most generous room at her house at 56 Collins Street.

"Professor Montague Caldicott, Mr. Edmund Caldicott, Miss Evangeline Caldicott and Mr. August Beauchamp, ma'am," the butler proclaimed and they stepped inside the ballroom.

Evangeline scoured the room. Thirty or more grey moustachioed men and generously bosomed ladies mingled, sipping sherry and anxiously awaiting the unveiling.

Disappointingly, Evangeline was by far the youngest guest in the room. Where were all the other young ladies interested in dead bodies? She couldn't possibly be the only one in Melbourne. How dull.

She spied a large box at the end of the room on a small stage. There it was, the sarcophagus shipped all the way from Egypt to Melbourne.

"Thank you, Farlow. Why Professor Caldicott, what a pleasure to see you." Mrs. Picklescott-Smythe was a woman of indeterminate age. Her heather-purple silk dress was ruffled and bustled in a passé style, her cloud grey hair piled with pinned ringlets. "I am so glad you could attend my little soiree."

The crepe-skinned woman, glittering with gems, held out her hand for the Professor to kiss. An acorn-sized sapphire sparkled on her gloved hand.

"I would not miss this event for the world." The Professor reached out with his clockwork right hand, taking his hostess's hand gently. "May I introduce my daughter, Evangeline."

"Miss Evangeline, I see we share an appreciation of purple." Mrs. Picklescott-Smythe gently patted Evangeline's forearm. "Although you look far more lovely in the shade than I."

Augie skilfully interjected. "You are far too modest, Mrs. Picklescott-Smythe. You are an absolute vision. I was only remarking to Edmund yesterday how vibrant you look. You must tell us your secret. Or is it too naughty?"

"Oh Augie, you devilish man." She playfully slapped him on the shoulder. "I am glad you are all here. Please partake of some refreshments. We shall begin with the unveiling soon."

Footmen appeared with silver trays laden with glasses of sherry and chocolate covered cream puffs on tiny porcelain plates. Evangeline politely refused.

"Do my eyes deceive me?" Uncle Edmund teased. "Evangeline Caldicott refusing a pastry? Are you unwell, my dear?"

"I'm far too excited to eat. When are they going to unwrap the body? What do you think it will look like? Like a prune? I once saw a mummified cat. It was all yellow like a husk."

"Evangeline!" hissed Augie with a frantic glance around the room. Uncle Edmund guffawed into his sherry.

The doors opened again and three more people entered.

"I didn't think she would be invited to this," Augie whispered. Edmund nodded.

A hush settled across the room as the new guests arrived and people whispered behind their gloves and hands. The woman was tall and statuesque with golden hair, a dress of deep scarlet with a matching Spanish lace hat. She strode into the room as though this party was her own. Two pale men tagged along behind her like little lambs.

"Who is it?" Evangeline asked.

"Madame Zsoldas. But don't stare."

Evangeline sighed. How could she not look? This was her first chance to inspect the infamous spiritualist.

"Mr. Beauchamp. How pleasant to see you again," Madame Zsoldas said with a thick Eastern European accent. Her eyes were hard and tawny like a lion. Her lips painted with a strong stripe of scarlet.

"Madame Zsoldas." Augie bowed slightly as she kept walking, slithering through the crowd.

"I didn't know you were acquainted," Uncle Edmund hissed.

Augie shrugged. "I know many people around town."

Edmund eyed him dubiously, but then, as the manager of the Prince Albert Theatre, Uncle Augie knew everyone there was to know in Melbourne.

"Frightful woman," the Professor said with a tut.

Edmund raised an eyebrow and smirked at his brother. "Oh yes. It was her, wasn't it? If only I'd been there..."

The spiritualist in scarlet headed towards the stage and Evangeline watched her every step. Then, with a knowing smile, the woman swivelled around and stared straight back. Evangeline's stomach tumbled and she immediately dropped her eyes. Perhaps all the stories about Madame Zsoldas were true.

A sarcophagus and a notorious spiritualist, two mysteries already and it was barely three o'clock. Today was turning out rather marvellous.

CHAPTER 2

A DESSERT FORK TINKLED AGAINST A glass. The
Caldicotts and all the other guests stopped their cordial
chit-chat and turned.

"Welcome, friends, to my humble home." Mrs. Picklescott-
Smythe stood on the low stage at the front of the room. The
guests closed in, politely manoeuvring for the best vantage point.

"I'm so thrilled you could all join me on this special occasion.
My nephew Jocelyn is a mad keen explorer and Egyptologist. I've
been haranguing him for simply years to send me a mummy from
one of his expeditions. And he has finally obliged. This sarcophagus
arrived last week by special dirigible, and I am pleased to be able to
share this exciting historic event with you all."

The clay sarcophagus was decorated with faded pictograms,
and terracotta and blue-green scribbles. A face with kohl-rimmed
eyes and long black hair was painted on the outside, arms folded
across his chest.

"And this afternoon, we are privileged to be joined by
the Eminent Professor of Archaeology from the University of
Sydney, Professor Walbottle."

A short balding man stiffly bowed.

"Professor Walbottle has travelled to Melbourne especially
for this afternoon's unwrapping soiree and will be providing a

commentary on the activities. Thank you for making the long journey, and we look forward to your enlightening lecture."

Evangeline wished the dull speeches would end and they would hurry up with the unravelling. The mummy unveiling was the most exciting thing to happen to Evangeline in at least a month. In recent weeks, life at 56 Collins Street had been rather dull. No monsters or anything.

"This mummy comes from the tomb of Pharaoh Al-hai-ti-po. My research suggests this is one of his lesser nobles..."

"I told you," whispered the Professor. "Nobody special."

"The Pharaoh is now proudly on display in the British Museum." Walbottle had a feeble expressionless tone, the type of voice which sent Evangeline immediately to sleep. She pitied his university students.

"Now, you may have heard some stories about mummies..."

Evangeline perked up immediately. He was finally getting to the interesting part.

"But we're all educated people here, living in a time of great scientific discoveries," he said, with a drone. "I hope we are all enlightened beyond that superstitious nonsense."

Evangeline narrowed her eyes. She could tell Walbottle a story or two. The world was a strange and unusual place, even here in Melbourne. One must keep an open mind.

"What makes this interesting is the evolution of the mummification process. This specimen comes from a period of transition from fats to beeswax and other resins for..."

Evangeline rolled her eyes and gazed around the room, smirking behind her glove as she caught other guests yawning. Then she locked eyes with Madame Zsoldas once again. The spiritualist stared directly at her with an intense curiosity. What had Evangeline done to attract her attention? They had not even been introduced.

"We shall now begin the unveiling," Walbottle said.

Two footmen stepped forward. One pulled a lever. There was a hiss of steam and a pneumatic elevator lifted the clay sarcophagus upright.

The Professor tutted under his breath.

"When will people realise the dangers of steam? I know he's an archaeologist, but I would have thought a fellow Professor would have more sense."

Evangeline said nothing. She knew her father's loyalties lay with the horological arts, but she thought the elevator looked rather useful.

Once the mummy was upright, the two footmen began cracking the sealed lid with crowbars. The lid slid open with a harsh grinding noise, and Evangeline and the rest of the room held their breath.

The lid of the sarcophagus slid open and all the guests oohed and aahed. Inside the clay box stood a tall figure, wrapped from head to toe in yellowed bandages.

"As you can see, the specimen is not encased in a wooden box. This means he was not of the richer classes," said Professor Walbottle.

"Our mummy is some old riffraff?" Augie huffed. "How uncivilised."

Walbottle and the footmen gently freed the body from the coffin, leaning him against a stand.

"A real mummy," Evangeline said to her father with a grin, her eyes as round as clock faces.

"Remarkable. Interred for more than a thousand years." The Professor leaned forward, re-positioning his pince-nez, and, with a few clicks, he adjusted his patent-pending magnifying lenses. Augie, the traditionalist, peered through a pair of brass opera glasses.

"I read a mummy is wrapped like a game of pass the parcel," Evangeline said. "There are hidden treats under every layer of bandage."

Walbottle held up his hand for quiet. "We have found the end of the swathing. We will now begin."

The footman carefully lifted up the first section of bandage with a set of tongs and started unrolling from the mummy's waist.

"My, what a pong!" Augie exclaimed, fanning his face.

As the bandages unfurled, a foul odour spread across the room. The stench of thousand-year-old rotten flesh growing stronger and stronger. The smell was reminiscent of the Melbourne streets after three or four days of baking summer heat. Evangeline gasped and scrambled for her lavender-scented handkerchief, Edmund coughed discreetly and the Professor pinched his nose. In the corner, a rotund lady in coral pink swooned and dropped to the floor with a thud. Footmen swarmed from all directions, armed with smelling salts and cushions.

Walbottle cleared his throat. "There appears to be a problem with the mummification. This... err... scent is highly unusual."

Augie pursed his lips as he dabbed his eyes. "Not only a nobody but a malodorous nobody."

The two footmen unrolled reams of yellowed bandage from the body, the tape pooling in a bundle at its feet. Despite the evil stench, Evangeline's excitement heightened as each layer peeled away. Some of the other ladies hid behind their gloved hands and fans, but Evangeline craned forward to catch the first glimpse of what remained of the mummy's flesh.

"I sense a presence," Madame Zsoldas called out across the room in a loud clear voice.

All the guests turned to stare.

"A dark presence in the room," she said with her rolling 'r's, her hands raised to the ceiling.

Evangeline glanced around, hoping to see a grey fog creeping along the wainscoting. But there was nothing out of the ordinary. Only a group of well-dressed guests wanting to see a mummy.

"Nonsense," muttered the Professor.

"It is strong. It is calling to me." Madame Zsoldas stepped forward with one hand gracing her forehead, the other hand outstretched, reaching out for something unseen.

"Is it the mummy?" cried Mrs. Picklescott-Smythe.

"I can taste sulphur."

"The devil," someone hissed.

"Only the horrid smell of a botched dead Egyptian," scoffed the Professor. "We can all smell it."

"The presence is growing stronger."

"Perhaps we should stop the unravelling?" Mrs. Picklescott-Smythe hurried over to Madame Zsoldas. The spiritualist stared out across the room with her unseeing eyes, ignoring the host. "Is this a warning to stop? Is it dangerous?"

Madame Zsoldas broke from her trance and touched Mrs. Picklescott-Smythe on the shoulder.

"All I see is darkness. All I feel is suffering."

"Maybe the stories were right. I should have known," Mrs. Picklescott-Smythe wailed. "I couldn't bear to bring any misfortune to my friends."

"Poppycock," called out the Professor, a little too loudly.

"Monty." Uncle Augie frowned, always the etiquette master.

"Don't tell me to be quiet, Augie. This is outrageous. This charlatan is spoiling this important scientific event with her mumbo-jumbo."

"Madame Zsoldas is a well respected spiritual healer. She is welcome in my home and her advice is appreciated," Mrs. Picklescott-Smythe said defiantly, glaring back at the Professor from her place by the stage.

"Respected," guffawed the Professor. "If only I'd brought my atervis detector. I'd show you all."

Evangeline watched with her mouth agape. Ordinarily, she was the one causing a scene. Watching her father's performance, she wondered if perhaps the trouble-making trait was hereditary.

"Monty. Please respect our host." Augie took the Professor's elbow with a conciliatory smile to the rest of the room. "We know you're anxious to see the body..."

"Well, get on with it." The Professor tugged his arm away from Augie's grasp. "We haven't got all afternoon."

"What do you think I should do?" Mrs. Picklescott-Smythe turned to Madame Zsoldas, her face flushed red.

Everyone else was distracted by the unfolding fuss, lapping up the gossip, even Walbottle and the footmen stopped tugging at the bandages to watch. Only Evangeline seemed to notice a movement on the stage. It was the mummy. It was moving. It was lurching forward right into the path of Mrs. Picklescott-Smythe. Evangeline gasped.

Somebody should do something.

CHAPTER 3

E VANGELINE HURTLED FORWARD, cartwheeling towards the stage in a flash of lavender satin. She bounced onto the stage and, with a kick, sent the mummy flying backwards. Mrs. Picklescott-Smythe squealed and the room was filled with gasps. The mummy came crashing down, right on top of Walbottle, knocking him over and pinning him to the ground.

"Get it off me," whined Walbottle. His legs and arms flailing.

But rather than helping the archaeologist, Evangeline found herself frozen to the spot, distracted by a rather peculiar feeling in her feet. Something vague but particularly odd.

"Miss Evangeline. Thank you ever so much," Mrs. Picklescott-Smythe said, her hands clasped against her chest, and a small round of applause broke out.

Forgetting about her feet, Evangeline smoothed back her hair and dropped into a dramatic deep curtsey. Then she stepped off the stage and joined her family in the crowd once more. Although not everyone was as impressed, Augie's lips were pursed as tight as a footman's breeches.

"I thought the mummy was attacking her," Evangeline said with a shrug. "It's only polite to help."

"Are you hurt, Professor?" Mrs. Picklescott-Smythe said as the footmen hoisted the stiff body off Walbottle and replaced it on the stand.

"Perfectly fine." Walbottle dusted himself off with a thunderous look on his face.

"This is all too risky," Mrs. Picklescott-Smythe said with a wobble in her voice. "Who knows what evil lies beneath those bandages. What do you think, Professor Walbottle?"

"It's completely safe," he said in between large gulps of sherry. "No need to panic. The footmen must have knocked the body over."

"I don't know." Mrs. Picklescott-Smythe shook her head. "My nephew knew Dougal Mendlesham. Some of you may have heard the stories. Within a week of bringing a mummy from the tombs of Luxor to his home in Berkshire, he shot off his own arm. Claimed it had turned evil with a mind of its own. His arm was planning to butcher the audience at the next village amateur dramatics society production. The curse of the mummy. I would be terribly upset if something rotten happened to one of my guests here tonight."

"Listen to the educated expert. Not this swindler," said Evangeline's father.

"Madame Zsoldas?" Mrs. Picklescott-Smythe said.

"I can still feel a strong presence. There is something strange here within this room. Like a black cloud."

Evangeline furrowed her brow. She felt something too, but it was ever so faint, nothing like Madame Zsoldas's description. So faint, she may have been imagining it.

"Too risky," Mrs. Picklescott-Smythe said. "Who knows what devilish spells were cast by the Pharaohs. Madame Zsoldas, you've convinced me. I must be cautious for the sake of my guests. We should stop right here."

The Professor groaned.

"Knickers," Evangeline said under her breath.

"I am sorry to disappoint you but it is for your own safety," Mrs. Picklescott-Smythe said. "I will not unwrap the mummy any further. Professor Walbottle, please place him back into his sarcophagus. Bring out the steam-organ, Farlow. Miss Sparkwell, could I bother you to play a little recital for everyone to lighten the mood?"

"This is ridiculous," said the Professor, puffing out his chest like a pigeon.

"This is my decision, Professor Caldicott. You are welcome to stay for more refreshments. But not if you continue to be so rude to my guests."

"Thank you for your hospitality, Mrs. Picklescott-Smythe, but I will not pander to this mountebank. Ludicrous," the Professor humphed, taking Evangeline by the arm. "We're leaving."

Her father pulled her towards the door, and Evangeline spied the tantalising sight of a table laden with golden pineapple jellies, chocolate eclairs and custard tarts. With the excitement of the mummy gone, Evangeline's hunger returned with a vengeance.

"But..." she said, trying to steer her father towards the sweets table.

"Come on, dear. I cannot spend another minute in this house."

"Just a little taste. Something small?" Evangeline pleaded. "A meringue?"

"Professor Caldicott. So good to see you again." Madame Zsoldas appeared with a wry smile, holding out her gloved hand. "When was the last time we met? Was it the lecture?"

The Professor pursed his lips, taking her hand as though he was handling a snake. "Madame Zsoldas. I am surprised you are still in Melbourne."

"It is a lovely city. Quite quaint. And so many interesting people."

With her father distracted by the spiritualist, Evangeline grabbed a coconut macaroon and shoved it in her mouth. Her shoulders shuddered with delight and she took two more.

"I must be going, Madame Zsoldas. I have work to do."

"Don't we all?" Madame Zsoldas said with a raised eyebrow, then turned to Evangeline. "And this is our little heroine. You are related? How interesting."

Evangeline felt the intense stare of the spiritualist again and smiled with closed lips, her mouth full of macaroon.

"Yes, my daughter Evangeline."

But before Evangeline could finish her mouthful and reply, the Professor was marching towards the door. "Come along, Evangeline."

"You know Madame Zsoldas too?" Evangeline said as she scurried behind him. "What lecture?"

"It was hardly a lecture. Some silly public debate." The Professor shook his head.

"What happened?"

"Never mind. Where's my brother and his halfwit friend?"

"I don't think they are coming."

"Deserters. Typical." The Professor grumbled as he led Evangeline through the front door and back home.

CHAPTER 4

THE SCRAPING OF CUTLERY ON plates was the only noise in the dining room at supper. There was a chill in the air and the biting winds from the South Pole were not responsible. The Professor and Augie had not exchanged a fully formed word since the scene at Mrs. Picklescott-Smythe's. The Professor kept his nose inside The Herald and Augie entered the room with an overly polite 'good evening' before focusing on his own post. Evangeline watched the two men out of the corner of her eye as she nibbled on her lamb. It was amusing to watch grown men behave so childishly.

"Another glass of cordial, Miss Evangeline?"

Miss Plockton hovered around the table, even more attentive than usual. Evangeline could tell she was burning with curiosity, desperate for any details on the mummy party. Apparently Miss Plockton's super-sensitive hearing did not extend beyond the house. Evangeline ignored her for the moment, she had her own business to attend to.

"Father? Do you have any spare hands?"

The Professor only had one real hand. His other hand was made entirely from brass, a fine example of his own clockwork engineering. To date, he had not been completely forthcoming about the events leading up to the loss of his hand. It somehow involved Big Ben.

"Have you been snooping around in my laboratory-workshop again?" he blustered.

"No, Father," she said. For once, Evangeline had not been ferreting around his laboratory-workshop. She learned her lesson last time when the Professor accidentally locked her inside, and his secret project at the dark end of the cellar began to move. The nightmares had stopped but she was still unsure whether there was something alive under 56 Collins Street. Her father held so many secrets.

"I had the most splendid idea last night for a new invention. I thought you may have some replacement spares for your own hand. Or old prototypes you no longer need?"

"Perhaps," he muttered.

"Sorry, I'm late." Edmund rushed to his seat at the table, Miss Plockton instantly producing a steaming plate of rosy lamb with brown gravy, peas and carrots.

The Professor and Augie grunted in greeting.

"You'll never believe what I saw outside. Across the road at Mrs. Picklescott-Smythe's."

"Well, it couldn't have been the mummy," said the Professor. "Foolish woman. Ruined my entire afternoon."

"It was the Zsoldas woman and her two companions."

"Leeching around again? 'I can feel a presence'," the Professor said in a heavily accented falsetto.

"She appeared to be moving in. She was standing on the footpath, giving orders and the footmen were unloading trunks from a carriage."

"What?" said the Professor. "That woman? In our street?"

"How modern." Augie rubbed his ample chins. "A bohemian element comes to Collins Street."

"Crooks more like it! She can smell Mrs. Picklescott-Smythe's money from a mile off. What respectable person moves house at suppertime?" The Professor shook his head. "Deplorable."

"I don't understand, Monty. Why this vehement disliking for Madame Zsoldas? Are you still vexed by that debate?" Augie replied. "She is a woman of service, providing comfort to the grieving. Relieving the suffering of the mourning. Assisting people to contact their lost loved ones."

"Pish posh. Don't be a goose, Augie. You really are a ninny sometimes. Can't you see through her facade?"

"How dare you speak to me like that? Edmund. Are you going to let your brother talk to me that way?"

Edmund, enjoying his lamb and minding his own business, put down his fork with a sigh.

"Monty. Mind what you say."

"This is my house, little brother. I'll do as I please."

The Professor glared at Edmund. Augie glared at the Professor. Evangeline's heart climbed into her throat.

"Please don't fight," Evangeline said softly.

The three men turned their eyes to Evangeline, their harsh expressions softening.

"You are right, m'dear. The supper table is not the place for this type of conversation. I'll have no more discussion of that woman in my house," the Professor declared. Edmund elbowed Augie and Augie reluctantly grunted in agreement.

"May I be excused, Father?" she said.

Her father nodded and shooed her away with a flick of his clockwork fingers. Evangeline picked up her skirts and ran to the parlour. With the men preoccupied on finishing their supper and hopefully reconciling, Evangeline had a chance to peek out of the lace curtains and investigate the activity across the road for herself.

She was just in the nick of time. The footmen were carrying the last trunk off the carriage and into the house, while Madame Zsoldas stood on the footpath. Under the street light in a scarlet turban and long flowing robes, she looked like an Arabian princess. Evangeline wished she could see into the travelling trunks, she wondered what exotic spiritualist apparatus lay inside. She didn't entirely know what a spiritualist did, but she imagined it involved shrunken heads and runes.

Madame Zsoldas started to follow the footmen inside the grand house. But before she stepped through the gate, she paused, turning her head and looking directly at Evangeline. She gasped and ducked her head below the window sill. How could Madame Zsoldas have possibly seen her? From that distance? In the dark? Through the window?

"What are you doing down there, Miss Evangeline?"

She jumped.

CHAPTER 5

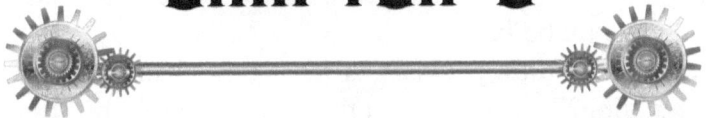

"IT'S NOT POLITE TO SNOOP, Miss Evangeline," Miss Plockton said.

"It's not really snooping. Merely confirming Uncle Edmund's story. I wanted to see what all the fuss was about."

"You must abide by your father's orders. He is most unimpressed with the whole situation and I must agree with him. It's all rather unsavoury. Spiritual healers taking advantage of a poor widow."

"She's very rich," Evangeline replied.

"Her soul is poor. As is often the case with the very wealthy," Miss Plockton said with pity. "I imagine her home is very extravagant."

"Enormous chandeliers and mountains of food. Although I barely got to taste any of it." Evangeline sighed, dreaming of the chocolate eclairs.

"Whyever not?"

"It turned out to be quite a strange afternoon. Not at all what I expected."

"In what way?" Miss Plockton leaned forward, her hands clutching at her chest.

Evangeline stifled a grin. It was a rare situation when she knew more than Miss Plockton about anything.

"There was a little kerfuffle."

"The spiritualist woman?" Miss Plockton's eyes were as round as saucers. "What did she do?"

Evangeline had Miss Plockton in the palm of her hand.

"I am so forgetful, Miss Plockton. In all the commotion and arguments, I left the supper table without any dessert." She rubbed her slim belly.

"I'm still a little peckish. Is there any chance I may have some pudding?" she said, with the innocence of a newborn. "If you've already tidied away the supper things, I'm happy to eat in the kitchen. I don't mind one bit."

Miss Plockton hesitated, raising a thin eyebrow.

"That's a shame." Evangeline sighed. "If there is no pudding left, I shall retire to my room for the evening. I do have some reading to continue with."

Evangeline started for the door. Miss Plockton grimaced. Under her frown, Evangeline could see Miss Plockton wrestling between her curiosity and her dislike of gluttony.

"Come with me," Miss Plockton said with an air of defeat.

She led the way down the corridor and into the kitchen.

"Cook. Please bring out the pudding for Miss Evangeline."

Evangeline sat at the wooden table as Miss Plockton spooned out a small serving of golden brown Baroness Pudding.

Evangeline narrowed her eyes. Miss Plockton tightened her lips and dolloped out another spoonful.

"Is there any custard?"

Cook produced a jug and poured generously. Evangeline picked up a spoon and tucked in.

"So you were saying, Miss Evangeline. There was a scene?" Miss Plockton said eagerly, sitting at the table alongside her. "Did you see the mummy?"

Evangeline started to speak but then remembered her manners. A lady does not speak with a mouthful of pudding. She shook her head instead. Uncle Augie would be proud.

"No? Was the coffin empty?"

Evangeline kept her mouth shut, savouring the delicious sweet raisins hidden inside the pudding. She held out her hands, as though she was sleepwalking.

"Hypnotism?"

Evangeline waggled her hand from side to side. This was turning into a game of charades. How fun. Evangeline pointed out to the parlour.

"Madame Zsoldas?"

Evangeline nodded. Miss Plockton was rather good at this game. Evangeline finished her mouthful and spoke.

"Madame Zsoldas said there was 'a strange presence in the air' and Mrs. Picklescott-Thingamie got all spooked and put a stop to the whole thing."

"Presence? What rot!" Miss Plockton said, her hand gracing the small gold cross around her neck. "But why is the Professor vexed with Mr. Beauchamp?"

"You must have some of this pudding, Miss Plockton. It's awfully good." Evangeline scraped her spoon along the bottom of the bowl. "Is there any more?"

Miss Plockton sighed and nodded reluctantly. Cook gave Evangeline a sly wink before loading up her bowl again.

"Father was very vocal in his scepticism about Madame Zsoldas. You could say he was a little insulting. Mrs. Picklescott-Macallit did not like it one bit."

"Heavens," Miss Plockton said with a flush in her cheeks. "A public altercation. And Mr. Beauchamp?"

"Father stormed out and Uncle Augie stayed behind."

"Oh dear," said Miss Plockton. "There has been some tension between the two of them recently. Ever since..."

As soon as the words left her mouth, Miss Plockton clamped her hand over her face. Evangeline buried a smirk by spooning more pudding into her mouth. It was funny to see Miss Plockton with her drawbridge down, ordinarily she was like the Tower of London.

"Oh, there you are," the Professor said, loitering in the doorway. A typical Victorian gentleman, he never entered the kitchen.

"Sorry, Professor. I was..." Miss Plockton blushed as red as a strawberry. How long had the Professor been standing there?

"Not you, Miss Plockton. Carry on. Evangeline? I found a spare arm for you. And by the way, have you seen my atervis detector?"

Evangeline popped another spoonful in her mouth and shook her head. It was her turn to blush red. The atervis detector was another of the Professor's clever inventions, a device for monitoring dark energy. It was a long brass tube like a telescope, but when you looked through the lens you could see dark energy: anything magical glowed with a silvery aura.

"Hmmm... I'm sure I saw it recently. It's just the device I need to prove what a charlatan that Zsoldas woman is."

The last time Evangeline saw the atervis detector, she had converted it into a more practical monocle and lost it in the Alchemist's mansion. It probably fell off somewhere, as she bounced about on her spring heeled boots. She had hoped the Professor had forgotten all about it.

"Botheration. I'll have to build another. Miss Plockton. Please go through my sketch archives and find the schematic. Right away. Before that woman fleeces Mrs. Picklescott-Smythe out of house and home. Someone needs to help that blasted foolish woman."

Evangeline scarfed down the last of the pudding and skipped after her father down to the laboratory-workshop. She headed straight for the battered wooden workbench where her father's spare hand lay.

"That arm got me through a lot of years," he said chuckling. His mood improved when he was in his favourite place, tinkering with his clockwork.

Evangeline splayed out the brass fingers and inspected the spare hand from every angle, testing the movement of each joint. This would do very nicely for her new invention and Evangeline got straight to work.

"Here you are, Professor." Miss Plockton appeared with a sheet of paper. Her cheeks still pink, her tone even more deferential than usual.

"Splendid," the Professor said and Miss Plockton scurried back upstairs. She knew when to make herself scarce. "Luckily, I have some leftover nuummite from the last device. Never throw anything away, Evangeline. You never know when it will come in handy."

Her father's mention of nuummite reminded Evangeline of her altercation with the Lady Alchemist. In order to escape, Evangeline had conjured up some type of energy of her own, but, ever since that incident, Evangeline had failed to recreate the power. It was a curious circumstance and then there was the vague feeling from the mummy this afternoon. She wondered whether her father had any experience with such matters.

"Do you ever get strange feelings, Father?"

"Sorry?" The Professor barely looked up from his schematic.

"Like a tingling sensation."

"I'm not sure what you mean, m'dear," the Professor stammered, looking up with a scared look on his face.

"A kind of warmth in your body."

"Err. Um."

"A tingling glow running through your limbs."

The Professor coughed. "Perhaps you need to talk to Miss Plockton about this type of question."

"Do you think Miss Plockton would understand? I thought she was far too religious for this type of thing."

"She may be prim but underneath she's still a woman."

"I'm rather confused, Father..."

"This is not a matter for fathers. I have no experience of being a young lady."

Her father stood up, his face a bright fuchsia and walked to the far end of the workshop. Evangeline wondered if she'd said something wrong, her father was acting rather strange all of a sudden. Perhaps he was tired. With the mummy unwrapping soiree this afternoon, the fuss with Madame Zsoldas and his battles with Augie, it had been quite an eventful and exhausting day.

She shrugged her shoulders and continued on with her invention.

CHAPTER 6

E VANGELINE TOSSED AND TURNED IN her bed, her tummy rather queasy, probably the result of too much pudding and the lingering scent of rotting Egyptian. She padded downstairs in her stockinged feet, in search of a soothing glass of milk.

The house was quiet, it was past midnight but a light blazed under the sitting room door. Evangeline poked her head in, finding Uncle Edmund in an armchair with a glass in his hand.

"Keep me company, little niece," Edmund said with a slight slur in his voice.

Evangeline gladly took a seat beside him. She rarely got any time alone with her Uncle Edmund.

"What a strange day," he said.

"I was rather disappointed about the mummy."

"What do you think about this business with Madame Zsoldas? Does the supernatural interest you at all?"

"Only from a scientific perspective," Evangeline said, trying to sound convincing.

"Very practical of you, my dear. Because there's a reason why you might be interested in it." Edmund took a long sip from his crystal glass. "The same reason why I might enjoy this little drink so much."

He held the glass up to the light, staring through the amber liquid.

"Has Monty told you about his mother? Our mother."

Evangeline's family history was unknown to her, she had only been reunited with the Caldicotts for six months and her father was not the divulging type. He had only made a couple of brief, unflattering comments about his mother, Lady Caroline Caldicott. Evangeline had the impression she was a stern cold woman, with little time for anything except for her horses.

"He has mentioned Grandmama once or twice."

"Never anything nice I suppose. Well, she is the wicked stepmother."

"Step?" Evangeline's mouth dropped open.

"Not our real mother."

"What happened to your real mother?"

"My knowledge is scant. Papa never speaks of her. And Monty rarely. All I know I've gathered from family gossip and Nanny Meaburn."

Evangeline leaned in, ears wide open.

"Our parents' marriage was quite scandalous. They met on the streets in London. My mother was singing and selling cut primroses. He was struck by her beauty, some say she cast a spell, and it was love at first sight. They were married within the week.

"It was an unsuitable marriage for a young landed gentleman. My grandparents must have been horrified; she was from a small fishing village in County Galway. But Papa loved her deeply and passionately. He never loved anyone like Geileish."

"Geileish," Evangeline said, rolling the unusual name around her tongue.

"It's Gaelic."

"It's beautiful. Go on, Uncle Edmund."

Edmund's shoulders sagged.

"Child birth is a dangerous business, Evangeline. For both the mother and the child. Despite all my family's privileges, our nice house in the country, the doctor and the nurses, my mother did not survive my birth."

"How terrible." Evangeline bit her lip.

"I never had a chance to know her. But Monty had five years with her."

"Did she look like you?"

"More like Monty than me. We have one daguerreotype of her. She was beautiful, a tiny little woman with jet black hair and pale blue eyes. Some people said she was part faery."

"Faery?" Evangeline gasped. "Did she have wings?"

Edmund chuckled.

"I'm not sure about the wings but she enchanted Papa. There were many strange stories about Geileish. According to the rumours, she would roam the countryside barefoot, talking to the wind and singing with the flowers. She had a fiery temper and could turn the milk sour inside the cows."

"Do you believe them?"

Perhaps Geileish was the reason why Evangeline felt the strange power in the cellar. Perhaps magic was in her blood.

"Sometimes people are jealous of true love and will do anything to destroy it." Edmund sighed, taking another swig. "Papa remarried quickly after her death. This time, he married a girl from the right type of family but it was obvious it was not for love. Monty was sent away to school and Papa spent more time in London building his political career. I don't think Papa ever recovered."

"Poor Father. Poor Grandpapa," Evangeline said.

"Monty understands the pain of losing a mother."

"Like me," Evangeline muttered.

"Like you." Edmund nodded.

"Do you know the story of how my mother met my father?"

"That is not a story for me to tell."

Evangeline sighed. It was worth a try but she knew Uncle Edmund was right. This was a story her father needed to tell her. But when? Being patient was such a bore.

"Where is Augie this evening?"

Edmund scratched his ear. "Promise you won't tell?"

Evangeline drew a cross on her chest. "Hope to die."

"He's across the road."

"At Mrs. Picklescott-Smythe's? So late?"

"I told him it wasn't a good idea. But Augie always does as he pleases."

"With Madame Zsoldas?"

"I believe so. He's desperate to attend one of her sessions."

"A séance?"

"Only a meeting of spiritualists, I believe. The group from the Messenger of the Dawn newspaper."

"Has Augie lost someone? He always seems so jolly. When he's not telling me off about my posture."

"We've all lost people. Death is a constant companion in this world."

Evangeline nodded solemnly.

"This conversation is all too maudlin for me." Edmund got to his feet. "I'm off to bed."

Evangeline followed her uncle upstairs and jumped back into her bed. There was a maelstrom of questions in her head, but she shut her eyes tightly. She needed a good night's sleep and all her wits in order to grill Augie in the morning. She must know all about the meeting with Madame Zsoldas.

CHAPTER 7

AFTER A FITFUL NIGHT'S SLEEP with strange dreams of faery grandmothers and mummies, Evangeline woke early. The sun barely peeking over the east and 56 Collins Street was as quiet as a museum.

Evangeline lifted up her eiderdown and stretched her sleepy limbs.

"Good morning, world," she said with a yawn.

She noticed a tightness in her muscles, probably after her exertion yesterday with the mummy. Her arms and legs were becoming rusty through lack of use. The Professor discouraged Evangeline from cartwheeling down the hallway, and it had been almost a month since her last sparring session with Mei. Evangeline could not allow herself to become complacent. As evident from the soiree, her acrobatic skills could be required at any moment.

"Right!" she said, slipping out of bed and onto the cold floorboards. "Let's begin."

Still in her nightgown, Evangeline leaned back. Reaching over her head, her hands touched the floor behind her with her palms laid down flat. She pushed herself back up to standing and then doubling over from the hips, touched the floor in front of her. She repeated her backwards and forwards stretch three times. Each time easier, as her spine warmed and remembered the moves. She leaned back one more time, placing her palms on the ground and began to scuttle up and down the length of her bedroom, like an upside-down crab.

"That will do for today," she said to herself. "But I will do more tomorrow."

Feeling virtuous, Evangeline moved on to her next activity for the day. The small clock on her mantelpiece showed there was ample time before breakfast to trial her new invention, the coiffure machine.

The coiffure machine would be a revolution for ladies across the world, bringing Evangeline fame and fortune. With the device, every lady would be able to style her own hair at home, quickly and easily, without the aid of a maid.

This morning, Evangeline would be the first test subject, arriving at the breakfast table perfectly groomed with thoroughly fashionable hair. She could not wait to see the delight on Augie's face.

"Here it goes," she said, turning the key on the box.

The mechanism clicked, the cogs whirred and ticked, and her father's leftover hand came to life. The clockwork fingers splayed one by one, as though limbering up before a piano recital. Evangeline turned the first dial, labelled in her own handwriting, to 'plait' and the second dial to 'twist'. She turned around and leaned back, slipping her head into the comfortably cushioned holder and waited for the clockwork fingers to perform their magic.

The fingers deftly twirled the middle section of her hair into a bun, leaving strands free around her face and down her neck.

"Ow," she cried as hair pins fired from the fingers like gun shots, the sharp ends gouging her scalp. She felt her skin gingerly, checking for blood.

"Minor adjustment needed. Reduce the force of the pins." She made a note in her little book by her side. A few teething problems. This was perfectly acceptable in the world of a famous inventress.

The fingers moved on and in a flash plaited up the remaining strands hanging down her neck. Evangeline stroked the long finished braid. It was neat and tight. Another tick for her new machine.

She noticed a funny smell and the brass fingers were growing increasingly warm against her scalp. But Evangeline sat still, waiting for her hairstyle to be complete. She couldn't wait to surprise her family with her fine hair at breakfast. There was a little discomfort but sometimes a lady needed to suffer for her beauty.

"Ouch."

The hand twisted the braid with a powerful jerk.

"Adjust the grip. A little too firm," she noted but the fingers continued to twist and twirl her braid, winding her hair tighter and tighter, pulling her head closer to the heat.

She sniffed, she could smell burning. Was her device singeing rather than styling her hair?

Panic building, Evangeline tried to lean forward but the strong fingers held her back, ripping strands of her hair out by the roots.

"Ow." She squealed.

The scent of scorched hair grew stronger as the brass fingers scorched against her scalp.

"Knickers," Evangeline said.

There was a gentle knock on the door.

"Breakfast."

"Miss Plockton. Help!" Evangeline cried.

The door flew open.

"What on earth? Is this machine attacking you?"

"Turn the switch to 'off' quickly."

"What is this torture device?"

"My coiffure machine. Only a few hiccups. I'll admit it appears to be working a little too well."

"Is it coal-fired? I smell burning."

"It might be me," Evangeline said. "Please help."

The little Scottish woman fiddled with the dials until the hand began to cool and the twisting stopped. Miss Plockton grasped Evangeline's braid. Pulling right and left, Miss Plockton grimaced as she tried to untangle Evangeline, but she was stuck firm in the grasp of the brass fingers.

"Let me get my scissors."

"No," cried Evangeline. "Let's try again, I'm sure we're almost there."

With a heave and a squeal, Evangeline jerked her head forward, wrenching herself free.

"See. No need for scissors. I'm perfectly fine."

Evangeline turned her head to see a chunk of her brown hair stuck in the brass fingers. She reached her hand up, feeling the charred broken ends of her hair and a bald patch of skin.

Evangeline ran to the looking glass to inspect the damage.

"Oh no."

"It can be easily hidden, if you pile it up like this," offered Miss Plockton.

"My hair is ruined." Evangeline sulked.

"No one will notice, Miss Evangeline."

"It will take forever to grow back. I'm half bald!"

"You know what the Lord says about vanity," Miss Plockton tutted.

"You wouldn't understand," Evangeline grumbled as she resorted to old-fashioned methods, twirling her hair into a bun with her own hands and carefully pinning a section to hide the burned patch.

"You look fine. Hurry along. Your eggs will be getting cold."

Evangeline stomped down the stairs after Miss Plockton, her dreams of being a famous inventress thwarted.

CHAPTER 8

C AN I SMELL BURNING?" AUGIE said as Evangeline slipped into a seat at the breakfast table. "Cook better not be burning my toast."

"Where's Father?" Evangeline changed the subject and patted her bun, checking her bald patch was covered.

"Still upstairs," Edmund said, mashing kippers onto a slice of toast.

"Good. I must hear all about the spiritualist meeting last night, Uncle Augie? Before Father arrives."

"Someone has a big mouth." Augie glanced at Edmund. Miss Plockton scowled, but hovered at the side of the room.

"Was there table rapping and spirits?"

"It was more like a church service than a séance..."

"What blasphemy," Miss Plockton spat under her breath and tugged at her cross.

"Or a lecture. Madame Zsoldas gave a talk about the latest scientific research and the evidence behind spiritualism. I didn't understand half of it but it was riveting stuff. She is quite the orator. Very engrossing and so very intelligent. She was one of the first women to obtain a science degree from the University of Budapest, you know. "

"So, no trances or messages from the dead?" Uncle Edmund teased.

"No, that will happen tonight." Augie wriggled with delight. "I can't wait. My first proper séance."

Evangeline was thoroughly jealous. She took a bite of her scrambled eggs. Miss Plockton was right again. They were a little tepid.

"She is absolutely above board. Cross my heart. She knows so much about spiritualism and the spirit world. We're so lucky to have someone like her, a world renowned expert, here in Melbourne. Her powers are ever so strong."

"Heathens." Miss Plockton tutted, placing a fresh rack of toast onto the table.

"You won't believe what she said. She swore she could see someone sitting by me. Right beside me. The spirit of a man who looked the very spit of me."

"Did you tell her about him?" Uncle Edmund said with disbelief.

"Believe me, I said nothing. I kept my mouth closed all evening. You would have been proud. She just knew. I'm telling you, Edmund. This woman is no fraud..."

"What woman?" The Professor strode through the door in a forest green waistcoat.

"No one," said Augie. "You wouldn't know her."

Augie took a teeny bite of toast.

"You better not be talking about you-know-who," the Professor harrumphed.

Miss Plockton fluttered around the Professor pouring him a large cup of tea.

"I don't understand your animosity against Madame Zsoldas, Monty. You are scientific compatriots."

"How dare you compare her to me." The Professor slammed his fist on the table. Four tea cups jumped into the air, splattering tea on the white tablecloth.

"Many other scientists like yourself take a keen interest in spiritualism. For instance that American fellow. The inventor."

Evangeline and Edmund gasped. The Professor's face flushed from red to purple. Augie was on dangerous territory.

Even Evangeline knew better than to mention the name of Hank Buchanan at 56 Collins Street.

"He is just like her. A thief!"

"She is doing admirable work. It's charity."

"Balderdash! I just passed by the window and saw that lawyer, Fortescue Williamson, arriving at the house across the road. As we speak, that woman is probably forcing Mrs. Picklescott-Smythe to change her will. Leaving all her husband's hard-earned fortune to a crystal ball gazer! Then she'll scare her to an early grave by tea-time tomorrow."

"Be reasonable, Monty. You really do have a bee in your bonnet about Madame Zsoldas."

The Professor took a long slurp of tea, sucking the drips from his moustache. He continued in a measured voice.

"It is well documented. There are phenomena which cannot be explained by science. Energy fields which exist but we do not understand. Yet."

Evangeline picked at her lower lip. Perhaps the faint tickle from the mummy was nothing unexplainable, probably normal like static electricity.

"So you agree it is possible to communicate with the dead." Augie stirred his tea.

"I am a man of science, I keep an open mind but I have yet to see solid proof. All I know is this particular woman cannot speak with the dead."

"How do you know? You have one little melee at a town hall debate and suddenly she's a charlatan."

"You want proof? I will prove it to you." The Professor rushed to his feet. "Miss Plockton, please serve my breakfast in my study. I have work to do."

Evangeline took a quiet sip of tea as her father bustled out of the room, Miss Plockton close behind him.

How did the Professor know Madame Zsoldas was truly a crook? What if her powers were real? This could be their chance to speak with the other side and prove the existence of spirits.

"You shouldn't antagonise my brother like that," Edmund said.

"He is the one being unreasonable. Just because Madame Zsoldas made him look silly in front of a room full of people."

Edmund shrugged. "This is his house."

"Perhaps it is time we got a house of our own."

"No," Evangeline exclaimed.

Edmund patted his niece's hand. Augie sat ramrod straight in his chair and defiantly tossed his head.

"I will go tonight. Regardless what your brother says. I must find out if she has a message from my twin brother."

Evangeline pressed her lips together. A séance on Collins Street? This was one show Evangeline could not possibly miss.

CHAPTER 9

E VANGELINE RAPPED LIGHTLY ON AUGIE'S bedroom door. His door was open and her not-real uncle sat at his writing desk in front of the window, the slate-grey Melbourne sky outside.

"May I speak with you, Uncle Augie?" Evangeline had been rehearsing her speech since breakfast.

"What is it, my dear?" He turned from his letter-writing, placing down his revolver pen. "You're not worried about my spat with your father, are you? We're a pair of stubborn old rams. Don't fret, it will all blow over soon."

"I don't often ask you for anything," Evangeline said.

"True. You are quite the self-sufficient young lady."

"And you are a modern gentleman? In favour of the education of young ladies?"

"To an extent. Only the exceptionally beautiful can get away with being complete dimwits."

Evangeline swallowed, plucking up her courage.

"Are you alright?" Augie said with a bemused expression.

Evangeline nodded but she was dumbstruck.

"You're not in some kind of trouble, are you?" Augie said, his brow furrowed.

Evangeline shook her head.

"Then what is it? Whilst your company is enchanting, I am rather busy," Augie said, gesturing to his pile of letters. "Every fool and halfwit wants a turn on my stage."

"I was wondering..."

As Edmund said, death was a constant companion of life and ever since the passing of her mother, Evangeline had been fascinated with the thin line between the two worlds. Everyone had a story of lost loved ones and plenty with their own tales of ghosts and spirits. Evangeline's last circus troupe even had its own resident ghost, Claude the French trapeze artist. Claude plunged to his death thirty years earlier in front of a full house. A man of discipline even in death, Claude could be seen maintaining his practice, the seat swinging when no one else was there.

But like her father, Evangeline needed solid proof. She needed to see it with her own eyes. Evangeline breathed in deep and blurted it out.

"...may I accompany you tonight? To the séance with Madame Zsoldas?"

With elevated eyebrows, Augie leaned back in his writing chair, whistling long and low between his teeth.

"Oh, my dear. I don't think that is possible. Your father would never allow it. He'd be terribly angry with me."

"Please. This is the closest I've ever been. A real chance to speak with the dead." Her lip began to tremble.

"It is not the place for an impressionable young lady like yourself. I am sorry."

"A chance to speak with my mother," Evangeline choked. "Speak to her one last time."

"Your father would be livid. Edmund too."

"Don't you want to help me?" Tears ran down her face like raindrops down a window.

"Dear girl. I can't." Augie took hold of Evangeline's shaking hand. "But I understand how you feel. I lost my own twin brother."

"Tell me about him." Evangeline cleared her throat.

"Almost eighteen years have passed but I still miss him terribly. Yes, twins but we were polar opposites, chalk and cheese as they say. He was so serious and calm, whereas I'm..." Augie smiled with sad eyes. "It happened a month before we were due to start at university. My family has a country house, and Horatio loved riding and hunting and all that fresh air business. Horses loved him back. Ordinarily. But one day, he was riding a new horse named Boreas. Boreas was frisky and unpredictable, but Horatio was convinced he could break him. But on this occasion, Horatio was wrong. A neighbour's low-flying dirigible spooked Boreas. He threw Horatio to the ground and trampled him, breaking his back. Horatio never woke up again."

Augie's brown eyes glistened. He took a monogrammed handkerchief from his pocket and blew his nose with a refined honk.

"I was away in London at the time, I had a holiday job as an assistant stage manager. It was my first taste of the theatrical world and I was madly in love. I had time for nothing else and had not spoken to my brother in months. We had a terrible row at Christmas. Horatio was a staunch traditionalist and could not bear anything but cranberry sauce with his turkey, but being the modern sort I am, I swore chutney was the way to go. Too much brandy and it got quite out of hand, we never resolved our quarrel. It pains me to this day, our last words were silly and spiteful. I can't even bear to see cranberry sauce. If only I could tell my brother I am sorry and I miss him."

It was Evangeline's turn to comfort her not-real uncle, patting him on the arm.

"I do understand how you feel, my dear. But imagine if your father found out. He would explode like a firecracker."

"His arm might blow right off." Evangeline giggled. Augie laughed too.

"I'm sorry." Augie sighed. "Even if I thought it was a good idea. There's a set number at the table. Only eight people are invited.

"But..." Evangeline tried one more time.

Augie shook his head and Evangeline knew she was defeated. With a heavy heart, she left him to his letter-writing and paced up and down the hallway, thinking. There had to be another way to get an invitation to the séance.

"Ah ha. Got you!" The Professor's voice carried down the hallway from the parlour. "I knew it!"

She raced downstairs and found him pressed up against the front window, the lace curtains pushed aside.

"Father?"

"I was right. There's nothing." He turned, a brass telescope-like cylinder held to his eye. He had built another atervis detector to replace the one Evangeline lost. "No silver aura. Not even an iota of dark energy. She is a pure swindler. Just as I suspected."

"Can I look?"

The Professor handed Evangeline the detector. She peered through the lens across the cobbled street to Madame Zsoldas standing by Mrs. Picklescott-Smythe's front gate, talking with sweeping hand gestures to a frock-coated man, dressed from head to toe in her signature scarlet.

"This proves it. She has no special powers. Where's Augie? I'll show him I was right."

Her father was correct. There was no sign of the silver aura Evangeline had seen when tracking down Lady Breckenridge-Rice, the Alchemist.

"Miss Plockton?" The Professor called down the hallway. "Can you bring down Mr. Beauchamp?"

With a new atervis detector in her hand and her father momentarily distracted, Evangeline had a thought. She peered through the eyepiece at her own hand. The very hand which months earlier had crackled with a strange power, a power she could not reproduce.

Her heart nearly stopped as she looked down. A thin silvery glow emanated from her hand. It was subtle but it was undeniably there.

While Madame Zsoldas was not, Evangeline was exuding dark energy.

CHAPTER 10

EVANGELINE LAY FACE DOWN ON her feather bed, tears drying tightly on her cheeks, her head foggy and muddled. Could it be true? What did this mean? Was she evil?

She had done many wicked things in her past, but there was always a well-founded reason. She stole and lied to eat, under duress with threats and beatings from her stepfather. But if she was honest with herself, even now when she had all she needed, she was far from perfect. Lies still fell so easily from her lips. Did this mean she was naturally bad?

If only she could speak to Mei. No one else would understand. Evangeline wiped her face and pulled the brass telegraph key from the hiding place under the floor, typing desperately to her estranged best friend across the laneway.

"Are you there?"

Nothing.

"I need to talk."

There was no reply.

The triangle sounded downstairs for tea. Evangeline cleaned away her tears with a splash of water and smoothed down her hair, her heart plummeting again as she touched the frayed burnt ends. But if she was riddled with evil, a bald patch was the least of her concerns.

She slumped downstairs and took her chair at the table.

"Good afternoon, Miss Evangeline," Miss Plockton said.

Evangeline grunted in reply and reached across the table, taking three large slices of seed cake.

"Manners," Miss Plockton tutted. Evangeline shrugged her shoulders and shoved a whole piece of cake into her mouth.

The Professor strode in with a whistle.

"I have asked Chief Inspector Pensnett to come and see me. We shall go across to Mrs. Picklescott-Smythe's house and unmask the charlatan Hungarian woman. Then it will be a matter for the police to deal with and everything will be back to normal."

Evangeline wolfed down three slices of caraway and citrus seed cake, before grabbing another piece.

"Rather hungry this afternoon?" her father remarked as he stirred his usual three sugar lumps into his tea.

Evangeline shrugged again and kept chewing.

"Please close your mouth as you chew," Miss Plockton said.

Evangeline screwed up her face.

"How I eat is none of your business," she said with a hard look in her eye and a mouthful of cake.

"Oh." Miss Plockton gasped, her hand fluttering to her heart.

"Evangeline!" her father retorted. "Apologise to Miss Plockton this instant. How dare you be so rude."

"Sorry," Evangeline said sarcastically, before cramming more cake into her mouth and washing it down with a loud slurp of tea.

"What has come over you? You are behaving like a pig at a trough," her father chided.

"Leave me alone," she grunted.

"What did you say, young lady?" her father bellowed. "To your room now. I will not tolerate such insolence in my own home."

"Fine." Evangeline grabbed a fistful of tea cakes and stomped upstairs to her room, slamming the door behind her.

She sat on the end of her bed, seething with self-loathing. She had been rude and ill-mannered but perhaps this was her true nature. She was not good enough for polite company and the genteel life at 56 Collins Street. Perhaps it would be better for everyone if she left and returned to her old life on the streets.

She pulled out her battered suitcase from under her bed. The only belongings she brought from London when she first came to live with the Caldicotts. A tear rolled down her cheek. She should have known this was too good to last. She was a fraud, she could never be the young lady her father wanted. She placed the tea cakes and a spare dress into the suitcase and snapped the locks closed. It had been nice for a while, but now it was time to leave.

CHAPTER 11

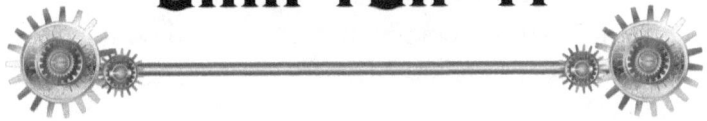

E VANGELINE HAD ONE FOOT POKING out her bedroom window when there was a gentle knock on the door. The handle turned and the door opened a sliver.

"Miss Evangeline?" It was Miss Plockton. "May I come in?"

Evangeline hastily closed the window and kicked her suitcase under the bed.

"Come in," she said, once she was nonchalantly seated at her writing desk.

Miss Plockton entered tentatively, her grey eyes softer than usual.

"I wanted to check on you. I wondered if you were ill. You were acting out of character at tea. Not your usual self at all."

Evangeline pursed her lips but stayed quiet.

"May I sit?"

Miss Plockton placed herself lightly on the very end of Evangeline's bed.

"I know I am only your father's personal secretary. I am merely an employee and not part of the family. But, I do have your best interests at heart. Sometimes I may be strict and appear old-fashioned and rigid. But please believe me when I say, my words come from a place of affection."

A lump clogged Evangeline's throat.

"I wanted to tell you I am glad you came to this house. You have brightened up the place ever so much. I thank the Lord you came to stay with us. I know your father feels the same."

Evangeline said nothing, holding in her sobs.

"This may be a confusing time as you settle into your life with us. But we are all glad God brought you to us."

"I am sorry, Miss Plockton, but..." she said with a choke.

"No need to apologise, Miss Evangeline. I know you are good in your heart."

Without another word, Miss Plockton rose to her feet and left the room. Evangeline flung herself face down into her pillows and sobbed.

There was a clattering under the floorboard. Evangeline jumped up and uncovered the telegraph key.

"I'm here." Evangeline typed.

"What's wrong? Liwei said there was something rattling in my room."

"I'm evil."

"What have you done now?"

Evangeline could picture her friend rolling her eyes.

"No. Truthfully. I've got the silver aura."

"Ballocks."

"I saw it myself. Through the detector."

"You can be a bit of an eejit now and then but you're not evil."

She shook her head vigorously. "What about the time I got us out of the cages? The magic I can't explain? And I had another strange feeling yesterday."

"Would I be friends with you if you were evil?"

Evangeline chewed on her lip. "Only if you're evil too."

"Good point. I hadn't thought of that."

She threw her hands in the air.

"You're not helping. I'm going to run away."

"You're hysterical. If I was there I'd give you a good hard slap."

"But."

"Come on, Miss Logic. Stop being such a featherbrain. Where are the facts?"

"I've done things I'm not proud of." Evangeline blinked, and a single tear splashed onto the brass keys like a water bomb.

"Exactly. If you were actually evil, you wouldn't care a bit. And I'm sure you'd have an evil laugh. Or a limp or something."

Evangeline sighed with a chuckle. "Maybe you're right."

"Of course I am. I'm always right. But I've got to go. Mama is still awake. I promise we'll spar again soon. I'm playing Perfect Daughter No.1. She's almost forgotten all about the fuss with the Bunyip. Bye."

"I miss you." Evangeline tapped back and put away her telegraph key with a smile.

If Miss Plockton and Mei believed in her, could she be so bad? Maybe the detector was wrong.

The storm clouds clearing from her head, Evangeline returned to her original plan. Obtaining a place at Madame Zsoldas's séance table was more important than ever. Fraternising with spirits and the spiritualists would be the true test of whether the dark energy lived within her.

CHAPTER 12

T HE PROFESSOR WAS NOT AS forgiving of Evangeline's
beastly behaviour. But there were benefits of being
banished to her room. It created the perfect alibi.

As soon as it grew dark and she heard Clarence the
grandfather clock chime seven times, Evangeline shimmied
down the drainpipe and dropped to the ground softly. This time,
Evangeline was dressed practically, shedding her bulky skirts for
a black Chinese jacket and trousers. A new sparring ensemble
smuggled across the lane by Mei's brother Liwei and perfect for
any nocturnal adventure.

She squeezed through the narrow gap between the red
brick house and the Nibthwaites' wall, past the camellia bushes
and out the front gate. She had no new inventions tonight,
but her lamp beam was squirrelled away in her pocket. The
perfect accompaniment for any nocturnal investigations, it was
compact, cast a penny-sized beam of light and was one of her
first inventions under the Professor's tutelage.

She darted across the road, spooking a horse pulling a
hansom cab, and vaulted over Mrs. Picklescott-Smythe's ornate
iron fence. A squeak from the gate would announce her arrival
and no one liked an uninvited guest.

She crouched in the rhododendrons and waited.

After a few minutes had passed and no one had come to investigate, she set off again, dodging the rose bushes and the bottlebrush before cautiously stepping onto the front verandah. She inched forward, pressed against the curtained windows and listened to the muffled voices inside.

Evangeline followed the verandah around the house, trying a window but the lock was firmly latched. She continued down three stone steps and through another gate into the back yard. She turned the corner of the house and noticed the back door was wide open, casting a rectangle of light onto the paving.

Crash!

Evangeline squashed herself flat against the wall.

"Bloody Nora!" exclaimed a woman. "You clumsy cow."

"I'm sorry," wailed a girlish voice.

"Brush the dirt off. Them lot won't notice."

A busy kitchen with an angry Cook was not the ideal entry point to the house, so Evangeline moved on. Ducking down low, she scuttled across the courtyard towards the conservatory.

Evangeline twisted the brass handle of the French doors but it was locked. Unperturbed, she pulled a pin from her damaged hair and fiddled with the lock until the door sprung open.

She tiptoed across the conservatory's wooden floors and paused by the door jam. Roasting meat and rosemary wafted up from the kitchen.

"Bagley?" called a familiar posh voice, followed by a swoosh of full skirts, grazing against the walls. It was Mrs. Picklescott-Smythe in another purple gown, this time a shade of iris. The lady of the house preoccupied with her preparations, passed by without noticing Evangeline hiding in the shadows.

Evangeline exhaled.

She heard the sound of little trotting feet scraping against wood and a small white terrier scampered down the hallway. The dog skidded to a halt outside the conservatory, bared her teeth and began to growl, her little body shaking and shuddering.

"Shh," Evangeline whispered. "Good dog."

The white terrier yapped, the shrill sound bouncing down the hallway.

"Petunia!" Mrs. Picklescott-Smythe called from down the hall. "What is it, dearie?"

Evangeline scuttled under the breakfast table and curled up into a tiny ball. The dog followed her, nipping at her toes and barking annoyingly.

"Shoo. Shoo. Go away." Evangeline hissed and waved her hands.

"Petunia." Mrs. Picklescott-Smythe called again. "Please be quiet. Bagley? Can you fetch Petunia? I hope she hasn't found another rat. Our guests will be here any moment."

Evangeline cowered under the table, as gaslight slowly illuminated the room and footsteps entered.

"Petunia. What's all this fuss about?" said an unfamiliar voice.

Petunia yipped and yapped.

Evangeline held her breath inside her chest, trying to think of a plausible explanation for why she was hiding under the table in Mrs. Picklescott-Smythe's conservatory.

CHAPTER 13

STOP BARKING, YOU STUPID LITTLE dog," said the voice again, this time in a hushed tone. "You better not have widdled on the carpet."

There was a scrape of claws and a yelp, as Bagley scooped Petunia from the floor and carried her away. Petunia's pathetic yapping fading away into the distance.

The grandfather clock in the hallway struck the half hour. The guests would be arriving soon. Taking advantage of the cover of the clock's carillon, Evangeline left her hiding place and ventured gingerly towards the front of the house. She scuttled into the grand foyer with the enormous chandelier and the grumpy portraits on the wall, glancing at the closed ballroom doors. Evangeline wondered what had become of the objectionable mummy. He was probably packed up and en route to Singapore already.

Footsteps sounded on the stairs and Evangeline squeezed herself beside the clock as it pealed its last chime.

A flash of scarlet stood at the base of the staircase.

"Chale?" Madame Zsoldas called out before entering a room on the left. "Chale? May I see you for a moment?"

She came straight back out of the room and started up the stairs, mumbling to herself.

"Where is he?"

The room on the left must be the location for the séance. Evangeline sprinted from her hiding place, across the foyer and in through the open door. The thick red velvet curtains were drawn and the room was dimly lit by tiny gas lamps on intricate brass sconces set into the wallpapered walls. A circular table was set in the middle of the room with all the other furniture moved aside, the walls lined with mahogany arm chairs, settees and chaise lounges upholstered in pear-green damask. More dark and dour-faced portraits hung on the walls, suspended by brass chains, and a spicy rich scent wafted through the air.

Evangeline darted into the farthest, darkest corner of the room and wrapped the heavy velvet curtains around her body like a mummy.

Rustling fabric and footsteps entered the room. The door closed.

"Is everything prepared, Chale?"

From her spot within the drapery, Evangeline could see Madame Zsoldas in her scarlet flowing robes and one of her companions, a grey-faced man with a matching emotionless voice.

"Yes, Madame. Exactly as you instructed. The table is set for nine."

"All your equipment is in place?"

"All in place, Madame."

The man pointed behind the sideboard near the door. Evangeline craned her neck but she could not see what he was referring to. What equipment did Chale need? Was he part of the séance? Despite the exotic incense in the room, this was beginning to smell fishy.

"Excellent. Now, we have three people with dead mothers." Madame Zsoldas referred to a sheet of paper in her hand. "One dead twin brother..."

Evangeline held in her gasp.

"...two dead children, one boy and one girl. And of course our hostess, Mrs. Picklescott-Smythe, with her dead husband."

Chale nodded.

"Seat the dead mothers on opposite sides of the table and the dead children together. We won't use the cards tonight. Only rapping and some spirit fluid. Perhaps the talking board if needed. Can we dim the lights further?"

Chale adjusted each lamp one by one and the room was lit by the merest glimmer of light, Evangeline could barely make out their faces across the room.

Madame Zsoldas reached up to touch one of the gas lamps.

"I like these new filters. They create exactly the right mood. Well done, Chale."

"I do my best, Madame."

"Excellent. This room is perfect for our session. Now, I want you to be subtle this evening. If all goes to plan, this will be the first of many sessions with our new guests. I want them to get a taste of the spirits but we will leave them wanting more."

"Of course, Madame."

"Show me the rapping."

Chale stood by the sideboard at the door. A loud rapping sound echoed across the room, yet Chale appeared to be standing completely still.

Madame Zsoldas laughed heartily.

"Excellent. We are ready for the show. Let's go and wait for our guests."

As the room was quiet again, Evangeline's heart fell. She would learn nothing about the spirits tonight. It appeared her father was right. Madame Zsoldas was another charlatan. Poor Augie will be so disappointed, he was so desperate to hear from his departed brother.

She sighed with frustration. There had to be another way to confirm whether there was dark energy coursing through her veins. Perhaps she should take a logical and scientific approach and return home to discuss the diagnosis with the Professor. This was the sensible option, her father would know what to do. Evangeline unfurled from the curtains and headed towards the door.

The front gate squeaked and Evangeline's heart clenched. Nervous laughter tittered on the doorstep and the doorbell chimed. Footsteps crossed the foyer and Evangeline scuttled back to her spot behind the curtain. With the guests arriving, there was no chance of escape.

If only she'd brought a bag of sweets. Humbugs would be the perfect accompaniment to Madame Zsoldas's show.

CHAPTER 14

C HALE OPENED THE PARLOUR DOOR and voices carried in from the foyer.

"Ah, Mrs. Woolpit, why, don't you look radiant this evening. Who says a lady cannot look chic in mourning black," said Mrs. Picklescott-Smythe. "You must pass on the name of your seamstress."

"Doctor Crawcrook, delighted to see you again," Madame Zsoldas purred. "I hope business is good. Any new interesting diseases?"

Evangeline wriggled to find a comfortable position. She may be here behind the curtain for a while.

"Ladies and gentlemen, it is time to begin," Madame Zsoldas announced. "Please leave your sherry glasses behind. The spirits can be mischievous. We do not want any damage to Mrs. Picklescott-Smythe's exceptional crystalware,"

"That sounds dangerous," stammered the porcine Mrs. Woolpit as Chale directed her to a seat at the table. "Are we in danger?"

"It is perfectly safe, Mrs. Woolpit," Chale replied. "Madame likes to take every precaution to protect her guests."

Mrs. Woolpit smiled weakly and cooled her face with a black lace fan.

"Why, it's awfully dark in here," said a familiar voice with a chuckle. "What are you planning to do with us?"

"So cheeky, Mr. Beauchamp," said Madame Zsoldas. "Please have a seat over here."

One by one, the room filled with guests. Some were cautious and took their seats with trepidation, others sat with beaming smiles, ready for the adventure. There were equal numbers of men and women; roly-poly but fashionable Augie, two men with thick grey beards and one with a pale blonde moustache, Mrs. Picklescott-Smythe in her iris gown sprinkled with gems as always, the red-faced Mrs. Woolpit with the fan, and two bony-chested women with similar buck teeth.

"Now, before we begin, a warning of sorts."

"I thought you said it was safe," flapped Mrs. Woolpit.

Madame Zsoldas smiled.

"There are risks with everything, Mrs. Woolpit. I implore you all to take a brief moment to consider what you are about to experience. You must come to this session with an open mind. You will see and hear unusual things this evening. Happenings which do not make sense in the ordinary world. But I ask you to be sympathetic and welcoming to whatever spirits speak with us tonight."

Mrs. Woolpit sighed, the buck-toothed sisters pursed their lips and Augie smirked.

"Once we close the door, we cannot allow anyone to leave the room until the session is complete. If the session is broken while the connection with the spirit world is in progress, someone or something may leak through into this world. It may lead to very dangerous consequences. So I must ask each and every one of you to agree to stay throughout the entire session."

The guests gulped and fidgeted, including Augie. The smirk gone from his lips.

"If you cannot promise to stay, please leave now."

Madame Zsoldas looked directly into the eyes of each guest.

"I will not be angry or disappointed if anyone wants to leave. But if you feel as though you cannot cope with contact from the other side, please leave now."

The room was silent as the participants sheepishly glanced at each other. Evangeline wondered who would be the first to leave. Even Augie, ordinarily the most confident man in any room, shuffled in his seat.

But no one said a word or made a move towards the door.

"We are all staying?" Madame Zsoldas asked. "We are all in agreement?"

There were small nods from all eight people.

"Excellent. We need full commitment from everyone to ensure that the session works. Close the door, Chale. We are ready to begin."

Chale obeyed and, with the door firmly closed, he took his place standing by the sideboard, statue-still with his usual blank face.

"Let us all hold hands."

The nine people sat at the round table, hand in hand.

With her eyes closed, Madame Zsoldas breathed in sharply through her nostrils and out again, with a hoarse unladylike rattle in her throat. The guests eyed each other nervously.

"I thank you all for coming this evening. We are about to experience a special event. We are opening the channel between our world of the living and the world of the dead. I ask you all to close your eyes and breathe deeply with me."

The guests followed her instructions, their eyes firmly closed, breathing in unison.

"Excellent. I can sense we have a welcoming group here tonight. There is a feeling of fraternity and openness to the wonders and wisdom of the spirit world. This is good. It fills me with welcoming energy. I can sense the door between the two worlds opening. Please repeat after me."

"We welcome spirits from the other side."

The guests repeated her words, in a cacophony of deep and high pitched voices and accents from all around the British Isles now at home in the Antipodes.

"Please share your wisdom with us," Madame Zsoldas said, her eyes firmly shut.

A few guests sneaked glances around the room before quickly closing their eyes again. Evangeline smiled as she watched the adults struggle with the strangeness of the proceedings.

"I can feel the door opening. The veil between our two worlds is thin. I am reaching through from here to there."

Madame Zsoldas's voice was deep and dramatic. Evangeline was impressed with the performance so far. With her acting prowess, Madame Zsoldas could easily star in one of Uncle Augie's productions at the Prince Albert Theatre.

The round table shifted on its legs, tilting up and down under the nine pairs of hands.

"What was that?" One of the bony-chested ladies squealed.

All the guests opened their eyes, horror and surprise across their faces.

Evangeline squinted hard through the dim light, scrutinising the legs of the table. At first glance, she could not identify how the trick was done. Then she remembered the steam pneumatic elevator from the mummy unveiling and wondered if the trick used a similar device, but stealthier.

"Someone is here with us. I knew this group was receptive to the spirit world. Ordinarily the spirits take time to become accustomed to new visitors. But our group is strong and someone is here to speak with us. Now."

Despite knowing this was all a sham, Evangeline felt a shiver of excitement. She could only imagine how the other guests felt, filled with fear, hope and trepidation. This was rather good fun.

Madame Zsoldas threw back her head and called out in a loud deep voice.

"Is there a spirit here in the room?"

The table jerked from side to side.

"We have a visitor, my friends. Are you speaking from the other side?"

This time, the table stayed still.

"Knock once for yes. Twice for no."

Bang.

A loud rapping sound rang through the room, a knock on wood. The same sound Evangeline had heard during their practice — somehow Chale was knocking against the sideboard.

The blond man gasped audibly.

"One knock. Yes, there is someone from the other side with us. Thank you for joining our group, spirit. We look forward to hearing your wisdom. Who are you, dear spirit? Are you known to anyone here in this room tonight?"

The room was silent.

Bang.

Another knock but this was a different sound. This was a rap on brass, a metallic ring like the strike of a gong.

For a split second Chale frowned.

"Spirit, you are known to someone in this room?" Madame Zsoldas continued.

Bang.

The clang of brass sounded again. This time twice as loud.

Chale's eyes darted around the parlour. A look of confusion briefly ran across his face before he hid his feelings away with his bland expression. If Evangeline didn't know any better, she would assume Chale had no idea what was going on.

But this was all part of Madame Zsoldas's act. Wasn't it?

CHAPTER 15

D O YOU HAVE A RELATIVE here at the table? A departed love one?" Madame Zsoldas continued.

Bang. Bang.

The answer was no.

Eyes opened around the table, the guests glancing at one another.

"You are not related to anyone in this room?"

Bang. Bang.

Two knocks on brass, not Chale's wooden knocks.

"I am confused, dear spirit. Are you related to someone in this room?"

A portrait began to rattle, thumping against the wall, flapping like a sheet in the wind. Evangeline's eyes grew to the size of dinner plates. How was Chale making the picture move?

"Great Uncle Charles!" Mrs. Picklescott-Smythe exclaimed, pointing at the painting of the grim faced old man with eyes like coal. "He was a very pious man. This must be a sign of his disapproval?"

Bang. Bang. Bang.

Chale jumped from his position at the door, a look of terror across his face. The brass knocking started again, but randomly.

Bang. Bang. Bang. Bang.

The lamps in the sconces flickered up and down, blasting the room with light so bright it hurt Evangeline's eyes, then plunging the room into darkness.

Bang.

The knocking was as loud as a thunderstorm. Evangeline covered her ears with her hands.

A deck of white cards fluttered across the room, showering over the table. Evangeline frowned. Had there been a change of plan? Madame Zsoldas said they were not going to use the cards this evening.

Augie picked a card from the table and read it aloud.

"Mother."

Three of the guests at the table gasped.

"Let me see," said a grey-whiskered man.

"No, us first," said the bony sisters in harmony, tearing the card from Augie's fingers.

"Whose handwriting is this?" asked one of the bony sisters. "It does not look like my mother's script."

"Nor mine," said the grey-whiskered man.

The temperature in the room plummeted. Like a London day in January, Evangeline could see clouds of her own breath. She was covered in goose pimples, the hairs on her neck standing on end. Evangeline reminded herself this was a performance, then why did she feel so afraid? She wished she could run over to her Uncle Augie for comfort.

The man with the blond moustache picked up another card from the table.

"Power," he read.

Gusts of wind blew through the room, lifting up the table cloth and billowing the curtains. Evangeline clung on for dear life, hoping the unknown winds would not give her away.

Madame Zsoldas remained calm, despite the chaos all around her.

"Dear spirit, may we know your name?"

Bang. Bang.

Two knocks like cannon fire.

"Is this a friendly spirit?" stuttered Mrs. Woolpit. "Or have we summonsed up something evil?"

Augie picked up a third card and read the message aloud.

"Miriam."

Evangeline's heart stopped dead.

"Does anyone here know a Miriam?" Madame Zsoldas asked.

All the guests shook their heads, except one.

"I know a Miriam. But she is not dead," said one of the grey-whiskered men stoically.

"Dear sister spirit, are you Miriam? Is Miriam your name?"

Bang. Bang.

Evangeline knew the truth. She knew who Miriam was. But how could Madame Zsoldas possibly know?

CHAPTER 16

T HE GUSTS OF WIND BLEW harder and harder, blowing the tablecloth right off the table, scattering the rest of the white cards and knocking Augie from his chair. Augie tumbled backwards onto the floor, landing by Chale's feet. Then everything stopped. The room was quiet and still, returning to an ordinary parlour.

"I say. What's this?" said Augie from his spot on the floor.

"Please return to your seat, Mr. Beauchamp," Madame Zsoldas said. "Remember you cannot break the circle. There may be consequences. Please do not remove yourself from the table."

Augie crawled across the floor on hands and knees and grabbed something from Chale's hand. It was a long metal staff with a lump of wood on the end.

"Turn up the lights," Augie demanded.

Chale did not move, his eyes directed at the floor.

"I said turn up the lights. Do you have something to hide?"

"Of course not," Madame Zsoldas said but she did not move.

"Then turn up the lights so we can see for ourselves."

"We are dealing with a spirit, Mr. Beauchamp. We must treat the spirit with respect, otherwise I cannot vouch for what may happen."

Augie scoffed.

Evangeline was confused, she wished everything would stop for a moment. What was happening? Was there a real presence in the room? A spirit with knowledge that no one else had?

"I suspect you are lying to us, Madame. Turn up the lights and prove me wrong."

Madame Zsoldas called out with her arms outstretched.

"Dear spirit. Are you still with us?"

This time there was no response. No knocking, no winds, no flickering lights. Aside from the knocked over furniture and the white cards scattered across the carpeted floor, the room looked like any other richly upholstered parlour.

"We thank you, spirit," Madame Zsoldas continued. "For revealing yourself and sharing your wisdom with us this evening. Wisdom we do not yet understand. But we thank you for visiting our world tonight."

Madame Zsoldas lowered her arms and spoke to the guests.

"The bridge between the two worlds has closed. The session is complete. It is safe to turn on the lights."

"About time." Augie pushed past Chale and turned up a gaslight dial. "What is this contraption? You were faking the knocks, weren't you?"

Chale said nothing, his face as bland as ever. He glanced across to Madame Zsoldas as Augie held up the lump of wood.

"You give me too much credit, Mr. Beauchamp. I am no thespian. How do you think I created the gusts of wind? And made the temperature drop?" Madame Zsoldas asked. "Please tell me how I managed to conjure up such an experience for you."

"Simple, my dear. I'm no clever clogs but all it would take is a clockwork fan and ice. We're no longer in the Dark Ages, you can't fool us with your superstitious claptrap." Augie banged open the sideboard drawers one by one. "Your device must be around here somewhere."

"Enlighten us, Mr. Beauchamp."

"I don't know," Augie blustered, as he opened doors and looked under chairs. "All I know is tonight was a sham."

But Evangeline knew Augie was wrong.

"I have nothing to hide, Mr. Beauchamp. Open the curtains. Light the rest of the lamps."

Evangeline froze.

The room was filled with light, as bright as day. The other guests roused in their seats as though awakening from a deep sleep.

Chale moved to the opposite window and flung open the curtains. Evangeline's heart started beating rapidly. She took a deep breath and prepared herself. Like a horse waiting for the beginning of a race, she was tensed and ready to strike.

"How did you make those brass clangs?" Augie peeked behind the settee and under the table. "I've spent twenty years in the theatre, I know a trick when I see one. I toured the Home Counties with Signor Blitz and his trained canaries, I've seen it all. There must be something here somewhere."

Chale moved closer to Evangeline, opening one side of the curtain. Then the other. Evangeline's hiding place was about to be revealed.

She burst from behind the curtain, pushing Chale aside and leapt across the room. Using a chair as a platform, Evangeline flung herself into the air and cartwheeled towards the door.

"And who was that man? Another one of your minions?" Augie said as Evangeline sprinted across the foyer and through the front door, Petunia yapping feebly in the background.

She darted down the front path, through the gate and across the road. She tumbled over her own front fence and hid under a camellia bush in the fallen leaves. She stopped to catch her breath and looked back across the road. All the front rooms of Mrs. Picklescott-Smythe's house now blazed with light.

"I am sorry." Mrs. Picklescott-Smythe called out as her guests left one by one, climbing into their carriages and instructing their drivers to take them straight home. "Please send your laundry bills to me."

Augie came marching across the road, flung open the front gate and slammed the front door. Evangeline waited a little longer under the bush before slipping around the side of the house and clambering back in through her open bedroom window.

She lay on her bed fully dressed, her mind racing. What had she witnessed in the parlour? Was it a real message from the spiritual world?

The name Miriam rang in her ears.

CHAPTER 17

E VANGELINE TOSSED AND TURNED, HER dreams filled with loud crashes, heavy red curtains and words adrift in the air. She jolted awake, with a plan fully formed in her head.

"I must know the truth," she said to herself, dressing quickly and sliding into her flat slippers.

She inched open her bedroom door. The rest of the house was sleeping except for Clarence, his steady ticks echoing down the hallway. She tiptoed downstairs to the Professor's study, switched on the desk lamp and began searching for the new atervis detector when a silver frame on the crammed bookshelf caught her eye. It held a daguerreotype of an elfin young woman, porcelain-faced with black hair, barely older than Evangeline herself. Was this her grandmother, Geileish? The heart of all the strangeness in her life?

She placed her grandmother back on the shelf and spied the brass telescope-like atervis detector. Now she could substantiate the existence of dark energy in the parlour and prove whether the evening had been a sham. Evangeline slipped the device into her pocket, once again lamenting the loss of her atervis monocle, and left the house by the front door, for a change.

Collins Street was deserted, lit only by a few pools of yellow gas light. Evangeline skipped over a mountain of horse mess and crossed the street.

A single light burned upstairs, far away from the front parlour, and the rest of the house was dark. Evangeline pushed on the front windows but they were latched from the inside.

She peered through the drawn curtains with the atervis detector. There was an ever so-slight silvery glow. So slight, she couldn't be certain whether it was merely the reflection of the moon on the window glass.

Testing the weight of the brass detector in her hand, she hoped Petunia was a heavy sleeper. With a quick jab, she cracked the window pane, then stopped and listened. The house was still quiet. The only noise was the sound of her own heartbeat thundering in her ears.

She prodded at the shattered pane until the shards fell away and with her hand wrapped inside her sleeve, reached through the hole, unlatched the window and stepped into Mrs. Picklescott-Smythe's parlour. She rushed to close the door, turned up a gas lamp and lifted the atervis detector to her eye. But before she had a chance to peek through the eyepiece, heavy footsteps came down the stairs. She hurriedly crouched beside the sideboard.

The door opened.

"Over there. In the sideboard," said Madame Zsoldas in a low voice.

Evangeline held her breath.

Chale pulled open a drawer and took out a tray of rattling silverware.

"It will have to do," Madame Zsoldas muttered.

Chale emptied the cutlery tray into a leather travelling bag.

"There has to be something else in here," Madame Zsoldas said. "This old sow is made of money."

The room started to spin as Evangeline's breath ran low. She hoped they would find nothing more and move on to the next room. Quickly.

"How about this, Madame?" Chale held up an old porcelain figurine with a tall white wig.

"Well spotted. Meissen. Wrap it very carefully," Madame Zsoldas said.

Her face turning blue, Evangeline could hold her breath no more. She opened her mouth with a gasp, the noise much louder than she anticipated. Chale turned instantly.

"Who are you?" He reached down and pulled Evangeline up by the shoulder.

Evangeline spluttered as she took a full breath.

"What are you doing here?" Chale thrust her under the light.

"I could ask you the same thing," Evangeline replied with a cough. "Let me go."

"I recognise you." Madame Zsoldas smirked. "Caldicott child. Now why are you here in this house in the middle of the night dressed in gentlemen's pajamas?"

Evangeline shirked off Chale's grip and stood up straight.

"I am here to find the truth about last night. Whether your séance was real."

"You were here?" Chale's brow furrowed.

"It was you," Madame Zsoldas said. "Very interesting. I wondered where it came from."

"What do you mean?" Evangeline frowned. "Was it real or not?"

"You are right. A spirit did visit us. I wondered if one of the guests had a latent talent. But you. It makes sense. I knew there was something strange about you, child."

"How rude." Evangeline huffed. "We've barely been introduced."

"This is a compliment. Such strangeness can be very profitable."

"What should I do with her, Madame?" Chale grabbed at Evangeline's arm.

"Be gentle, Chale. The Caldicott child could be very useful."

Chale grimaced and dropped his grip.

"Thank you very much," Evangeline said with a toss of her head, dusting down her jacket. "So, Madame Zsoldas. You are obviously a charlatan and didn't conjure up the spirit yourself. Then what was in the room? How did it know about Miriam?"

"You tell me."

"How should I know?"

"You know more than you let on. I know lies when I see them. We are alike, you and I."

"Rot."

"Don't be so hasty. As I said, strangeness like yours, events like last night, could be very profitable indeed. In fact, I have a proposition for you. Have you ever been to Vienna?"

"Austria? I don't understand?"

"Come with me and I will show you how lucrative mesmerism can be."

"Absolutely not."

"There is a dirigible departing for Batavia at six o'clock. Join us. I know many people, rich and powerful, desperate for the type of experience we had last night. I will introduce you to the wonders of the Empire. The real Empire."

"But what if she is evil, ma'am?" Chale stuttered.

Madame Zsoldas laughed.

"You are a simpleton, Chale. Who is evil and who is good?" Madame Zsoldas concentrated on Evangeline with her tawny eyes.

"I will never go anywhere with you." Evangeline stared back.

Zsoldas shrugged.

"I gave you a choice." She turned to Chale. "Tie her up. It's time we left."

CHAPTER 18

L EAVE ME ALONE."
Chale lunged forward but Evangeline struck back with
a sharp elbow to his ribs. He groaned and doubled over.

"Need a little help, Chale?" Madame Zsoldas said.

"I can handle it, Madame." Chale grimaced and grabbed for
Evangeline again. This time his grip was like iron and it was
Evangeline's turn to groan. She kicked back like a donkey, her
dainty heel connecting with Chale's bony shin.

"Oh dear, Chale. A little girl is showing you up. Hurry along
now. We haven't got much time."

Chale grabbed Evangeline by the shoulders and flipped her
face first onto the settee.

"Get off me." Evangeline writhed, her voice muffled by the
upholstery. Chale gripped her hands securely behind her back
and bound her wrists together with a tasselled curtain tie.

"I will never help you," Evangeline spat as Chale hoisted
her upright. Madame Zsoldas unwound a scarlet scarf from her
throat and stuffed it into Evangeline's mouth. Chale finished the
job by tying up her feet.

"We shall see about that."

Evangeline protested but only mumbles emerged through
her silken gag. Her eyes were flinty but underneath her heart

was galloping. No one knew she was here in this house, and she wouldn't be missed until breakfast. By then, she'd probably be half way to the Dutch East Indies.

"I gave you the choice to come freely. But I cannot let a golden goose like you get away so easily. You'll have plenty of time to reconsider my proposal on our long journey to Vienna. Come, Chale, let's complete our packing. I have just the right sized trunk."

Somewhere else in the house, a heavy weight thudded to the floor, shaking the floorboards. Madame Zsoldas and Chale paused, Chale with his hand resting on the door knob.

"Probably the old woman falling out of bed." Madame Zsoldas shrugged. "Come on."

Another bang was followed by a long scrape,

"Who'd be moving furniture at this hour?" Chale said.

"Never mind. Perhaps it's a burglar. Let's go."

Evangeline writhed on the velvet settee, pulling at her restraints. She hoped it was the police. She was already concocting a vivid story of how the spiritualist had kidnapped her from her bedroom for the white slave trade.

Crash. The sound of delicate pottery shattering into a hundred pieces and Chale's ordinarily aloof face was crumpled in concern.

"Very well. Go and investigate, Chale." Madame Zsoldas sighed. "But it sounds as though you missed something valuable. Pay closer attention next time."

"Yes, ma'am," gulped Chale.

He inched open the parlour door and a nightmarish scream echoed across the grand foyer. It was a two-toned bellowing shriek, both high pitched and low growl at the same time.

"Oh my heavens," Chale squeaked, slamming the parlour door and leaning up against it. "This is all your fault. I should never have got involved with you. You said it was harmless. All an act, you said. What was I thinking? Meddling with the dead."

"What are you blathering about?" Madame Zsoldas scoffed.

"You were right. At the unwrapping party. You were right," Chale spluttered.

Through the closed door, something slowly dragged and scraped its way across the foyer. Chale rushed to the end of the sideboard and pushed, heaving with all his might. Evangeline's chest tightened. She recalled the strange faint feeling from yesterday. It wasn't real, was it? Surely, she had imagined it.

"He's coming for us."

"Don't be ridiculous."

The screeching roar blasted once more, and this time it was accompanied by a smell. An evil stench coiled under the door and up inside Evangeline's nostrils. She coughed, choking on her silken gag. This was a familiar smell, a smell she could never forget.

"The tingle. I should have known," Evangeline muttered to herself. She moaned and kicked her legs against the wooden chair legs but they paid her no mind.

The smell reached Madame Zsoldas, her confident mask slipping for a moment. She hurriedly joined Chale, pushing the sideboard. The two groaned with effort but it was solid oak, their combined weight barely budged the sideboard an inch.

"The table?"

Chale tipped the round table on its side and pushed it against the door. Evangeline wriggled and rocked on the settee, trying to attract their attention. But she tipped too far, sliding off and thudding onto the oriental carpet.

The low slow scraping drew closer, the thick stinky fog grew stronger. Chale and Madame Zsoldas pushed their weight against the table, desperately holding back the door.

"Should we untie the girl? She could help."

From her place on the floor, Evangeline nodded violently and groaned.

"Leave her. She's a perfect present. Wrapped up like a bon-bon."

Evangeline banged her heels against the ground, glaring at Madame Zsoldas with the best vitriol she could muster. But the spiritualist's attention was far away.

Bang.

Bang.

Bang.

Three knocks shook the heavy door, shuddering on its hinges, propelling Chale and Madame Zsoldas forward. A fist burst through the panelling, wood smashing into the room, kindling and splinters flying in all directions.

The door was no protection.

CHAPTER 19

A BANDAGED FIST REACHED THROUGH THE hole, striking Chale. His eyes rolled back and the grey-faced man slithered to the ground like a pool of water.

Madame Zsoldas shrieked and exclaimed in an indecipherable language. From her expression, Evangeline gathered it was not a comment for polite company.

"Chale. Wake up." The spiritualist kicked him. "This is not the time for resting."

The mummy's hand retracted back through the hole, out of sight. With another wail, the door flew from its hinges, crashing into the middle of the room. Zsoldas was fleet-footed, skipping aside and escaping without a scratch.

The mummy yowled.

Silhouetted in the doorway, the creature stood over six foot tall, with spools of stained bandages pooling around his feet. His outstretched fingers were the colour of strong tea, his finger joints like knotted wood, his eyes blazing red lights, hidden deep within the layers of rotting swaddling.

He swiped the table aside like a bothersome blade of grass and lumbered into the centre of the room. Madame Zsoldas held a fluted sleeve against her nose and stood her ground.

"Go. Go now," she ordered, in her authoritative voice. "I have not wronged you. I did not bring you here."

The mummy screeched in reply and lunged out with his hands. Madame Zsoldas squealed and jumped aside.

"Ma'am?"

Chale was back on his feet, albeit unsteadily, rubbing his forehead. He teetered within kicking distance of Evangeline and she shoved him with her boots. He looked down at her with unfocused eyes.

"If you're not too busy. I could do with some help here," Madame Zsoldas said, fending off the reanimated Egyptian with a fire poker.

Evangeline kicked Chale again, reinforcing her message.

"Leave the girl."

Chale swivelled between Madame Zsoldas and Evangeline with a confused expression. The mummy swung wildly, knocking the chandelier from the ceiling. A cloud of white plaster dust descended and a small white ball shot into the parlour with a growl. Petunia grabbed at the bandaged leg of the mummy, tearing at the strips of fabric. The mummy bent at the waist, swatting away the terrier. But Petunia was too quick, dodging the mummy's lumbering swipes.

Chale bent down and untied Evangeline's hands.

"What are you doing?" cried Madame Zsoldas, trying to sneak past the mummy while the little white dog nipped at his ankles. The creature glanced up at the last moment and lunged at the spiritualist. She jabbed the poker straight at the creature's heart but the metal bounced off his chest without a flinch.

Evangeline rubbed her wrists and pulled the gag from her mouth.

"Thank you," she said with a croak, as she freed her ankles.

The mummy turned her way, ignoring the yapping dog and the spiritualist, staring with his fiery eyes. Evangeline stumbled to her feet, dancing from one leg to the other in a desperate attempt to recirculate the blood.

He lurched towards her. Evangeline deflected his grapple with a defensive forearm swing. The mummy surged forward again but Evangeline was ready, striking the Egyptian right in the belly.

"Ow," she cried, nursing her wrist against her chest. It felt as though she'd punched a piano.

He roared and reached out with his bandaged hands, grabbing Evangeline by the ruffled throat and lifting her off her feet. His other hand reached over her head, grabbing her jaw. Evangeline kicked and grimaced, his fingers icy-cold against her cheek. Her heartbeat thundering in her ears with the fear he would tear her head clean off.

Petunia struck again, nipping at his heels. The mummy groaned in irritation and threw Evangeline across the room. Colliding with the wallpapered wall, she smashed into one of the grumpy portraits, crashing to the ground in a shatter of glass.

"Petunia. Where are you?" called a loud familiar voice. It was Mrs. Picklescott-Smythe calling down the stairs.

The mummy was in the centre of the room, lashing out at the tenacious dog, while Madame Zsoldas, still trapped in the corner, tried again to sneak past towards the door.

"Do you know any incantations?" Evangeline called out. "Anything we can do to stop him?"

"If I did, I would have used it by now," Madame Zsoldas grunted as she darted to one side, avoiding his grasp.

Evangeline's education was light on enchantments but a few months earlier, somehow she'd freed herself from a spellbound cage, conjuring up something mysterious. But, despite all her efforts, she'd failed to replicate the power. Should she take the chance and try again? But the silver aura? What might happen if her dark energy met a reanimated Egyptian?

"One more try," she said with a determined nod, while the mummy took another swipe at Petunia.

From her resting place on the floor, Evangeline strained. She contracted every muscle in her body, from her toes to her forehead, squeezing with all her might, wishing the tingling would return.

She ground her teeth and grunted but there was nothing. Not a jot of power and the mummy was coming her way again. Evangeline's shoulders slumped with a sigh.

Luckily, she had practical skills to rely on.

Evangeline reached down to hoist herself upright and felt cold metal against her fingers. She picked up a foot long piece of copper picture wire, an idea sparking in her head. But was it enough?

Evangeline fumbled in her pocket for the lamp beam, grinning as she felt the little cylindrical shape. She unscrewed the brass casing and emptied out the battery.

"Pass me the chandelier," Evangeline called to the spiritualist. "I think I can stop him."

"I don't need your help," Zsoldas retorted.

"Yes, you do," said Chale.

At the sound of Chale's voice, the mummy swung around, walloping him in the process. Chale's knees buckled and he cracked his head against a carved chair arm. The mummy turned his attention back to Madame Zsoldas, pushing her back towards the fireplace.

"I guess I'll have to make do." Evangeline grumbled.

She hurriedly bent the picture wire into a clumsy coil and wrapped one end around the battery.

"Here goes."

Evangeline crossed her fingers and toes, held out the wire like a dowsing rod and pressed the button.

Nothing.

"Knickers," Evangeline said.

CHAPTER 20

P ATHETIC," CALLED OUT MADAME ZSOLDAS, now brandishing a brass shovel and an occasional table.

The mummy pushed past her sword and shield and thwacked the spiritualist across the face. She slammed into the window and crumpled like a discarded napkin.

Evangeline inhaled sharply and the mummy heard her swallowed cry. He lurched forward but Petunia pounced, chomping at his calf. Evangeline regretted her harsh words for the little dog earlier in the evening, she promised to bring a meaty treat for Petunia when she next visited Mrs. Picklescott-Smythe. Petunia was the bravest of them all.

With Petunia distracting the mummy, Evangeline fiddled with the copper wire and the battery.

"Loose connection, of course," she muttered and pressed the button again.

Zap.

A spray of electricity flashed along the coil and Evangeline smirked. The mummy staggered towards her, both arms outstretched, Evangeline ducked her head and stabbed the wire into the mummy's chest cavity.

The mummy jerked slightly, like a single attack of the hiccups. He roared and grabbed Evangeline by the shoulders, tossing her across the room again. She tumbled over the side of the settee and crashed into a bookcase. The objet d'art on the bookcase had already been cleaned out by Chale and Madame Zsoldas and a lone candelabra tumbled off the mantelpiece, clocking Evangeline in the head.

"My poor baby. Save my baby." Mrs. Picklescott-Smythe wailed down the stairs. "Fifty pounds for the man who rescues my Petunia"

There was a thunder of boots on the stairs and three footmen burst into the parlour, immediately skidding to a halt. Their mouths hung open when they spotted the mummy. It welcomed the newcomers with another ear-splitting screech.

Evangeline crawled along the floor, looking for her battery and copper wire.

Evangeline found her battery under an armchair and made an additional quick turn of the wire.

"Stand back," she cried.

Holding the candelabra high, Evangeline took a run-up and leaped forward, thrusting the three silver prongs into the mummy's back.

He screeched and flinched, and Evangeline pressed the battery button. Coils of electricity surged through the three prongs, shoving Evangeline backwards. But the electricity rolled along the coil and through the silver, pulsating through the mummy over and over. The bandaged figure convulsed and jerked, screeching and shivering with electricity before crumbling into a smouldering pile of ribbon on the floor.

There was a loud knocking at the front door. One of the footmen grabbed Petunia under his arm and more servants piled into the parlour, gagging at the smell, the room filling with smoke from the flaming bandages. Someone opened the front door and three bobbies with truncheons rushed into the room. Questions and raised voices came from all directions. Evangeline lowered her chin to hide her face as the room filled with people. She glanced over at the unconscious Madame Zsoldas, but she was gone. The velvet curtain pushed aside revealing the window Evangeline had broken.

In the confusion Evangeline skipped out of the broken window, down the path and into the street. A flash of scarlet jumped into a carriage and sped away, presumably towards Flemington, destined for the 6 o'clock dirigible to Batavia.

"Can I help you, sir?" said a bobby, waiting by a paddy wagon. He blinked as his eyebrows scrunched together and Evangeline remembered her unladylike black attire. "Sorry, Miss…"

"Follow that…" Evangeline said pointing to the disappearing carriage, but then the bobby stepped into the light. She recognised his face and ducked her head back into the darkness. She knew this policeman, it was Constable Kane. She met Kane on the night Mei went after the Alchemist, telling him a legion of lies to put him off the scent. Kane was a nice young man, a little too gullible for a policeman, but even he would have trouble believing Evangeline this time. He would quite rightly suspect she was part of Madame Zsoldas's monkey business and Evangeline would be the one facing a trip in the Black Maria. She dropped her arm by her side.

"Never mind," she mumbled.

"Please go back to bed, Miss. Leave this matter to us."

Evangeline nodded her downcast head and crossed the quiet street. She hesitated for a moment, she was letting Madame Zsoldas escape. Should she face her lies, turn back and raise the alarm? The lies were coming back to haunt her. Perhaps this was the revenge of the dark energy in her veins.

"Constable!" called a voice from the house and Kane disappeared inside.

Her moment to confess had passed. With a guilt-heavy heart and weary limbs, Evangeline slipped around the side of 56 Collins Street, climbed back to her own room and collapsed on her feather bed. Her slippers had barely hit the ground when she began to doze off.

"My lamp beam," she said, bolting upright with a start. "And the atervis detector. Not again."

Losing her inventions and her villains was becoming a habit. She vowed to be more careful as she drifted off to sleep, trying not to think about Miriam.

CHAPTER 21

The next day

"THERE'S NOTHING HERE ABOUT LAST night's ruckus," the Professor said, rustling The Argus.

"The Nibthwaite's kitchen girl said it was those Little Lon larrikins." Miss Plockton tutted as she poured the tea. "Melbourne used to be such a safe place."

"In league with that woman, I'll bet." The Professor shook his head with tightly pursed lips.

"She said the bobbies caught one of the bandits," Miss Plockton said. "Thank the Lord."

"So it wasn't the mummy?" the Professor said with a twinkle in his eye. "Coming to life?"

Miss Plockton tittered and Edmund guffawed, while Evangeline dabbed at her brow with her napkin. Luckily, Uncle Augie bustled into the conservatory with a flamboyant flourish and changed the subject.

"I have an apology to make to you, Monty," Augie said, drawing himself up to his full impressive height.

"Really?" The Professor put down his paper.

"You were right about Madame Zsoldas. She is a charlatan."

Evangeline sipped her tea and kept her mouth closed. The Professor chuckled into his moustache.

"I went to her 'performance' last night. What a total sham! I've seen better local amateur dramatic productions. She treated us like children, knocking on doors and flinging around cards with random nonsense on them. Ridiculous."

"So, no spirits materialised then?" Edmund asked.

"Hardly. I am so embarrassed, Monty. To be taken in by such a woman. I ought to have my head read."

"Well, no harm done, Augie old chap. I just hope Mrs. Picklescott-Smythe realised the truth too."

"Oh, I expect Madame Zsoldas will have disappeared in the night. One of the other guests is the sister of the editor of The Herald. I shan't be surprised if the truth about Madame's shows appears in print very soon."

"Good riddance. We can all get back to normal." The Professor smoothed his moustache with his brass fingers.

"The mood has been awfully sombre around here over the past few days. Let's take an outing and have some fun. My treat. St. Kilda Beach?"

"Can I go ice-skating?" Evangeline perked up.

"Of course. Very graceful pastime," Augie said. "I almost forgot. This should be good for a chuckle. I took a few souvenirs from last night. In case I needed some type of evidence."

From his jacket pocket, Augie pulled out a stack of white cards and spread them across the table. Edmund and the Professor leaned in. Evangeline gasped a little, hiding her reaction behind her tea cup.

The top card read 'Mother'.

"Oh, that could apply to anyone. Everyone has a mother," the Professor scoffed. "Classic trick used by fortune tellers."

"Exactly," Augie replied. "No magic there. Madame Zsoldas claimed she did not recognise the handwriting either. Apparently it was not her hand or any of her minions."

The next card read 'Power'.

The men all chuckled. Evangeline stayed quiet, anxiously awaiting the next card.

Then Augie laid down the third card. "Miriam." Augie chuckled.

"No one in the room knew a Miriam. One person did but apparently their Miriam was very much alive. This was the final nail in the proverbial coffin, revealing Madame Zsoldas for the crook she is."

The Professor and Edmund turned open-mouthed and stared at Evangeline. Evangeline looked back with eyes as wide as saucers. It was obvious they were as confused as she was.

Augie chuckled, oblivious to the shocked expressions around the table and picked up the final card.

"Um, Augie..." started Edmund in a quiet voice.

"And this one. Some gibberish. I don't know what it means."

Augie laid the card down. This was a card Evangeline had not seen from her hiding place behind the curtain.

The card read 'Geileish'.

This time, the Professor audibly gasped and Edmund brought down his tea cup on the saucer with a crash.

The room was filled with awkward silence.

"What's wrong?" said Augie.

No one spoke for a long time.

CHAPTER 22

E VANGELINE SAT AT HER WRITING desk, pretending to complete her comprehension exercises. But she was staring out the window, watching the clouds flock and separate, while her mind wandered in a hundred different directions.

There was a soft knock at the door and the Professor entered. He sat on the bed with a sigh.

"Well, this has been an unusual morning."

"What does it mean, Father?"

"Edmund told you about my mother?"

"He said you lost her when you were a small boy."

"She was taken far too young. I have never known anyone like her." Her father smiled wistfully.

"But how could Madame Zsoldas know? About your mother. About me. What does this mean? No one in Melbourne, except for you and Uncle Edmund knows that my name used to be Miriam."

"This is a baffling situation."

"Did your mother really have powers? Uncle Edmund mentioned the rumours. Is this why you are still open to the possibility of magic?"

"Yes. No." The Professor shrugged his shoulders and puffed his self-combusting pipe. "It's all quite confusing. I was only a child. Perhaps it was the sorrow of a young boy, trying to cope with the loss of his mother. Perhaps my mind created the magic. But I am not sure."

"I have felt a strange feeling," Evangeline confessed. "A few months ago. Something I cannot explain."

The Professor frowned.

"A power tingling through my fingers. It allowed me to do something which was impossible." Evangeline skipped over the finer details of the escape from the Alchemist's cellar. "I looked at my hand through your atervis detector. I saw silver and now I am petrified, Father. What if the energy is dark? What if I am evil?"

The Professor reached out, clasping Evangeline's hand with his real hand.

"Where did you get such silly ideas? No daughter of mine is evil. I am your Father. I am here to look after you. Whatever happens," he said with conviction. "Everything changed so rapidly for you. A new country, a new family, a new name. Of course, you'll be a little out of sorts."

"And it becomes curiouser every day." Evangeline sighed.

"These are strange times." He nodded. "I can't fully comprehend or explain but you have my support. As long as you mind your table manners and there is no repeat of last night's tea-time beastliness."

"Thank you, Father. This is a great comfort to me."

"Perhaps we can do a few experiments," he said.

Evangeline grimaced, imagining herself trussed like a poor dissected frog.

"Who would have thought such strangeness would follow us out here to the new world. But I must go. I have my meeting with the Governor. We shall talk about this later."

The secret project.

"Is your project finished?" Evangeline forgot her other worries. She burned to know what was under the tarpaulin.

"Nearly, my dear. I shall be able to tell you all about it soon." The Professor grinned. "Oh, and this letter came in for you in the post."

The Professor handed over a white envelope with Evangeline's name written on the front in an unfamiliar copperplate hand. He stood up and closed the door.

Evangeline felt a weight lift from her narrow shoulders. It felt good to tell the truth and she vowed to do it more often. Her father did not think she was evil and he understood about her strange feelings, perhaps there was a rational explanation for everything. She wished Grandmama Geileish was still alive to explain. Perhaps Geileish had already tried. Last night in Mrs. Picklescott-Smythe's parlour.

Evangeline padded downstairs to find a letter opener. She found Miss Plockton at her desk in the kitchen and borrowed her little silver blade.

"An invitation, Miss Evangeline?" Miss Plockton probed. "Perhaps from one of those lovely young ladies from your watercolours class."

Evangeline shrugged. The paper was thick and excellent quality, but the post mark was indecipherable. She slipped out a single sheet of paper folded in half. She opened and read.

Dear little urchin,

I apologise for my lack of correspondence, but after our last meeting I was whisked away on other business.

I have had the pleasure of meeting up with our mutual friend again and he wants to pass on his well-wishes. He is missing you very much and I understand he is planning to come to visit you in Melbourne very soon.

I hope our paths will cross again soon.

Yours faithfully

Lady Violetta Breckenridge-Rice.

Evangeline let the paper slip from her fingers and drop to the bluestone floor.

"Is it bad news, Miss Evangeline?" Miss Plockton asked with concerned eyes.

"I think it is," Evangeline said.

EVANGELINE
AND THE
MYSTERIOUS LIGHTS

MYSTERY AND MAYHEM IN STEAMPUNK MELBOURNE
(THE ANTICS OF EVANGELINE BOOK 4)

CHAPTER 1

E VANGELINE CLOSED HER EYES AND rocked with the rhythm of the open-top carriage, happily filled with strawberry ice-cream.

"What a splendid afternoon," said her father, the Professor, rubbing his rounded belly.

Evangeline murmured in agreement, eyes half closed, dreaming of another pink scoop.

"A delightfully grey day," said Evangeline's Uncle Augie, perfecting the angle on his straw boater. "All this Antipodean sun can be such a bore. Today reminded me of good old Brighton. Civilised. With no unseemly perspiration."

As the sun sank, ribbons of plum and apricot unfurled across the May sky. The horses clopped across the Swanston Street bridge, returning from the St. Kilda seaside and headed for the home they all shared at 56 Collins Street. St Paul's Cathedral bells pealing, Evangeline stared up into the sky, watching the stars emerge one by one.

"I'm still not used to this night sky," Uncle Edmund said, screwing up his face. "I can't find any of the stars I know. It's all topsy-turvy."

"We had stars in London?" Augie raised an eyebrow. "How could you see through the smoke?"

"It's perfectly logical, little brother," said the Professor, pointing into the air with his clockwork hand. "That one is Scorpius, a scorpion. And over there, Centaurus. And that magnificent grouping is known as the Southern Cross."

"A cross?" Miss Plockton, the Professor's efficacious personal secretary, said throwing a tartan blanket over Evangeline. "Isnae that lovely?"

"This new sky will take some getting used to," Edmund said. "For example, what on earth is that?"

Edmund pointed to the east where the sky was darkest. Three brilliant white lights blazed far away in the distance, bigger and brighter than any other stars in the sky.

Evangeline leaned forward, squinting, while her father clicked and flicked, selecting the ideal lens on his pince-nez.

"Curious." The Professor stroked his moustache with his brass fingers. "I am not familiar with that particular constellation. But we're all learning about our new surroundings."

"But Father, the lights are moving," Evangeline said. "Coming towards us."

"No," scoffed her father. "That's impossible. An optical illusion, m'dear."

"She's right," Edmund said. "They're getting bigger."

"Probably just dirigibles," said Augie with a yawn, barely glancing up from his fingernails.

"They're awfully bright..."

Augie shrugged. "Another disaster perhaps? Tragic but the price of progress."

"But isn't the dirigible field over there? West. In Flemington? They don't usually fly over town."

"Perhaps they're taking a new route?" Augie lay back with his eyes closed. "Are we home yet?"

"What's out there to see? Only trees and bush," Edmund said. "There is something very strange about those lights. Not like a dirigible at all. Do you have your opera glasses on you, Augie?"

The Professor, Evangeline and Edmund stared up into the inky sky. The lights pulsing as they hurtled closer to the town centre, swapping positions like a street magician's cup and ball trick.

"How very peculiar," the Professor said. "No airship I know can manoeuvre in that way. Absolutely fascinating."

"What could it be?" asked Evangeline, perking up in her seat.

"I don't know," the Professor said, his voice trailing away into thought.

Evangeline licked her lips. Strange lights in the sky and something her father did not know? Was a new mystery unfolding before her eyes?

"Perhaps there is another explanation." Miss Plockton tugged at the gold cross at her neck and muttered the Lord's Prayer.

"Now my curiosity is well and truly piqued. Hurry along, man!" The Professor shouted to the carriage driver. "We must get home quick sticks."

The carriage driver slapped the reins, the horses picked up their pace, and the leisurely afternoon carriage ride was over.

"I have just the instrument. If we hurry, we can solve this mystery here and now."

CHAPTER 2

"HURRY, MAN," THE PROFESSOR EXCLAIMED.
The three lights hurtled closer, flying in from the east. The size of oranges in the dark sky. The four wheeled carriage sped along Flinders Street, the murky Yarra River on one side, *The Herald* newspaper building, the Allied Steamworks Factory, and the sandstone wool stores along the other. The carriage turned up Exhibition Street, then Collins Street and stopped in front of the red-brick Caldicott residence at number 56.

The portly Professor leaped from the carriage, racing through the iron gate and in the front door. Evangeline scrambled along after him, not wanting to miss a moment.

"Come on, Uncle Edmund."

"Wait for me," panted Edmund, closely behind her skirts.

They ran downstairs into the Professor's laboratory-workshop, an underground cellar filled with neatly categorised supplies and equipment. Rows of trunks lined the bluestone walls and, in the farthest corner, the Professor's secret project, hidden under a locked beige tarpaulin. The secret project, which, on occasion, moved all by itself.

The Professor rushed over to a microscope in the corner of the room.

Evangeline frowned. "But..." She pointed into the air.

Mumbling to himself, her father twiddled a sequence of dials and knobs. "Blast. Can't see a thing."

Only then did Evangeline spy three brass pipes leading out of the instrument, up the stone wall and through the ceiling.

"Cursed birds nesting over my peephole. Remind me to get Miss Plockton to clean out the gutters tomorrow." Turning away, he hurried across the room, diving head first into the nearest trunk and started rummaging. "I only saw the infernal thing the other day. I knew it would come in handy."

"Is this it?" Evangeline held up a long brass tube.

"Ah ha." The Professor grabbed the telescope with his clockwork hand, charging it in the air triumphantly. "As fine as the Great Melbourne Telescope. Hurry along."

Evangeline, the Professor and Uncle Edmund scrambled back upstairs and onto Collins Street.

"Where are you, ruddy lights?" the Professor muttered, squinting into the telescope.

Evangeline scoured the sky with her naked eye. Looking east and then west, she spotted Scorpius, Centaurus and the Southern Cross, but her father was right. The strange blinking lights were gone.

"Give it here. You were always rubbish in the outdoors," Edmund said. "Remember the hedgehog."

"How many times do I have to tell you, it was ferocious." The Professor huffed, handing over the telescope to his little brother.

"Dang it. You're right, Monty," Edmund said, scouting about the sky. "They were moving at an awfully fast clip. Perhaps they've already flown over?"

"The back garden?" Evangeline suggested.

Her father and uncle barged through the house, pushing past a bemused Miss Plockton, knocking a silver calling-card holder to the floor with a clang.

Out the back kitchen door and into the courtyard, the three Caldicotts stopped, their necks craned upwards. Evangeline searched every corner of the sky but the three bright lights were well and truly gone.

"Knickers," Evangeline grumbled.

"We lost it," the Professor said, sighing. His shoulders drooping, the telescope swinging by his side.

"A dirigible couldn't move that fast?" Edmund continued to stare up into the sky. "We only lost sight of it for a few moments."

"Most unusual. A real brain-twirler. What could it have possibly been?" The Professor stroked his ample black moustache.

Taking the telescope from her father's hand, Evangeline peered up into the empty sky. "Look, Father," she said, pointing to a faint trail of smoke. "Pink vapour."

"Why yes." The Professor rubbed his chin. "How curious."

"Tea time, Professor," Miss Plockton called through the open kitchen door.

"Splendid. I'm parched." The Professor clapped his hands. "Ample stimulation for one day. Especially for a Sunday."

"What could it have been, Father?" Evangeline asked as they headed into the warm house.

"One of Miss Plockton's fine brews and a pipe will reveal the answer. Mark my words." The Professor pulled up a chair and held out his tea cup to be filled.

The room settled into a contemplative silence, the Caldicotts and Augie stirring and slurping their milky tea, each absorbed in their own little world. Evangeline traced her upper lip as her mind whirred. Bright lights, mysterious manoeuvres, pink smoke, strawberry ice-cream. A delicious new mystery unfolding, begging to be solved. But where should Evangeline begin? She tilted her head to the side. One thing she knew for certain, another ham and pickle sandwich would definitely aid her thinking process. She leaned across the table and grabbed another.

CHAPTER 3

The next day

"THE HERALD AGREES THEY WERE dirigible lights," Edmund said with a crisp nod.

The air in the Conservatory rustled with newspapers and the scent of crispy bacon. The Professor grunted in agreement.

"Other people saw the lights too?" Evangeline said, taking a seat at the breakfast table and a generous serving of bacon. The news was a pleasant surprise, she was often disappointed by the lack of curiosity in other people.

"Half of Melbourne was staring into the sky last night. Those three peculiar lights have caused quite the stir." The Professor's eyes gleaming like Christmas morning.

"But the dirigible companies claim there were no flights over the east last night." Edmund scratched his jaw.

"The Argus says it was a dirigible, escaped from its moorings," the Professor reported from his own copy.

"A runaway airship?" Evangeline said leaning in, her butter knife stopped in mid-air.

"Are we still talking about those lights? How tedious." Augie huffed as he swanned into the room.

"Cripes!" Edmund said, grabbing the sides of the breakfast table. "This fellow claims it was a French scouting party. We should all be preparing our defences for an invasion!"

Evangeline and Augie's eyes widened, as big as bread and butter plates. The Professor shook his head, chuckling.

"Come. Come, little brother. A little far fetched. Although..." the Professor said, smoothing down his voluminous black moustache. "That fool President Questembert does fancy himself as the new Napoleon."

"Even on the other side of the world, we cannot escape the power tussles of Europe." Augie sighed.

"Never fear, Augie. There is only one true Empire," the Professor said, thrusting out his chest.

Evangeline listened as she chewed, digesting all the abounding theories. Runaway airships? Corrupt companies? Warmongering Frenchmen? Where should she begin?

A knock on the front door interrupted Evangeline's thoughts. Miss Plockton appeared, handing a note to the Professor.

"Tell the man to send Chief Inspector Pensnett right over." The Professor folded up the note and grabbed another triangle of toast.

Chief Inspector Pensnett? Evangeline wriggled in her seat. Now something exciting was bound to happen.

"Miss Plockton? Set the Chief Inspector a place at the table. I imagine he's spent half the night running about after rogue lights. He's probably missed his breakfast."

Evangeline said nothing, sitting as still as she could manage. If she remained quiet, her father might forget she was there. She couldn't bear to miss out on another conversation with the police. On his last visit to 56 Collins Street, Chief Inspector Pensnett brought the mystery of the fake gold, eventually leading Evangeline to the Lady Alchemist. What excitement would Pensnett bring today?

"Must dash," said Edmund slurping down the rest of his tea. "Off to explain why I can't change my drawings to another half-wit Minister."

"I must be off too." Augie rose to his feet. "I have a little secret project of my own. An exciting new production coming to Melbourne. But I have all this beastly correspondence to complete before I can breathe a word. But believe me, it will be blood-curdling." He growled and clawed the air with his fingers before flouncing from the room.

The best friends left Evangeline and the Professor alone in the Conservatory. Evangeline grimaced. There was nowhere to hide.

"Now Evangeline," the Professor said, clearing his throat. "I've been meaning to have a word with you."

Evangeline's shoulders flopped as she waited for her marching orders from the breakfast table. Didn't her father realise how helpful she could be?

"You have been with me for over six months now."

"Seven."

"Exactly. While there were a few bumps in the road. I'm willing to forget your early reckless acts." The Professor raised an eyebrow.

Evangeline longed to interrupt. The incident with the explosion in the outhouse was not her fault. But she kept her mouth closed and listened.

"New country, new family and all that. Such an upheaval in a young lady's life. A few rough moments are to be expected. But you have proven yourself to be extremely trustworthy over recent months."

Evangeline nodded, hiding her mouth with a sip of her tea. The Professor did not know the half of her adventures since arriving in Melbourne. But fathers didn't need to know everything about their daughters. Where was the fun in that?

"You've excelled in your studies. Quite a brain you've got there, my girl." The Professor grinned, rubbing his brass hand with his real one. "You're a real Caldicott. And you've proven yourself to be very handy in the workshop. You have talents which must be nurtured."

Evangeline's heart thumped, holding her breath.

"I've been thinking long and hard. About your future..."

Evangeline's face fell. She slumped further into her chair.

Only last week, a third girl from her watercolours class left Melbourne, heading for one of the new girls' boarding schools. Apparently, the education at St. Agnes was top-notch, providing instruction on everything a practical young lady needed to know; mathematics, physics, archery, the works. Was her father sending her away too?

She bit into her toast to hide her trembling lip, she did not want to go anywhere. She'd only just arrived.

CHAPTER 4

T HE PROFESSOR'S EYES GLEAMED WHILE Evangeline returned his gaze, holding back tears.

"Remember my old pal, Wilby? He put the idea in my head. Made me wonder if perhaps I was being too old-fashioned."

Wilby was her father's adventurer friend, who invited Evangeline to join his Bunyip-catching expedition. Although Wilby proved he was not quite the hero her father believed.

Evangeline's heart cantered. It was obvious. Her father was sending her away. Maybe all the way back to England.

"My plate is rather full, with all my research and experiments etcetera. And I could do with a hand." The Professor wiggled his brass fingers. "So I have a proposal for you. Would you like to become my assistant?"

Evangeline jumped in her chair, clasping her hands to her chest.

"You're not sending me away?"

"Of course not! Whatever gave you that idea?" the Professor chuckled. "So will you accept the position?"

"Yes, Father!" Evangeline grabbed her father's real hand. "It would be an honour."

"Excellent. You'll be a real help to me. Until you get married and start your own family, of course. Then I'll have to cope on my own."

Evangeline sneered at the mention of marriage. She was only seventeen, she planned to have a whole life of adventures before stuffy old husbands and noisy nurseries.

"We shall start with a probationary period. But remember, if you act out or go off on one of your little misadventures, the offer will be withdrawn tout suite."

"I understand." Evangeline nodded, her voice low and firm. Perhaps she should put aside her plans to investigate the lights, for the moment. Or be so remarkably clever, he would not find out.

"There'll be long hours in the laboratory-workshop, and I am not the easiest man to work with. Ask Miss Plockton. But I am confident you will bring a valuable contribution to my inventions."

"Thank you, Father." Evangeline leaped up and wrapped her arms around him, placing a kiss on his bristly cheek. In all the excitement, he must have forgotten to visit Cornelius the barber.

"That's settled."

"When do we start?"

The knocker on the front door pounded loudly.

"Bring the Chief Inspector straight in, Miss Plockton."

Heavy footsteps thumped down the hallway, and a man marched into the room, his plush greying beard flowing.

"Sorry to intrude so early on a Monday morning, Professor, but we have an emergency."

"Perfectly fine, Chief Inspector. Please sit. Toast? Eggs and bacon? Miss Plockton can rustle up some kippers if you're so inclined."

"You are very thoughtful, sir. I haven't had a chance to breakfast this morning," Pensnett said, grabbing a chair with swift determination.

"A man cannot think properly on an empty stomach, Chief Inspector. Miss Plockton, please arrange a full breakfast for our guest."

"You've already seen the papers," Pensnett said, gesturing to the mess of newspapers strewn over the table and spilling onto the floor. "I am here to talk to you about the very same topic. The mysterious lights."

"We saw them ourselves." The Professor nodded, plucking his self-combusting pipe from his waistcoat pocket. "On returning home from St. Kilda last night. Most peculiar."

Evangeline clutched her hands together. She knew Pensnett would bring excitement to the house.

"The Governor is very concerned. As are the police, of course," Pensnett said, waving his forkful of fried egg and toast.

"Indeed. I saw the outlandish theory about the French."

"Reckless reporting." Pensnett shook his head. "Frightening people with tales of invading forces. It could lead to absolute bedlam."

"Panic in the streets of Melbourne." The Professor nodded, lips pressed together tightly.

"We need to quash these stories and find an explanation post-haste. And this is my reason for troubling you, Professor. We'd be grateful for your professional advice, yet again."

"I do have a little experience with dirigibles," the Professor said, adjusting his tie.

"You are being modest, sir. I understand you developed the engine for the Tobermory Mark Three. The first clockwork engine ever to win the Towcester to Timbuktu Rally."

"Eons ago. But, yes," the Professor said, smoothing his waistcoat over his ample belly.

"I have a proposition for you, Professor. It's rather unorthodox. But you are the ideal man for the job," Pensnett said, mopping his whiskers with a napkin.

"Do tell."

Evangeline leaned forward in her chair, wondering whether a Professor's assistant should take notes. Pensnett stopped and narrowed his eyes, staring directly at Evangeline as if noticing her for the first time.

"This is quite sensitive, sir. Are you quite sure your daughter should be present?"

"Absolutely. I have just engaged Evangeline as my new assistant," the Professor said, drawing himself to his full height in his chair. Evangeline followed his lead, lifting her chin up high.

"Very well." The Inspector raised his eyebrows. "I have a particular favour to ask you."

"Anything for the Constabulary."

"Would you consider going, as we call it, 'undercover' for the police?"

"Undercover?"

"Yes. Basically act as our spy."

Evangeline's eyes widened, imagining clandestine meetings with secret code words, capes and sword fights. She wriggled in her seat.

"Visit the dirigible companies to find out the truth behind the lights. But don't tell them you are working for the police. They're close-lipped with us, but they may be more forthcoming with a reputable inventor like yourself."

"You mean lie?"

"A little white lie." The Inspector shrugged. "For the greater good."

The Professor stroked his handsome moustache with his brass fingers and pursed his lips.

"Now, Evangeline," he said. "These are unusual circumstances. Don't take this as my endorsement of lies and fibbing. Sometimes, one needs to stretch the truth to help others."

Her father failed to remember she was rather worldly, perhaps more worldly than him. She knew a trick or three about bending the truth, but Evangeline nodded her head obediently.

"Miss Evangeline will be joining you? Do you think this is a good idea?"

"Absolutely. She's my assistant. Although it is her first day."

"Some of the dirigible folk can be a rough lot. Please do not be shocked by their language."

Evangeline hid a giggle, remembering the colourful language of the street and the circus troupes. She could curse in seven different languages at least.

"Thank you for your concern, Chief Inspector. I will be sure to look the other way," she said with her straightest face.

Pensnett raised an eyebrow at Evangeline before turning back to the Professor. "That's settled. When can you start, sir?"

"As soon as I am finished my tea. This is a matter of utmost importance."

Evangeline restrained herself from clapping her hands with glee. An invitation to help her father and investigate the night lights.

Grabbing another slice of toast, she twirled and twisted the knife around her fingers, before slapping on a thick layer of butter and marmalade. A lady needs a full stomach to think clearly and unravel the truth behind the mystery lights.

The day was turning out splendidly already, and it was barely nine o'clock.

CHAPTER 5

D RESSED IN HER BEST COAT, parasol and hat, Evangeline and the Professor marched up the path towards the Ingloss & Company depot, the first dirigible company on their list.

The Melbourne dirigible depots sat together on a flat expanse of green grass in Flemington. Arriving and departing dirigibles, of every size and model, dotted the fields like grazing cows. The late autumn air was crisp and bracing but Evangeline pinched her nose, warding off the earthy whiff of the nearby racetrack and cattle sale yards.

Ingloss & Company operated from a squat practical red brick building, with plain eaves and simple windows, decorated with hand painted signs advertising journeys to Bendigo, Sydney Town and Adelaide.

Evangeline and the Professor stepped through the glass front door and a frock-coated man with a chinstrap beard sidled straight up to them.

"Professor Caldicott, I presume." The man bowed deeply and efficiently. "An absolute pleasure. On behalf of Mister Ingloss, we are thrilled you have chosen to visit our humble establishment. I am the Manager of Ingloss and Company. My name is Mister Snore."

Evangeline stifled a giggle behind her gloved hand.

"Thank you, Mister Snore. Most kind of you." The Professor nodded. "May I introduce my assistant, Miss Evangeline Caldicott?"

Evangeline beamed each time her new title was mentioned. Although she was not entirely sure what being a Professor's assistant entailed.

"Firstly, I must apologise to Mister Ingloss for my neglect." The Professor continued. "Terribly slack of me. Failing to visit Ingloss and Company until today. I've been rather distracted by other projects, you understand. Today is the first day I happen to have a few spare moments for a tour. I'm keen to see what your fine company is up to. Please lead the way to your maintenance workshop."

"Absolutely, Professor." Mr. Snore nodded, his necktie as snug as a noose around his neck. "But as you can imagine, our workshops are quite busy and dangerous." Mr. Snore peered down his nose at Evangeline.

"Don't worry about my assistant, Mister Snore. She is very familiar with working workshops."

Evangeline held her chin high.

A white-aproned young lad rushed across the foyer. "There's another one of them journalists here, Mister Snore, sir. 'E's askin' all kinds of questions, 'e is," the lad said, wringing his hands.

"Send him away, boy," Mr. Snore barked. The young man cowered and scuttled away. "Useless."

The Professor and Evangeline shared a knowing sideways glance.

"The newspapers have gone quite mad. Did you see all the hoo-haa in the morning editions?" Mr. Snore gestured towards a door, and they followed him through the dirigible depot foyer. Past rows of bleary-eyed and plainly-dressed people yawning on hard wooden benches.

"Yes, the lights. Quite peculiar."

"I didn't see them myself. I was at evensong as all God-fearing Christians should be. If you ask me, it all sounds like the result of too many afternoon rums," Mr. Snore grumbled. "This way, sir."

Exiting the main building, they followed a dirt road towards a vast wooden shed, the size of a railway station.

Dirigible was the fastest way to get around the world in 1882. Evangeline travelled the many-legged journey from London by dirigible seven months earlier with Edmund and Augie, to start her new life in Melbourne. Her journey across the world in the latest technology kindled her interest in the possibilities of science. She quite fancied herself as a dirigible captain, living a life on the high skies and having adventures.

Inside the shed, six dirigibles of different sizes and models were lined up under the corrugated iron roof. Some with rigid structured domes and some with deflated balloons but each airship crawling with maintenance men. The cloying scent of oil paint in the air. One group with brushes in hand, touching up the gondolas with the canary yellow company colours. Evangeline barely heard a word over the clang of metalwork, the revving of engines, and the whoosh of inflating balloons.

"Splendid." The Professor hurried up to the first dirigible, a broad grin on his face. "I'm extremely pleased to see none of that silly faddish steam. Most people do not appreciate the dangers. Now, what's going on here?"

"Our ships only travel short domestic distances. We stay local. Every ship comes in for maintenance at least once a week. Some repairs are routine. Replacing ropes and repainting. But every now and then, they need a complete overhaul, and we have to practically rebuild from the ground up."

The Professor whispered to Evangeline. "Have a look around, I'll deal with Snore."

"What am I looking for?"

"Anything suspicious. These ships are all old and battered. Nothing which could travel at the speeds of the mystery lights. Perhaps they have some experimental ships somewhere. Look for something brand spanking new."

Evangeline gave her father a little salute, somehow it seemed appropriate, and headed off.

"So Snore, tell me about these Gnattington engines. I hear they can be a little temperamental when put into second gear?" the Professor said, steering him away.

"Ah, yes. So refreshing to speak to a man of your intellectual stature, sir. The Gnattingtons are quite troublesome creatures..."

Evangeline skipped behind the largest dirigible and began inspecting every inch of the gargantuan shed for any hint of advanced technology.

She stopped to take a closer look at one of the smaller dirigibles. With long wooden benches and small portholes, this was a far cry from the luxurious sleeper dirigible Evangeline took from London to Melbourne, with its restaurant car and bunk bed compartments. No new technology in this basic model dirigible.

"'Allo there, Miss." A young man swaggered towards her, doffing his cap. "Nice to see a pretty face around here. Makes a change from all these ugly mugs."

She nodded demurely and continued on. His fellow gondola painters chuckling and elbowing the brash young man.

"Get back to work," yelled another voice, hidden somewhere underneath a deflated balloon.

Evangeline was not as inconspicuous as she hoped, more stealth required to be a proper undercover spy. But she continued on, wandering past all six dirigibles, looking for a secret door in the wall or a locked room. But there was nothing.

Evangeline called up to a young man fastening wire supports. "Excuse me, sir."

The dark haired man with a handsomely hooked nose jumped down to the ground and wiped his greasy hands on a rag.

"Sorry to trouble you but I'm a bit lost," she said, batting her eyelashes. "I am looking for your newer ships. Where can I find them?"

"New ships, Miss?" he said, his brow furrowed, a curious lilt to his voice. "I do not know of Mister Ingloss buying any new ships."

"Nothing from Bavaria?"

He shook his head and frowned. "Only the ones you see here. The others are in the sky."

"I must be mistaken. Thank you, sir."

The man bowed and Evangeline turned to walk away, but she paused. There was something strange about the way he spoke.

It was his voice, his accent. He was not English or Irish or Scottish like everyone else. He was French.

A Frenchman in a dirigible company?

CHAPTER 6

E
VANGELINE SQUINTED, INSPECTING THE
FRENCHMAN top to toe. She gasped. His white shirt
front smeared with a faint pink stain. The very same shade
of pink as the vapour trail in the sky last night. The newspaper
report was right. An invasion was imminent. Someone ought to
do something.

Evangeline glanced down the length of the shed towards her
father. He was hundreds of yards away. He would not hear her
voice over the ruckus of repairs. It appeared Evangeline was on
her own, but luckily, she was a rather capable young lady.

She spun around, parasol in hand and tripped the unsuspecting
Frenchman. He tumbled to the ground in a heap, grunting.

"Why did you do that?" He scowled up at her.

"You know why," Evangeline said. "There's no point
pretending. I know who you are."

"Quoi?" He held out his hands.

"Exactement." Evangeline nodded.

"You are mad." He shook his head. Evangeline narrowed her
eyes. The Frenchman's left hand was fumbling behind his back,
groping for a weapon of some kind.

"No, you don't." Evangeline lunged forward, striking him
across the face with her gloved hand.

"Help." The man cried, his hands above his head, a stripe of red blood on his bottom lip. "I'm being attacked by a madwoman!"

"No one will help you. Especially when I tell them you are a spy and a traitor."

"I don't know what you are talking about, Miss."

Evangeline grabbed the Frenchman in a headlock and dragged him towards her father and Mr. Snore. She struggled for a few feet, but he was a good deal taller and heavier and it was a long way to the end of the shed.

"On your feet," she ordered.

"Non," he said, slumping to the ground. "Leave me alone."

Evangeline swung her parasol from the crook of her elbow and clicked the button three times. This was no ordinary parasol, this was one of her very own inventions. Evangeline lost the original version of her vicious parasol in her battle with the Bunyip, but her new model was ruffled and in this season's colour: arctic blue.

A bayonet blade extended from the ferrule and the man jumped up like a rabbit, hands in the air.

"This way," she said, pointing the bayonet tip right at the young man's Adam's apple.

"Why are you doing this?" he said, his head bowed as she marched the French traitor towards the other end of the shed. The shed grew unnaturally quiet as, one by one, the workers stopped and stared.

"Evangeline!" her father exclaimed. "What is going on?"

"This man is a spy. A French spy."

"I am not. I do not know what..." the Frenchman said, his palms in the air.

"Be quiet, traitor." Evangeline thrust the blade closer to his face.

"Evangeline, put that thing down. Let the man speak."

"Father." She frowned.

"This is Jean-Pierre," said Mr. Snore, shaking his head. "He's no spy. He is one of my best workmen. And he's Belgian."

"How well do you know him?" Evangeline said with hands on hips. "He could be here gathering intelligence to start an invasion."

Jean-Pierre and Mr. Snore burst out laughing. Evangeline narrowed her eyes.

"Father, look at his shirt. Pink smudges."

The Professor leaned forward, grabbing his pince-nez from his pocket. "So, it is..."

Jean-Pierre looked down, his cheeks reddening. "I can explain."

The Professor reached out his hand and touched the pink stain, sniffing the residue on his fingers cautiously. His brow crumpled. "Roses?"

Jean-Pierre dropped his chin to his chest. "My wife."

"Jean-Pierre is a newlywed," Mr. Snore said, his mouth pinched. "And perfectly respectable."

"Right." The Professor cleared his throat and adjusted his collar. "I think we need to leave, Evangeline."

"I agree, Professor. Otherwise I will be forced to call the police. And we wouldn't want a scene. Would we?" Mr. Snore sneered. "You can show yourselves out. Good luck with your assistant. Quite a handful, you have there."

The Professor grumbled under his breath and gripped Evangeline by the elbow. She frantically pressed the button on her parasol, retracting the blade as her father dragged her away.

"What were you thinking?" the Professor hissed as they marched through the main building and back out to the road.

"You said look for anything suspicious. His accent. It was French. And the pink?"

"Belgian. Where did you get that implement?" The Professor pointed with wide eyes.

"Isn't it magnificent? I made it myself. I call it the vicious parasol." Evangeline thrust out her chest. "It's awfully handy. For all manner of difficult situations."

"Aptly named. Don't use it again." He frowned.

"But, Father."

"Ever. Give me your word?" He pointed a brass finger.

"I promise." Evangeline pouted and her father shook his head.

"Where did you learn such behaviour? Man-handling that poor fellow? What did I say earlier about your probationary period? Trouble already and it's not even time for elevenses."

CHAPTER 7

E VANGELINE SLOUCHED SULKILY BEHIND THE
Professor as they continued down the road to the next
dirigible service company, Egmere Brothers.

The Egmere Brothers premises was a two-storey sandstone
building with gleaming curved windows, moulded arches and
eaves, flanked by precisely clipped hedges. A uniformed man
with white gloves opened the door as they approached.

"Welcome to Egmere Brothers, sir. May I take your luggage?
Oh, no luggage. Travelling on a whim, sir? How spontaneous."

"I'm Professor Caldicott. I'm here to speak with the man in charge,"
the Professor said, sweeping straight into the foyer. The doors opened
up into a waiting room with lofty cathedral-height ceilings. Tasteful
chamber music played softly, and fashionably dressed passengers sat
on upholstered chairs sipping tea. The waiting rooms should have
been familiar to Evangeline, the Egmere Brothers depot was her first
stop on Australian soil. But on that momentous day, her head was so
clouded with fear and excitement, she could barely recall a thing.

"Do you have an appointment, sir." The man with the white
gloves scurried after them.

"I sent a telegraph but didn't receive a reply. But I'm sure
he will make time to see me." The Professor drew up to his full
height, shoulders back.

"I'm afraid Mister Clumber is not available, sir." The man bent so low his white gloves almost graced the floor. "He is extremely busy managing the maintenance of our ships. Ensuring our passengers have the best and safest possible voyage."

"Please tell him I am here. Professor Montague Caldicott. He'll know who I am."

The white-gloved man bowed and darted away.

"I can't stand impertinence," the Professor grumbled. "Where can I get a cup of tea? I'm simply desiccated."

"Attention, please. Ladies and gentlemen," a calm voice announced. "The half-past-ten dirigible bound for Shanghai is now ready for boarding. Please assemble at Door Two with your tickets ready. We hope you have a pleasant journey and thank you for travelling with Egmere Brothers."

The white-gloved man returned with another deep genuflection.

"My apologies, sir." He cowered. "Unfortunately, Mister Clumber is not taking any visitors this morning."

"There must be some mistake, boy. Are you sure you pronounced my name correctly? Cal-di-cott."

"Quite sure, sir. He mentioned you were an eminent engineer, but unfortunately, his schedule does not allow any interruptions."

"Poppycock," the Professor said and barged through the side door. Evangeline followed closely behind, smirking.

"Sir! Sir!" the man called after him.

Through the door, the Professor and Evangeline arrived in a large open office. Hat-less women sat in rows like a school room, their fingers moving swiftly over typewriters in a symphony of clattering keys.

"Where is this Clumber fellow?" the Professor said loudly, scouting up and down the room, frowning. The typists did not look up or miss a single keystroke. Evangeline shrugged. The Professor pursed his lips and pushed through another door into a corridor.

"I'm looking for Clumber." The Professor poked his head into a small office, startling a whiskered man at an abacus.

"Probably out in the maintenance sheds," the man said, blinking. "The door on the right."

The Professor harrumphed, and without breaking stride, marched through the door and across the gravel towards a row of warehouses. The stiff breeze flapping his moustache like a hairy bird.

The Egmere Brothers sheds were built from the same creamy sandstone as the main terminal building but twice as large. Inside, a row of identical spotless airships sparkled in the gaslight.

"Who are you?" said a worker with blackened hands. "You can't just come in here."

"Are these Dinkelsbuhl? Fantastic." The Professor rushed at the nearest airship with the enthusiasm of a small boy, flipping the lenses on his pince-nez.

"Oi, mate. Get out." Another man stepped forward, towering over the Professor like an oak tree.

"I am looking for Mister Clumber."

"Well, he ain't here. So sod off."

The Professor gasped and covered Evangeline's ears. Evangeline sharply inhaled, pretending to take offence, but she'd heard worse insults from children barely out of nappies.

"Sir. There are ladies present."

The oak-sized man shrugged his shoulders and walked off, leaving the Professor standing with his hands on his hips. "More impertinence."

Evangeline glanced around the warehouse while her father upset more people. In the corner, a man carefully padlocked a small shed.

"Look. Over there, Father." She pointed.

"Exactly the type of suspicious behaviour we're looking for. Come along."

The Professor made a beeline for the suspect shed, but before Evangeline and the Professor were half way there, three men came running, blocking their path.

"You are trespassing, sir," said one of the men. His words were polite but his pale blue eyes were hard. "We must ask you to leave."

"I have a simple request. I only want to speak with Clumber. I don't understand why it is so difficult."

"You've been told repeatedly, he is not available, sir. We must insist you leave our property at once." The three men stood in a row with their arms folded.

"What has he got to hide?" The Professor thrust his chin in the air.

While the men were distracted, Evangeline took a stealthy side-step towards the shed. With all the arguing and name-calling, no one noticed Evangeline yanking at the padlock. It was locked firm. But unperturbed, she grabbed her hat pin.

"Nothing, sir. Mister Clumber is a busy man. If you will not leave willingly..."

Evangeline glanced down as she tussled with the lock, spying a puddle on the brick floor. The liquid was pink. Her eyes widened.

"Then what?" The Professor glared. "Are you threatening me, sir? I'll have you know I'm a..."

The oak tree man reappeared, grabbing the Professor in a bear hug and lifting him from his feet.

"Get your hands off me, you thug." The Professor kicked as the man carried him across the gravel.

Evangeline gasped, abandoning the lock and hurrying towards her hamstrung father. "Put him down."

Evangeline scuttled along beside him. "Can I use the parasol now, Father?"

"No, I can handle this." The Professor wheezed and writhed. "This is outrageous. I have never been so insulted in all my life."

The big man said nothing, depositing the Professor onto his feet on the street outside the Egmere Brothers property line.

"I shall speak with the Governor! And the police!" The Professor shook his fist, his face post-box red. Newly arriving passengers heading into the terminal building averted their eyes and quickened their pace.

"Are you hurt, Father?" Evangeline rushed to her father's side, smoothing his sleeve.

"What are they hiding?" he grumbled, dusting himself off. "Hmmm. That did not unfold quite as I expected."

"I saw..."

"Miss Caldicott?" said a voice.

Evangeline frowned, glancing up to find a familiar set of bushy black eyebrows.

"Mister Middlehall. What a surprise." Evangeline blushed an unfashionable shade of red, wondering if Albion Middlehall witnessed her father's little melee. At least, this time she wasn't covered in mud. Unlike the time she accosted the thieving footmen at the Easter Ball or when wrestling the Bunyip on the banks of the Yarra. "Are you taking a dirigible? Summering in Europe perhaps?"

"Only boring old business, I'm afraid. No travel plans."

Albion gestured to his three companions. Their faces and suits solemn and monied.

"With the Egmere Brothers?"

"I believe so." One of his colleagues grimaced and Albion nodded like a puppy. "I'd love to stay to continue our conversation, but I really must dash, Miss Caldicott. Chancing upon you was a lovely surprise. May I call on you in the coming weeks, perchance?"

"Of course," she said as Albion pressed his lips to her gloved hand. Evangeline scrutinised Albion as he walked away. Another clue. The Middlehalls, the richest family in Melbourne, in business dealings with the Egmere Brothers. This could only mean one thing, money and lots of it. But what was the scheme?

She turned back to the Professor. "While you were... erm... conversing with those men, I saw a pink puddle outside the locked shed. And it wasn't rouge this time. We should come back later and investigate," Evangeline said. "After dark."

"A midnight raid. Capital idea." The Professor stroked his chin. "I knew you'd make a valuable assistant."

Evangeline patted her hair. Her experience with nocturnal adventures would come in very handy. Again. She wondered which one of her inventions would be most useful.

"We'll regroup and return under the cover of darkness. Expose the dirty little secrets of the Egmere Brothers. That'll teach them to disrespect Professor Montague Caldicott."

"And his daughter," said Evangeline.

"Indeed. But first, luncheon."

CHAPTER 8

"WHAT A PAIR YOU ARE!" Augie guffawed as the Professor relayed the morning's adventures at the dirigible depots.

"Like father, like daughter." Edmund snorted into his soup. "Show us your weapon, Evangeline."

"It was not all in vain." The Professor frowned. "We have one lead."

"The French?" Edmund chuckled.

"No. No. Silly idea. What would the French want with Melbourne? Terribly far from Paris and not a stinky cheese for ten thousand miles." He shook his head. "We suspect the Egmere Brothers are experimenting with new ships. Probably something prohibited. This explains all the secrecy. And Evangeline found a clue. A pink clue."

"Hae you considered other possibilities, sir?" said Miss Plockton as she cleared the soup tureen from the table. "Aside from the French. Other invaders, perhaps?"

"What other invaders could there be?" The Professor crumpled his brow. "The Austrians? Why would we ever be at war with them?"

"Further away," Miss Plockton said, blushing to the roots of her salt and pepper curls. "Hae you considered other invaders from the skies?"

"Of course..." Edmund nodded, rubbing his chin. "Killer birds."

The Professor tilted his head, squinting. "Angels?"

"Do you mean from the stars?" Evangeline offered.

"Yes," Miss Plockton said, a nervous wobble in her voice. "We arenae alone."

"Star men?" Augie burst out laughing.

Evangeline stifled a smirk. But she knew first hand the world was filled with phenomenon not easily explained. Her own experience, a tingle of power through her fingers, was as elusive and unreliable as the Melbourne weather.

"Have you been reading those novels again? I warned you. They're filled with gobbledegook." The Professor sighed.

"They are written by scientists like yourself," Miss Plockton said, her face deadly serious. "And based on scientific theory. Do you deny the possibility of other life in the universe, sir?"

"The lights did move in a rather odd way." Edmund nodded.

"Don't encourage her, Edmund," the Professor said, frowning. He sighed. "Whilst it is mathematically probable there is other life in the universe, the chances of anything coming from the stars are a million to one, I'd say. Especially here to Melbourne."

"But Monty, it moved diagonally. What airship can move like that?"

"Exactly, sir. Imagine the advanced technology. If they could travel all that way through the darkness. What else are they capable of?" Miss Plockton's eyes gleamed.

"Miss Plockton. That is plainly ridiculous. I am surprised a God-fearing woman as yourself would entertain such fancies. What would your pastor think?"

"Reverend Inverpepper lent me the books in the first place. He is a great believer," she said, her hands pressed together. "Star men are still God's creations."

The Professor shook his head.

Miss Plockton continued. "The men from the stars would be very sophisticated. They could easily conquer us. I am surprised the Governor isnae more concerned." Miss Plockton narrowed her eyes. "Perhaps he has more information. Information he isnae telling us."

"You make an interesting point, Miss Plockton." Edmund nodded slowly.

"Edmund!" the Professor exclaimed.

"Cripes. What if the Governor is one of them?" Edmund slapped a hand against his cheek. "It could explain a lot."

Evangeline tittered but the fun was interrupted by the chime of the mantelpiece clock. She wished she could stay longer to hear more of Miss Plockton's star men theories, but she had an appointment in the laneway.

Through the back door and into the laneway, Evangeline gingerly tip-toed over piles of rubbish and night soil, firmly clasping her nose. Even in this genteel area, people tipped their potato peelings, tea leaves and chamber pots into the cobbled lane.

Mei was nowhere to be seen. Evangeline stood by the red brick wall, juggling her weight from foot to foot, hands at the ready, glancing in all directions. Mei could creep up from behind and strike a sneaky blow at any moment. Evangeline grinned. It had been ages since Mei and Evangeline sparred. As the events of this morning showed, her fighting skills may be required at any moment. She couldn't risk getting soft and complacent.

"Girl from the park. Bunyip catcher," said a familiar voice.

It was the tall Aboriginal elder she'd met in Yarra Park. His walnut coloured skin, toga-like robe and gnarled stick, out of place against the red bricked walls of the cobblestoned laneway.

"You saw him, didn't you?" The elder approached her.

"Yes," Evangeline said in a small voice, recalling her struggles for breath as the Bunyip dunked her head under the water, again and again.

"Bush is very quiet now. But he be back." He nodded.

"Not too soon. I hope." Evangeline gulped.

"You see the Min-Min last night?" The elder pointed to the sky with his nobbled stick.

"Min-Min?" Mei appeared, resplendent in a coral day dress, trimmed with white braiding.

"There you are. Usually I'm the tardy one," Evangeline said. "A new dress?"

Mei shrugged her shoulders, even her hair was in a neat chignon rather than the usual snake-like plait.

"Min-Min. Them lights in the sky. Over the east."

"You mean the airships," Evangeline said to the elder, then turned to Mei, eyes gleaming. "Did you see them last night? You'll never believe what happened this morning, Father and I went to Flemington..."

"Not airships. Min-Min." The elder chuckled.

"What is Min-Min? Some type of bird?" Mei raised an eyebrow.

"Killer birds?" Evangeline shivered.

"Them spirits."

"Ghosts?" Mei frowned.

Evangeline gulped again. This time, her heart palpitated recalling the séance in Mrs. Picklescott-Smythe's parlour. The truth behind the visiting spirit still unknown.

"Are they malevolent?" she asked, eyes wide.

He shook his head slowly. "The Min-Min are the spirits of my dead people. Children."

Evangeline nodded, lips pursed, but Mei broke into a wide smile and gaily waved down the lane.

A young gentleman came running along the cobblestones, dressed in a morning jacket and bowler hat. "You! Old man! Get out of here," he shouted, waving his arms. "Away from the ladies, you pest."

"Excuse me, sir." Evangeline glared at the gentleman, hands on hips. "There is no need to be so rude. My friend and I are quite capable of handling ourselves."

The elder turned, cackling, and shuffled away down the laneway.

"What do the Min-Min want?" Evangeline called after the elder as he disappeared. "Please stay."

"Good riddance." The young gentleman shook his fist and turned to Mei, taking her hand to his lips with a deep bow. "Are you alright, Miss Fang? He didn't try to hurt you, did he?"

Mei shook her head and blushed a beetroot red.

"They're trouble. All of them," he said. "They belong out in the bush. Not wandering among civilised people."

Evangeline grimaced.

"Miss Evangeline Caldicott. May I introduce Mister Nathaniel Applecross?" Mei said, giggling girlishly. Nathaniel gave Evangeline's hand a cursory shake. "His father owns Applecross Brothers Grocers on King Street."

"Pleased to meet you, sir," Evangeline said in an overly polite manner. "I know your father's establishment. My father's personal secretary raves about the quality of your salted cod. She says it's the best she's tasted outside of Inverness."

Nathaniel barely looked up, brushing invisible dust from his lapel.

"But while your cod is good, it appears you are lacking in manners."

"Evangeline." Mei hissed.

"How dare you? I was protecting you from a menace. You should be more grateful, Miss Carmichael."

"Caldicott," Evangeline said, with narrowed eyes.

With a haughty half-shrug, Nathaniel turned to Mei. "Shall we go, Miss Fang? My auto-chariot is parked on Spring Street. I don't want to leave it on the street too long."

"Sorry, Evangeline, I have to go," Mei said, shrugging.

"Oh. I thought we were having the afternoon together. I have simply loads to tell you, and you promised to teach me some long-fist moves. I was hoping..."

"Tomorrow?" Mei said, beaming over at Nathaniel as he tapped his foot. "Can you cover for me? My mother wouldn't approve."

"Never mind your mother, I'm not sure I approve." Evangeline tutted.

Mei crossed her arms and clenched her jaw.

"Is this the reason why you didn't come to St. Kilda yesterday?"

"Mister Applecross and me don't get much time together."

"You missed a lovely day out." Evangeline kicked at the ground with the toe of her boot. "There was ice-cream."

"Miss Fang and I had a perfectly pleasant day in Williamstown instead," Nathaniel said, loudly exhaling. "Let's go, Miss Fang."

Evangeline tugged Mei aside by the elbow and whispered in her ear. "Are you sure you want to do this?"

"He's very handsome." Mei nodded. "And he's got an auto-chariot. One of the brand-new models. It's ever so fast."

"You can't be seen alone with a young gentleman! Unchaperoned. What will people say?"

"When did you get so uppity?" Mei pulled her arm from Evangeline's grasp.

"I thought we had an appointment. I was so looking forward to... Cook's baking scones." Evangeline's shoulders slumped.

"I'll make it up to you. I promise. We'll spar soon. Can I count on you?"

"Yes." Evangeline sighed, head bowed.

Mei beamed.

"Miss Fang? Are you coming?" Nathaniel started off down the laneway.

"I'll tap you tonight. I owe you," Mei said as she skipped off down the cobblestones after him. "Comin', Mister Applecross."

Evangeline was left all alone in the laneway. It appeared the mysterious lights would be another mystery she would have to solve without her best friend.

CHAPTER 9

H ER AFTERNOON PLANS DASHED, EVANGELINE sat
in the sitting room, distractedly leafing through a book on
combustion engines. Her mind wandered, thinking of Mei's
welfare, when a letter tumbled out from the pages and onto her lap.

Evangeline opened the letter, written on thin cheap paper,
her heart stopping as she recognised the clumsy handwriting. It
was the hand of her stepfather, Charlie Drigg.

This was the letter that started it all.

*"Dear Sir. You do not know me, but I know about you. I
know the sordid secrets of your past..."*

Evangeline's eyes widened, a slight tremor in her hands.

*"...your torrid affair with a maid which lead to the birth of
a child out of wedlock. A young girl by the name of Miriam."*

Evangeline clutched at her throat.

*"Such a child would bring shame on any gentleman like
yourself. Any well-respected man would not want his shameful
past known to the rest of the world."*

Her heart ached for the Professor. What a terrible way to learn he had a daughter.

"But I am a man who knows how to keep secrets. For the right price..."

Evangeline's shoulders tightened. The lengths her stepfather would go for an easy purse.

"For five hundred pounds, I can promise you I will never tell another living soul about the real father of Miriam...."

Evangeline vividly remembered the next part of the story.

***

Seven months earlier

Evangeline, or Miriam as she was known then, lived with her stepfather in an abandoned squat house. Living alongside twenty or more ne'er-do-wells, where the walls shook with singing, shouting and barneys. Her days devoted to tumbling, thieving and trying to avoid Charlie's boot.

But one night as Evangeline hurried along the dirty canals, sneaking away from the out-cold Charlie, a finely dressed man called out to her from the shadows. The posh man had a strange tale, claiming he was her uncle and Charlie Drigg was not her real father. At the time, Evangeline snorted and walked away, thinking he was one of those gentlemen Charlie warned her about, those who fancied young girls.

She quickly forgot the queer man and his story. Life returned to normal, doing as she was told and trying to keep Charlie happy. Life was slightly easier this way. But every night, Evangeline said her own version of a prayer. She wished Death would visit during the night and take Charlie away. But Evangeline had never been lucky and every morning when she woke he was still there.

"Get me another, you useless cow!" Charlie bellowed. She ducked her head. Luckily, his throw was wide and the empty bottle smashed against the wall. "Now!"

Grabbing a handful of coins off the table, she scampered out the door, down the narrow alley past the painted ladies towards The Rusty Sparrow.

Her body tensed and her hand on her blade, she approached the front door of the ramshackle pub. The door flung open and three large and hairy men tumbled out, punching and kicking one another. Evangeline jumping aside just in time.

"Miss Miriam?"

She turned, her hand gripping her knife handle. It was only the posh man again. Edmund, wasn't it? She exhaled and stepped over the wrestling men in the puddles, opening the pub door.

"Wait."

"What do you want? I'm busy," she said with hands on hips.

"You didn't let me explain."

"My father is waiting for me," Evangeline said, one foot inside The Rusty Sparrow.

"He's not your real father. But you know that," Edmund said with shining eyes.

"Leave me alone. I need to go." She waved him away.

"Here." Edmund thrust a piece of paper into her hand. The paper was folded over, dog-eared and well-worn.

"What is this?" She held the letter between two fingers.

"You can read?"

"Of course," Evangeline snapped. She opened the letter.

"This is the proof, I'm telling you the truth. My brother is your real father."

Evangeline shook her head. This man was barking mad, but she opened the page and started to read.

The letter was dated seventeen years ago. Her breath caught in her chest as soon as she recognised the childish handwriting.

"My dear Monty.

I have to go away. I am sorry I could not say goodbye to your face. But it would be too sad. You are a good man and I will always remember our time together. It is better I say goodbye now. I hope you have the good life you deserve.

Love always Peggy."

Evangeline grabbed at the door, her knees turning to jelly. Unexpected tears pouring down her face.

This letter was from her mother.

"Where did you get this?" She frowned.

"From my brother. Montague. Monty." Edmund nodded and handed over a white handkerchief.

"How?" Evangeline dabbed her nose.

"Your mother was a maid at my brother's university digs. They became close."

"I know nothing about this. She never said..." Her voice trailing off as she rubbed her forehead. "Why did she leave him?"

"This was the last contact Monty had from your mother. But now after all these years, he finally knows the reason why she left."

"Charlie Drigg is not my real father?" Evangeline said, running her hands over her ears and down her neck.

"Montague Caldicott is your father. He lives in Melbourne. In the Colonies. He has sent me to find you and take you to him. Start a new life with him in Melbourne."

Her head spinning, she carefully folded the paper and handed it back to Edmund.

"You're telling the truth..." she whispered.

"Come with me now," he said, eyes wide.

"He'll find me. He always does. You don't know what he's like." She shook her head, her hands touching her ribs. Four times she'd run away from him, but each time Charlie found her and each time, her punishment harder. Her ribs still ached on cold nights following her last failed attempt.

"We can be off to the Colonies as soon as possible. Thousands of miles away." Edmund placed a hand on her shoulder. "You'll be safe there."

Evangeline leaned against the wall of The Rusty Sparrow. Everything was topsy-turvy. Edmund was offering a chance to escape Charlie, leave London and start a new life with a well-to-do family, a Professor no less. But if Charlie found her and dragged her back a fifth time, she'd get a thrashing she would never forget.

"I need my locket. I have to go back," she said, her voice calm.

"I'll come with you." Edmund stepped forward, but Evangeline held up her hand.

"No. Wait here."

Ignoring Edmund, the wrestling men in the mud, and everything else around her, Evangeline marched along the alleys to the squat house. She slipped under the makeshift front door and into the hallway.

"About time." Charlie stood outside their door. "Where's my bottle, stupid girl?"

Charlie glared at her with red rimmed, flashing black eyes. She glared back.

"What? Nothing to say?"

Evangeline clenched her jaw. There were no words to describe how much she hated him.

"No excuse? No one stole your coins?" He snorted. His arm outstretched, blocking the entrance to their room.

With a heavy sigh, Evangeline looked down at her worn boots. She was a fool for coming back, but she couldn't bear to leave her keepsake behind.

"Useless."

He lunged out, backhanding her across the face and knocking her off her feet. She crashed against the wall and collapsed into a heap. She looked up at him, expressionless, hair strewn across her face, wiping blood from her nose.

"You want some more? I'll teach you."

He staggered towards her. She scrambled to her feet and ducked under his arm into the room.

"Where are you going?"

He grabbed for her hair but she was too quick. She ran to the corner of the room where she kept her belongings, scurrying through her coat pockets until her hand felt metal.

"Are you deaf as well as stupid?"

She groaned, his toe cracking against her rib. She tumbled to one side, still clutching her coat, wrapping her fingers around the chain and wrenching it from her pocket. She leapt to her feet and slammed a handful of coins down on the table.

"Get your own," she said, with hard eyes.

"What!" he roared.

Instinctively, she put her arms over her head. But he fooled her, punching her deep in the stomach. Dry retching, she doubled over.

"You ungrateful little..."

He clipped her around the ears. She wobbled on her feet, her ears ringing. All she needed to do was get past him and a new life was waiting for her. She clenched her fists, swallowed down her tears and slipped the chain around her neck. She had all she needed.

He struck again, knocking her to the ground, her head hitting the dirty wooden floor. He grabbed her neck, his fingers threading around the locket's chain. He tugged hard. The chain snagged around Evangeline's throat, digging into her skin. She spluttered, but the chain snapped, sending the small oval locket tumbling through a crack in the floorboards.

"No," she cried, as the locket slipped out of sight.

He held up the broken chain and flung it against the wall, sneering. Evangeline took a deep breath, said goodbye to the locket, and crawled towards the door.

"Where do you think you're going?"

He blocked her path. She got to her feet and stood up to her full height.

"I'm leaving," she said.

"You never learn." He guffawed. "Where are you gonna go? No one wants you."

He doubled over, his laugh throaty and mean, shaking his head.

This time Charlie Drigg was wrong.

Evangeline lunged across the floor and picked up an empty bottle. She smashed the bottle against his skull, connecting with a satisfying crack. He howled, clutching the back of his head.

Evangeline ran.

Nursing her ribs, she ran as fast as she could. Down the hall, through the door, across the canal. She didn't look back or wipe the blood from her face. She didn't stop until she saw her new Uncle Edmund waiting for her outside The Rusty Sparrow.

"Let's go," she panted, ignoring Edmund's aghast face.

She stepped into the hansom cab and the door closed. The horse clopping away from The Rusty Sparrow and transporting her to a new life. Evangeline settled back into the soft upholstery and caught her breath. Her smile widening with every step away from him.

CHAPTER 10

M ISS EVANGELINE." MISS PLOCKTON APPEARED in the doorway, dragging Evangeline away from the past. "Your father requests your assistance."

Evangeline extracted herself from the overstuffed armchair and headed for the laboratory-workshop.

"No, this way." Miss Plockton directed Evangeline along the hallway, into the Conservatory and through the open French doors.

The courtyard was covered, corner to corner, by a taupe tarpaulin. A large lump hidden underneath.

"Evangeline. Is that you?" said her father, his voice muffled under the canvas. "Can you fire up the engine? On the left there. Turn the crank."

Evangeline lifted up the fabric and grabbed hold of the crank handle with both hands. She turned the handle. After a series of clicks, the engine popped and snapped to life.

"Splendid," the hidden Professor exclaimed over the whirr of the engine.

The tarpaulin slowly inflated into a long oval shape and began rising from the earth.

"Fasten the guide ropes! Otherwise she'll fly off on us."

Evangeline looped the ropes around pins, hammered into the garden beds. The balloon and gondola drifted into the air, stopping short once the ropes were taut. The Professor emerged from the other side with a big grin.

"What do you think?"

"She's magnificent," Evangeline gasped, admiring the small airship, barely larger than a four wheeled carriage, with two propellers at the back and a keel underneath. On closer inspection, the airship was more like a rusty dinghy than one of the elegant Egmere Brothers' gondolas. The hull was a patchwork of mismatching steel, sewn together with rivets of all sizes and colours. But Evangeline didn't mind one bit. She clapped her hands and bounced on her toes, her heart brimming. "You really are the cleverest man alive, Father."

The Professor flapped his wrist. "No great shakes, m'dear. Cobbled together from a few bits and pieces floating about the workshop." He knocked on the steel hull. "I still remember the old Tobermory basics. Acid. Iron. Voila, hydrogen."

"Our very own family-sized airship. Everyone will be ever so envious. Can we go for a ride?" Evangeline tugged at her father's sleeve.

"Are you sure it's safe, Professor?" Miss Plockton tutted.

"Of course," the Professor said, his chin in the air. "I haven't tested it but I'm sure it is. Safe enough to protect us from your star men, Miss Plockton. Despite their advanced science."

Miss Plockton pursed her lips and disappeared back inside the house.

"Change of plans, m'dear. I had a rather spiffing idea while I was cleaning my pipes. Rather than mucking around in the dark in Flemington, I thought we'd catch those scallywags red-handed. In the sky." The Professor puffed out his chest. "As soon as it's dark, we'll go looking for them."

"In our own airship, Father. What an excellent idea."

And so much more fun. Evangeline couldn't wait until the sun set.

Luckily it was May and night came early.

"We'll leave as soon as we've finished our tea." The Professor grinned. "I'm keen to get up there. See what our little dirigible can do."

"Hopefully no one mistakes us for the mystery airships," Evangeline said, before taking the last bite of her fourth honey-covered crumpet.

"Or men from the stars." The Professor chuckled.

"It disnae hurt ta keep an open mind, sir," Miss Plockton said, collecting the plates from the table, her lips drawn into a thin white line.

"Not too open." The Professor raised his eyebrows. "Ready, m'dear?"

"One moment, Father."

Evangeline dashed from the room, up the stairs and into her bedroom. Another one of her new inventions sat on the writing desk, a set of magnetic bracelets, made of leftovers from the Bunyip catcher. She slapped the bracelets on her wrists, grabbed her parasol and headed back downstairs. Her father was waiting for her, dressed in a tweed three-piece walking suit, a leather cap with earflaps and a pair of brass goggles.

"Here. Safety first." He handed Evangeline a cap and a set of goggles of her own. "All that soot and smoke up there. Terribly irritating."

Evangeline pulled the cap over her head, but it would not fit over her chignon. She unpinned her bun, carefully constructed to hide the frazzled bald patch from her failed coiffure machine, and tied her brown hair in a long plait like Mei's. This time, the cap slipped on her head easily.

"You won't be needing that." The Professor pointed to the parasol.

"I might." Evangeline pouted.

"Blades? Gas balloons?" the Professor said, eyebrows raised.

"Perhaps you're right." Evangeline's shoulders slumped. She did not want to be responsible for piercing the balloon and incinerating her own father. That would be rather unfortunate.

"Let's go solve a mystery. All aboard!" the Professor said.

They rushed into the courtyard, the Professor cranked the handle and the airship engine whirred into action. Evangeline opened the gate and stepped inside the gondola. The interior was completely sparse. Two long metal benches running down each side and at the stern end, the controlling lever and three dials. A few soft furnishings wouldn't go astray.

The Professor jumped inside, closed the door and took his place at the lever.

"May God be with you," Miss Plockton called as she released the rope. The Professor saluted her and slowly released the lever with one hand, then turning a dial to inflate the gas balloons with the other.

Goggles on, Evangeline's stomach tingled as they left the ground with ease. Gracefully drifting past the first floor bedrooms, the second floor attic where Miss Plockton slept, and over the terracotta roof tiles into the air above the homes and buildings of Collins Street.

Evangeline sighed as she watched Melbourne sweep beneath her. The gas-lit streets were quietening, people heading indoors, curtains drawing and woodsmoke spiralling from chimneys. Melbourne was inside having its tea and all was right with the world. Except, of course, for the mysterious lights in the sky, but Evangeline and the Professor were on the case.

Switching on a gas-lamp, the Professor accelerated, and the airship forged through the sky. Heading east over the sandstone Parliament House, the neighbouring Ministry buildings with their classic Greek columns, and Fitzroy Gardens, where the last of the amber leaves drifted from the trees.

A telescope fixed to his eye, the Professor scanned in all directions.

"Ha. Ha. There!" he exclaimed. "Past Normanby's house."

Evangeline squinted. She could see nothing over the imposing gothic home of the Governor.

Then she looked harder.

Three lights blinked in the distance, growing bigger with each passing moment and heading their way.

CHAPTER 11

"THEY'RE COMING TOWARDS US! FAST!" Evangeline said, with a gasp and a grin.

The three lights flew in a straight line, catapulting towards them.

"Peculiar." The Professor stroked his substantial black moustache with his clockwork fingers. "By my rough calculations, they are flying faster than any airship I know. It must be some interesting new style of engine. But let's see what our little craft is capable of, eh? Come on, old girl."

The Professor revved the engine and the little dirigible lurched forward.

The lights merged together and swapped positions, from a straight line to a diagonal formation.

"What on earth?" Evangeline murmured.

"Golly," said the Professor. "That's rather nifty. I can't wait to inspect their rudders."

The lights began to circle and spin, around and around, like a Catherine Wheel in the sky.

"Now, that's just showing off," the Professor said with a furrowed brow.

"What kind of airship can manoeuvre like that?"

"None I know," the Professor whispered. "It's almost unnatural."

"You don't suppose…"

Evangeline and her father looked at each other with wide eyes and clenched jaws.

"Miss Plockton could be right?" the Professor said hesitantly.

Evangeline and her father went quiet for a moment, then shook their heads and replied in unison.

"It's not possible."

"Of course not."

A chill ran down Evangeline's spine.

The lights came closer and closer, three comets barrelling towards them. Evangeline shaded her eyes against the glare, her heart galloping under her bodice as she realised the lights were heading straight for them.

"Are we going to collide?" she yelled, over the roar of the whirring propellers.

"Not if I have any say in this matter." The Professor wrenched the lever and changed direction. "That should do the trick. We're out of their trajectory now. They'll pass right over us."

But one light followed, peeling away from the others, adjusting its path and coming right for them. Evangeline's heart thumped in her chest like a marching band. How vulnerable they were, in their little steel boat in the sky, battling an unknown assailant. Next time, Evangeline would insist on cannons.

"Hold on. I'll shake them."

The Professor pointed the small airship towards the ground, Evangeline clutched the outer railing with white knuckles

But again like a reflection in a looking glass, the light followed their lead, descending rapidly.

"Persistent fellow, aren't you," the Professor grumbled.

"It's awfully close" Evangeline said, shakily. "Should we…?"

Crash!

The gondola jerked forward, throwing Evangeline and the Professor from their feet. They hit the steel deck with a thud.

Evangeline bounded back to her feet, counting her limbs, fingers and toes. Thankfully, everything was in its proper place.

"Father?" She turned.

The Professor lay flat on the deck with his eyes firmly closed.

"Father. Father." She rushed to his side, patting his plentiful cheeks and gently shaking him, but his body was limp. His leather cap providing little protection against the hard steel floor.

The light loomed over them again. The dark sky lit up like a blazing January day. The earth was the safest place for them and her father urgently needed a doctor.

Evangeline rushed to the controls and stared at the three unfamiliar dials. She chewed on her lip.

"Next time," she said to herself. "Driving lessons before we depart."

She took a deep breath and a firm grip on the lever.

"Here goes nothing."

She pushed the lever down.

Crash!

A second strike and the gondola lurched on its side, sending Evangeline and the unconscious Professor skidding along the steel floor. Evangeline toppled up and over the metal bench. She thrust out her hands and clutched hold of the edge of the ship. Her body flailing in mid-air, her fingers the last defence against plummeting to the ground.

Acrobatics were Evangeline's forte, but she'd never been very good at aerial feats. She wasn't scared of heights, merely a healthy respect for gravity.

Foolishly, Evangeline glanced down to the streets and roofs below. She gulped. One slip and she'd splatter on the cobblestones like an overripe apple.

She gritted her teeth. Her hands howling under the strain. She set her jaw, tensing every muscle. But one by one, her fingers gave up, until there was nothing left and Evangeline tumbled out of the gondola into the sky.

CHAPTER 12

S ILLY ME," EVANGELINE SAID, GRIMACING.
As her fingers gave way, she flung out her wrist. But her magnetic bracelet failed to connect with the hull and she bounced over the steel surface.

"Knickers."

She swung her other wrist above her head as she fell.

Clunk.

The bracelet locked hard, jolting her to a stop. Fixing her wrist to the hull, the rest of her body dangled like washing on a line.

Crash!

For a third time, the airship rammed the little Caldicott sky dinghy. But this time Evangeline was attached to the hull like a barnacle.

The sky went black, the airship's harsh headlamps snuffed out. She glanced up and caught her first proper glimpse of the mysterious craft. Painted black, it was bigger than any of the airships they'd seen in Flemington, its full shape hidden against the dark sky. The ship slipped left, darted right and then hovered in one position. Waiting for something. Or someone.

Gravity was unforgiving as always. Evangeline's shoulder screamed with pain as the weight of her body tugged her arm from its socket. She slung her right hand behind her head and her other bracelet latched onto the hull tightly.

She heaved and grunted in a very unbecoming way as she strained to release her wrist from the hull. But her bracelet was stuck firm. She grimaced and tugged again, screeching like a laneway cat. This time, the magnet released, and she inched herself towards the deck, slowly scaling up the hull like a two-legged crab. She kept her eyes closed, learning her lesson. The wind billowed, flapping and lifting her skirts for all the world to see. But modesty was the least of Evangeline's concerns.

After what felt like an eternity, but probably less than a minute, she reached the edge and flipped back over into the little dirigible. Her heart beat like a hummingbird's wings as she rested against the side, panting and perspiring, rubbing her aching wrists.

"Father?"

She glanced around and found the Professor crumpled under the bench, still out cold. Stretching him out flat on his back, she placed her hand against his forehead. She was hardly Florence Nightingale but his temperature seemed normal and his breathing natural. If she ignored the nasty red swelling on his forehead, he might be enjoying one of his afternoon snoozes.

Her heart ached in her chest, seeing her father in such a vulnerable state. Here was the man who saved her from her squalid life with Charlie Drigg. A man she owed everything to. She pecked him on the bristly cheek and stood up straight, scowling into the sky towards the big black shape looming above her.

"Scaring Melbourne with mysterious lights is one matter. But knocking out my father is simply unacceptable," she said, waving a fist in the air. "No one crosses the Caldicotts and gets away scot free."

She raced to the controls and wrenched the lever, pulling the nose higher into the sky and towards the mysterious ship.

"Two can play at this game."

The balloon hissed, filling with hydrogen, coming into line with the bigger black craft. Evangeline tied the lever into place, twisting her cap and goggles into a makeshift rope. She stood up on the edge of the bench and looked across at the black gondola, gleaming menacingly. With a deep breath, she leaped out into the air, stretching out towards the other airship. This time, fingers crossed, her magnetic bracelets would connect straight away. She didn't dare think of the consequences if they failed again.

For a brief moment, Evangeline was flying, weightless and carefree like a leaf on the wind. Every drop of fear evaporated from her body and an enormous smile spread across her face.

Thud!

Her bracelets connected and she jerked to a bone-rattling stop. "Hoorah," she said. "But... ow."

Ignoring the pain, she pressed on, scaling up the side of the black ship with her magnetic bracelets.

Unlike the little Caldicott dinghy, the black gondola was fully enclosed with a row of portholes along the sides. Evangeline peered inside, finding a lamp-lit room with oriental carpeted floors, flocked wing chairs and buttoned chesterfields. Only the whiskey and the pipes were missing. This dismissed Miss Plockton's star man theory, unless gentlemen's studies were fashionable across the universe. But the room was also deserted.

Hauling herself across the hull and finding a door, she turned the handle and blinked with surprise as she stumbled inside. Jumping to her feet, she flattened herself against a wall, listening for signs of life. But besides the constant rumble of propellers, the ship was quiet.

In front of her, a long passage stretched out with doors on either side. She opened the first door on her left and stepped inside the well-appointed study she'd seen through the window. She tip-toed inside to get a better look.

"Why hello there, Missy," said a voice. "And who might you be?"

CHAPTER 13

A FACE POKED OUT FROM ONE of the flocked armchairs and a man with a natty moustache stepped into the light.

"Don't you know it's rude to drop in uninvited?" he said, smiling widely, with the sparkle of a single gold incisor. "Although I'm mighty impressed. That was quite an entrance. What have you got there? Magnets on your wrists?"

The man wore a leather waistcoat over his plain white shirt and his accent was not English. He wasn't French either.

"Cat got your tongue, Missy?" He blew a plume of cigar smoke into the air.

"Who are you?" Evangeline said. "Why did you ram my dirigible?"

"I asked first," he said, folding his arms.

Evangeline stood up to her full height. "Miss Evangeline Caldicott."

"Caldicott? Caldicott?" The man hooted with laughter and slapped his knee. "Caldicott. I should have known it was him snooping around. Where is the old fool?"

"How dare you speak of my father in that way?"

"Where is he?"

The man inched towards her. Evangeline glimpsed a pistol at his waistband.

She narrowed her eyes. "What is this airship?"

"I'm testing out a new prototype. She's pretty dang swift, ain't she? She's gonna dominate the skies."

Of course, he was American.

"She's the best thing I've come up with in ages. But I've had a little help with this one. A secret weapon, you might say. You like airships? You take after your father?"

"I am his assistant." Evangeline tossed her head.

"Perhaps you'd like to come and see the controls."

"If you are testing out new ships, why the cloak and dagger treatment? Why is it painted black?"

"I don't want any one stealing my ideas. The company I'm working with wanna protect their investment. And hey, a little mystery and a bit of publicity ain't such a bad thing? Did you see those headlines? Awful good fun." He clamped his cigar butt between his teeth. "In a few months, she'll be ready for production and everyone will want one. And I'll be the most famous inventor in the world. Again."

Evangeline raised her eyebrows. There was only one famous inventor in her eyes, Professor Montague Caldicott. Her father. Until the day Evangeline takes over the mantle herself, of course.

"Don't believe me? I'll show you. She's revolutionary," he said. "This way."

Evangeline cautiously followed, her eyes darting left and right. Along the wall, the portholes opened out to sweeping views of the gas-lit Melbourne streets. Low shelves running underneath, stocked with leather-bound books and objet d'art. Evangeline paused, chewing her lip as a particular pear-shaped terracotta bowl caught her eye.

"Come on. I won't bite." The man beckoned.

"You never did tell me your name," Evangeline said as the man led through one door and then another, down the corridor.

"The control room," he said, holding a door open for her.

Evangeline entered a triangular room with windows on all sides. Much smaller than the bridge on the dirigible which brought her to Melbourne, there were only two chairs, bolted to the floor in front of a bank of dials and levers. One of the chairs was occupied, a pair of hands resting on the controls.

The chair swivelled and Evangeline's jaw dropped.

"Hello, my little street urchin. How kind of you to drop by again. You've saved me a trip."

It was Lady Violetta Breckenridge-Rice, the Lady Alchemist and fake gold swindler, kidnapper and birthday ruiner. Of course, the terracotta vase was an aludel, the signature implement for alchemists.

"The secret weapon," Evangeline whispered.

Lady Breckenridge-Rice stood up, sporting a penny-brown leather coat, cinched at the waist with puffed sleeves. On her legs, blousing knee-length bloomers and tall brown boots. Evangeline nodded appreciatively, the Lady Alchemist knew how to blend fashion with practicality. She wondered whether bloomers would be appropriate attire for Professors' assistants.

"We meet again," Evangeline said, with a little smile. Here was her chance to bring the Lady Alchemist to justice. She would not get away a second time. "I thought you were out of town."

"I am here. I am there. Thanks to the wonders of our modern age and of course, the convenience of new airships. What do you think of her? Isn't she spectacular?"

"Me and the Lady are a winning combination." The American draped an arm across Lady Breckenridge-Rice's shoulder.

"It's powered by alchemy?" Evangeline frowned.

"Of sorts. I can do more than turn boring old iron into gold," Lady Breckenridge-Rice said, swishing a hand through the air. "This ship is a little experiment. A brand new power source. Better than silly old steam. Or archaic clockwork."

"But is it safe?" Evangeline said, narrowing her eyes.

"What's a few explosions." The Lady shrugged.

"We're ironing out the kinks," the American replied.

"I don't believe you." Evangeline folded her arms.

"And your opinion matters how? You're not going to have a chance to tell anyone." The Lady laughed. "I can't have you spoiling things a second time. This little venture will make Hank and I very rich."

"Hank?" Evangeline gasped. "Hank Buchanan?"

"At your service, ma'am." The American bowed, doffing an imaginary cap.

Hank Buchanan. Her father's nemesis. The exact details were scant, but as far as Evangeline could gather, Hank stole one of her father's patents. Any mention of his name sent the Professor into apoplexy.

"The thief?"

"I ain't no thief." Hank's nostrils flared. "Is Caldicott still cut up about that? Just a misunderstanding. The Amalgamaton was a dud anyway. Total flop. No one wants their meals all blended up into a drink."

Evangeline narrowed her eyes. She was positive there was more to this story. "And where have the other two ships gone? There were three…"

"Miles away." Hank waved his hand. "Now if you'll kindly step this way, Missy. The Lady's right. We can't risk you opening your big mouth and telling the world our little secret. We can't have copycats spoiling our grand prize."

"What are you going to do with me?" Evangeline gulped.

"I haven't quite decided," Lady Breckenridge-Rice said, taking a thin cigarillo from her lips and blowing a heart-shaped ring of smoke into the air. "I have a few other experiments which could use a human subject. What do you think, Hank darling?"

"Whatever you want, sweetie," Hank said, gold tooth gleaming.

Evangeline's heart battered under her rib cage. She scanned the small room. There was only one door out and Hank was within arm's reach.

"Excellent. I'm bored of frightening the people of Melbourne. Now it's time for a different type of fun."

The Lady smirked.

CHAPTER 14

EVANGELINE HAD ONE OPTION.

She lurched out, backhanding the Lady Alchemist across the chin, the square metal edge of her bracelet clipping Lady Breckenridge-Rice across the jaw. Evangeline's new invention had multiple uses. The Lady Alchemist wailed, toppling back into the pilot's chair.

"Well, I wasn't expecting that," Hank said, nodding. "Nice shot."

Evangeline followed through with a kick to Hank's nether regions. The American tumbled forward, clutching his crown jewels.

"You little..." he groaned.

She thumped her fists on the back of his neck and he collapsed to the ground.

Lady Breckenridge-Rice lunged forward, screeching. Her fingernails extended like claws, she grabbed hold of Evangeline's hair and flung her against the wall. Evangeline's head cracked against the wood panelling, and she stumbled in a daze, the room spinning before her eyes.

"Get her." Hank grunted from his foetal position on the floor.

The Lady grabbed Evangeline's hands and secured them behind her back. She writhed and wriggled but the knot was tight.

"Now, that was extremely rude and very sneaky behaviour, young lady," the Lady said, rubbing a red welt on her chin. "Although I should have expected it from a guttersnipe like you."

Evangeline screwed up her face, desperate to respond but spitting or swearing would only prove the Lady right. She stifled her unladylike urges and resorted to a hate-filled glare instead.

"I have no choice but to punish you. Take her to the engine room."

Hank staggered to his feet, groaning.

"Is that wise?"

"Where else?" the Lady said, hands on hips.

With a half-shrug, Hank lifted Evangeline to her feet and pushed her back into the corridor.

"You are putting your reputation on the line by associating with that woman," Evangeline said.

"Thanks for your concern but I can look after myself, Missy. Sometimes you gotta take a few risks for the big pay off."

Hank kicked aside a gold and emerald carpet revealing a trap door. He pulled on the brass ring and the door creaked open, releasing an astringent pink fog. The same shade as the smoke from the sky. With nostrils burning and throat tickling, Evangeline began to cough.

"Get inside." Hank shoved her towards the open cavity.

"Stop right there," said a voice. "Where are you taking my daughter, Mister Buchanan?"

Evangeline's cough turned into a chuckle. The Professor stood by the door, a pistol in his clockwork hand and a puce egg-shaped lump on his temple.

"Are you alright, m'dear," the Professor said softly.

Evangeline nodded with a grin. "But very glad to see you, Father."

"Monty. How are ya, old fella? Glad you could join the party. Long time no see," Hank said, with open arms.

"If only you had the decency to stay away longer. You did not answer my question, Mister Buchanan."

"Your daughter here. She's a real bobcat. She's been snooping around and making a right nuisance of herself. Then she attacked my lady companion and kicked me in the you-knows. That ain't good manners. So we're gonna teach her a lesson."

"That's where you are wrong, Mister Buchanan." The Professor stepped forward, aiming the pistol at Hank. "You are going to unhand my daughter and come with me."

"I've done nothing wrong," Hank said, raising his hands in the air. "It's only science, Monty. You understand."

"Father. As we suspected, there's some type of experimental chemical engine down there," Evangeline said.

"Nothing, eh? Illegal experiments. Endangering lives. Air highway code violations. And I'm sure Chief Inspector Pensnett will have a cavalcade of other charges to lay."

Hank chewed his lip and then burst into a smile. "I'm going nowhere with you, Monty."

"Watch out. Lady Breckenridge-Rice!" Evangeline shouted.

"Who?" The Professor frowned.

"Me." The Lady Alchemist appeared, pushing a pistol into the small of the Professor's back. "Pleased to meet you, Professor Caldicott. We've not been formally introduced but I've heard so much about you."

"Who is this woman?"

"Trouble," Evangeline muttered.

The Professor put his hands into the air.

CHAPTER 15

"ENOUGH TONGUE WAGGING. INTO THE engine room. Both of you." Hank shoved Evangeline towards the open trap door, knocking her to her knees.

"And you. Your gun?" Hank turned to the Professor, palm open.

"You're making a grave mistake, Buchanan." The Professor huffed as he handed the pistol over. "You won't get away with this."

"But that's where you're wrong, Monty old fella. This is the big one. The lovely Lady Vi is an A1 genius, with all the right connections. We've got a desperate patron with deep pockets and an engine powerful enough to blow every other fathead right out of the sky."

"But how does it work?"

Hank leaned in, finger in the air. "It's simple but ingenious. I'm sure you've heard of rubidium? Combine that with a little everyday household ingredient, cheap as dirt and..."

"Oh, do be quiet, Hank. You feckless fool." Lady Breckenridge-Rice pressed her pistol against the Professor's bulbous nose while Hank narrowed his eyes. "You Caldicotts really are awfully tedious. All of you. Now do as you're told and get inside."

Evangeline looked through the trapdoor and down the ladder, the pink chemical cloud obscuring the floor below.

"My hands?" she said.

"Ah yes. We're not complete monsters." Hank smiled, loosening the restraints.

"Ballocks," said Evangeline.

Her father barked out a laugh.

"Inside." Hank pointed.

Evangeline covered her nose with her sleeve and descended down the ladder. The Professor close behind, complaining and grumbling.

The ladder led to a humid windowless room with four clear glass barrels at the far end, each the width of three men. The barrels filled with simmering pink liquid, bubbles ominously popping and spluttering inside. A tangle of tubes, traversing in all directions, joined the barrels together and ended at two large metal boxes, with external propellers rumbling underfoot.

The trapdoor clunked shut and a lock clicked. Evangeline climbed back up the ladder and pushed on the door.

"Locked," she said, but raised an eyebrow. "We'll see about that."

Inhaling deeply, exactly the way Mei taught her, she slammed her fist into the door, producing a satisfying thump. But the wood barely flexed under the force of her blow.

Evangeline chewed her lip. "There must be another way out."

Back down the ladder, she patrolled the room, knocking on walls and searching for any possible escape routes. But the walls seemed solid and the trapdoor the only exit.

She harrumphed and slumped down next to her father on one of the metal boxes. The box hummed as power flowed from the barrels out to the propellers. Evangeline closed her eyes, her head woozy with the thick chemical scent and thin air.

"Pensnett will be here any moment. I'm sure of it. Hundreds of people would have seen the lights from the ground." The Professor wiped his damp forehead with a handkerchief.

"Do the police have their own dirigibles?"

"Hmmm. They could commandeer an airship?"

"Or wait til we crash," Evangeline said, her shoulders rounded.

"Now, now. What's with all this glum talk? We'll find a way out of..." The Professor's words trailed off, engulfed by a hacking cough. "If only we brought the nasal protectors with us."

"Or my parasol," Evangeline said with downturned lips. But her father did not reply, instead collapsing into another round of violent coughs.

Evangeline tore a strip of fabric from her underskirts. "Tie this around your face, Father."

"Stand and deliver," he said with a feeble grin, tying the material over his nose and mouth. "I always fancied myself as Dick Turpin."

"What about your screwdriver, Father?" Evangeline perked up. "You always have your screwdriver close at hand."

"Alas no. I distinctly remember leaving it on my workbench." The Professor let out a long sigh. "A shame. The screwdriver would have come in awfully handy."

"Have you ever thought of converting your brass fingers into tools? Then you would never lose anything. A screwdriver, a knife, scissors..."

"And a bottle opener!" the Professor exclaimed, slapping his tweed covered knee. "What a capital idea. We simply must get out of this predicament. This is too good an idea to waste."

"But how, Father?" Evangeline said, her chin to her chest.

"There must be some way. We can't let some ruddy American get the better of us."

Evangeline smiled wanly. She wished she had her father's confidence but her head was swimming. Her usual optimism was running low. Perhaps it was the sweltering heat or the cloying chemicals, but she could not see a way out of this quagmire.

One of the glass barrels started shuddering and vibrating, belching geysers of liquid to splatter against the side.

"Oh, dear," said the Professor. "I don't like the sound of that one bit."

"What is rubidium?" Evangeline said, tracing the flow of liquid through the tangled web of tubes.

Sucking air through his teeth, the Professor shook his head. "A world of trouble. When will people learn? At least you can rely on good old cogs and pins. Solid. Stable. And safe. We'll have to tread very carefully, my dear. One slip and Guy Fawkes Night'll come early this year."

Her whole body felt heavy. If Evangeline had been more like Miss Plockton, she would have dropped to her knees and asked for help from a higher power. And not the star men.

"We're not going to escape, are we?" Evangeline said, her chin trembling.

"I don't know, my dear," the Professor said, his voice a mere whisper, a dribble of sweat running down the side of his nose. "We are in rather a pickle."

"If this is the end. I'm glad to be here with you, Father." Evangeline closed her eyes and rested her head against her father's shoulder.

"And I, you, dear little Evangeline." The Professor said before coughing heartily.

"There is something you can do for me."

"Anything, m'dear."

"I need to hear the story of you and my mother."

The Professor chuckled, his voice a rusty rasp. "You have me in a corner. There's no way out now."

"Please, Father. Tell me the story of how you met."

CHAPTER 16

P EGGY." HE SIGHED.

"Is it a terribly sad story?" Evangeline leaned forward.

"Sad. Happy. Life never turns out as one expects. Good can turn to bad, but bad can be good in disguise." The Professor wheezed as he spoke. The bottle nearest them shuddering erratically. "We met in London. 1864."

"The year before I was born?"

"Indeed. My first year at King's College. I always knew I wanted to be an engineer. I was never one for games and the countryside, not like Wilby or even Edmund. In those days I was quite obsessive."

Evangeline raised an eyebrow.

"I dismantled every contraption I could lay my hands on, especially anything clockwork. Drove Mama half-mad. She hated being late for anything."

"Mama?"

"Step mama." The Professor corrected himself. "My hard work and single-mindedness paid off. I secured a place in the engineering school at King's College. So I left for London and took a room in a hostel. Where I met Peggy."

The glass bottle rattled loudly, the vibrations building up speed.

"How long can that hold?" The Professor winced. "Perhaps we can strengthen the bottle. More strips of petticoat, my dear?"

"If you think it could help." She nodded, her head as heavy as a cannon ball. "But please carry on, Father."

She couldn't allow him to get distracted, not now, when she was finally on the verge of learning how she came into this world.

"University life was not quite as I hoped and dreamed. My studies were difficult and demanding. No longer the cleverest boy in my year, I was barely average, no matter how hard I worked." He shook his head.

Perched on the edge of the metal box, Evangeline tore strip after strip from her petticoat. Her eyes fixed on her father.

"London was big and grey and friendless. Every day was the same. I would go to my lectures and come straight home to my small room in the hostel or walk the foggy streets, barely sharing a word with another soul. One day, I was struck by a rather melancholy mood and left my lectures early. I returned to my room in the late morning and disturbed Peggy cleaning. We exchanged a few words, mainly profuse apologies on both parts and she scampered off. I have to admit I was a little smitten by her. Such lovely dark curls. Just like yours." His hand reached out towards Evangeline's hair, but he pulled his hand away at the last moment.

"Let's reinforce the glass," the Professor said, standing, and Evangeline handed over a stack of cotton strips.

"Go on with the story, please, Father," Evangeline said, as they slapped the first makeshift bandages around the jittering barrel. "I'm listening."

"I was young. Inexperienced. Absolutely no idea how to talk to the female of the species. But there was something beguiling about Peggy, I wanted to know all about her. I made a habit of missing lectures, in the vain hope of seeing her again. I left little gifts for her on the dresser, posies of violets or bags of boiled sweets. Eventually I teased a few words out of her, then full sentences and one day I convinced her to stop her work and have a cup of tea with me. She was reluctant at first. It was rather improper and daring of us. A girl, even a maid, uncharoned in my room was highly irregular. But despite all this, our friendship blossomed."

The Professor and Evangeline wrapped the glass with petticoat strips, glued down with condensation.

"Then one day I came home late and found her waiting on my bed in tears."

Evangeline's hand clasped over her mouth.

"I was angry and scared. I thought something horrid had happened. London is never a safe place for a young lady... but you'd know that better than I would."

Evangeline nodded, pushing aside the memories of her own narrow escapes.

"When I saw the tears running down her face, I could not help myself. I took a seat beside her on the bed and comforted her. Brash and reckless, I know but I didn't care. I only wanted to make Peggy smile again. She told me a horrid tale. She'd gone along with her sister, and half of London, to Newgate Prison to watch the hanging of Franz Muller. The railway killer. She was such a sensitive soul, your mother. So good hearted. She said she wanted to see justice prevail. Sometimes justice provides little comfort. It can be just as brutal as the deed itself."

The Professor sighed. Evangeline stuck on the last cotton strip and crossed her fingers. Their efforts only wrapping the large barrel with a thin belt.

"But she was shaken by what she'd seen. I didn't know what else to do. I wrapped my arm around her, then placed my lips on hers and then..." The Professor blushed a deep pink. "You don't need to know the rest."

Evangeline stifled a giggle.

"It was foolish but having your mother in my arms is one of the happiest moments of my life."

"You skipped a part, Father. When did you propose? You were engaged to be married, weren't you?"

The Professor cleared his throat. "Not quite. My father wouldn't have approved."

Evangeline furrowed her brow. "But what about my grandmother, Geileish? Wasn't she a flower seller from a village in Ireland? Your father overlooked her position to marry her?"

"With tragic consequences. On the day she died, my father's heart died with her. He was a different man by this time. Rigid and unwieldy. He would never have understood about Peggy." The Professor shook his head. "But I never got a chance to tell him about her. Within a few weeks, she was gone. Leaving only a letter. I never had a chance to say goodbye."

Nodding, Evangeline's eyes filled with tears. Not quite the romantic tale she'd hoped, her father comforting her mother after a gruesome hanging, but in the topsy-turvy life of Evangeline Caldicott, somehow, this beginning made perfect sense.

A cracking noise made Evangeline and her father turn their heads. A thin hairline crack sliced down the side of the convulsing barrel, tearing right through their attempt at reinforcement.

"Oh, dear," the Professor said. "That's rather worrying."

CHAPTER 17

E VANGELINE GLANCED AT THE CRACKING glass, then up at the locked trap door, then scouted the windowless room one more time. A droplet rolled down her cheek, tears of sadness turning hot with frustration.

"Come here, m'dear. Chin up, old girl." The Professor opened his arms, and she rested her head against his shoulder, breathing in the scent of pipe tobacco and tea.

"What's this?" she said, feeling a hard lump in his pocket.

"Oh, what a first class duffer I am," he said, fumbling about in his internal jacket pocket. "In all the excitement, I plum forgot. I wanted it to be a surprise. A gift for your first day as my assistant."

The Professor opened his palm. Evangeline squealed and grabbed his arm, eyes shining.

"But how?" She stammered. "I saw it fall."

The Professor grinned and tapped his nose. "I am a man of mysterious ways."

"Oh, Father." Grabbing the locket from his hand, she clutched it close to her chest, feeling the familiar silver necklace against her skin. "Oh, how I've missed you."

"Open it."

Wiping aside a tear, she opened the locket. Rather than a daguerreotype or a lock of hair, a square of paper was folded tight on the inside. She brushed the paper with her fingertips, she did not need to unfold it.

"Are you sure, Father? The letter is yours."

He nodded, smiling, but his eyes were moist.

"Oh, Father. How can I ever thank you?"

The Professor squeezed her hand. Evangeline beamed, her finger tracing the lark engraved on the front.

"Wait. Silver?" Evangeline raised an eyebrow. "Too soft?"

"Plated. Nickel underneath." His eyes twinkled. "We can get it repaired again. I think she would approve."

Opening the locket wide, Evangeline unscrewed the pin from the hinge with her fingernail.

"Look after this for me." She handed the dismantled necklace back to the Professor and scooted up the ladder like a monkey.

Holding her breath, she set to work on the trap door hinges. The pin was slim and her hands slippery, she gripped it, but the pin skidded across the head of the screw. Grasping tighter and gritting her teeth, her fingers cramped and seized under the strain. But the little nickel pin was sturdy and after four failed attempts, the first screw began to loosen. Evangeline let out a brief yippee before finishing the job with her fingernails. One by one, the screws delightfully clanging onto the floor below.

"Nice work, m'dear," said the Professor, standing at the bottom of the ladder.

"With a little help from Mother. Let's get out of here." Evangeline placed her palms under the trap door and pushed with all her might. She groaned and strained. But nothing. The door remained stuck fast.

"Knickers," she muttered.

"What? It should have opened," the Professor said, leaping to his feet. "Give me a turn."

Evangeline moved aside as her father scampered up the rungs and shoved the door, brass elbow bonging. But again, the door barely budged.

"One more." The Professor tried again. A thump and a grunt but still nothing. "There is something unusual about this door. A second set of hinges?"

Evangeline's shoulders slumped. "I should have known. She's put a spell on it."

"Did you say spell? Magic?"

The Professor knew nothing about Evangeline's first altercation with Lady Breckenridge-Rice and her escape from the cages in the cellar.

Smash.

The cracked glass barrel shattered, a river of pink liquid flooding the floor. Quickly, the liquid rose up to the first few rungs of the ladder, bubbling and simmering under their feet. The clouds of pink gas thickened, provoking fresh rounds of coughs.

"I hope it's not corrosive," Evangeline said as they both clung to the ladder, watching the pink sludge pool beneath them.

"I'm not keen to find out," the Professor said, shuffling back up towards the trap door. "Oh, dear. Rock and a hard place."

Evangeline had one last chance. The circumstances looked insurmountable but she had beaten the odds before. She had one last possibility but it was slippery and unpredictable, and may even unleash something evil.

She closed her eyes and concentrated, banishing away any thoughts of death or failure. It would not work if she pitied herself, she needed every scrap of strength, perseverance and grit. She had the mettle, she'd survived and escaped Charlie Drigg. Lady Breckenridge-Rice would not cut short her new life with the Professor. They'd not even celebrated one of Evangeline's birthdays yet.

Evangeline ground her teeth, drawing up every ounce of determination. Thinking of her mother and grandmother watching over her, wherever they may be. It was not the time, the three generations would not be reunited today.

"Are you praying?" the Professor asked, with a shrug. "I guess it's now or never."

Evangeline steeled herself. This was the chance to prove her latent power was not dark or wicked. Her power could save her father and herself.

She felt a tingling. Was she dreaming? Was she concentrating too hard and fooling herself again? Was there truly energy flowing through her fingers? Had the power finally returned?

"Gadzooks!" said the Professor. "What on earth..."

Evangeline opened her eyes and gasped.

The amber glow was there, pulsing through her fingertips. Her father's mouth flapping like a fish on land.

Wasting no time, Evangeline placed her palms on the trapdoor and pushed. It slid out like a knife through jelly, the door toppling onto the floor above.

"I'll explain later." She climbed out of the trapdoor and called down below. "Come along, Father."

The Professor stepped out of the hole and onto the wooden floors, gulping and wiping his brow.

"This way. I'm sure we can take them by surprise."

"Let's go home," he said, rubbing his neck. "I've had enough excitement for one night."

"But we can't let Hank and the Lady Alchemist get away!" Evangeline frowned.

"Let Pensnett deal with it. I'm not sure I'm cut out for this type of caper."

Evangeline hesitated. Sometimes she was not her father's daughter. She could not let Lady Breckenridge-Rice get away a second time.

Bam!

Light blasted through the trap door, rocking the airship from side to side, throwing them off their feet and sliding across the wooden floors.

"Buchanan. Sloppy as always. Let's go," her father shouted, helping Evangeline to her feet.

Plumes of darker purple smoke emerged out of the trap door hole.

"But the others?" she said, pulling her father back towards the dirigible's bridge. The Professor tugging the other way.

"The next blast will blow us all to Kingdom come. Forget about Buchanan. We must save ourselves."

Evangeline chewed on her lip, looking left and right.

"Come on." The Professor disappeared into the smoke.

Screwing up her face, she followed him. She hated leaving anything half-finished.

She fumbled blindly through the smoky air, running her hand along the wood panelled walls until her hands met a handle. "Here. The door." She wrenched it open, welcoming the rush of fresh air with big greedy gulps.

The small Caldicott airship was moored alongside the burning ship. Evangeline and the Professor jumped across the strait into their dinghy and Evangeline set to work on the guide rope, unwrapping it from the wire support. Her father grabbed the dials, sending a gush of hydrogen into the balloon and grabbing the lever.

"Ready?" he shouted.

"Not quite." Evangeline said, tugging at the guide rope. Rather than coming loose as she pulled, the rope only snagged tighter.

"Knickers," she muttered as she yanked.

"Hurry," the Professor said. "She might..."

Blam!

Another explosion burst from the engine room. The black gondola reverberated, ramming the smaller airship and knocking Evangeline to the deck. She scrambled onto her knees, crawling along the steel floor.

"Are you hurt?" her father called, his hands still firmly on the lever.

"Shipshape, Father." She righted herself and grabbed hold of the guide rope once more. The knot was firm and unforgiving, and an inch out of reach.

"Hurry," the Professor said.

Evangeline took a deep breath and stepped up onto the rim of the ship, the toes of her boots poking out into the air. She leaned forward, looking straight ahead. Wind rushing all around her, loose hair blowing into her eyes, her torn skirts flapping. She groaned, stretching her fingers as far as they would reach. But she was still not close enough.

Drawing in deeply, pushing aside any thoughts of the hard ground below, she balanced on one leg, straining for just an extra inch of reach. This time her fingers grazed the rope. Her heart leapt but she was not done yet. She fumbled and grappled to untie the knot, gritting her teeth. A pearl of perspiration trickled down her cheek, fingers aching and seizing up under the pressure.

"If you could get a wriggle on, m'dear."

The knot finally loosened under her fingers. "Hoorah." She panted in relief. But she was leaning out into the air on one foot and her ankle was wavering. She took a firm grip, squeezed her eyes shut and jumped blindly backwards. Her derriere smacking on the steel deck.

"Ready, Father." She grimaced, rubbing her bruised posterior.

"Righty-oh!" The Professor pulled the lever.

"Let's get out of here," shouted another voice, as a pair of boots hit the steel deck of the airship with a ring.

It was Hank.

CHAPTER 18

H ANK BRUSHED HIMSELF OFF, GOLD tooth flashing.
"You really are the most annoying chap," the Professor said.
"You can't get rid of me so easily, Monty old pal." Hank
smirked. "I can explain everything."

"Save it for the police," the Professor grumbled.

Hank shrugged. "I don't see any uniforms. Who's gonna
hand me over? You? Don't make me laugh, old man."

Hank and the Professor stood toe to toe, their chests puffed
out like pigeons. Half a head shorter, the Professor craned his
neck to stare into the American's face.

"You always were a reprobate." The Professor poked his
finger into Hank's lapel.

Evangeline shook her head. Grown men and their school boy
antics. It was up to her to stop this silliness. The guide rope in
her hand gave her an idea.

"You high falutin' old fossil." Hank narrowed his eyes.

Twirling her fingers, Evangeline looped a noose. A
technique she'd learned from one-armed Hattie, the lead trick
rider in the Tockholes Circus Troupe. No one knew horses, and
ropes, like Hattie. Unfortunately she came to a rather sticky
end, involving a backwards triple somersault, a bloodthirsty
tiger and a mislaid cutlass.

"Old? Who are you calling old?"

Evangeline launched the rope into the air, spinning the noose over her head and picking up speed. She tossed the rope towards Hank, the lasso slipping over his shoulders like a quoit over a pin.

"Hey." He moaned as Evangeline tugged the rope back tightly, securing his arms. "How'd you learn to muster cattle?"

"She is a lady of many talents," called out a voice.

Evangeline, the Professor and Hank turned to see a figure standing in the open door of the large airship. It was Lady Breckenridge-Rice, surrounded by smoke. Evangeline sighed.

"I could do with some help here, honey." Hank struggled.

The Professor raced back to the controls and pushed down on the lever. Evangeline ran to the dial for more gas.

"Hold tight there, Hank," Lady Breckenridge-Rice said, laughing heartily.

"Hurry," Evangeline muttered as the two ships separated at the pace of a snail. "Get a move on, old girl."

"Coming."

Lady Breckenridge-Rice stretched out her arms and leapt from the airship door, a perfect swan dive into the open night sky. Evangeline held her breath as the Lady Alchemist glided through the air, closer and closer to their dirigible. Evangeline narrowed her eyes and squared her stance, ready to take on Lady Breckenridge-Rice once again.

But the Lady Alchemist sailed right past their little airship.

"Next time!" she called as she soared, quickly falling out of view.

Evangeline ran to the side of the ship but Lady Violetta Breckenridge-Rice was gone, disappearing into the blackness of the night sky.

"She got away again," Evangeline grumbled.

The Professor chuckled.

"Looks like your Lady friend has flown the coop, Mister Buchanan."

Hank grunted.

Bam!

The mystery airship exploded, a roaring great fireball bursting across the sky. They ducked as a wave of heat blasted over their heads. The ship tearing into a million pieces, floating about like black snow.

The force of the explosion smashed into the smaller airship, shunting them towards the ground.

"Father?" Evangeline gasped. The wind howled in her ears as the dirigible picked up speed, charging towards the cobbled streets below.

"Yes. I'm well aware." The Professor wrenched at the lever. "Just a little sticky."

"Quickly, Monty. Fix it, will ya?" Hank said. "I don't wanna die."

"It's not working." The Professor groaned and pulled, but the lever held firm.

"I've got an idea." Evangeline took the lever from her father's hands. "Hold on. It might not work."

"Does she know what she's doing?" Hank gulped as he and the Professor clutched onto the sides with white knuckles.

"Of course she does. She's my daughter." The Professor thrust out his chin.

"Here we go," Evangeline shouted.

The ship swerved sharply to the left, tilting and tipping. The tiled roofs, brick chimneys and cobbled streets rushing far too quickly towards them. Evangeline closed her eyes tight and hoped she was right.

Thud!

The ship came to a shuddering stop. Yowling, Hank skidded across the deck on his shoulder. The Professor and Evangeline toppling over and landing on top of the cursing American.

"Get off me," Hank grumbled.

"It worked." The Professor grinned and bounced up to his feet.

Evangeline smoothed back her hair. Just as she calculated, the iron spire of a church steeple pierced right through the balloon, skewering the ship in place. But her celebration was cut short. Gas hissing from the hole like a kettle on the boil.

"Quickly." The Professor held out his hand. "Hydrogen."

Evangeline jumped over the side of the ship, onto the tiled roof of the church.

"You're not going anywhere, Buchanan." The Professor shoved Hank overboard and followed closely behind him, his clockwork hand clamped firmly on the rogue's shoulder.

"But Monty, old friend..." Hank raised his hands.

"Do be quiet," the Professor and Evangeline said in unison. Hank hung his head.

"Well done, my dear," the Professor said, his eyes gleaming. "We solved the mystery of the airship and captured the perpetrator."

"Well, one of them," Evangeline said, shaking her head. "My first day as your assistant has been rather eventful."

"Indeed." The Professor continued, "Don't expect excitement like this every day."

"Of course not, Father." Evangeline said. But in her heart, she knew her father was wrong. There would be many more adventures to come. She was sure of it.

"She would be proud of you," her father said, squeezing Evangeline's hand.

"And you, Father." She squeezed back.

"I hope so."

Waiting for Chief Inspector Pensnett and his men to arrive, the three of them sat on the church roof, admiring the Camberwell skyline. Evangeline sighed. The moon began to rise and everything was in its proper place in the Antipodean sky. For now.

CHAPTER 19

"TERRIFIC JOB, PROFESSOR," CHIEF INSPECTOR Pensnett said, placing down his teacup. "Governor Normanby is extremely pleased with your assistance in this matter."

"Anything to help." The Professor smiled, reaching out and patting Evangeline on the arm. "Although I cannot take all the credit. I couldn't have done it without my assistant."

"Thanks to you and Miss Evangeline, Mister Buchanan will be deported back to New York tomorrow."

Evangeline beamed, crunching into another gingersnap.

"Good riddance," said the Professor.

"The Egmere Brothers are denying all knowledge of Mister Buchanan. And with the explosion of the airship, we do not have any hard proof of their involvement. But we will be keeping a close eye on them. They will have to mind their Ps and Qs from now on."

Evangeline frowned. She wondered about Albion Middlehall's role in this caper. Had she underestimated him? Was he in league with Hank Buchanan and the Lady Alchemist? Perhaps he was not as innocent and trustworthy as he appeared. She would have to keep a close eye on him in future.

"But there was more than one. What of the other airships?" the Professor said. "And the woman?"

"There's been reports of strange lights from Wynyard and Broken Hill and across the Tasman in Dunedin and Greymouth but unfortunately, no word of Buchanan's accomplice. She's disappeared into thin air."

Evangeline pinched her lips together, robbed of another chance to bring the slippery Lady Alchemist to justice. But Evangeline knew in her bones this was not their last encounter.

But one mystery remained. A month ago Evangeline received a letter from Lady Breckenridge-Rice. Her letter referred to a mutual friend, planning to pay Evangeline a visit. Who was this mysterious friend? It couldn't be Hank Buchanan. He knew nothing of Evangeline until yesterday. If not Hank, who? Who was on their way?

Evangeline shuddered, hoping with all her heart it was not him, the man she never wanted to set eyes on again.

"You never did explain your acquaintance with that woman? She seemed to know you rather well," the Professor asked Evangeline, passing the plate of raspberry tarts and lowering his voice to a whisper. "Or that other strange business with your hands?"

"Stories for another day, Father," Evangeline said, popping another pastry into her mouth. The Professor was not the only one with secrets.

"When I spoke to the Governor," Chief Inspector Pensnett said, "he mentioned you were close to finalising your secret project."

"Oh, yes. I'm making the final adjustments."

Evangeline perked up in her seat. The secret behind the moving tarpaulin in the laboratory-workshop would be finally unveiled?

"Next week. In fact." The Professor grinned.

"As your assistant, I presume I get an early viewing?" Evangeline said, leaning forward with wide eyes.

"Not this time, m'dear. I am sworn to secrecy. You'll have to wait like everyone else."

Evangeline sighed. Being patient was such a bore.

Perhaps she could sneak downstairs and catch a glimpse before the great unveiling. Maybe later but first things first. She reached for another raspberry tart. They were rather good.

Thank you for reading
The Antics of Evangeline
If you enjoyed this book, please leave a review
and share the word.

***

Want more of Evangeline?
For updates and news, connect with
Madeleine D'Este at:

www.madeleinedeste.com

ABOUT THE AUTHOR

Madeleine D'Este grew up in Tasmania and is now based in Melbourne. After studying law (but never practising) and travelling the world, Madeleine now lives a double life, working in corporate Australia by day and writing female-led speculative fiction by night.

The Antics of Evangeline is a collection of the first four novellas set in "Marvellous Melbourne."

Published Titles

- Evangeline and the Alchemist
- Evangeline and the Bunyip
- Evangeline and the Spiritualist
- Evangeline and the Mysterious Lights
- The Antics of Evangeline: Collection No.1

ACKNOWLEDGMENTS

It takes a community to write a book.

I'd like to thank my beta readers for their valuable advice, encouragement and occasional tough love; Claire d'Este, Karen Jakubec, my British Science Fiction Association Orbit critique group (Steve Turnbull, John Keane, Alex Weinle, Dom Dulley and Terry Jackman), Andrew Clarke, Romy Winter and extra special thanks to Scott McAteer.

Thanks to Vanessa Ricci-Thode for her magical editing skills and the Deranged Doctor Design team for their design skills.

Finally, thanks to the following writers who inspired the Evangeline stories; all the writers of classic Dr Who, Joss Whedon, Gail Carriger and Lucy Maud Montgomery.